THE ADVENTURES OF WESLEY JACKSON

By William Saroyan

Novels

THE HUMAN COMEDY

THE ADVENTURES OF WESLEY JACKSON

Stories

DEAR BABY

MY NAME IS ARAM

SAROYAN'S FABLES

PEACE, IT'S WONDERFUL

THE TROUBLE WITH TIGERS

LOVE, HERE IS MY HAT

LITTLE CHILDREN

THREE TIMES THREE

INHALE AND EXHALE

THE DARING YOUNG MAN ON THE FLYING TRAPEZE

Plays

GET AWAY OLD MAN

RAZZLE-DAZZLE

THE BEAUTIFUL PEOPLE

SWEENEY IN THE TREES

ACROSS THE BOARD ON TOMORROW MORNING

THREE PLAYS

MY HEART'S IN THE HIGHLANDS

THE TIME OF YOUR LIFE

LOVE'S OLD SWEET SONG

WILLIAM SAROYAN

The Adventures of
Wesley Jackson

HARCOURT, BRACE AND COMPANY, NEW YORK

THE ADVENTURES OF WESLEY JACKSON

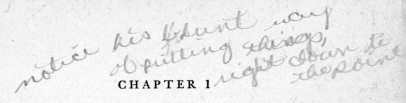
*notice his blunt way
of putting things,
right down to
the point*

CHAPTER 1

Wesley Sings Valencia and Gets an Important Letter

MY NAME is Wesley Jackson, I'm nineteen years old, and my favorite song is *Valencia*. I guess everybody in the world gets himself a favorite song sometime or other. I know I've got mine because I keep singing it or hearing it all the time, even in my sleep. I like the way the fellow hollers at the top of his voice:

> *Valencia!*
> *In my dreams*
> *It always seems*
> *I hear you softly calling me!*
> *Valencia!*
> *Dat tarrata*
> *Dat tarrata*
> *Dat tarrata, dat ta ta!*

You can't get away from songs in this world because there's always some kind of trouble going on in everybody and trouble goes with singing. My pal Harry Cook sings *If I had my way, dear, you'd never grow old*. He sings it to people he doesn't like, and he means if he had his way they'd be dead, he doesn't mean he wants them to stay young forever. At the same time he sings the song as if he meant it the way the writer of the song meant it—as if he were singing it to his bride and was broken-hearted because he couldn't keep her young and pretty forever. But the man Harry's sore at knows what Harry means, only he can't do anything about it because it's a clean song and nobody could ever prove that Harry wasn't singing it to the girl who is going to be his bride some day. There's no law against singing to your sweetheart.

Nick Cully sings:

> *O Lord, you know I have no friend like you—*
> *If Heaven's not my home, O Lord, what will I do?*

Angels beckon me to Heaven's open door
And I can't feel at home in this world any more.

Nick sings his song two ways too—serious and kidding. From the way Nick sings you know he means, "I don't like this life," but at the same time you know he also means, "I don't like it, but I want to keep it, so if I've *got* to go, for God's sake, let me go to a better place than this place—let me go to Heaven." You know Nick's homesick for some kind of impossible life, and you know he's making fun of his homesickness. Every time I hear Nick sing that song or remember him singing it, I get so sad I wish I was somebody else instead of who I am. I wish I was a Chinaman or an Eskimo or anything except what I am—an American born in San Francisco whose mother came from Dublin, whose father came from London, met in San Francisco, fell in love, got married and had two sons, myself and my brother Virgil. I get sick of my life when I hear Nick Cully asking the Lord what will he do if Heaven isn't his home, either.

Everybody I know has a song that he remembers from somewhere, that means something special to him. I like to wonder what kind of songs famous men sing to themselves when nobody's around. What a man sings in church is one thing and what he sings when he's alone is another.

So far you know my name, my age, and my favorite song, but you don't know the most important thing about me there is to know: I'm ugly. I'm not a *little* ugly like some fellows, I'm *all* ugly. Why this is so I don't know, but it's so and that's the end of it. Every time I go to shave I get a surprise. I can't believe *anybody* could be so ugly, but there he is right in front of my own eyes, and it's *me!* It's Wesley Jackson (39,339,993), it's not somebody else. I didn't know how ugly I was until I started to shave three years ago and had to look at myself every two or three days, and that's what I've got against shaving. I don't mind doing it, I don't mind trying to get neat, but I've got to look at myself when I shave and what I see makes me so sick I don't even bother to wish I was an Eskimo, I wish I was dead.

On account of this I took it into my head three years ago to stay out of sight as much as possible. I took long walks and read a lot of books. Walking gets you to thinking and reading puts you in touch with the thoughts of other men—most of them ugly men too, most likely. After you walk a lot and read a lot and think a lot you get to talking to yourself, only it isn't exactly to *yourself,* it's to the fellows you came to meet in the books. Pretty soon you get a hankering to talk to somebody alive, but when you go to do it, well, they don't know what you're talking about because they haven't been reading the books you've been reading or thinking the things you've been thinking, and chances are they think you're crazy. Maybe you are, but who knows who's crazy and who isn't? I wouldn't take it upon myself to say any man was crazy. I might be mistaken.

Next, you go to thinking you ought to write a letter to somebody, and that's what I did. I mean I *thought* I ought to write a letter, only I didn't know who to send it to. Mom had been separated from Pop most of my life, and I'd gotten out of touch with her.

As for Pop—hell, I didn't know where Pop was. As for my brother Virgil—what could you tell a fellow only thirteen years old even if you knew him, which I didn't? If I wrote to the President, wouldn't *he* be surprised?

I didn't know anybody else well enough to write to, so at last I wrote to Mrs. Fawkes who used to teach Sunday School in San Francisco.

Pop made me go to Sunday School because he claimed he'd lost the way to the good life and was afraid I'd lose it too if I didn't get a little assistance from somebody. He said it was up to me to find the way for the two of us, but hell, *Pop* was the drunkard, not me. *He* should have gone to Sunday School.

I wrote Mrs. Fawkes a long letter and told her some of the things that had happened to me since I had seen her last which was nine years ago. I didn't think she would remember me, but it seemed to me I ought to write to somebody, so I wrote to her. What's the use being in the Army if you don't write a letter once in a while and get one back once in a while? If Mrs. Fawkes wrote back, O.K. If she didn't, O.K.

One night about a month after I had sent my letter to Mrs. Fawkes there was a big commotion at Mail Call because there was a

letter for me. Vernon Higbee started the fuss. Instead of throwing
the letter to me the way he did for everybody else, he said he
wanted to present it to me officially. The boys liked the idea of
making it official and I didn't mind particularly, so when they made
a path for me to the platform, I walked down the path and up
onto the platform beside Vernon, the way they expected me to do
it. I knew they wanted to have a little fun and when a lot of fellows
in the Army want to have a little fun the best thing to do is let
them, because if you don't, they have *more* fun, and you don't have
any at all. But if you let them, then you have a little fun yourself.
If people laugh at you, who are they laughing at? I laugh at myself,
why shouldn't a lot of fellows in the Army laugh at me too? Everybody learns to laugh at himself after the age of eighteen, I guess.

Well, when I got up onto the platform beside Vernon everybody
was laughing and having fun, so Vernon stretched his arm out the
way public speakers do who've got control over their audience.

"Quiet, everybody!" he said. "This is the most important occasion
of my career as Mail Clerk of Company B. I have the honor to announce that a letter has come through the American Postal System
—and I have the further and greater honor to announce that this
letter is addressed to Private Wesley Jackson. Three cheers for
Private Jackson please."

The fellows cheered and I kept wondering what Mrs. Fawkes had
to say in the letter. At the same time I kept hearing the fellow hollering *Valencia.*

After the cheers somebody said, "Who's the letter from?" And
somebody else said, "Don't tell us even Wesley's got a girl."

But I didn't care.

"One thing at a time please," Vernon Higbee said. "With Private
Jackson's kind permission I will tell you who the letter is from. As
to the matter of whether or not Private Jackson has a girl, the
affirmative or the negative of that circumstance is not involved in
this ceremony which is official. The letter I hold in my hand, which
is the private property of Private Jackson, is very clearly addressed
to him by title, which is Private, by name which is Wesley Jackson,
and by Army Serial Number, which is 39,339,993—all in accordance
with Army Regulations. Three cheers for Army Regulations."

The fellows cheered the Army Regulations, and then Vernon

said, "Now. Who is the letter from? The letter is from the Seventh Avenue Presbyterian Church of San Francisco." Here Vernon turned to me.

"Private Jackson," he said, "I take great pleasure in presenting to you on behalf of the Nation this letter which has come to you from the Seventh Avenue Presbyterian Church of San Francisco, a city close to my heart, only nine miles across the bay from my own home in San Leandro, and almost two hundred miles from this Army Post."

Vernon clicked his heels and came to attention. For some reason every one of the fellows standing around waiting for their own mail, about a hundred of them, did the same thing. They didn't follow Vernon's *example*, they clicked their heels and came to attention *with* him, the way a flock of sparrows will fly from a telegraph wire together. It was a game, but I didn't mind at all. I even liked it a little because I never saw those fellows so smart before, not even on parade. If it's for fun, a fellow can do almost anything in a smart way. Besides, Mrs. Fawkes had answered my letter and pretty soon I'd be reading it.

Vernon bowed, handed me my letter, and everybody roared with a kind of laughter you don't hear anywhere except in the Army, or maybe in a penitentiary. I could still hear them laughing as I ran to the woods I used to go to when I was at that Post. When I got to the woods I sat down under a tree and put the letter on the ground in front of me and looked at it.

It was the first letter I had ever gotten in my life, and my name and everything was typed out on the envelope, *oh Valencia!*

After a while I opened the envelope to see what Mrs. Fawkes had to say, but the letter wasn't from Mrs. Fawkes, it was from the preacher of the church. He said he was sorry to tell me that Mrs. Fawkes was dead. She had passed on in her sleep three months ago, aged 71. He said he had taken the liberty of opening my letter, and he said he had read it a half dozen times. He was sorry he had never met me because judging from my letter I was a fine Christian young man (which was something I never knew until he told me and something Pop would be glad to hear). He said he was going to pray for me and he told me to pray too—but he didn't tell me to pray for *him*. He said a lot of other things that I read while the tears came out of my eyes because Mrs. Fawkes was dead, and then he said, "There is one thing I have decided after careful considera- tion to tell you, which I hope you will have the courage to accept with dignity and resignation: *You are a writer.* I have been writing for the better part of forty years, and I must say that even though my work has not gone altogether unheeded (I published a small inspirational book fifteen years ago at my own expense called *Smiling Through in Spite of the Tears* which Reverend R. J. Featherwell of Sausalito, California, used as the subject of a sermon in which he said, 'Here is a book the world has long been waiting for—a book whose gentle light a dark and evil world stands very much in need of')—even though, as I say, my work has not gone altogether unheeded, I must tell you that your writing is better than mine, therefore you must write. Write, my boy!"

Well, I thought the man must be foolish, but after a while I found myself taking his advice, and that's how it happens that I am writing this story which is about myself mainly, since I don't know anybody else very well, but about others too as far as I know them.

I was pretty careful of my language in my letter to Mrs. Fawkes —and my thoughts too, I guess—but I don't have to be careful any more and I mean to say what I think is right at the time, no matter what it comes to.

CHAPTER 2

Wesley Explains What the Army Does to a Fellow, Says Something He Thinks Is Right, and Can't Sleep

I SAID the letter I got from the preacher in answer to my letter to Mrs. Fawkes was the only letter I ever got in my life, but that isn't quite the truth, although it's not a lie either. I got a letter from the President once, but I don't think he knew very much about it, so I didn't count it. It wasn't personal anyway. It didn't seem sincere either. I read the word *Greetings* and wondered why it wasn't *Good-bye,* considering it meant I was going to be in the Army very soon. I'd heard that if you could breathe, the Army wanted you, and I used to breathe just fine. I'd heard a lot of other things about the Army, some of them funny and some of them dirty, but all they ever came to was that I'd soon be in uniform because I had no criminal record, I wasn't insane, I didn't have a weak heart, my blood pressure was fine, and I had all the fingers and toes and eyes and ears and different things I was born with, all of them O.K. It seemed as if I had been cut out to be a soldier all the time and was only hanging around the Beach and the Public Library in San Francisco waiting for the declaration of War. All the same, I wasn't raring to go. I was raring *not* to go.

One or two times I thought I'd hide away in the hills somewhere and wait for the War to end. One time I even got the stuff I'd need for a life like that and tied it up into a bundle and took a street-car as far out of town as I could go. I got out on the Great High-way and a fellow gave me a ride sixty miles south to Gilroy, but when I looked around I was still in the same country and every-body was still excited about the War. Everybody seemed sick with the excitement, and the excitement seemed obscene. I bought a hamburger and a cup of coffee, and then I hitch-hiked home. I didn't tell a soul what I'd done. I didn't even mention how I'd looked over my shoulder at the Coast Range Mountains where I thought I'd go to live during the War and felt so lonely and help-less and ignorant and cheap and disgraceful that I began to hate the whole world, which is something I don't like to do because the world is people and people are too pathetic to hate. I just moved along with everybody else, and when the time came I went down to 444 Market Street and got took into the Army.

But that's all ancient history now, and I don't propose to fool with any ancient history in this story. Some day this whole War is going to be ancient history and I am going to want to know what the consensus of opinion is going to be about it then. I am going to want to be interested in the outcome. I wouldn't be a bit sur-prised if this War turned out to be the turning point, as they say on the radio. The trouble is if you think about a turning point three or four minutes you come to the conclusion that there is nothing in the world that *isn't* a turning point, and the only thing that's important about a turning point is what it's a turning point from, and what it's a turning point to. If it's a turning point from nothing to nothing, what good is it? Maybe it might have been ignored even, although I can't see how anybody who isn't lame or mad can ignore a War, considering the mail he gets and the complications that come into his life once he's opened the mail and looked at it.

I remember before the War started that nobody in the whole country knew I was alive or cared much one way or the other. Nobody invited me to pitch in and help solve the problems of peace. And yet I was always the same fellow and always in need of a little ready cash. That's why the big-family spirit that comes over a whole country when there's a War makes me a little suspicious of the people who throw the party because it seems to me they are always smiling and full of hope and too quick to be heroic, whereas the fellows in uniform are confused and miserable most of the time and only begin to smile when there's nothing else to do, and are never terribly hopeful because they don't know very much about what's going on or what it means or what the outcome is likely to be—for themselves, I mean—and never in a hurry to be heroic because with a little bad luck they might be both heroic and dead. And when a fellow knows a thing like that he can't enjoy a party with all his heart and soul. Henry Rhodes used to say when he and I were at the Reception Center together for the first few days of our life in the Army, "This is the bum's rush, Jackson, and you and I are a couple of the bums."

Henry Rhodes was a Certified Public Accountant who worked in an office on Montgomery Street in San Francisco until he was drafted. He was no kid. He was forty-three years old, but in those days they took them all.

I said I was going to say whatever I think is right, no matter what it is. Well, the time has come for me to say something that I think is right, but here I am scared to death to say it. *I'm* scared because I'm in the Army, but what the hell's scaring the people who aren't in the Army? The minute a War starts everybody seems to forget everything he ever knew—everything that's worth a hoot—and shuts his mouth and keeps it shut and just groans with agony about the lies he hears all over the place all the time.

From the beginning they scare you to death in the Army. They begin scaring you with the *Articles of War*. They don't mean to be human about any of the difficulties a fellow is apt to get into, they just naturally threaten to kill you, that's all. They tell you so while you're lifting your arm to take the oath. They tell you before your arm is down, before you're *in* the Army, "—the punishment is Death." They are your own family, the same people who tell you so many other things, so many of them so confusing after you've been told what the punishment is. Of course they hardly ever have to give a fellow that punishment, but the word Death is forever after hanging around in the whole idea of Army law and order, and pretty soon it seeps down into every little irritating rule it's possible for a fellow to break, so that if he goes to get a drink of water in the afternoon they call it Absent Without Leave, which is very serious, and for which the punishment, although called Extra Duty, is actually Death. Or if he lets the tap water run while he's washing instead of filling the basin, again the punishment is Extra Duty, but that's just another term for Murder as far as I'm concerned. You get six or seven months of that kind of law and order and if you aren't scared to death, or full of confusion and anger, you're a better man than I am because even though I'm easy-going about all things, and by rights shouldn't be scared or confused or angry, I am scared, I am confused, I am angry. I don't like it, but I just can't help it.

Anyway, I was talking about Henry Rhodes and the thing I felt I ought to say about him because I felt it was right but was afraid to say because I am in the Army was this: Henry Rhodes was sore at the government for drafting him into the Army.

I was afraid to say a little thing like that.

I'm ashamed of myself.

I can't sleep from thinking about these things, but sometimes when I can't sleep it's on account of the noise the fellows make in the barracks all night, talking, telling dirty stories, singing, or playing games on each other, like the game Dominic Tosca and Lou Marriacci play on Dominic's brother Victor who sleeps in the bunk between them.

As soon as Victor falls asleep Dominic on one side and Lou on the other start whispering in his ear: "I don't want to be in the Army. Why did this happen to me? I was minding my own business. I don't want to be a soldier. I don't want to kill anybody. I want to go home. I don't want to die." They whisper louder and louder until poor Victor wakes up and says, "Ah cut it out, will you? I'm going to tell Mama on you Dominic." All the fellows in the barracks roar with laughter, even me, and I don't think it's funny at all.

CHAPTER 3

Jim Kirby of the U.P. Teaches Harry Cook and Wesley the Art of War and Sends Them Flying to the North

I THINK Harry Cook's a funny fellow, though.

One evening I was sitting on the pile of timber in front of our barracks reading around in a book I'd found in town called *The Art of War,* and Harry was over at the other end of the pile of timber lying on his back. The timber was a good place to sit or stretch out, but what it was for nobody ever knew. From the color it had turned you could see it had been there a long time. Well, Harry kept saying just loud enough for me to hear, "Private Cook reporting as ordered, sir. You can take the Army, Colonel, and I think you know what you can do with it."

So after a while I said:

"Who you talking to?"

"I'm talking to the Colonel," Harry said. "The son of a bitch."

"*What?*"

"You heard me."

"You can get court-martialed for that."

"You heard me," Harry said again.

"What have you got against the Colonel?"

"He used to be the credit manager of a department store."

"How do you know?"

"His stenographer told me. She looked it up."

"What did you have to see him for?"

"The Captain sent me."

"Why?"

"The Lieutenant."

"What'd you do?"

"The Sergeant told the Lieutenant I had made derogatory remarks about the Army."

"What'd the Colonel say?"

"Said I ought to be ashamed of myself. Said the only reason he wasn't having me court-martialed was that he didn't want to give the Post a bad name. So I gave him a bad name, and you know what it is."

Harry rolled down onto the next layer of timber, out of sight, so I went back to the book I was reading, but just then I saw a handful of Army men with one civilian among them come around the corner from the Post Exchange, headed straight for the timber. From the way they moved, I could tell they were important. You can tell an officer from a Private from the way he walks. It's not that the officer walks any better than the Private, it's something else. Even from a distance you can see that an officer feels he is being watched, either by superior officers or by the rank and file, and you can see that he thinks he is a pretty important man in this man's world, as he puts it—not as important as a Captain if he's a Lieutenant, but more important than the great majority of men in the Army, or in the world for that matter. I didn't have to see the tin chicken on the shoulder of the Colonel to know he was a big man, I knew it from the way he occupied his space among the other men in the group. He occupied his space a little more importantly than the Major beside him did, and the Major occupied his space a little more importantly than the two Captains beside him occupied theirs. The First Lieutenant was just a little trashy in that company, but the man who was most important of all was the civilian. He was the youngest of the lot too, probably no more than twenty-six or twenty-seven.

I got a little panic-stricken when I saw so many important men because I was out there in the open where I could be seen. I didn't know whether to scramble down from the timber and throw the lot of them a salute, or duck down a layer or two and hide. I didn't like saluting in those days and I didn't like needing to think about it all the time, but nowadays it doesn't bother me at all because I go according to the way I feel. If I see a little old Colonel coming down the street who seems to be lonely and confused, almost as if he were no better than a Private, well, I catch his eye and give

him a smart salute and move on down the street. But if I see some
rollicking young fool charging up the street, on the verge of changing the history of the world from something sad to something
hideous, I just naturally get lost in thought, or turn to look into
a shop window, or lift my eyes to the sky, and move past the im-
becile. I'll salute if the spirit moves me. I've saluted old beggars,
children in the streets, beautiful girls, drunkards hanging onto
lampposts, elevator operators in uniform, and all the fellows in the
Army I like, regardless of rank, but I didn't like the group coming
down the company street, so I ducked down, around, and out of
sight. I crawled over to Harry Cook.

"What's the matter with *you?*" Harry said.

"The Colonel," I whispered. "Four other officers and a civilian."

We heard their voices now, and Harry made a face.

"Let's listen to 'em," I said.

But they didn't say anything worth listening to, so I started
reading again, and Harry started singing very softly *If I had my
way, dear, you'd never grow old*. I knew he was thinking of the
Colonel.

The men were very cheery with one another in that special way
that Army men have, but at the same time they were very careful
too—not so much of what they said as of the tone of voice they permitted themselves to use. Every once in a while I'd hear the Major
talking too brilliantly for his rank, and then I'd hear him change
his tone of voice out of deference to the Colonel. It was that way
with every one of them excepting the Colonel himself and the
civilian. The Colonel was quite brilliant for a man who had only
recently left the credit department of a big department store, but
the stuff he said sounded pretty silly to me. I gathered that the
civilian was a newspaperman who'd been sent by his paper to write
a series of stories on how men in the Army live. Then I heard him
say:

"Colonel Remington, I wonder if I might have a word with one
or two of your men—anybody at all."

Then I heard the Colonel say:

"By all means, Jim. Lieutenant Coburn, will you fetch our friend
Jim here a couple of our men? Use your own judgment, Lieutenant."

I heard the Lieutenant make the usual reply and hurry away. The men went back to being cheery, but of course not too cheery. Pretty soon the voices got too close to be comfortable and the first thing I knew the whole bunch of them were all the way around the pile of timber, right where they could see Harry Cook and me. Before I could decide what to do, they saw us! Every one of them saw us, but the Colonel especially. Harry pretended that he didn't know they were there and began to sing louder than he needed to in order to sound as if he didn't know somebody was near by. So it was up to me to do the right thing, only I didn't know what the right thing was. I jumped to my feet and discovered that I was standing a little over the heads of the men which made me feel foolish. Even so, I took the book from my right hand, so I'd be free to salute, and I saluted. Everybody excepting the civilian returned the salute, and the Colonel said, "At ease, son," so I knew he wanted to impress the newspaperman. He wanted the newspaperman to get the impression that he was a regular fellow. So, noticing the book, he said, "Catching up on your home-work?"

By this time Harry had stopped singing. He had spent some time looking up at me and then around at the group. He got to his feet, and when it was absolutely silly to do so, he saluted, but he did it as if he had all the time in the world. Well, there was an awful awkward moment there because Harry had saluted so slowly that the automatic reaction that takes place in Army men when they see a smart salute was upset. Nobody moved to return Harry's salute, and Harry wouldn't give in. He just stood there on the timber and held the salute. After a lot of fidgeting the Colonel returned the salute in a very irritated way, and all the other officers followed his example. By now they were all rattled and wished they hadn't run into us, I guess. It was so long since the Colonel had asked me if I was catching up on my home-work I didn't think a reply was in order, so I just stood there too. The newspaperman broke the tension by saying, "Colonel Remington, have I your permission to speak to these men?"

This time the Colonel didn't feel so cheery.

"I want you to speak to any man you please," he said. "Any man at all."

The newspaperman looked at Harry, smiled, and said, "How do you like the Army, Mac?"

Harry didn't smile.

"I don't like it," he said, "and my name's not Mac, it's Harry."

"What's your last name?"

"Cook."

Harry stepped down from the timber. I thought he was going to stand with the newspaperman and the officers and answer some more questions, but without another word he turned and walked away. I guess he went to the Post Exchange or to the movie. So that left me. I could see the Colonel was sore as hell at Harry for saying what he'd said and for doing what he'd done, so I decided to try to improve matters a little—first for Harry, and then for the Colonel himself, because I hate to see a man upset that way, no matter who he is.

"Harry got a letter from his father this afternoon," I said. "His mother's very sick, and his father thinks she's going to die. He's been crying all afternoon."

I got down from the timber as I spoke. I kept my eye on the Colonel to see how he was taking it, and sure enough he was taking it the right way. He was relieved, for one thing, and I got the feeling that he was thankful to me for getting him out of a tough spot. Newspapermen are a nuisance to Army men. They can make a lot of trouble for a Colonel who's bucking for a B.G. Men out of uniform, especially newspapermen, take Colonels and even Generals with a grain of salt—their hero is the little man. The Colonel was smart enough to see that his best chance to keep the good name of the Post, and his own good name, was to be unhappy about Harry's unhappiness. But at the same time I could see how happy he was that Harry's mother was about to die because that meant that Harry didn't really dislike the Army, he didn't like the idea of his mother dying, which was something else again.

"Yes," the Colonel said looking at the newspaperman, "I thought that poor boy was going through some sort of emotional crisis. Major Goldring, will you please see that Private Cook is given a special furlough home? I want that boy to get on the next train out of town and go home for a few days. I want every man on this Post to understand that we—the Commanding Officers—are their friends. Get Private Cook home immediately, Major."

"Yes, sir," the Major said. "I'll attend to everything the first thing in the morning."

"The first thing in the morning be damned!" the Colonel said. *"Now!* Immediately!"

The Colonel turned to me.

"Where is Private Cook's home?" he said.

Well, I knew Harry's home was in the Sunset District of San Francisco, not far from where Pop and I used to live. But I didn't want to make any trouble because I knew there were two or three trains to San Francisco every night. I thought if I told the Colonel where Harry's home was, and the Major got Harry on the next train, pretty soon everybody would find out that Harry's mother wasn't sick at all, and Harry and me would both be in trouble. So I thought I'd say Harry's home was far away—so far away that the Colonel would drop the idea of getting Harry home on the next train and be satisfied to let him go on being unhappy.

"His home's in Alaska, sir," I said. I said that because when I saw the trouble coming I got to wishing I was somebody else instead of who I am, and that made me think of Eskimos, and Eskimos made me think of Alaska.

"Alaska?" the Colonel said.

"Yes, sir," I said. "He's an Alaskan."

I could see the Colonel had a problem on his hands now, and I was ready to believe the whole matter would be dropped and forgotten. Now, if the Lieutenant would only show up with two men his own judgment told him were appropriate for an interview with a newspaperman everything would be fine, and I'd go look for Harry. The Colonel looked over at the newspaperman, and if I ever saw a face you couldn't figure out it was the face of that newspaperman. It was a real honest-to-God poker face. The Colonel smiled at the newspaperman, but the newspaperman didn't change his expression, so the Colonel knew he was still on the spot.

"What city in Alaska?" he said.

"Fairbanks."

"Major Goldring," the Colonel said, "find out what planes are scheduled to go to Fairbanks, and get Private Cook on the next

one—give him a special priority, and if he needs any money, attend
to it for me personally."

"Yes, sir," the Major said and went off.

"Young man," the Colonel said to me, "go find your friend. He's
going home."

"Yes, sir," I said and turned to go, but the newspaperman said,
"Excuse me—what's that book you have?"

"*The Art of War*," I said. "By Clausewitz."

"May I ask how it happens that you are reading that book?" the
newspaperman said.

"The intelligence of the average enlisted man in this Army,"
the Colonel began to say, but the newspaperman cut him short.

"Sherman said War is hell," the newspaperman said. "Clausewitz says it's an art. What do you think it is?"

"I don't know very much about it," I said.

"What do you think of Clausewitz?"

"He's easy to read."

"What do you think of his ideas?"

"I think they stink."

"What's your name?"

"Wesley Jackson."

The newspaperman wrote my name on a little pad that he got
out of his coat pocket. For a while the Colonel had been pleased
with me, but when I got to talking freely—even though I didn't
mean to—I saw that he didn't like it at all. It seemed to him that
this fool newspaperman was going to go to work and write about a
Private instead of about *him*.

"Where you from?" the newspaperman said.

"San Francisco."

"What'd you do as a civilian?"

"Nothing."

"Nothing?"

"I spent some time looking for work, I worked once in a while,
but most of the time I loafed. My father was in the last War. He
got a pension because he'd been wounded, so he and I always had
enough to get by on."

"What's your father do?"

"Nothing."

"What's his trade or profession?"

"Hasn't got any. He was at college when he got drafted, but when he came back he didn't feel like studying any more."

"How do you know all that?"

"He told me. We were good pals until this War started."

"What happened then?"

"Well, Pop always liked to drink, but when they started drafting everybody again he didn't do anything *else*. He wouldn't even eat."

"What was your father's injury?"

"Gas, shrapnel, and shock. He's got some metal on the top of his head where some shrapnel almost scalped him."

"Do you like your father?"

"Sure."

"What'd you fight about?"

"We didn't fight. I tried to get him to stop drinking for a while, but he couldn't stop. He wanted to, but he couldn't. He'd go off on a drunk for three or four days, and when I'd ask him where he'd been he wouldn't be able to remember."

"If you didn't fight, how'd you happen to stop being pals?"

"He didn't come back."

"What'd you live on, then?"

"I found myself a Saturday job—three dollars. I lived on that."

"Where's your father now?"

"I don't know."

"Anybody else in the family?"

"My mother and my brother."

"Where are they?"

"They're in El Paso. My mother's brother—my uncle Neal—he's got a farm-implement business in El Paso, and my mother and my brother have been staying with him about ten years now, I guess."

"But you stayed with your father?"

"Yes. We've been together since I was nine."

Well, the newspaperman kept asking questions and I kept answering them, telling the truth every time and feeling more and more like a fool, hoping the Lieutenant would show up with the two men who would give the Post a good name instead of the miserable name Harry and I were giving it. But the Lieutenant didn't show up, and my hands kept sweating and I kept wishing I was an Eskimo, and the fellow kept hollering *Valencia!* because that was the song Pop used to sing when Mom first went off to El Paso with my brother Virgil, and Pop and me were dying of loneliness. After Pop and I got over the loneliness, Pop stopped singing *Valencia,* and I forgot all about it, but I remembered it again when Pop didn't come back, and by the time I was in the Army I kept hearing it all the time.

I thought I didn't like the newspaperman, but once we got to talking I could see he was straight, so I got over not liking him. For some reason the Colonel and the other officers just let us go on talking, but I'll be damned if I know why. Maybe they thought it was interesting.

"One more question," the newspaperman said. He looked at the Colonel out of the corner of his eye. Then he said, "How do you like the Army?"

Well, hell, there it was. Harry Cook had told him, so now he wanted me to tell him too. If I told him the truth the Colonel would be more unhappy than ever, and if I didn't tell him the truth I'd be a coward. I don't know why I didn't want the Colonel to be unhappy, considering I didn't like him any more than Harry did, but I know I didn't want the Colonel to be unhappy. It just seemed wrong to make the Colonel unhappy. I don't know how to explain this, but it seemed worse for me to make the Colonel unhappy than to be a coward. So then I got to thinking of the things I liked in the Army, but there were so few of them I knew I couldn't make them an excuse for saying I liked it, and the more I thought about it the more confused I got. I got to feeling sick too, but I had to make a decision real soon, so I tried to seem cheerful and earnest at the same time and I said, "I like it fine."

Just then the Lieutenant came up with the two men he'd selected, so I turned to go, but the newspaperman took me by the arm. The Lieutenant introduced the two men he'd selected. They were a couple of fellows who were permanently stationed at that Post. They did office work. I'd seen them around but I didn't know them. The newspaperman asked them how old they were and where they were from and what kind of work their fathers did, but he didn't write down any of the answers they made. The whole atmos-

phere got nicer and nicer, and the Colonel got to being cheery
again, and then the Major came back and said, "There's a plane
leaving for a field about a hundred miles from Fairbanks in three
hours, sir. I've got Private Cook's furlough, travel orders, and
money in this envelope."

I guess I must have looked pretty sick when I heard that, and I
guess the newspaperman caught on to how I felt because he turned
to the Colonel and said, "A fellow going all that distance on an
airplane alone—" He turned to me. "Don't you think you ought to
go along with your pal, considering his mother's so sick, and he's so
unhappy?"

"I guess so," I said. "I guess I'd like to see Alaska all right."

By this time the two fellows who did office work were feeling
cheery too, so one of them said, "Alaska? Who's going to Alaska?"

"Private Cook," the Major said. "We're sending him home. His
mother's very sick."

Well, hell, I knew I was in for it now.

"Private Cook?" the office fellow said. "What Private Cook is
that?"

"Private *Harry* Cook," the Major said.

Well, that newspaperman, he was O.K.

"Colonel," he said, "I'd like a word with you alone. Don't go
anywhere," he said to me.

"By all means," the Colonel said to the newspaperman.

The Colonel and the newspaperman went around to the other
side of the pile of timber and the rest of us stayed where we were
and kept looking at one another. The two fellows from the offices
knew something was fishy, but they didn't want to go too far with
what they knew because in the Army they teach you not to go too
far with anything no matter how right it is, just in case it might
make trouble for somebody higher up because then he might thank
you very much for informing him but after a week or two you
might find yourself in some God-forsaken part of the country that
you don't want to be in at all, so the fellows from the offices didn't
say anything more about where Harry Cook's home was, even
though they were sure it wasn't in Alaska.

The Major, he knew what was going on too, and every once in
a while he'd sneak a look at me. I'd sort of smile at him, but he'd

turn away quickly as if to say, "Steady now—don't weaken—don't say anything. The Colonel's in charge here. This is his show. Let's not embarrass the Colonel. He's talking to the newspaperman now. He'll make a decision for himself and give his orders. And we'll carry them out too."

The two Captains and the Lieutenant, they all got the idea too, so the only thing we could do was stand there and wait. We couldn't talk because if we did we might make a lot of trouble for the Colonel. Well, I wanted to go to Alaska all right, but I wasn't sure Harry Cook wanted to go. I wanted to go anywhere, just so I could get away from the Army for a while. I was fed-up with the Army, and if they flew Harry and me to Alaska that would be just fine because besides the change maybe I'd see an Eskimo at last.

Pretty soon the newspaperman and the Colonel came back. I could see they were on excellent terms now, so I felt pretty sure the newspaperman had promised to write a fine piece about the Colonel and help get him his B.G. Even though neither of them was smiling I knew everything was O.K., no matter where Harry Cook's home was, no matter who knew it.

The Colonel looked his men over, and they all acknowledged that he was Chief. Then he said, "Major Goldring, I want Private Jackson here to go along with Private Cook to Fairbanks, so please attend to the necessary details. Private Jackson will go as a courier." The Colonel turned to me and said, "Go find your friend and tell him the good news. Then I think the two of you had better hurry and pack your duffle bags. Lieutenant Coburn, will you arrange for transportation to the airfield?"

Everybody stood at attention and saluted the Colonel. He returned the salute, and the group broke up. I went straight to the barracks on the chance that Harry might be lying on his bunk, and sure enough he was. He was asleep. I shook him and when he opened his eyes I said, "Get up—you and I are going to Alaska in an airplane in three hours."

Harry said he and I were going to do something that I won't mention here. He turned over to go back to sleep. I was trying to get him to understand that what I was telling him was the truth when the newspaperman came into the barracks.

Lucky for Harry and me the only other fellow in the barracks was Victor Tosca and he was asleep on his bunk away over at the other end of the big room. The newspaperman looked at Harry and said, "I'm sorry I called you Mac. I didn't mean anything by it. How about shaking hands?"

"Sure," Harry said.

"Where's your home?" the newspaperman said, but I didn't care.

"San Francisco," Harry said. "I live in the Sunset District, just below Red Rock Hill."

"How's the family?"

"O.K."

"Any letters from home lately?"

"I got one this afternoon from my mother. She's made a cake and she's going to send it to me."

"Do you like cake?"

"Hell yes—but this is a special cake," Harry said. "Dates and raisins and walnuts and rum and stuff like that in it. Don't you like cake?"

"I like cake too," the newspaperman said. He looked at the two of us. "I know *your* names," he said, "so I think you ought to know mine. Jim Kirby. I write for U.P."

"Union Pacific?" Harry said.

"United Press," Jim said.

"What do you write?"

"Well, the boss wants me to write about soldiers. *You* fellows. Not the big shots, the *little* shots, you might say. I'm supposed to start out with a series of articles on life in Army Camps at home, and then move along with the mob."

Harry looked over at me and said, "Jackson claims we're going to take an airplane ride to Alaska in three hours."

"That's right," Jim said. "How do you like the idea?"

"I like it fine," Harry said. "Always did want to see the Klondike. But how come?"

"Well, your friend here," Jim said, "he and I went to work on the Colonel, and between the two of us we fixed it."

"No fooling?" Harry said.

"No fooling," Jim said. "And don't worry about anything. It's O.K. Well, you've got to pack your bags, so I'll say so long. Hope I'll be seeing you again."

We said so long to Jim Kirby and he turned and walked out of the barracks. Harry and I started packing our bags and Harry kept saying, "For God's sake, what did you tell the Colonel?"

It was a fine journey, going and coming, and it was a pretty nice place to be for a change, but the only Eskimo I saw worked in a saloon in Fairbanks. His name was Dan Collins, he was a Christian, and he looked more like an American than an Eskimo. I don't suppose the trip was a waste of time and money for the government because the Colonel had me carry some parcels and do a few things for him while we were up there. I went around to a half dozen Army Posts with the Colonel's stuff, and I took stuff back with me from every place I went to.

When Harry found out how and why we had got sent to Alaska he said, "Well, what do you know? The world sure is crooked, isn't it, Jackson?"

We were gone five days all told, and the minute we got back we went right on with our Basic Training, and every night Dominic Tosca and Lou Marriacci played games on Dominic's kid brother.

CHAPTER 4

Victor Tosca Makes a Bright Crack, Sergeant Cacalokowitz a Stylish Speech

VICTOR TOSCA was the best-looking boy in our Company. His brother Dominic was a hoodlum, but Victor had beautiful manners. Dominic and his pal Lou Marriacci spent a lot of time and energy playing games on Victor, but all he ever said was, "Ah cut it out will you fellows?"

Dominic was past thirty, and his friend Lou Marriacci was almost forty. Before they had gotten into the Army they had worked together in San Francisco. They had both been up for trial, they had both served short sentences, but they had never gotten into any serious trouble.

Victor was my age. In comparison with his brother Dominic he was a baby.

Any time there wasn't anything for him to do Victor would go to his bunk, stretch out, and go to sleep. He used to go to sleep at the Training Films we used to have to see all the time—how to salute; how to take care of yourself if you'd had a woman of the streets; how to revive a man from shock or drowning; how to find cover and concealment; how to disarm a man and kill him; and all the other things they wanted us to know about. None of the things they wanted us to know about were things we wanted to know about, but we were always being asked to see the films just the same.

The minute they turned the lights out to show us one of the films, Victor's head would drop and he would go to sleep. If we went to an orientation lecture, Victor would go to sleep. If we had to hang around on a Saturday morning, all fixed up for Inspection, he'd go to sleep on his feet. They tell you the best soldier is the soldier who learns to wait—well, if anybody had a talent for waiting it was Victor. He could go to sleep anywhere, any time.

His brother Dominic used to say, "He's scared—my poor little brother's scared to death. That's why he goes to sleep all the time."

And Victor used to say, "Ah cut it out will you Dom? Some fellows can sleep and some can't. I can. I'm not scared. I'm just not interested."

Like everybody else, Victor had a favorite song, and if he *had* to be awake—if we were out on a hike, or on a detail of some kind, or standing guard—he would sing the song:

> *Everybody calls me honey—*
> *Don't know why they do.*
> *Maybe it's because my Mama*
> *Calls me honey too.*

Once in a while there would be an entertainment of some sort and the Company Commander would tell us at Retreat, "I'm not ordering you to attend the entertainment tonight, but it would be a good idea if every man in this Company attended it. There won't be a roll-call, but just in case somebody isn't there, word is liable to reach me, and of course that will make me unhappy, if you know what I mean. This is not an order, you understand. You can go or stay away, as you please—but I suggest that every one of you take advantage of the opportunity to be entertained. Dismissed."

At first a few of the fellows didn't care to be entertained and stayed away, but they soon found out it wasn't a nice thing to do because they got Extra Duty. So pretty soon everybody went to every entertainment that came along, and one night it was a woman who was supposed to be famous, but none of us had ever heard of her. She hadn't talked two minutes and we knew we were in for a messy hour. It happened that I sat next to Victor Tosca who was sitting next to Dominic and Lou Marriacci.

Well, Victor went to sleep almost before the woman had said ten words. I saw Dominic turn and look at his brother. The expression on his face was one I had never seen before. If ever a brother loved his brother, Dominic Tosca loved Victor—that's what I saw in his face. When somebody stares at somebody who is asleep you can tell how he feels about that person, so when I saw Dominic looking at his brother I knew why he played games on him. I knew the games weren't to amuse Dominic and Lou Marriacci.

The woman's idea, I think, was to whoop up our drooping spirits —cheer us up.

We had gone to the hall frowning. We had sat down frowning. And when the woman began to talk we had frowned worse than ever. I don't think anybody wanted to hear what she had to say. She was going along at a pretty good inspirational clip when all of a sudden she said:

"Science tells us that twenty-seven muscles of the face are exercised when we smile, whereas almost twice as many, or fifty-one, are exercised when we frown."

She paused a moment and then said:

"So why should we frown?"

At this moment Victor Tosca opened his eyes.

"Because it's more exercise," he said.

Everybody busted out laughing and cheering and applauding and somebody said, "After all, it's more and more exercise we're after, isn't it?"

The Company Commander got up and hollered, "At ease!" So everybody shut up.

"Who made that bright crack?" he said.

Victor Tosca moved to get to his feet, but Dominic grabbed him and pushed him back into his chair.

Then Dominic got up.

"Report to my office," the Company Commander said, so Dominic left the hall.

He was confined to quarters for a week, plus Guard Duty every night.

"My brother!" he said. "The nicest kid in the world—a kid who'd be polite to somebody who wanted to stick a knife in his heart— Goes to sleep at a lousy lecture— Wakes up just in time to think of something sarcastic— Instead of keeping it to himself like us loud-mouths would do, he *says* it!"

One evening when the Sergeant we had in those days whose name was Cacalokowitz had bawled us out for half an hour he pushed his lower lip out the way he did whenever he was trying to choose his words carefully, and then he said, "The Company Commander has ast me to mention something that ain't on the record. It's off the record—between you and me. The Army don't want no fairies—so any of you boys that's fairies come to me after this formation because the Company Commander says it ain't your fault. The Army don't want you, that's all. Everybody got that?"

Everybody had it, but didn't say anything, so the Sergeant said, "Dismissed."

It was the custom to gather around Cacalokowitz after these evening sessions to find out what the gossip was around the Post, and to kid around with him—so of course everybody gathered around him now. They were kidding around about the excellent choice of words he had made for his latest announcement when the Sergeant said, "Where's Private Victor Tosca?"

Victor was walking down the company street with Nick Cully when everybody started hollering, "Hey, Victor—the Sergeant wants to talk to you."

So Victor came back. The Sergeant had a little trouble choosing his words again, but finally he said, "Where was you last night?"

"When?" Victor said.

"Around ten, I think they said."

"*Who* said?"

"Well, where was you?"

"I was sitting on the bench outside the movie listening to the music because I'd seen the picture. Why?"

"Who was with you?"

"Nobody."

"Then what happened?"

"What do you mean?"

"Didn't somebody come along and sit down beside you even though there was a hundred yards of benches both sides of the path to the movie?"

"Oh yeah," Victor said. "I forgot. A Captain came over and sat down."

"You *forgot?*"

"Yeah. Why?"

"You heard that last announcement I made, didn't you?"

"Sure I heard it. Why?"

"What did the Captain say?"

"I don't remember. I got up to salute him, but he said, 'Forget it.' So I didn't salute him. Can't salute an officer if he tells you not to. What's the matter?"

"What do you think they're going to do with that Captain?"

"What are they going to do with him?"

"Kick him out of the Army."

"Why?"

"Don't you know?"

"How should I know?"

"You were there, weren't you? It was you and him, wasn't it?"

"I don't know what you're talking about," Victor said. He looked around at everybody and they were all making dainty faces, having fun, so then he knew what Cacalokowitz was trying to tell him.

"Don't be silly," he said.

He turned and walked away, and the boys said, "Hey, Sergeant, what happened? Tell us what happened."

"I wasn't there," the Sergeant said, "but they tell me the Captain and Victor had a flirtation—at least the Captain did. I guess Victor didn't even know what was going on. He sure must be dumb."

"Somebody probably framed the Captain," Vernon Higbee said.

"Naaah," Sergeant Cacalokowitz said. "He's fruit all right. They looked him up. Any of you guys had anybody flirt with you around here lately? The Army don't want 'em."

Everybody busted out laughing, and Joe Foxhall said, "You're the only guy that flirts with us, Sarge. You not only flirt with us, you f—— us every day."

"You f——ing well right I do," Cacalokowitz said, "and any of you guys don't like it you can go f—— yourselves. You been flirted with lately?"

"Who?" I said.

"You," Cacalokowitz said, so I knew he was talking to me, which I was afraid he was doing because I knew the boys would kid me.

"Him?" Joe Foxhall said. "You mean Wesley Jackson? Who the hell would flirt with a guy that ugly?"

"I suppose you guys think you're better-looking than he is," Harry Cook said. "I suppose you guys think you're irresistible to men and women alike. Why don't you take a good look at yourselves when you shave? You're no bargains, you know. Beautiful women ain't *all* fools, you know, and a guy like Wesley's got a better chance of getting himself a good wife than any of you lunkheads —he's got something besides looks."

"But he's got looks too," Joe Foxhall said. "Hey, Wesley—what do you think of your pal sticking up for you like that? Insulting, isn't it? Why the ugliest fellow in Bakersfield used to get the prettiest girls—who doesn't know that?"

"All right, you guys," Cacalokowitz said. "Remember all this stuff is off the record—between you and me. We don't want this scandal to get around."

"What scandal?" Joe said.

"Never mind what scandal," Cacalokowitz said. "I made the announcement the Company Commander ast me to make."

"And you did it with style too," Joe Foxhall said. "You're a European, Sarge, that's what you are."

"What's a European?" Cacalokowitz said.

"You mean to say you don't know what a European is, Sarge?"

"I'm a Pole," Cacalokowitz said.

"You're a man of the world," Joe Foxhall said. "That's what you are."

"O.K.," the Sergeant said. "You wise guys from colleges and places like that can make fun of the way I talk if you want to, but don't forget I'm the guy who sits down in the little office and decides who does what dirty work, and I know your name Private Foxhall."

"You wouldn't do a dirty trick like that, Sarge," Joe Foxhall said. "Not to a graduate of Bakersfield High School, would you?"

"Don't give me that Bakersfield High School stuff," Cacalokowitz said. "I look up every man's classification card in this outfit. You got a degree from the University of California. I'm ignorant all right, but don't forget I'm Sergeant too."

"O.K., Sarge, I won't forget," Joe said. "But don't you think they ought to show us a nice two-reel Training Film on how to cope with homosexual Captains? Victor Tosca didn't know what to do. He thought he was supposed to salute."

"Never mind," Cacalokowitz said. "You guys just keep this scandal under your hat, and don't forget it."

CHAPTER 5

Joe Foxhall Tells Wesley About the Business of Living

THE NEXT night Joe Foxhall and I were on Guard Duty together, and he got to talking about the life we were living. "After you get over the first shock of being a sheep and begin to get back your own little ego—something every man in the world needs and ought to have—well, I guess the worst thing about the whole business is the waiting. The little waiting and the big waiting. Waiting to eat, waiting to get inoculated, waiting for Inspection, waiting for a pass. And then the big waiting—waiting for mail, waiting to know where you're going next, waiting for the War to end—and of course biggest of all, waiting to be killed, or spared. You remember the boys in the jeep that went off the road over the cliff in the dark—well, they were a million miles from the War, but they were waiting to know if they would be killed or spared, and they weren't spared."

We were sitting on our bunks in the Guard House—the Guard House isn't the jail, as most people think, it's where the fellows on Guard Duty wait to go on duty and where they sit or sleep four hours after two hours of duty. We were waiting for ten minutes to go by when the truck would come along and pick us up and take us out to where we were to go on duty.

"The whole business of living," Joe said, "is a business of waiting, and of course unconsciously every man born into the body of a human being is waiting for that body to wear out and go back to the mud. He's waiting to die. But since he knows he's apt to have the use of the body for thirty or forty years more, he goes to work and waits for other things. When he's a boy, he waits to be a man. Then he waits for a wife. Then he waits for a son. Then he waits to talk to his son. Or if he doesn't want to wait for a wife at first, he waits for some girl who will do something to the stuff that keeps his body alive—something that will make him feel that he is more than just a half dozen kinds of juices ebbing and flowing through a body—make him feel more than just another foolish, feeble, ridiculous animal in a suit of clothes—make him feel immortal. In other words, he waits for experience—he waits to fall in love—for the wisdom he suspects will come to him through love. Or if he doesn't want to wait for a wife, or for the wisdom of love, maybe he goes to work and waits to *do* something—make something of himself, as the saying is: make himself known to a great many people instead of only to his family and a small circle of friends—make himself known to God, as a matter of fact—write a song, make some great discovery in science or poetry—reveal truth—compel the blessing of God. But all it ever comes to is that he wants to live. He wants to beat the rap. He knows he's going to die sooner or later no matter what he does, but he wants to get the best of death if he can. Everything we've got in this world has come out of this struggle of man with death—all our song, all our poetry, all our science, all our truth, all our religion, all our dancing, all our government— everything: commerce, invention, machinery, ships, trains, airplanes, weapons, rooms, windows, doors, door-knobs, clothes, cooking, ventilation, refrigeration—shoes. Do you follow me, Jackson?"

"Sure I follow you," I said. "How did you happen to figure all that stuff out?"

"How?" Joe said. "I'm *telling* you. I want God to smile at me. I want to be handsome. I want the eyes of children to fill with light when they see me. I want beautiful women to like me. I want to

live as greatly as it's possible for me to live in the carcass I've got,
which is now so loaded down with impertinent junk."

"What did you study at U.C.—philosophy?"

"Philosophy!" Joe said with contempt. "I studied *myself* at U.C.,
that's what I studied, and while I still don't know very much, I
learn something new every day. The more I learn about myself, the
more I learn about you."

"How come?"

"You and I are the same, that's how come. Not you and I *alone*
—you and I and the other fellow too—*everybody*. Cacalokowitz, Lou
Marriacci, Harry Cook, Vernon Higbee, and the millions more all
over the world that you and I have never seen and never will."

"You mean everybody in the world is the same?"

"I do."

"Eskimos?"

"Yes."

"Chinamen?"

"Everybody."

"Germans?"

"Everybody."

"Japanese?"

"Listen," Joe said. "You and I are a couple of Japanese."

Joe didn't say anything then, so I knew it was my turn to say
something, but I didn't know what to say because only that afternoon at the Orientation Lecture the Lieutenant had said the Japanese were monkeys, not human beings. He had said they were cow-
ards. He had said they were cannibals. He had said they weren't like
us. He had said they weren't fighting for freedom, they were fighting for the Emperor who was mad. He had said they were fanatics
who were willing to die like dogs by the thousands for their Emperor whom they worship as we worship God. The Lieutenant had
said it was up to us to understand who we were fighting, to learn
to hate him, so we could kill him when we met him in combat. I
didn't know what to tell Joe Foxhall.

"Do you know what I mean?" he said at last.

"I don't know whether I do or not—*exactly*," I said.

"Listen," Joe said. "All the people of the world are the same, and
they're all waiting for the same thing—to die. In the meantime

they're waiting to do one or another of the other things I just spoke of. If you hate yourself, O.K., hate the Japanese too. Hate the Germans, the Italians, the Hungarians, the Bulgarians. Hate anybody you like. It happens that I don't hate myself because I can't see anything in it for me. Since I don't hate myself, I can't hate anybody else. I may have to kill somebody some day because if I don't he'll kill me, but I'll be damned if I'm going to hate him too. I'll be damned if I'm going to think I've done a fine thing, either. I'll be damned if I'm going to think I've accomplished something for myself, or for you, or for my family or your family, or for our country, or for the world, or for truth, or art, or religion, or poetry. Do you follow me now?"

"I guess so," I said. "Are you a conscientious objector, Joe?"

"Oh poppycock," Joe said. "Conscientious objector my ass. To object to War when it's going on is like objecting to a hurricane that's lifted your house off the ground and is carrying it up into the sky to let it fall and smash after a little while—with you inside. If you object to that, it's a cinch your objection is conscientious. What the hell else could it be? But a hurricane is an act of God. Maybe a War is too—I don't know yet. But my hunch is that a War is an act of man. I don't like it. I hate it with all my heart. But when its fury grabs hold of me, I don't see how I can do anything about it—except hope that I'll be spared, and you can be sure that that's what I'm hoping."

Well, then the truck came by and we picked up our rifles and went out with the other fellows and got in. Joe and I sat together. I didn't know what to tell him, so I offered him a cigarette which he took. I lighted it for him and I lighted one for myself. After he'd inhaled very deeply and exhaled he said, "We're waiting to die— and even these cigarettes help us wait."

It was almost midnight. We would go on duty at twelve sharp, walk our ground for two hours, at which time the truck would bring our relief and take us back to the Guard House where we could rest or sleep for four hours. At six we would go back for two more hours.

"Cigarettes are good things," Joe went on. "You couldn't get men to fight a War without them. They kill you a little, you see— just enough to make it possible for you to get a little more killed without going mad. Because something in you doesn't want you to get killed, and you've got to soothe it—you've got to give it little doses of death—sleep, forgetfulness, distraction—with cigarettes, or alcohol, or women, or work, or whatever it might be. You've got to keep soothing it all the time because it's very sensitive. It might scream if you didn't put it to sleep. Ordinarily you put it into a pleasant sleep by soothing it for reasons that aren't offensive, but in a War you've got to put it to sleep any way you can manage for reasons that *are* offensive. You've got to slug it into unconsciousness if the worst comes to the worst. But the mischief begins when you go too far and instead of putting it to sleep you murder it, because then you're dead yourself—your body is still alive, but the real life in it is dead—and that's the thing I don't like about this monstrous monkey business."

CHAPTER 6

Wesley Longs for Love and Freedom, and Sergeant Cacalokowitz Disgraces the Uniform

WE CAME to the place I was supposed to guard, so I said so long to Joe Foxhall and got out of the truck.

"We wait," Joe said. "That's what we do all our lives. For the next two hours you'll wait for two hours to go by. Two hours a million years old."

"See you when they've gone by," I said.

"O.K.," Joe said. "Look at the sky. Don't forget to do that."

"O.K.," I said.

I went through the formalities of changing the guard with Lou Marriacci who kept shaking his head the way fellows like him do when they are getting a kick out of something they think is silly. When the formalities were over, and he had walked the area with me so I'd know what the area was and I had become the official guard of that area for the next two hours and Lou was unofficial, he said, "Now take it easy, boy—don't go to work and get scared and shoot the first man who comes along and looks like a spy and can't talk from being just as scared as you are."

"O.K., Lou," I said.

"A fellow like you should always try to stay out of trouble," Lou said. "Never murder anybody. Ask the man in a nice way to identify himself and let him go to bed. He'll be some private just back from a lay in town, so don't murder him. He's got a mother."

"I won't shoot anybody," I said.

The fellows in the truck hollered out to Lou, "Come on, come on—let's get going. We can't hang around all night."

"I'll walk back to the Guard House," Lou hollered back. He handed one of the fellows in the truck his rifle, and then the driver of the truck shifted gears and the truck banged away down the road.

I thought Lou was going to start walking back to the Guard House right away, but he stayed beside me, walking in step with me and talking.

"Slow down, boy," he said. "Take it easy. Two hours is a long time. You've got nowhere to go—this is it. Around and around." So I slowed down. I guess I was walking too fast for a guard. Guarding isn't walking, it's guarding—it's being on hand. Well, it was late November, cold and clear and so lonely a fellow felt a dozen different ways at once, but mainly sorrowful and grieving, the way a little boy will grieve around Christmas-time without knowing what he's grieving for.

The sky was something to look at all right. It was bigger and deeper than I had ever seen it before. There were only a half dozen stars out, but they were big and bright and good to see. I was fresh from all the things Joe had said about waiting, so I couldn't help wondering about the waiting stars do—the waiting they've already done—and the waiting they'll do a hundred years after all the people of our world are dead and forgotten, and the same old world is still underfoot.

"What are you dreaming about?" Lou said.

"Nothing," I said.

"Well, where do you think you're going?"

"What do you mean?"

"You're off the area."

Lou took me back to the area, and then he said, "I got a little something I want to talk to you about."

"It's against the rules to walk with me when I'm on Guard Duty," I said.

"I know," Lou said, "but don't worry, I won't get you into any trouble. There's nobody around. If anybody shows up I'll disappear."

The area I was guarding was about a block long and half a block deep, full of all kinds of Army trucks. Two blocks away was a cluster of barracks under construction, and then there was nothing around but open country and the woods I used to go to to be alone in once in a while. It was a big Post, out in the country, about seven miles from Sacramento over lonely little roads and a main highway with almost no traffic on it at that hour.

Sometimes I could see a light moving along the main highway, away over in the West, and I wondered who it was in the car and where he was going. I envied him for being free, for having a car, for being on the lonely highway at that hour of the night, for having a home and family to go to. I thought of him as if he were alone in a whole secret world of Winter love, getting home in his car, putting it away, going inside to his wife who had food waiting for him on the kitchen table. I could see him holding her in his arms and kissing her, and then sitting down with her and talking quietly —talking about nothing important, nothing like the stuff Joe Foxhall had talked about. Just little things—where he had been and what he had done. I could even *hear* them talking, and I knew they didn't feel they were waiting to die at all. *Oh beauty, here we are —here we are!* And I wished to God I was the man. I wished I was the one who was there. I wished to God I was home and had *my* woman. I wished to God the War was over, and I was there—*oh my darling, the War's over, and here it is November again, and here's the cold sky again, and the bright stars my darling. Here we are, and nobody to bother us.*

I got so carried away thinking about the wonderful luck of some people and the poor luck of others that I guess I forgot what I was supposed to be doing because all of a sudden Lou grabbed me and shook me and then disappeared. I saw somebody coming along that it was my duty to challenge, so I said, "Halt—who's there?" But my voice was so bad I had to say it again. Well, even then the man didn't stop, so I got scared because I expected the man to stop and answer me and I didn't know what to do. I guess Lou understood what was going on because he jumped up from somewhere and took my rifle and told the man to halt, and the man halted.

Then Lou got the man to identify himself, and it was the Sergeant himself, Cacalokowitz, drunk and dead to the world of law and order.

"Why you old son of a bitch," Lou said. "I should have shot you."

"Shot me?" Cacalokowitz said. "What for?"

"What for?" Lou said. "For not halting when I told you to halt."

"I halted," Cacalokowitz said.

"Yeah," Lou said. "After I'd told you three times. You can thank God I didn't shoot you after the second time."

"Shoot me for what?" Cacalokowitz said.

"For being Sergeant," Lou said.

I stayed out of sight because it would look funny if two fellows were guarding the same area at the same time.

"A fine Sergeant you are," Lou said. "A fine example you're setting for the boys from good families in San Francisco and Oakland and cities like that. I think I'll turn you over to the Sergeant of the Guard."

"Sergeant of the Guard?" Cacalokowitz said. "What for?"

"For not halting when challenged," Lou said. "For being drunk, and for having sexual relations while off duty."

"Sexual relations?" Cacalokowitz said. "I just come from church."

"You just come from a cat-house," Lou said. "I can smell the perfume on you from here."

"Polish church," Cacalokowitz said.

"You're drunk," Lou said. "Well listen, Sergeant, it's my duty to make an example of you, and I'm going to do my duty as you have always asked me to. I've done my duty when you've asked me to do Kitchen Police, and I've done my duty when you've asked me to clean the barracks, and I've done my duty every time you've asked me to do it, so I've got to do my duty now too. You'll be busted back to a private in the morning."

The Sergeant was drunk, but not so drunk he couldn't understand he was in trouble—not so drunk that Lou couldn't have a lot of fun with him out there under that wonderful lonely November sky at midnight. After a while the Sergeant got around to talking terms with Lou and Lou's terms were hard. From now on he wanted no more nonsense from the Sergeant—no more K.P. or any other kind of Extra Duty for him, or Dominic Tosca, or Victor Tosca, or Wesley Jackson.

"Wesley Jackson?" Cacalokowitz said. "What's he got to do with it?"

"Never mind what he's got to do with it," Lou said. "Just see that he's included in the deal, that's all."

"O.K.," Cacalokowitz said, so I knew I was either headed for better days or more trouble. If the Sergeant happened to forget everything in the morning when he was sober again, or if he remembered everything but decided to get even on Lou and the rest of us, what could we do? But I hadn't figured on Lou knowing his business so well.

"What have you got on you?" Lou said. "To make it a contract, legal and irrevocable?"

"Legal and irrevocable?" Cacalokowitz said.

"Come on," Lou said. "What have you got on you? Bring the junk out of your pockets."

Cacalokowitz brought the junk out of his pockets and Lou went over everything and picked out all kinds of valuable odds and ends —identification cards, dog tags, and other things the Sergeant needed badly in order to go on being Sergeant—and he put them away in his own pockets. There was a big assortment of things to put away because Lou kept everything except money.

"I'll hand you back what I don't need in the morning," Lou said. "I'll do it when nobody's around. I'll get you to your bunk and put you to bed, but from now on I want you to be nice to me and Dominic and Victor Tosca and Wesley Jackson—understand?"

"O.K.," Cacalokowitz said.

"Just be nice and everything will be all right," Lou said. "I'm being nice to you, so you be nice to us. We're only four. We'll be wanting extra passes and other little favors. We'll be nice all the time, so you can say we are being rewarded for good behavior in case anybody gets nosey—understand?"

"O.K."

"And you can thank God I didn't shoot you," Lou said. "You've

got no idea how close I came to shooting you. You look just like a
German spy."

"Polish," Cacalokowitz said.

Lou handed me back my rifle.

"I'll come back in a little while," he said.

"Come on," Lou said to the Sergeant. "You're out on your feet.
Hold on to me. I'll take you home."

He went off with the Sergeant, and I could hear him badgering
the poor man, nagging at him for being drunk and no different
from any other unhappy man, Sergeant or not.

CHAPTER 7

*Wesley Makes an Astrological Bargain, Sees a Star,
and Learns a Secret*

I WATCHED Lou Marriacci keep Sergeant Cacalokowitz on his feet
as they went up the road together. There was something almost
wonderful about it, although I couldn't figure out what it was.
Maybe it was what the Sergeant said to Lou when they began
to go.

"Walk slowly," he said. "I'm wounded."

"You ain't wounded," Lou said. "You're drunk."

"No, I'm wounded," the Sergeant said. "I'm bleeding somewhere."

Drunkards say strange things sometimes. I know because I remember the things Pop used to say when he was drunk. Half the
time I didn't know what he was talking about, but I always knew
it wasn't as silly as it sounded. Cacalokowitz wasn't wounded and
he wasn't bleeding, but I knew what he meant, and I guess Lou
knew too because he slowed down. Lou started out with Cacalokowitz as if he was angry at him, as if he didn't want to waste any
more time than he had to on a man who got so drunk he couldn't
walk straight or talk sense—but I knew Lou was only having fun.

Pretty soon I couldn't see them any more, so I was alone. I didn't
mind being alone, but I would be a liar if I didn't say I was scared.
I walked around the area once, hoping nobody would come up to

be challenged because I didn't like doing it. I didn't mind *being* challenged, but I didn't like challenging.

I remembered the instructions we always got when we were about to go on Guard Duty.

At the same time I kept looking into the sky at the stars and dreaming of the lucky man who was free.

The instructions were always the same—at least in spirit, if not in words. "Remember, men. This is serious. You're not going out there for fun or punishment. Doing Guard Duty is an honor any man in this man's Army has got to be proud of. It's a great responsibility too. You go out there to guard your country against the enemy. Challenge in a clear strong commanding voice. If your first challenge is not acknowledged, challenge again. If your second challenge is not acknowledged and you think something's funny, shoot—and shoot to kill! You will have done your duty, no matter who you've shot—Major or Colonel or General. If you don't think something's funny—if you think it's a drunk, or if you can see who it is and *know* he's O.K., well, don't shoot—use your judgment. But don't take any chances. The enemy is in our midst. He may put on the uniform of an American soldier, and you may *think* you recognize him, but don't be a fool—don't take any chances—it may cost you your life. If your second challenge is not acknowledged it is not only right for you to shoot, it's your duty."

I didn't like the instructions. A few people had been shot, but not one of them had been the enemy. Most of them had been Enlisted Men. We heard stories all the time of fellows on Guard Duty shooting innocent people. Most of the stories came from other Army Posts, but one night one of our own fellows shot a fellow from another Company. The fellow who'd been shot died before they could do anything for him, and the fellow who'd shot him was sent home on furlough, so he could get over feeling the way he did, but he never came back to our Post. They sent him to another Post, so nobody would know he'd killed another fellow in the Army.

Pretty soon I'd walked around the area three times. A dozen different ideas had gone through my head, and then I began to hum something, only I didn't know what it was or where I'd heard it. Then I knew, because I remembered the words that went with it:

Oh boy oh joy where do we go from here? It was Pop's, from the other War.

Next I got to wondering what Lou wanted to tell me. Then a little cur-dog came up from somewhere and tagged along at my heels. I was thankful for him. It was very still all around, only myself making a little noise with my heavy shoes as I walked, and the little cur-dog making no noise at all. Once I stopped, even though it was against the rules, to talk to him. "Hello, boy," I said, but the little dog ran off. He slowed down, stopped, and little by little came back. I could see he didn't feel sure of me. You find little cur-dogs all over the place around Army Posts.

I got to feeling I ought to have a smoke, but I knew it was against the rules, so I didn't have one—but pretty soon I felt too miserable not to take a chance, so I got a cigarette to my mouth, got it lighted, and began to smoke and feel better, just like Joe Foxhall said. I'd been on duty only thirty-five minutes, but it seemed a lot longer.

I decided to see if I could figure out a game to help me pass the time, so I said, "From here to where I turn is exactly one hundred and thirty-three steps," and I began to count. But I was wrong. It came to one hundred and fifty-four steps.

Then I said, "If I guess within ten steps how many steps there are from this end of my area to the other, well, then—"

"Well, then the War will be over by morning."

But I knew that was silly, so I said, "No. If I guess right, I won't have anybody to challenge and I'll go back to the Guard House and Joe Foxhall and I will feel glad that we've got half our duty done, and maybe instead of going to sleep we'll sit down and smoke and talk."

But I figured I'd be seeing Joe in the Guard House anyway, and I figured we'd sit down and smoke and talk anyway, so I wasn't satisfied with that bargain either.

So then I said, "If I guess within ten of the right number, Pop's all right. He's gotten over the awful way he was feeling when he went away, and he's safe and sound in some furnished room somewhere."

But even that didn't satisfy me, although I wanted Pop to be all right.

So I said, "I'll find the girl for me before this War's over—*my* girl, *my* bride, *my* wife. I'll find her and she'll love me as I love her and we'll set ourselves up somewhere and not care what the people of the world do to themselves."

By that time I had walked the whole distance and hadn't tried to guess how many steps it was, so now I was walking the depth of the area which was not long enough to bother with, too easy to guess, I thought, so I waited until I had walked that distance and was ready to turn and walk the length of the area.

When I was near the turn I said, "It's exactly three hundred and ninety-three steps. If I've guessed within ten of the right number, I'll find her."

I turned the corner and began to count.

The reason I picked that number, three hundred and ninety-three, is that I like the number three and have felt for a long time that it's my number, and that all numbers into which three is evenly divisible are my numbers. My Army Serial Number is all threes and nines. When I was little I liked the number seven, but I guess seven was too many because I stopped liking it and started liking three. I saw all things in threes, and it seemed right to me.

Well, I hoped I was right in my guess because you get to believing in numbers, but pretty soon I could see I had overshot the mark, so then I began to take shorter steps, but even then I was away off the mark. All it came to was two hundred and eighty-four steps, including the short ones, and that is a number that means nothing at all to me. If you divided three into two hundred and eighty-four, you got ninety-four and two-thirds, but that's no good either. The nine in ninety-four was better than nothing, though, so I decided that that gave me a right to try to make another bargain, but since I had failed in the one that meant (if I had not failed) that I would find my girl, I decided to make a new bargain, so I said, "This time if I see a new star come out in the sky, or if I see a star fall, well then—"

I knew there was a bargain I wanted to make, but I just didn't seem to know what it was.

But pretty soon I knew, and I knew for sure.

"If, in the time it takes me to walk once around my area, I see a new star, or one that falls, I won't get killed in this War."

So then I got excited because I wasn't sure I hadn't given myself the worst of it. Walking as slow as a guard ought to walk, or even a little slower, it took about eleven minutes to walk around the area, and even though I had been looking into the sky most of the time I'd been on duty I hadn't seen a new star come out and I hadn't seen one fall. But a bargain is a bargain and I'd made it, so I was going to keep it. I felt it would be better to have a little the worst of it, so that if I won, I'd know for sure that I wouldn't get killed in the War because it seemed to me the odds against my being spared were pretty great, so it seemed right not to have the best of it in the bargaining.

I didn't let myself look into the sky while I was thinking about all this because if a new star came out before I had given the bargain my hand in solemn agreement, it wouldn't count anyway, so then I gave my hand, noticed where I was, looked up into the sky and said, "If I see a new star before I have passed this point again, or if I see a star fall, I, Wesley Jackson, won't be killed in this War."

I decided also not to cheat by walking slow, or slower than I had been walking, because I didn't think there was any use trying to cheat God. If I wasn't going to be spared, I might as well know it. I wouldn't feel fretful about it any more. I'd just say to myself, "Well, I guess that's going to be so," and forget it.

I looked into the sky and walked, and pretty soon I was more than half way around my area. I hadn't seen a new star come out and I hadn't seen one fall.

I didn't feel discouraged, though.

I don't know why I felt I'd see a new star come out before I'd gone all the way around, but I did, I felt *sure* I'd see one—I wouldn't see a star fall, I'd see a new one come out from somewhere away out in the sky, millions of miles away, and then I'd know I wouldn't be killed. I didn't care what the odds against me were, I knew there would be a star out for me to see—a brand new one in the sky—my own star—to tell me that I was going to be O.K.

Well, then I began to look where I believed the star was going to come out—away over in the East—about twenty feet above the line of the land. Now I don't know anything about stars. I don't know where they are in the sky from one month to another, or where they move, or what their names are, so you've got to appreciate what an awful chance I was taking by keeping my eyes on that one area. But I wasn't worried. I knew my star would come out, so don't think I'm telling a lie when I tell you my star *did* come out. It came out long before I had walked all the way around my area too. I saw it as clearly as I saw the other stars in the sky, and I saw it exactly when it came out too.

"This is a miracle," I said. "That star came out for me. God made it come out for me. Of course it was always there, only something was in the way, but God heard the bargain I made. He took the stuff away that was keeping the star from being seen, and it came out and I saw it, and I'm not going to get killed in this War."

I felt so happy I hollered *Oh boy oh joy where do we go from here?* The little cur-dog didn't seem afraid any more, and I wasn't afraid any more, either—of *anything*. I got out another cigarette and lighted it and smoked it, and I didn't even care if somebody came up the road to be challenged.

Then somebody came down the road.

I knew it was Lou Marriacci, but I shouted, "Halt—who's there?" anyway.

"That's right," Lou said. "Holler it out."

So I hollered it out again, just for the devil of it.

CHAPTER 8

Lou Marriacci Asks a Difficult Favor of Wesley

LOU AND I walked along and I wondered what was on his mind.

"I see you've lost your pal," he said of the little cur-dog which had just run off. "I like a fellow dogs like. I know he's O.K."

"A lot of dogs *don't* like me," I said. "A lonely dog will make friends with *anybody* at this hour of the night."

"Oh no," Lou said. "The minute I came up that little dog ran off, and now he's gone. He's not hanging around near by, figuring to come back, either. He won't come back until I go."

"You mean he doesn't like you?"

"I *know* he doesn't."

"Why not?"

"Well," Lou said, "it's like this. A dog'll go on a hunch. He may be wrong, but chances are he's right. I walked this area for two hours before you did. I saw that dog a couple of times away off sniffing the air trying to make up his mind if he ought to come up and make friends. Well, he never came up. He smelled me and didn't like it."

"What do you mean?"

"Dogs want somebody to be right. I'm all right for myself, I guess, but I'm not right for dogs any more. Maybe you're right for yourself and dogs too. If you are, you're a good man, and I figure you are. That's the reason I want to talk to you."

"O.K., Lou."

"First of all, don't let on to anybody what happened here a little while ago between me and the Sergeant. I put him to bed and everything's O.K. He'll be nice to us from now on. He's never been a son of a bitch with any of us, but it's always good to have something on somebody who might get a notion into his head to *become* a son of a bitch. Cacalokowitz is a good guy, but he's got a job to do, so every once in a while he's got to give us orders—you know, Police the Grounds, Barracks Orderly, Kitchen Police, Guard Duty, and all the rest of it."

"I guess everybody's got to take his turn, Lou."

"You're a good boy," Lou said. "Sure you guess everybody's got to take his turn. On account of that the little dog likes you. But I *don't* believe everybody's got to take his turn. I know everybody *doesn't* take his turn—and that bothers me because if there's anything in the world I don't like it's for me to be sucker."

"What do you mean?"

"In a War everybody *ought* to take his turn—and I mean *everybody*—unless somebody's kidding. *I'm* in the Army, but a lot of guys I know who ought to be in the Army, well, they're not, and never will be."

"How come?"

"They're smart," Lou said. "They ain't suckers. If a War's on the level, every man in the country ought to be in it, especially the guys with the most dough, the most to lose—but they're not in the War at all. They want you and me to fight the War, but *they* want to go right on making money—out of *us*. They don't care how many of us get killed just so they keep what they've got and get more. They're very patriotic too—ten times more patriotic than we are. They love the War and we hate it. They read about it in the papers and magazines and they know more about it than we'll ever know. They know all about other Wars too. They study them, to find out how to make more money out of *this* War."

"I guess some people would rather have money than anything else."

"A *lot* of people," Lou said. "Too many of them. But it isn't money alone they're after—they use a War to get other things too —more power, more importance, more reputation. We become numbers in the Army—you can't tell one of us from another at a distance of ten yards. But to hell with that. What I want to tell you is this."

We walked along in silence a moment and then he said: "I want to get out of the Army. I know I can do it. But I need a little help, and I'm asking you to help me."

"I couldn't do that, Lou," I said. "They could shoot both of us for something like that."

"Don't think I don't mean to do something for you," Lou said. "I do."

"I won't do it," I said. "Maybe I'm a sucker to be in the Army, but I'm in it, and I won't do anything crooked."

"Suppose it *isn't* crooked?"

"But it is," I said. "I know it is."

"All right," Lou said. "Let's say it is a little crooked. Do you think everything else in the Army, in the government, in the whole country is on the level? It's *all* crooked—always has been—always will be as long as people are the way they are. People stink."

"Maybe they do," I said, "but sometimes they don't."

"Sometimes *I* don't," Lou said. "I've got a wife that I love, that means everything in the world to me, that sits at home and cries all day. I've got three kids that I love. I don't stink when I'm with my wife and kids. I'm forty years old. Some son of a bitch in my neighborhood doesn't like me, so he gets me into the Army. He finds out I've put away a little money and he says it's enough to keep my family O.K. for five or six years—so he sits down with the other sons of bitches and they decide to *get* me—they decide to put me in the Army as a punishment. The country's at War, every-body's excited, hundreds of thousands of guys are going into the Army, so why not me too, they figure. One's a cheap lawyer, an-other's a tinhorn Judge, another's a ten cent business man—but they're on the Board, so anything they say goes. The mob's with them—not with me. I get thrown into the Army the way a thief gets thrown into the penitentiary. Well, I've cut a few corners, but I never stole a dime from any man in my life. I paid my debts. I loved my wife, and I brought up my kids."

"What'd you do before you got into the Army?"

"A little of everything," Lou said. "I've got a bar on Pacific Street in San Francisco. I used to have a little gambling in the back room. And I knew some girls who liked to make a little easy money once in a while."

"What kind of easy money?"

"You know what I mean," Lou said, and I did too. I guess I should have hated somebody like that, walking with me and telling me things like that about himself—first his wife and kids—and then all that other stuff. But I guess I'm lowdown because I didn't hate Lou. Maybe it was because I knew he wasn't lying to me. Maybe it was because he was telling me everything, and I had to admire any-body so honest. If I'd done things like that, I guess I'd be ashamed to tell anybody. I guess I'd lie about it, or skip it, but Lou wasn't lying, he was telling the truth. It seemed to me that if everybody told the truth, if everybody was straight that way no matter who they were or what they did, the world would be a lot better off, and maybe that's why I didn't hate him. I'm not sure, though. Maybe I didn't hate him because I'm just naturally lowdown.

"Well, what do you want me to do?" I said.

"You tell me what I can do for you."

"Oh that's all right. You don't have to do anything for me, but if I can do anything for you that won't get me shot, I guess I'll do it. What are the names of your kids?"

"The oldest is Lou too. Then there's a girl, Rosa, because that's my mother's name. And then the baby, two years old, Michael, be-cause that's my grandfather's name."

"What's your wife's name?"

"Marta."

"What do you want me to do, Lou?"

"I'm supposed to come back on Guard Duty here at four."

"Yeah."

"Well, I won't be in the Guard House, and I won't be here."

"Where will you be?"

"I'll be lost," Lou said. "They'll find me in two or three days. I won't remember anything. So they'll go back and find out who saw me last. Well, you did. When I took the Sergeant to his bed I thought somebody would see me and I'd let this stuff go until some other time, but nobody was around. Everybody was asleep. Nobody saw me. Here's the Sergeant's stuff. All of it. What I want you to do is give it back to him in the morning. If he wants to know how you got it, remind him that he was drunk, that he came up the road and didn't answer your challenge, so you almost shot him but recognized him just in time. Tell him he wouldn't go home but kept giving you his things. So you kept them for him."

"He'll remember that you took him to his bed," I said.

"Not too clearly," Lou said, "and that's what I want. He'll *sort* of remember, but he won't want to bring the matter up."

"Suppose he says somebody put him to bed?"

"He was drunk. He imagined it. He won't tell anybody about it, but when you give him his stuff he may take you to one side and ask you. Tell him he gave you his stuff and went home."

"Suppose he just looks at me and doesn't ask me anything?"

"All the better. It may happen that *nobody* will ask you anything—all the better."

"Do you think you can do it, Lou?"

"I've *got* to do it," Lou said. "My wife cries all day. My brother writes and tells me the truth. My wife—she writes *beautiful* letters —everything's fine—she tells me lies and prays for me every morning and night."

"She *prays?*"

"Sure," Lou said.

"Where you going? Where will you be?"

"See those woods?"

"Yeah."

"Ever been there?"

"Yeah."

"Well," Lou said. "For the next couple of days and nights I'm going to be in those woods."

"Got anything to eat?"

"I don't want anything to eat. A man who loses his memory from being worried about his wife and family doesn't take a lunch with him."

"All I got to do is give Cacalokowitz his stuff, is that it?"

"And if anybody asks you if you changed the Guard with me, you did. That's the truth. If they ask you if I got on the truck to go back to the Guard House, I didn't. *That's* the truth. Did you see me walk toward the Guard House? You did. You'll see me walk toward the Guard House in a few minutes, so *that* will be the truth too."

Lou waited a little while and then he said, "Do you want to do it?"

"I'd be a liar if I told you I *wanted* to do it, because I *don't*. I've never been in anything crooked in my life. I don't think I could tell a real lie if I wanted to. I hate lies. If somebody lies to me I get sick to my stomach—I don't know why."

"I'll go back to the Guard House," Lou said. "We'll forget all about it. I know how you feel. I'm a poor Catholic but not so poor I don't respect an honest man."

"I'm not finished yet," I said. "I don't *want* to do it, but I'll do it. I'll try to stick to the truth—but if I've got to lie, well, I guess I'll lie."

"I hope you don't have to lie," Lou said. "I'll remember this."

Well, then Lou walked off toward the Guard House, and I was alone again. I thought a lot of time had gone by, but it was only twenty-five past one, so I still had thirty-five minutes to go.

CHAPTER 9

Wesley Challenges Colonel Remington Who Curses the Democrats and Has a Yapping Duel with a Dog

BEING ALONE again I got to feeling sore at myself for siding with Lou, but I knew I wouldn't double-cross him no matter what hap-

pened to me, so that made me sorer than ever. I was a liar. I'd do
what Lou asked me to do—I'd answer the questions, telling the
truth or telling lies—but after Lou got out of the Army—if he did—
well, then I'd go and turn myself in, that's what I'd do.

But how could I do it? If I turned myself in, they'd want to know
what for, and all I'd be able to tell them was that I lied about Lou
Marriacci, so then they'd go after Lou—home with his family by
then—and bring him back—bring him back in disgrace, or take
him to jail.

No, I'd never be able to tell the truth again. It would hurt too
many people for me to start telling the truth once I'd lied. It would
hurt Marta Marriacci and her two sons Lou and Michael and her
daughter Rosa. I'd be a liar forever, that's all.

Well, I felt so poorly about being a liar that tears came to my
eyes and I wished I'd never been born. What's the use being alive
if you're going to be a liar?

I began to cry the way I used to cry when I was no more than
six or seven years old—softly and secretly, with nobody to talk to.

While I was crying I heard somebody coming up the road. I was
so sore at myself, I got mean and hated everybody, especially the
man I was going to challenge. I wasn't scared any more because
now I didn't care what happened. I didn't even care if I got
killed, because if I did then I wouldn't have to tell any lies, and
Lou would know I hadn't double-crossed him. I was so mean when
I said, "Halt—who's there?" the man almost fell down. He stopped
right where he was.

"Colonel Remington," the man said, and by God it *was* the
Colonel. *He* was drunk too.

Well, Colonel or no Colonel, I was sore. And some day this very
man—this old fart who'd gotten drunk in town the same as Cacalokowitz, the same as any ordinary Private in the Army—would go
to work and put me through some terrible inquisition that would
disgrace me forever, so I didn't stop being mean. I told him to advance and identify himself, which he did. When everything was in
order and he was free to proceed to his quarters, the Colonel looked
at me and said, "You're Private Jackson, aren't you?"

"Yes, sir."

"Well, I'm proud of you," he said. "I've never seen a better job of challenging on this Post, and I'm going to mention it to your Company Commander in the morning. As long as young men like yourself stand guard at the portals of our great country, our people need have no fear for their security. Private Jackson, the glory of our nation lies in the firm brave hearts of such young men as yourself, not in the sickly wishy-washy hearts of such men as—"

I thought he was going to tell the truth and say "—such men as *myself,*" but he went on to say:

"—Benedict Arnold."

Well, I hadn't checked up on Benedict Arnold, so I didn't know if his heart had been sickly and wishy-washy or not, but it was all right with me at that hour of the morning.

"Yes, sir," I said.

"And furthermore," the Colonel said, "we will fight the enemy until he has been brought to his knees, and corruption has been driven from the face of the—"

Well, then the Colonel refused to finish the sentence, which was so easy to finish. I was about to finish it for him when he made the kind of face a man makes who remembers something that disgusts him, and he began to swear under his breath, "Dirty little small-town slut." So I figured the Colonel was guilty of having had sexual relations while off duty too, the same as Sergeant Cacalokowitz— maybe with the same girl, considering Cacalokowitz had come by so long ago.

I didn't want to be rude, but it seemed to me that if I was to go on being all the wonderful and brave things he'd said I was I ought to go on with my duty, so I said, "Good night, sir," and began to walk.

Well, then the Colonel went a little mad, I guess, from the drinking he'd done, and the other things, and he began to make a speech that sounded a lot like a speech the President had made over the radio once. The Colonel used the same words the President had used, he used the same tone of voice, and he tried to sound as if he were the President. Well, I'd heard different Privates in the Army do that. Almost every man in the Army does that at one time or another, especially where the President said he knew War, had seen the dead bodies of American soldiers, hated War, and wanted to assure American mothers and fathers that he was going to see to it that their sons would not go to War, and so on and so forth. Every man in the Army who'd heard that speech remembers it and sometimes imitates the President making the speech, or at least goes over it in his mind. I've gone over it in my own mind, but I haven't been sore at the President, I've just wondered why things turn out the way they do—even the greatest elected man in the country unable to control anything any more—everybody in the world helpless to stop the War, even the President of the United States, the political leader of the greatest, richest, freest, most advanced and best people in the world.

To make matters worse the little cur-dog showed up and listened to the Colonel, wondering what the noise was all about. I guess the dog decided the noise was no good because he began to bark at the Colonel. Maybe he was protesting, maybe he was joining in. Whatever it was, the little dog didn't want to get any closer than he could help—and he kept going off a little, and coming back, and yapping. Well, the Colonel heard the dog yapping, and started yapping back at the dog. This excited the dog, and then the noise got to be something awful. I don't know who yapped the best, the dog or the Colonel, but it was close all the way. Finally, the Colonel won. The dog went off and didn't come back.

Victorious at last, the Colonel said at the top of his voice, "To hell with the Democrats, I'm a Republican." Well, I never could tell a Democrat from a Republican, so I didn't care about that. I suppose he was a Republican if he said so, but in addition to being a Republican, he was a Colonel, next to the biggest man at our Post, and I thought he ought to remember it. The only man bigger than him was a Brigadier General who only came out of hiding when there was something fussy doing—a dedication of a new building or something like that. They told me he was a West Point man, past sixty, who'd never seen combat in his life and never would, on account of his advanced years. It didn't seem to me a Colonel ought to carry on that way, imitating the President on the one hand, and on the other yapping at a lonely little cur-dog.

So I stood there, about twenty yards from the Colonel, and listened. So many confusing things had happened to me since I'd gone on Guard Duty I thought I'd shoot the man and be done with it—which goes to show you what crazy ideas go through a fellow's head when he's in the Army and there's a War going on in the world. Just because I had a loaded gun in my hands and the Colonel was making a mish-mash of everything they had taught me to believe about the Army, I got the notion into my head to shoot him—as if that would do anybody any good. The idea was a terrible surprise to me.

I decided to make up for having had such an ugly idea in my head by going back to the Colonel to see if I couldn't keep him from disgracing himself any more. If somebody came along and saw him in that condition and heard him imitating the President, yapping at the dog, and denouncing the Democrats, well, it might not be so good for him, or it might make for more crookedness than ever—so I went back and stood at attention near him. He went right on denouncing the Democrats. He said they were hypocrites, money-changers, Episcopalians, and Fascists, but after I'd stood at attention half a minute or so he fell silent and it seemed to me he was trying to gather his feeble wits about him. At last he said:

"Private Jackson, you are the best soldier on this Post, and I'm going to speak to your Company Commander in the morning."

"Yes, sir," I said.

"Who are *you* going to speak to about *me* in the morning?"

"Nobody, sir."

"Who are you going to *write* to about me in the morning?"

"Nobody, sir."

Well, then the Colonel waited a moment.

"You're a good soldier, Private Jackson," he said. "Good night."

"Good night, sir," I said.

From the way he went up the road I knew he was sober again. In less than three minutes I was back to feeling sore at myself for the bargain I'd made with Lou Marriacci, so then I got to crying again because pretty soon I was going to be a liar. I cried a long time, but after a while it wasn't only because I was going to be a liar, it was because of other things too: poor Pop lost; a beautiful night full of ugly and half-mad people like Cacalokowitz and the Colonel instead of handsome people; Lou Marriacci scheming against the government to get back to his broken-hearted wife; the lonely cur-dog yapping at the Colonel instead of finding a friend and a home; Joe Foxhall knowing so much about the way things are with people; my star in the sky, that came out just for me; the man in the car on the highway going home to his wife with nobody to take him by the arm and say, "You've had enough happiness, come along with me"; the President talking over the radio long ago and everybody imitating him, and everything turning out different from what he thought; hell, what sense does the world make? What's a fellow to do to save his soul? When is he ever going to get time enough to reach a little peace and beauty and love and truth? How could anybody like me, born ugly and foolish, find time to grow handsome somewhere or other in this life?

CHAPTER 10

Wesley Escapes a Life of Lying and Dreams a Terrible Dream

PRETTY SOON the truck came by and a new fellow came out and went through the rigmarole of Changing the Guard with me. I walked him around the area, then got into the truck and sat down beside Joe Foxhall who was smoking a cigarette. I got one out and lighted it and the truck moved on up the road.

"Anything doing?" Joe said.

"Nothing much."

"Did you look at the sky?"

"I sure did."

"Did you like it?"

"Sure."

"Get any ideas of any kind?"

"One or two."

"Like what, for instance?"

"Like what a sad lot human beings are."

"How'd you happen to get *that* idea?"

"I don't know. I just got it."

"Challenge anybody?"

"A couple. How about you?"

"Not one, for which I thank God."

"Why?"

"Who am I to ask who's there? *I'm* there, that's who. I'm there every time. Did you get tired of waiting?"

"A little."

"Want to go to sleep?"

"Not for a while."

"I think I'll sit up a while too. Sing any old songs?"

"Valencia."

"Say any old prayers?"

"Our Father."

"Remember any old times or old friends?"

"When I was six or seven, and Pop."

"Any laughs?"

"A few."

"Any tears?"

"What?"

"Any tears—inside or out?"

"Both."

"About what?"

"Everything."

"Same here," Joe said. "Did a dog come up and make friends?"

"Yeah. Did he come up and make friends with you?"

"Yeah," Joe said.

"What makes a dog do that?" I said.

"What do you mean?" Joe said.

"Why will a dog make friends with one fellow and not another?"

"A dog will make friends with anybody."

"I hear a dog won't make friends with somebody who doesn't smell right."

"There isn't a man in the world who doesn't smell right," Joe said.

"Well, maybe he doesn't smell right for the dog, then."

"That may be," Joe said, "but the sense of smell in a dog is a poor means by which to judge human beings, who get their odor from the world."

"I guess so."

We came to the Guard House and had some coffee and sandwiches and sat down and talked a long time. Then we stretched out and went to sleep. When it was almost six they got us up and we went back in the truck to our areas and stood watch again for two hours.

It was almost half past eight when I got back to the Company area, so I went straight to the Orderly Room to give Sergeant Cacalokowitz his stuff. He was at his little desk looking over the Sick List. He looked pretty sick himself. When he looked up and saw me I didn't smile or anything. Nobody was around, so I got his stuff out of my pocket and handed it to him. He looked at me as if to see if he could tell how much I knew, and I guess he decided I knew plenty because he said, "Thanks, Wesley."

I was so glad I hadn't had to lie I thanked God, but when I turned to go he said very quietly, "You seen Lou Marriacci?"

I got scared because I was sure I'd have to start telling lies now and keep it up to the end of my days.

"When?" I said.

"This morning."

"No, I haven't," I said, which was the truth, but getting closer and closer to lies.

"I want to talk to Lou," the Sergeant said.

So there it was. I'd never escape. I thought I'd ask the Sergeant what he wanted to talk to Lou about, but I changed my mind because I was afraid asking questions would lead me into lying all the quicker and I wanted to postpone that as long as possible.

Then the Sergeant said very casually, "Lou's being sent home. He's out of the Army."

"What?"

"He's past thirty-eight. A new directive from the War Department came out a couple of days ago. He'll be home in three or four days. He's on this list. If you see him, tell him, will you?"

"I'll tell him," I said.

I don't think I've ever felt as happy as I felt that morning because Lou was going home anyway and I didn't have to be a liar. I couldn't wait to get out to the woods, but I didn't want to run because then somebody would wonder why I was running, so I strolled. I took all the time in the world and I kept feeling better and better every minute. Pretty soon I was in the woods, and after a while I was in the heart of the woods where I figured Lou would be, so I started whistling *Valencia*. I wanted Lou to hear me and know nothing was wrong, but I guess I wasn't near enough for him to hear me because he didn't come out of hiding, and it seemed to me I'd walked straight through the heart of the woods. Even so, I kept walking and whistling and waiting for Lou to show up.

After a while I got worried. Suppose he'd gone home? Suppose somebody picked him up for being Absent Without Leave and things went wrong because he didn't know he was out of the Army anyway, and he pretended he'd lost his memory, and everybody got suspicious and called me in, and I had to be a liar after all, even though he was out of the Army anyway?

I got so scared I stopped whistling. I began searching for Lou, getting more and more scared all the time. That would be just my luck, and Lou's too—to disgrace ourselves when we didn't need to. Well, then I thought I'd call out to him, so I called out a couple of times, but my voice scared me worse than ever.

I sat down to think things over. I must have fallen asleep because all of a sudden I was home with Pop and he was O.K. again. He was singing *Valencia,* and he wasn't sore at anybody. He was happy. Pop was fixing one of those suppers he used to fix for us when we were together and everything was O.K. We sat down and ate the supper and talked. Then somebody knocked at the door, and I got scared to death. Pop opened the door and a fellow said, "I'm looking for Wesley Jackson."

"Who are you?" Pop said.

And the fellow said, "You know me. I don't have to tell you who I am."

I got so scared I began to cry, only it wasn't like the crying a man does when he's awake, it was that awful crying that gets the tears flowing out of everything in the whole world and shakes everything with terrible sobs—because I knew who the fellow was, and I didn't want to go with him. Pop didn't want me to go with him either, but there was nothing he could do about it, so he took a drink out of a bottle. The fellow came and stood beside me, but I wouldn't look at him. Then he took me by the shoulder and shook me gently and said my name as if he were the best friend I had in the world instead of who he really was.

"Wesley," he said.

Pretty soon it came to me that maybe I was sleeping, and *oh beauty* that made me feel better. I began to remember little things that made me know I must be sleeping—the woods, Cacalokowitz drunk at night and sober in the morning, and then I was *sure* I was dreaming, so I moved around a little this way and that in my sleep, feeling better, and then I opened my eyes, and there was Lou Marriacci holding me by the shoulder.

I shook my head a couple of times and then smiled at Lou, but I guess he was too worried to smile at me. He didn't say anything. He just waited.

"You're out of the Army," I said. But he still didn't say anything. "I came to tell you, but I couldn't find you. I guess I fell asleep." I waited for Lou to say something, but I guess he just couldn't, so I said: "I gave Cacalokowitz his stuff like you told me to, and he said thanks. He didn't ask any questions, so I didn't have to tell any lies. So then he wanted to know if I'd seen you, and I got scared. But I'd made a bargain and I was going to keep it, only I hoped I wouldn't have to tell any lies to do it. So then he said you were out of the Army because you are over thirty-eight years of age. He said a new directive had come out a couple of days ago, and a list had come from headquarters with your name on it. He told me to tell you, if I saw you. So I came to tell you."

All of a sudden Lou began to smile.

"I love you like I love my own two sons," he said. "You're the handsomest man in the world."

"I sure am glad you're going home," I said.

"I've got to do something for you," Lou said. "I've got to do a *lot* of things for you."

"The *Army's* sending you home," I said. "I didn't do anything."

"You were *going* to," Lou said. "I've got to do a lot of things for you. You've got to tell me what I can do for you."

"There's nothing I can think of, Lou. Thanks just the same."

"Think hard," Lou said. "I'll see that you get pocket money—a little every week. But that's nothing. Think hard."

"I don't want any money."

"You've got to tell me what I can do for you," Lou said. "I'm a Catholic. I asked you to lie for me, and I know you're not the kind of fellow who likes to lie, but you said you'd do it for me because you wanted me to get home. I've got to do something for you to atone for my sin. I always do something to atone for my sins—every one of them."

So then I remembered Pop.

"Maybe you could find my father," I said.

"I'll find him," Lou said. "Tell me about him."

I told Lou everything and he said, "Don't worry. I'll find your father. I'll take care of him too. I'll write to you about him, and I'll get *him* to write to you."

We went back to the Company area, and Lou Marriacci went into the Orderly Room to see Sergeant Cacalokowitz. Three days later I went down to the station with Lou to say good-bye. Dominic and Victor Tosca were there too, and when the time came for Lou to get on the train there were tears in his eyes. He put his arms around Dominic and said something in Italian to him, and then he put his arms around Victor and slapped his face the way they do—three or four times, with love. And then Lou came to me.

"Don't worry about anything," he said. "I'll find your father. I'll find him before I do anything else."

So then Lou Marriacci got on the train, and the three of us walked out of the depot to a bar.

I drank a lot of beer and got drunk for the first time in my life, and Dominic and Victor Tosca took me back to the Post in a taxi and put me to bed.

CHAPTER 11

Harry Cook and Wesley See a Beautiful Girl

WHEN HARRY COOK and I flew to Alaska because Jim Kirby the newspaperman fixed it for us with poor old Colonel Remington (who wanted to get himself into the papers) we swore to stick together through the whole War, but we hadn't figured on the Army having other plans for us, so when we had finished our Basic Training, which was not long after Lou Marriacci went home, Harry Cook found out that he was going to a Post in Missouri, and I found out that I was going to a Post in New York.

"What part of New York?" Harry said.

"Cacalokowitz says *in* New York—in the city. What part of Missouri you going to?"

"Some place near Joplin."

Well, we both felt sorry, but that's how things go in the Army. Dominic Tosca was going to Missouri too, but his brother Victor was going to New York. The fellows going to New York felt luckier than the fellows going to Missouri, or somewhere else—Louisiana some of the fellows were going to. Everybody felt sorry to be going but at the same time eager. The reason the fellows who were going to Missouri envied the fellows who were going to New York is that everybody in America wants to get to New York some day, I guess. I know I always thought I'd like to get to New York some day, so when the gossip reached me that I was on the list to go to New York I felt pretty good. But when I heard that Harry Cook wasn't going with me, I went to Cacalokowitz and told him if Harry couldn't go to New York with me, could I go to Missouri with him? Cacalokowitz said every man had been classified and assigned, and there was nothing he could do about it.

"What am I classified as?"

Cacalokowitz got out my card and looked at it.

"It doesn't say *exactly*," he said. "But you're going to New York. I guess they'll have you do office work or something like that because you know how to type. Where'd you learn to type?"

"Polytechnic High School, San Francisco."

"How come?"

"It was a mistake. I tried to tell them I hadn't elected typing and shorthand, but they didn't care about that, so I learned both—typing better than shorthand, but I got passing marks in both."

"Ever work in an office?"

"I worked for the Southern Pacific Railroad two weeks once during school vacation. It's on the card."

"I guess that's why they're sending you to New York," Cacalokowitz said.

"Why can't I go to Missouri with Harry Cook?"

"Because you're in the Army."

"What's Harry going to do in Missouri?"

Cacalokowitz got out Harry's card and looked at it.

"Lineman," he said. "His I.Q. is pretty low."

"How's mine?"

"Pretty high."

"How's yours?"

Cacalokowitz looked at me, but he wasn't sore.

"Mine's lower than Harry's," he said. "I guess that's why I'm Top Sergeant out here in this wilderness. You fellows of Company B are the fifth lot I've trained and sent along, but I'm still here. You're pretty lucky to be going to New York. I wish I was going too."

Well, we thought we'd be leaving in a day or two, but it wasn't until the middle of December that we finally left. Before the Company broke up a picture was taken, and everybody had everybody else sign his name on the picture, so everybody would remember everybody else. Harry and I promised to write to each other and we spent a lot of time together in town on pass. Everybody on pass went to Sacramento, but Harry and I always went to Roseville which was smaller and a better place to spend time because there were fewer soldiers there.

One night we were sitting at a table in a little restaurant and bar that we liked when a girl came in that I thought was the most beautiful girl I had ever seen. She was so beautiful I lost my breath and gulped a couple of times. If I had tried to talk to her I know I wouldn't have been able to say one word. The girl was dark, with long soft black hair reaching to the bottom of her neck, and a red ribbon in her hair. She was Spanish, I guess, or Spanish and Mexican, but she was so beautiful I was ashamed to look at her because of the way she made me feel. She made me feel I ought to be alone with her somewhere and tear her clothes off. She had a drink at the bar—a real drink—straight whiskey—and every once in a while she turned and looked the place over.

Well, Harry and I had been talking about our visit to Alaska, remembering the fun we'd had up there and how amazed I was when I saw the Eskimo Dan Collins. We didn't want to let each other know how the girl made us feel, so we tried to go right on talking.

"Red Collins," Harry said. "He sure didn't look like an Eskimo, did he?"

"You mean Dan Black," I said. So then I knew Harry had noticed the red ribbon in her hair, and I had noticed how black hair was, but I didn't say anything.

"Well, whatever his name was," Harry said, "we sure had fun up there in Roseville."

I almost didn't notice that he'd said Roseville instead of Fairbanks because I knew what he meant anyway, so it didn't matter.

I never knew things to matter so little so suddenly that had always mattered so much, and that seemed very strange to me. I kept looking at the girl's body inside her dress and I kept seeing it naked, and that kept blinding me all the time. I was too ashamed to let on, but trying so hard *not* to let on only made me more ashamed and made the way I felt more noticeable than it would have been if I had been lucky enough not to feel so all-fired crazy about the girl. I didn't care about myself any more. I didn't care about Pop being lost any more. I didn't care about people being in trouble all the time, or poor, or broken-hearted, or sick any more. I didn't care about good luck or bad luck, being alive or being dead or anything else any more. All I cared about was the awful need I felt to get near the girl, and that didn't make sense at all.

The girl had another drink and Harry and I went right on talking as if both of us weren't smitten sick by her beauty. I had no idea what we were saying, but I knew we were getting everything wrong. I had no idea what we were saying because what we were saying was only an excuse for what we were feeling, which we couldn't possibly talk about, and I thought, "I guess this is what happens to men to make them the fools they are, but I guess it's worth it."

First thing I knew she had come over to our table and was having a drink with us. Well, then something happened that amazed me. I began to hate Harry because he could talk to her so easily and I couldn't. I was jealous of his good looks too. I decided she was nothing but a common street-walker, but that didn't make me feel any better. So then I thought, "Harry's I.Q. is very low." After a while I said to myself, "This sort of thing is for animals," but I knew I was trying to make up for being so ugly. Then I said, "Some day I'll go to work and make something of myself in the world, and Harry Cook will be nothing, or nothing more than a lineman with syphilis." But no matter what I said to myself I didn't feel any better, and I would have given anything in the world to change places with Harry because the girl seemed to like him so. Pretty soon the girl turned to me.

"What's the matter with *you?*" she said. "You look as if you ate something that didn't agree with you."

"Oh hell," I thought. "Oh damn me!"

I don't think I ever felt so little in all my life. I thought I'd get up and go out of the place, but I knew if I got up I'd run and maybe stumble and fall and be the biggest fool that ever lived. I thought Harry was going to laugh at me too, because it seemed to me that if I was in his place and he was in mine I would have laughed at him—or at least felt proud of myself. But Harry didn't laugh at me. He had been smiling at the girl, but when he looked over at me he stopped smiling.

"Want to go?" he said. He spoke so softly I could hardly hear him. I couldn't say anything, so Harry got up and said, "Let's go." So then I got sore at myself for being such a lunk.

"Hell no," I said. *"You* don't have to go. I want to take a little walk around town. I'll see you later." I felt proud of myself then, and didn't hate anybody any more, and I didn't feel the way I had been feeling about the girl any more, so I could look at her and smile, and sure enough she smiled at me.

"Maybe I'll see you both later on," I said.

I went out of the place. I didn't run. I didn't stumble or fall. I didn't want to tear the clothes off the girl any more, and a lot of things started to matter again. I stood in front of the restaurant, trying to figure things out, and then I began to walk up the street. Before I got to the corner I heard Harry holler out, "Hey, Jackson, wait for me."

Pretty soon we were walking together. I wanted to say a few things, but I didn't know where to begin. How do you tell a pal you're sorry for having hated him because his I.Q. is low, and he's handsome and you're not, and women of all kinds like him and don't like you, and stuff like that?

At last I said, "She was a nice girl. I wish I hadn't been there to spoil things for you."

"She was a dog," Harry said. But the way he said it I knew he wanted to go back, so I said, "Go on back, Harry. I'll see you in the barracks."

Instead of answering me he took hold of a lamp-post and began to vomit in the gutter. When he was all through he said, "The wine we had at supper made me sick. Let's walk back to the Post."

We walked the whole six miles back to the Post. At first we didn't talk very much, but pretty soon we got to talking about our visit to Alaska, and then we got to singing, and before we got back to our barracks we were O.K. again, and we promised to write and look for each other in San Francisco after the War.

CHAPTER 12

Wesley Remembers His Last Days of Freedom, His First Days of Imprisonment

WHEN I took my physical examination at 444 Market Street in San Francisco there was an old civilian doctor there who said, "Anything the matter with you that you want to tell me about?" I thought, "The only thing the matter with me is that I'm alive and don't know what to do about it," but I knew I couldn't tell him that, so I told him I was O.K. He was in a hurry anyway, because they were examining seven or eight hundred of us and there wasn't time to dilly-dally.

Before we knew it we had gone through the whole machinery of examination and were sitting on benches on one side of a big hall. Somebody called out the name of a Mexican who was told to sit on the empty side of the room. Then the same man called out my name and told me to sit beside the Mexican who said, "I know why we're sitting here, away from the others."

"Why?" I said.

"Because we've been in jail before."

Well, *he* had, but I hadn't, so they wouldn't let him get in the Army. They sent him home, but they sent me back to the other side of the room.

Later in the afternoon they asked every man who had been examined if he wanted to go straight to the Reception Center in

Monterey or take a two-week furlough first. A lot of the fellows wanted to get started right away because they'd heard that the first four or five weeks are the toughest and the sooner they got those weeks out of the way the better, but I wanted the two-week furlough because I wanted to see if I could find Pop and say good-bye to him. And I wanted to walk around San Francisco once more, like I used to do before the War started.

I remember the fellow in front of me in that line. He was asked what he wanted, a two-week furlough or to go to Monterey right away, but he didn't understand, so the fellow who was asking the questions said, "Where do you want to go?"

"Oakland," he said.

The fellow in uniform put this man down for a furlough, but a furlough wasn't what the man wanted at all. He wanted to go home, and he lived in Oakland.

"Can I go home now?" he said.

"Home?" the fellow in uniform said. "You'll take the oath just as soon as the Major shows up."

Well, the man couldn't understand that at all. He was supposed to get out of the way so the rest of us could let the fellow in uniform know what we wanted, but he wouldn't move.

"I want to go home," he said.

"Move on," the fellow in uniform said. He had a lot of work to do and he wanted to get it over with.

"I'm a conscientious objector," the man said.

"Move on," the fellow in uniform said. "You're in the Army now."

So the man moved on and everybody began to say to himself or to the fellow next to him, "You're in the Army now."

The Major didn't show up until three hours later. He was a little drunk and very bored and tired, but he read the required passages from the Articles of War and the other stuff. We were all in the Army then for sure because we had taken the oath.

There's no use saying I didn't feel trapped because that's exactly the way I felt. I felt the way a bull in a corral must feel that knows something funny's going on and gets to thinking he's being taken to slaughter.

But I had two weeks, and I thanked God for them. I went to all the saloons Pop used to go to and I asked about him but nobody had seen him lately or knew where he might be. I looked all over the city for Pop, especially the streets where homeless men go— Third Street and Howard Street and all around in there. I saw a lot of men who might have been Pop, but I didn't see Pop himself.

The days and nights were going by and I didn't know what to do to make the most of them. If I started to read something I had always wanted to read pretty soon I'd remember how little time I had and I'd jump up and go out to the Beach and walk there and look for bright pebbles and watch the sun go down. And then all of a sudden every now and then I'd think I ought to have somebody to say good-bye to, and then remember that I didn't know anybody. I'd get desperate and think I ought to *find* a girl and say good-bye to her. I'd leave the Beach or the Public Library and get on a street-car and go off in any direction looking for a girl to love and say good-bye to. I saw some that I thought I could love all right, but when it came to striking up an acquaintanceship with them I just couldn't do it.

Finally I remembered a girl who had been at Polytechnic High School when I'd been there. I'd been in love with her secretly for a year a long time ago. I decided to look her up. That was early in October, in 1942. The weather was bright and wonderful, with cool fog coming in from the Pacific every evening. It was sundown when I found the girl's house, but when I got to the door I decided I must be out of my head. I didn't even know if the girl had ever noticed me—most likely she hadn't—and there I was calling on her to ask if I might fall in love with her and say good-bye. Even so, I pressed the button of the door-bell, and who should come to the door but the girl herself—Betty Burnett—prettier and prouder than ever. Well, she was in a hurry, the way pretty girls always are when they're near somebody they don't like.

"Remember me?" I said. "Wesley Jackson? Polytechnic—"

"I'm afraid I don't," the girl said. "And I'm in an awful hurry." She closed the door, and that was all. I walked on out to the Beach.

I don't think I felt sorry for myself or anything like that, but I *did* feel sore at myself for getting so panicky about not having a girl to love and say good-bye to. And when I'm sore at myself I'm a better man than when I'm hopeful and not sore at myself.

So then I thought I'd write to Mom. I sat down to do it a couple of times, but I got ashamed and didn't do it because I hadn't written to her in all the time she'd been separated from Pop and me. Now, just because I was going into the Army I wanted to write to her. It seemed a cheap thing to do, so I didn't do it. I always liked Mom, and Pop always liked her. "A finer woman couldn't have been your mother," Pop said. "Too bad she had to marry a man like me. Too bad I had to be your father." But hell, that didn't make sense at all.

One morning the days of my furlough were all gone. I said good-bye to the landlady of the house where Pop and I had lived, but she was having trouble collecting rent from one of her roomers and was too worried about the six dollars he owed her to tell me to take care of myself or anything like that. I packed Pop's stuff into some boxes and the landlady agreed to keep them in the basement until Pop showed up, or until I came home after the War, and that was that.

I took a street-car to Third and Market, transferred to the cross-town street-car and got off at the S.P. Depot. A lot of fellows were already there and more were coming in all the time. Pretty soon we got aboard the train, but it didn't begin to move. I got restless and wondered what the matter was. I didn't know that that was the way it was going to be all the time in the Army—hurry and wait, as the fellows say. We sat in the train long enough to get half-way to Alaska by airplane before it began to move. I remembered a hundred things I should have done but hadn't during my last two weeks, and then at last the train began to move.

Well, there were all kinds of people on the station platform waving good-bye. All of a sudden I heard a crash, so I went to see what it was. It was a man who had punched the window of the train. His wrist was spouting blood and nobody knew what to do. Somebody pulled off his coat, and then his shirt, and wrapped the shirt around his wrist. Everybody was excited and a little sick. The train stopped, and there we were not even out of the depot yard. I tried to find out what had happened, and this is what I learned.

The man had had a couple to drink, and so had the woman who had come to say good-bye to him. He had been standing at the window of the train looking at her. All of a sudden she had begun to

cry and he had shouted at her, "Don't cry!" But she couldn't stop.
Well, then the man got angry and kept shouting at her not to cry,
but the more he shouted the more she cried. So then the man became very angry and doubled his fist and began hitting the air with
his doubled fist because he didn't want her to cry. When the train
began to move he was jabbing the air but jabbed too hard and too
far and punched his fist through the window. He lost so much
blood before somebody who knew what to do got to him that he
passed out, and then it was serious. We stayed in the depot yard
about forty-five minutes, and then an ambulance came and the
man was put on it and taken away.

There isn't much to tell about the Reception Center at Monterey
except that I was sick all the time because I couldn't get used to
living that way, being herded around for examinations and tests
and inoculations and the issuing of clothing and equipment, and
standing in line to eat, to get a haircut, to wash, to sit on the toilet,
to take a shower. It was like cattle. I was sick the whole seven
days and nights I was there.

A lot of strange things happened in those seven days. I saw a
fellow take out his glass eye late at night and look at it with his
good eye and wash it and say to himself, "I'm right-handed and my
right eye's glass—what the hell am I supposed to do in the Army?"
I heard men crying at night, and I saw them sitting or lying on
their bunks in the daytime going mad. But there were comedians
too, especially the Italian and Portuguese boys from Santa Clara
Valley.

There was one fellow with us who was famous. He had been in
the movies, and quite a few fellows remembered him, but I didn't.
Well, this fellow hated the Army more than anybody else. He had
all kinds of money and was always shooting craps with the Negroes
and Filipinos and changing a little game to a big one in two or
three passes. Whether he won or lost he was always the same, so
you could see he wasn't after money, he just wanted something to
take his mind off the way he felt about being in the Army. He was
a lot older than most of us—thirty-five or so, I guess—and every once
in a while he would mention the name of some big man in the
moving picture industry and he would say, "That dirty double-
crossing son of a bitch."

I heard him say that of two or three dozen different executives of one sort or another. He wasn't a leading man, he was a character actor, so he looked a lot like the rest of us. If somebody hadn't told you he was an actor in the movies, you'd never have guessed it. Well, when they ordered him to get the regulation haircut, he didn't like that at all, and he took to swearing at a whole new category of people in Hollywood. He had started out with the business men, but pretty soon he had moved on to the leading men, and then he had taken up the character actors, and then the directors, and finally when it was time for him to get the regulation haircut he took up the actresses, but he called them sons of bitches too. He mentioned all the pretty women he knew, that he'd worked with at one time or another, and he swore at them all. There was a Chinese civilian cutting hair and that's the barber who cut this actor's hair. Well, the barbers were all bad—all ignorant, not like the good barbers of San Francisco—but the Chinaman was the worst of all. When the actor got out of the chair and looked at himself and saw what the Chinaman had done to his head he was so mad he didn't know who else to cuss in Hollywood, so he cussed the animal actors, the dogs and horses.

He paid a half dozen boys from Santa Clara Valley fifty cents a day to salute him whenever they passed him, which they were happy to do, but part of the bargain was that he didn't have to return the salute.

"Officers have to return the salute," he said. "For fifty cents a day I get saluted all day and don't have to lift a finger—the sons of bitches."

Those seven days and nights were the longest I ever lived through. They were a nightmare. I was glad when they put a gang of us on an old broken-down bus and drove us to the Post outside Sacramento. When the bus got near San Francisco I thought my heart would break—but lucky for me, it went north the other way, through Hayward and Oakland, so I didn't see San Francisco again. When Harry Cook and I flew to Alaska the plane landed at the Municipal Airport of San Francisco, and we got out a minute or two, but we didn't see the city, although we had seen the lights of it from away up. Just being near it made us feel better because San Francisco—that's home.

The fellow I spent most of my time with at Monterey was Henry Rhodes, but he went one way and I went another. If Henry reads this, I hope he remembers me, and I hope he's O.K. I hope he's out of the Army and back at his old job on Montgomery Street in San Francisco. I hope every man who was ever drafted into an Army is still alive, out of the Army, back home, and O.K. I mean Russians, Germans, Italians, Japanese, Englishmen, and all the other nationalities of the world. Military men and politicians like to refer to the dead as the *brave* dead or the *heroic* dead or some other kind of dead. I guess I don't understand the dead, because the only dead I can imagine are the dead dead, and that's going too far. I can understand the brave *alive,* though. I can understand them a *little,* and they're a pretty sad lot.

CHAPTER 13

Company B Throws a Farewell Party and Dominic Tosca Says Good-bye to His Brother Victor

WHEN WE all knew where we were going next the atmosphere around our Post grew sombre because so many of us who had come to be pals were going to be separated. We had already been separated from many things, so now we were going to be separated from the friends we had made in the Army too. Sergeant Cacalokowitz knew how we felt because one night he said, "If you guys in Company B want to throw a party before you leave this Post, O.K., throw it, but hurry up because some of you will be leaving here before you know it."

We decided then and there to chip in and buy a lot of beer for a party the following night.

At the party Dominic Tosca came over to me and said, "Keep your eye on my brother for me, will you?"

"Sure," I said.

"Lou Marriacci likes you and if Lou likes you I like you, so look after Victor for me because he's my brother. I'll go get him."

Dominic went and got his brother and said to him, "Here's your pal in New York—and don't forget it." He put his arms around us and squeezed very hard. Victor and I had to laugh because we had always been pretty good pals.

"Babies," Dominic said. "If I was in Frisco, I wouldn't even let you hang around me. So now the government wants you to win the War."

He pushed us away and went and got another bottle of beer and drank it. Then he came back and pointed at Victor and shouted at him, "Hey—you! Stay awake, please. Take care of yourself. Don't be afraid. Write to Mama. Say your prayers. Go to confession. Understand?"

"Ah cut it out will you Dominic?" Victor said.

"You listen to me," Dominic said. "Be a good boy. You're too good-looking for a big city like New York. Take care of yourself. Stick with your pal. Hey, Wesley—pretty soon I won't be seeing you any more. Hang around with my brother in New York. Let me know anything goes wrong." Then he turned to Victor.

"O.K.," he said. "Good-bye, baby. But first, sing the song."

"What song?"

"You know what song. Sing it for your brother once more."

So then Victor sang *Everybody calls me honey*. Dominic listened and tears came to his eyes.

"Mama calls you honey," he said.

He was so overcome he waved a rebuke at the lower things and went back for more beer.

Then Cacalokowitz came over to listen.

"Sing with him," he said to me. "That's a good song. Why don't you sing with him? You can sing, can't you?"

I was a little drunk, so I began to sing with Victor. Pretty soon Cacalokowitz got Dominic to help him push a lot of other fellows over by us, and then almost everybody in Company B was singing with Victor. But no matter how many of us sang, it was always Victor's song, and you could hear him singing better than anybody else. The song was just right for him, and he sang it only one way —straight—while a lot of the other fellows made fun of the song and themselves as they sang.

Well, then Nick Cully sang his song, *Oh Lord, you know I have no friend like you*—and we all joined in on that one too.

The party was a good party because no officers were allowed.

Everybody got drunk and swore to remember everybody else. Harry Cook came over and said, "I'll see you in San Francisco after the War for sure—don't forget. And don't forget to write."

Two days later Harry Cook and Dominic Tosca and Nick Cully and Vernon Higbee and a lot of the other fellows of our Company started their journey to Missouri. Victor Tosca was lying on his bunk when it was time for Dominic to get aboard the truck that was going to carry them to the depot, and from there little by little to the War. I was sitting on my bunk looking down at my shoes when I heard somebody come into the barracks. I looked up and saw Dominic. I saw him begin to walk to his brother. Then I saw him stop. I saw him look at his brother a long time. Then he turned and motioned to me. I went out of the barracks with him, and he put a wad of currency in my hand.

"Pocket money from Lou and me for you and Victor. I ain't got the heart to say good-bye to him again, so tell him I said good-bye, will you?"

"O.K. I'll give him this money too."

"No no," Dominic said. "He's got money. Spend it on each other, but keep your eye on him. You're both babies, but *you* got something upstairs. All he's got is heart—no head at all."

He put his arm around me and squeezed, then he hurried up to the Orderly Room where the truck was waiting.

I thought I'd go along and take one last look at my pal Harry Cook, but I was feeling so low I decided to count the money and go back into the barracks and sit on my bunk instead. The money was ten five-dollar bills. Lou Marriacci had sent me a letter every week for three weeks with a ten-dollar bill in it, but he hadn't had any luck finding Pop. So now I had eighty dollars besides some left-over money from my Army pay. If I knew where Pop was, I'd send him the money because I knew he could use it. He could buy better stuff to drink for a change. I went back into the barracks and sat down. Pretty soon I heard the motor of the truck start. I ran out of the barracks and up the Company Street, and there the truck was going away with Harry Cook and Dominic Tosca in it somewhere, and all the other fellows going to Missouri. When I turned around Victor Tosca was standing beside me.

"Want to go to Roseville for a drink?" he said.

Cacalokowitz gave us passes and we went to Roseville, to the restaurant Harry Cook and I used to go to. We didn't want to eat, so we just sat there and drank. Pretty soon the Spanish girl Harry and I had seen that night came in, and pretty soon she sat down at our table. She liked Victor very much, and the first thing she said was, "Don't I know you from somewhere?"

One thing led to another, so then Victor told her his name.

"Anything to Dominic?" she said.

"I'm his brother."

"Well, what do you know?"

When she heard that Dominic was in the Army she said, "Oh for heaven's sake!"

She got up and smiled and said, "Now take care of yourselves. See you in Frisco sometime maybe. Be good." Then she went out of the place.

"Who is she?" I said.

"I don't know," Victor said. "I guess she's one of Dominic's old girls."

"You mean his sweetheart?"

"Hell no. Dominic never had anything to do with his girls. Do you like her?"

"I thought I might write a letter to her once in a while."

"What for?"

"I don't know."

"We can find her if you want to write to her."

I thought about it and decided I'd better wait for somebody else to write to, but I felt awfully unhappy about the whole thing. Victor didn't, though, and that's what I couldn't understand. It didn't seem as if he wanted to tear her clothes off, and it didn't seem as if he felt unhappy about her, either.

"Don't you feel sorry for a girl like that?" I said.

"She's all right," Victor said. "What's there to feel sorry about?"

"Don't you feel sorry about her living a life like that?"

"I don't suppose she's very good at anything else."

"Wouldn't she be pretty good as a mother?"

"Maybe," Victor said. "Maybe she'll get married and have a family some day."

"You mean a girl like that can still get married?"

"If somebody happened to like her a lot and didn't know, or liked her enough not to care anyway, they could get married, I guess. He'd be somebody who'd been around a little himself, I guess."

"Would a marriage like that work?"

"Maybe," Victor said. "You got a girl?"

"No."

"Here's a picture of mine."

Victor brought a snapshot out of his wallet and handed it to me. Well, the girl in the snapshot was even prettier than the girl who'd had a drink with us. Besides being prettier, there was something good about her that had lasted a long time and would last a long time longer. You could see it in her face as sure as you could see her face.

"She sure is beautiful," I said. "Who is she?"

"She's the daughter of my mother's best friend, our neighbors. She's only seventeen now, but we've been in love a long time, and right after the War we're going to get married."

Well, Victor and I sat there and drank and talked. After a while I began to understand him and his family, but it was pretty confusing all the same because so many different kinds of things were going on in them at the same time. They themselves always seemed to manage to stay neat and O.K., though.

CHAPTER 14

Joe Foxhall, Victor Tosca and Wesley Spend a Night in Chicago on Their Way to New York

THE GOOD day came at last for the three of us from Company B who were going to New York to get on the train and go: Joe Foxhall, Victor Tosca, and myself. And Joe started talking right away.

"One thing I forgot to tell you about," he said, "is the continuous feeling of oppression that badgers a fellow's spirit the minute he begins to be changed from a free human being into what some officers in the Army like to call a 'fighting man.' There's no doubt a fellow gets to be a fighting man soon after he's in the Army, but

I don't think he's quite the same kind of fighting man the Army men mean. He fights boredom and hopelessness and a whole army of little persecutions that seem to be determined to reduce him to something not quite human—an ape with a number.

"In other words," Joe said, "he fights for the freedom of his own little nationality, which is *himself* and no other man in the whole world. And it never seems to him that he is fighting for too little. He fights all the little troops of conditions and circumstances that seek to ambush his spirit and if possible destroy it. He fights being insulted and outraged. And since he fights a losing battle because there is no end to the enemy's resources he is always oppressed. No matter what else goes on in his life, or in his sleep, he's also oppressed all the time. It's like a sickness you can't get rid of. The only cure for it is peace in the world and the information that you are no longer required to do what you are told to do, that you can go home and be happy or unhappy, or anything else you please. Of course there's always the other cure, but not for me. Death is also the cure for measles, but I don't recommend it."

The three of us felt pretty good when the train pulled out of the station and started us on our long journey across the country. It was Christmas week too, and that is my favorite week of the whole year.

Joe Foxhall had been across the country before, so it was old stuff for him, but it was new stuff for Victor and me.

It was new and beautiful stuff for us, and we couldn't get enough of it. The train was crowded of course—troops of all kinds from all over the country getting on and getting off all the time—but Joe pulled a few strings with the conductor, we paid a little extra money, and they put us in a private compartment. It was very small, but you get used to very small areas in the Army. We tossed a coin to see who got what bunk, and it turned out that Joe Foxhall got the worst of it but didn't protest or ask to make it two out of three, the way some fellows do. I got the best of it, and Victor got the next best. That is, I got the lower, so that meant I could look out the window at the landscape all night. Victor got the upper which was as good as the lower except that it was up and had no window. And Joe got the bench across from the lower which the porter made into a bed any time you were ready. When we got up in the morning the porter came and broke down the lower and put a table between the seats, so we had a place to rest our elbows.

We could sit at the table and eat, or talk, or play cards, or read, or write letters—or poems, even. Joe Foxhall wrote poems, but he wouldn't read them to us or let us read them. He said they weren't good enough to read. I asked him how good a poem had to be to be read and he said it had to be as good as the best poem that was ever written. I asked him what that poem was, and he said it was a poem by James Joyce called *Ecce Puer*. He said that that poem said almost everything that could ever be said, and it was only eight lines long. I asked him to recite the poem to us, but he said he'd forgotten it, so then I asked him how he could feel the poem was so great when he couldn't even remember it, and he said he didn't know how, but it was so just the same. He had read the poem in *The New Republic* six or seven years ago, and he had known ever since that he had read the greatest poem in the world.

Victor hadn't ever heard of James Joyce or *The New Republic* and he had never suspected that poems had enough importance to be discussed at such great length, but he listened anyway and didn't say, "That's a lot of hooey," the way so many fellows who don't know very much about something do. Victor just listened and didn't think Joe and I were crazy. Eight lines of poetry—forty words or so—the greatest poem in the world. Victor didn't say, "So what?" He came from a good family, a simple people who had always stayed neat and O.K.

Joe Foxhall had his portable typewriter with him, but he hardly ever used it. He preferred to write his poems quietly, he said. If a man made that much noise to write a poem, he'd better be sure it was great. Before that journey was over Joe said a lot of things, and I wish to God I hadn't forgotten so many of them because Joe almost always said something worth remembering. We played cards, we sang songs, and every time we got to a station where there was time enough to see the town, we hurried out into the town and saw it and brought back a lot of things to put on our table and eat, so we wouldn't have to stand in line to eat in the dining car.

The first town we stopped at was Reno, but we were there only long enough to see the lights and feel the excitement of the people

in the streets of a wide-open gambling town. Then we saw Salt
Lake City, Denver, Omaha, and then Chicago where we changed
trains and stayed overnight.

Victor and I had a lot of money and Joe had enough, so we went
to a good hotel and had food served in the two rooms we'd taken.
We had supper and breakfast served to us. Living that way seemed
a lot different from the way we'd been living, but it seemed absolutely right for us too. I wasn't surprised by the furniture or anything. The first thing Victor did was hand half-dollar pieces to
everybody who did anything for us, and he gave the waiter who
brought us our supper two one-dollar bills. After supper he gave
the same man another one-dollar bill when he brought us brandy,
which Joe felt was in order. It seemed to me Victor's family didn't
know how to be careful about money, and I thought that that was
just about as nice a quality as a family could have.

Joe said he thought we ought to see if we couldn't get somebody
to send up three beautiful girls. I didn't know he was kidding, so
I was a little surprised, but Victor wasn't surprised at all. He said
somebody could be found to send up the girls all right. He didn't
say he wouldn't have anything to do with any of them, but I knew
from the way he talked that he wouldn't. He just didn't want to
spoil anything for anybody else. I didn't know whether or not I'd
have anything to do with any of them, so I was a little worried
about the whole thing.

But Joe was only kidding, which made me feel foolish.

After supper we went out to look at the town. We went to a lot
of places and had a drink or two in each place, but only Joe did
any real drinking. Victor and I took to drinking beer after the
brandy, but Joe stayed with brandy all the time. I wasn't sure I was
keeping my eye on Victor the way Dominic had asked me to. It
seemed to me that Victor might keep his eye on *me* because the
more beer I drank the more I kept noticing how beautiful every
woman I saw was, and I wondered why, with all the beautiful
women in the world, I shouldn't have one.

Pretty soon we were all tired and sleepy, so we walked home and
said our prayers and went to bed. Joe Foxhall was the one who said
we had to say our prayers.

He was a funny fellow that Joe Foxhall, but he was always serious too. He was more than serious, he was sad. That's how it is with a lot of fellows who are funny, I guess.

It was three o'clock in the morning by the time we got to bed, but Joe had picked a good late train for us instead of an early one. When he turned out the lights he said, "We can sleep as long as we like because we're taking the evening train. We'll have breakfast when everybody else is having lunch."

We had breakfast at one in the afternoon. It was a thick steak apiece, with potatoes and onions fried together which Joe knew about, called Lyonnaise, boiling hot coffee and apple pie. It was just about the finest breakfast I ever ate. Joe made the waiter bring up a whole big pie, still in its baking tin, so we each had two big pieces. There was enough coffee for a dozen growing boys, but we spent a lot of time at the table, eating and talking, and we drank it all.

"A man about to sit down in the electric chair is given a breakfast something like this," Joe said.

Well, Victor and I were enjoying things so much we didn't bother to try to figure out what Joe meant, but a long time afterwards I remembered the remark and I knew what he meant. We just went on eating the pie and drinking the coffee and feeling thankful to God for Jesus whose birthday the whole Christian world would soon be celebrating.

After breakfast I looked in the Chicago telephone book and found a fellow named Wesley Jackson, but I didn't mention it to anybody. I thought I might find Pop's name in the book too. I had agreed beforehand that if I did, I would call up whoever it was and talk to him. But Pop's name wasn't in the book. There were a lot of Jacksons of course—two or three Andrew Jacksons, at least one each of the usual names like Joseph, Edward, William, and so on—but not one Bernard. Bernard (NMI) Jackson. (NMI) is the Army's way of getting it clear that your whole name is your given name and your family name. It means No Middle Initial. Pop didn't have a middle initial, and neither did I. Well, then I got to turning the pages of the Chicago telephone book, and it was wonderful thinking of all the people with names and telephones.

Names are like poems, I guess, and the poem by James Joyce that

Joe Foxhall liked so much may be the greatest poem in the world, but I like the poems names are too.

We all shaved and took showers and put on fresh clothes, and our Army shoes which Victor had had the valet shine for us because we had always had to shine them ourselves, and our uniforms which Victor had had the valet press.

If only there hadn't been a War, we would have felt even better than we did. Deep down we knew we weren't kidding anybody—this was only a little sport because we happened to have enough money to be able to afford it, and because Joe Foxhall wasn't the kind of nuisance a lot of fellows in the Army are and didn't make us get on the earliest train as if we had to get to New York just in time to be told to wait around for five or six days while somebody tried to figure out what to do with us. We knew this was a little make-believe that couldn't last very long, and we knew we weren't kidding anybody.

We got on the evening train O.K. Joe had already arranged for another compartment for us, so we tossed a coin again, and everything evened up very nicely because this time Joe got the lower, I got the upper, and Victor got the bench.

That journey across the country to New York with Joe Foxhall and Victor Tosca was one of the nicest things that ever happened to me.

CHAPTER 15

Wesley Gets Pneumonia for a Christmas Present, Meets a Brother in the Hospital, and Finds Out from Victor What the Post in New York Is Like

CHRISTMAS JUST about breaks the heart anyway, let alone Christmas in New York, three thousand miles from home. When I went out to walk in the streets I could even *smell* how far away San Francisco was. It was too far to reach immediately, which is all the time I wanted to take, so I knew I was homesick. Christmas makes a fellow homesick even when he's home sometimes, but there I was with all that land between myself and home. The streets were covered with snow and full of beautiful girls I didn't know. One after another I saw them and never saw them again. It was awful, cold and lonely, and there wasn't one girl for me to kiss on Christmas morning.

That's why I got pneumonia, I guess.

They took me in an ambulance to the Army Hospital on Governors Island in New York harbor, and they put me in bed in a big room full of men in pain—oh that was no Christmas for Wesley Jackson! It was just my luck to come down with pneumonia when I wanted to go through the streets singing *Silent Night* and kissing all the Christmastime girls. It was just my misfortune to fall sick in body when the whole world was supposed to be full of song and love.

There wasn't much song or love in that hospital. *Oh Blessed Infant*, it was hell. Any time you see a movie about an Army Hospital and the nurse is beautiful and full of tenderness and understanding—well, they're fooling you. The nurses are *not* beautiful, and they are *not* full of tenderness and understanding. Most of the time it's not nurses that take care of you anyway—it's other fellows in the Army. But those nurses—God forgive them. They are policemen, they're not women at all.

A Red Cross woman with a cold wet nose and a moustache under it came to my bed and woke me up to ask if I wanted taffy kisses. I couldn't help saying what I said.

"No," I said. "I just want to lie here and die."

If you want to know who took care of the sick in that hospital, I'll tell you. The sick took care of the sick. The less sick took care of the more sick. They didn't take medicine to them, but they took healing to them. They went to them and sat beside them and waited. They didn't say anything. They just sat there and when the very sick ones woke up there was somebody there a fellow hadn't seen before who was a brother just the same. I know, because when I woke up my brother was sitting there. He was a Japanese boy who was in the American Army. He didn't smile and he didn't say anything. He just sat there, better now, waiting for me to get better too.

He had a dried-up little old orange in his hand for me, but he knew I might not want it just then, so I didn't even have to shake my head to let him know. He just knew, and he put the orange on the table, so I'd have it when I wanted it. After a while I went to sleep again, and when I woke up he was still there. We're animals, that's what we are. Sick animals understand each other even if they don't belong to the same family, and they care about one another. Whoever he was, that Japanese boy was my doctor in that hospital. I never did see him too clearly because I was too sick, and by the time I was well enough to sit at attention when the Army doctors made their morning rounds, he was gone. But there were three dried-up little old oranges on my table that he'd left for me. I thank people everywhere for the goodness of their hearts, which came out so abundantly and quietly in that boy. The Army doctors gave me medicine all right, but they might just as well have given it to something in a cage or a test-tube. Sickness isn't all in the body, you know.

One night in the hospital I heard that it was now 1943, but hell, I didn't know what had happened to 1942. Victor Tosca had tried to visit me, but they'd told him he couldn't—first because I was too sick, second because they didn't allow visitors in that ward. So I didn't see him until I was out of the hospital, trying to keep my legs steady, and by that time it was almost the end of January.

I wanted to see Joe Foxhall right away, but Victor told me Joe had gotten in trouble and they'd shipped him to a Post in Ohio as punishment.

We sat down in a little restaurant in the Battery and had coffee.

"What kind of trouble?" I said.

"He had some words with the Company Commander," Victor said.

"What sort of words?"

"They had an argument about something," Victor said. "At first they were going to court-martial him, but after a while they decided not to. They sent him to Ohio instead."

"What sort of a Post is it?"

"You'll find out."

"Is it that bad?"

"They keep threatening you."

"What do they threaten to do?"

"Send you to North Africa or the Pacific."

"Who are they?"

"They're a mob who beat the draft by volunteering and getting direct commissions as technical experts. I think that's the excuse they give—technical experts."

"Who's the Company Commander?"

"Fellow from Universal."

"What do you mean?"

"Universal Pictures."

"You mean he's an actor?"

"No. His mother's brother is on the Board of Directors."

"Well, what's *he?*"

"They say he used to carry film from one part of the studio to the other."

"I don't get it."

"The whole Post is like that. It's a Club, and it's not easy to join."

"What are the requirements?"

"I'm not sure. All I know is that not one of them knows how to hold a rifle."

"What have they got you doing?"

"K.P.," Victor said. "Barracks Orderly, Guard Duty, and I go to school."

"What are they teaching you?"

"Map Reading and Army Organization."

"What's the Sergeant like?"

"He's Army. He's the only fellow in the joint who knows what he's doing. He had to be Army or the whole place would collapse. He's a very unhappy man."

"Why?"

"He's doing everybody's work."

"Why?"

"Because they're all from Universal, or Warner's, or Columbia, or Metro, or R.K.O. They're the happiest people I've ever seen."

"You're kidding."

"No," Victor said. "You'll go to work and throw one of them a salute and he'll call you back and tell you to do it again—it wasn't good enough. 'How long have you been in the Army?' he'll ask you. He came from Hollywood by airplane four days ago and just got into his pink pants. A Major."

"What about the Enlisted Men?"

"There are Members, and Non-Members."

"What's the difference?"

"Members get ratings, so they won't have to do any of the dirty work—and they go along with the officers, calling them by their first names and talking about Sam Goldwyn and L. B. Mayer, and laughing their heads off."

"What happens to the Non-Members?"

"There's a War on. This is a time of National Emergency. The Non-Members do their duty, as it is pointed out to them in official, printed orders. They go here and there."

"How do you like it?"

"I'd like to get three of my brother Dominic's friends to capture the Post for America, that's how I like it."

"Have you done much K.P.?"

"Too much. Smell my hands. That's from four days ago. The stink won't get out of my skin. And the men in the pink pants come around to see that I get all the grease out of the corners of the baking pans."

"How's New York?"

"They can have it."

"What do you hear from Dominic?"

"He hit a Lieutenant for calling him a Wop."

"Things are pretty bad."

"I'm ready to go over the hill."

"Any mail for me?"

"These two letters from Lou."

Victor handed me the two letters and I put them in my pocket, to read later on. I was still a little sick from the pneumonia and the hospital, but I was on a two-week convalescent furlough, so I told Victor I wanted to get myself a room in a good hotel, where should I go?

"Come to my hotel," Victor said. "We'll get a couple of adjoining rooms."

"Do they let you live off the Post?"

"Not officially. I've got to stand Reveille at six in the morning, but I get a little privacy almost every day. I've got to keep a bunk in the barracks, keep it clean, stay in for Friday Night Clean Up, and so on."

"That's pretty good, isn't it?"

"But they keep threatening you," Victor said. "They can't stop you from having a room at a hotel if you can afford it because all the Members live off the Post, but they *know* who sleeps in his bunk and who doesn't, and if you don't sleep in your bunk and aren't a Member, they like you to know there's a War on. Think of the fellows in the Pacific getting their heads blown off all the time. Think of that."

"What are you going to do?"

"I don't know, yet. I don't like being threatened, that's all."

We got a taxi and Victor told the man to take us to The Great Northern Hotel on 57th Street.

"It's not as good as the hotel in Chicago," he said, "but I couldn't go to a better hotel because they wouldn't like it."

"Why not?"

"They don't want it to get around that anybody at that Post isn't sacrificing his life all the time. They're very touchy about that. You and I are in Company D. That means we are on the Adjutant General's list, and that means we're available for shipment at any time. The Members are in Company A."

"What's that mean?"

"That means that their mothers' brothers are on the Board of Directors, and *they* are not on the Adjutant General's list, but can throw a snappy salute and talk a crushing defeat for the enemy."

"If you went over the hill, where would you go?"

"I'm not going over any hill," Victor said.

"We can get transferred to another branch of service."

"Don't even think of it. They're very sensitive about that too, and if you fill out the form and hand it in, it hurts their feelings. It hurts their feelings so much they get excited about the way the War's going and feel it's their duty to get you overseas as soon as possible."

We got out of the taxi and went into The Great Northern Hotel. Victor knew everybody. When he told them we wanted adjoining rooms, they all got busy. In less than ten minutes Victor's stuff was in the new place, so we moved in, and it was two good rooms.

I didn't like the way that Post sounded, but I was too tired to think about it, so I stretched out on my bed and Victor stretched out on his. By the time I had read the two letters from Lou Marriacci and wanted to tell Victor the good news, he was sound asleep. The good news was that Lou had found Pop in the Army Hospital at the Presidio in San Francisco. He'd been pretty sick. But Lou had gotten him out of the hospital and put him in a little furnished apartment over his saloon on Pacific Street, and given him money. He said Pop was O.K. now and was going to write to me very soon. He said not to worry, he liked Pop and Pop liked him and everything was going to be all right, so I went to sleep too.

CHAPTER 16

Wesley Gets Off to a Poor Start at the New Post Because He Doesn't Know How to Answer Military Questions, Reads Ecclesiastes, and Remembers the Vow He Made When He Was Sick

AFTER MY furlough of two weeks I felt half-way alive again, but I still got tired easily.

The day I returned to duty fell on a Saturday, so I had to stand Inspection. When the Company Commander showed up I saw a man all dressed up in fine clothes who walked as if he was the one man in the whole world who was going to smash Hitler—and then he slipped on a pebble and I knew he wasn't. The fellow standing next to me in the Inspection Formation kept talking all the time. When the Company Commander showed up he said, "Look at him, will you? Now, there's a fighting man for you. Look at those pants. Notice how proud he is. He's proud because he's winning the War." When the Company Commander slipped on the pebble, this fellow said, "That might have happened to anybody. Things like that happen in a War. Notice how quickly he recovers himself. He's a born leader. The son of a bitch couldn't lead you to the latrine. The no-good conniving little son of a bitch."

During the furlough Victor and I had talked things over, and we had come to the conclusion that the only thing for us to do was

try to get along, no matter what. We decided to make a game of it
and wait for the War to end. If we get rousted around, we decided
to imagine it was happening to somebody else. We decided to
watch the show, because that's what it was: watch the boys in the
pink pants make fools of themselves, which they did all the time.
They helped win the War all right, but the front they fought on
was on no map and was mentioned in no dispatches. It was a hell
of a War, though, and many a man earned the admiration of his
Uncle on the Board of Directors.

So the great soldier began to inspect his troops. And his troops
were a peculiar lot. On the one hand there were his friends who
called him by his first name. They were scenario writers who had
never written anything, not even a scenario; directors who had
never directed anything; and producers who had never produced
anything. On the other hand there were fellows who knew something or other about photography, or the cutting of film. Or fellows who were projectionists. I didn't know where they planned to
fit me into that picture, so I decided they would do about the same
with me as they'd done with Victor Tosca—office-boy, messenger,
or technical assistant—that is, a fellow who would move a chair or
a piece of equipment, or just be on hand to do something none of
the officers wanted to ask their friends to do while these others
made Training Films.

Well, if that was how they wanted me to do my duty, it was O.K.
with me.

Pretty soon the Company Commander reached our row. All of
us tightened up, so we'd pass Inspection and not get some kind of
Extra Duty. When he came to the fellow next to me he said, "Why
aren't your shoes shined?"

The fellow looked down at his shoes, so then the Company Commander said, "Eyes straight ahead." He said it in a very military
manner.

The fellow didn't get much of a look at his shoes, but he said,
"I thought they *were* shined, sir."

The Company Commander turned to the Sergeant who put a
mark after the fellow's name, so the fellow knew he was going to
get Extra Duty.

Then the Company Commander came to me.

"What's your name?"

"Wesley Jackson, sir."

"How long have you been in the Army?"

"Three and a half months, sir."

"And yet you don't seem to know that you *are* in the Army."

I didn't know what he meant, so I didn't say anything because I knew if I started a discussion I'd get Extra Duty.

"Do you?" he said.

I didn't know what else to say, so I said, "Yes, sir."

"Yes, sir *what?*"

"Yes, sir, I know I'm in the Army."

"Well, then answer my question."

"What question, sir?"

I knew I was in for it now, for sure. I'd gone to work and *asked* a question, and that's the worst thing a fellow can do when he's at attention, in formation.

"*My* question," the Company Commander said.

"My name is Wesley Jackson, sir," I said.

"See me in the Orderly Room after this formation," he said.

So there I was, off to a poor start on my first day. After the formation I went to the Orderly Room and the Sergeant told me to wait. The Sergeant was bored and tired and very unhappy, just as Victor had said.

"What'd I do wrong?" I asked him.

"Should have told him your rank."

"He asked me to tell him my name."

"Should have told him your rank."

I waited an hour, and then the Sergeant told me I could see the Company Commander.

"Do you know how to present yourself to him?" he said.

I said I did, so I walked to the Company Commander's desk, stood at attention, saluted, and said, "Private Jackson reporting as ordered, sir."

I expected him to say, "At ease," but he didn't.

"How does it happen," he said, "that you don't know you're in the Army?"

"I know I'm in the Army, sir."

"Do you know what your rank is?"

"Yes, sir. It's Private."

"Do you know what branch of the service you're in?"

"Yes, sir."

"Do you know what Post this is?"

"Yes, sir."

"Do you know the function of this Post?"

I didn't, but I said I did.

Then he said, "You don't seem to know you're in the Army, and I think there's something to be done about that. The Sergeant will tell you what it is. That's all."

I saluted, about-faced, and went to the Sergeant's desk.

"You're on K.P. tomorrow," the Sergeant said. "Be in the mess-hall in your fatigues at four in the morning." I didn't say anything, so the Sergeant said, "You've just come back from hospital furlough, so go on up to the Dispensary for a physical."

I went up to the Dispensary and sat on the bench three hours, waiting to be examined. At a quarter to twelve the Medical Officer arrived and looked at the fellows who were on Sick Call. There were about thirty of them. He asked one fellow after another what was the matter, but he was in a hurry, so one fellow said "Cold," another "Ear," another "Stomach," and one fellow said something that made the Medical Officer very angry. This fellow said, "Nightmares."

"Nightmares?" the Medical Officer said. "What are you doing up here? Get back to your unit. Hurry now."

The fellow got up and went away and the Medical Officer turned to one of the Enlisted Men who worked with him and said, "Let me know who that was. We'll get rid of his nightmares for him."

Then he came to me. I told him I'd just returned to duty from a furlough after a month in the hospital with pneumonia.

"Feel all right?"

"I don't know, sir. The Sergeant told me to come up for a physical."

"O.K.," he said. "Report to your unit."

I went back to the Sergeant.

"Are you O.K.?" he said.

"What do you mean?"

"Did you get your physical?"

"I sat there three hours," I said. "When the Medical Officer arrived he asked me how I felt and I told him I didn't know, so he told me to report to my unit."

"You've had your physical," the Sergeant said. "You're O.K." He shook his head with amazement and anger.

"What's my unit?"

"Don't know yet. The Company Commander's been looking at your card. He wants to talk to you again."

I moved toward the Company Commander's desk, but the Sergeant said, "Not now—later. I'll let you know when he's ready for you."

"I'm a little hungry," I said. "Can I go to lunch?"

"Better wait," the Sergeant said.

I sat down on the bench and pretty soon Victor came and sat beside me. I told him what had happened and he said, "The dirty little son of a bitch. I'll do K.P. for you tomorrow—you're not well enough to do K.P. yet."

I told Victor I wouldn't let him do K.P. for me. I told him it was a good thing I'd gotten off to a poor start because I'd get used to being rousted all the sooner, and it seemed to me I ought to get used to it as soon as possible. Victor asked the Sergeant if he could do K.P. in my place because I'd had pneumonia, but the Sergeant said no. Victor sat down and looked over at the Company Commander.

"I guess I'll just have to kill the son of a bitch," he said.

I laughed and reminded Victor that we had agreed to try to get along, no matter what, so he said, "O.K., O.K., I'll see you at home."

I waited an hour for the Company Commander to see me, and then he went to lunch. The Sergeant told me to go to lunch too, but to hurry back because if I wasn't on hand when the Company Commander wanted to see me he'd be very angry. I said I ought to have an hour for lunch the same as anybody else, but the Sergeant said to come back as soon as possible. I thought I'd have lunch in the mess-hall to see what the food was like, but the fellow at the door said lunch was from half past eleven to one. I told him it was three minutes to one, but he said it was too late, so I went out of the building and found a little restaurant two blocks away. I sat down to eat some lunch, but I was so sore about my bad luck and so hungry for something really good to eat that I couldn't eat at all—I just drank two cups of black coffee and then went back to the Orderly Room.

At a quarter to three the Company Commander came back from lunch. With him were three other officers, all in pink pants, and just as Victor had said they were calling each other by their first names, remembering other happy people, and having a fine time. The four of them chattered for about an hour. The Sergeant looked over at them every once in a while, and then at me—and I began to be pretty sick and tired of it. I didn't feel happy at all.

After a while the Company Commander's friends went off, so I felt sure I'd see him soon and get it over with, but then he began to make telephone calls. He called his mother who had just come to New York to be near him, and they talked a long time. Then he called a girl or a woman named Stella. He talked with her the way men of that kind talk to women they know—fast and clever and full of jokes and gossip and laughter and the word *listen* again and again. I asked the Sergeant what time we'd stand Retreat. He said Retreat was at six every night ordinarily, but there probably wouldn't be any Retreat tonight because it was Saturday.

"I don't feel so good," I said. "I think I ought to lie down and rest."

"What's the matter?"

"I get tired easily ever since I had the pneumonia," I said.

"Where's your bunk?"

"I haven't got one yet."

"Where do you figure to lie down, then?"

"Home."

"Home?" the Sergeant said. "Where's that?"

"Victor Tosca and I are staying at The Great Northern Hotel."

The Sergeant didn't like that very much, but I guess he remembered that everybody who could afford it was living off the Post, so he didn't make anything of it.

"O.K.," he said. "But be sure you're in the mess-hall at four sharp—not ten minutes after four—otherwise you'll be A.W.O.L., and that won't be so good for you."

"I'll be there," I said. "Can I go home now?"

"Hell no," the Sergeant said. "Are you out of your head? The Company Commander wants to see you."

Well, the Company Commander was still talking to Stella and still telling her to listen. "Listen, Stella," he kept saying and laughing. I don't usually go to work and hate anybody, but I hated that son of a bitch.

When it was almost half past five the Company Commander nodded to the Sergeant, so then the Sergeant said I could see him. I went through the presentation rigmarole again, and this man who'd been so charming on the telephone with Stella became very military again, very determined to face the Germans with a stout heart. He hadn't stopped thinking for a moment what difficult times our country was going through, what a terrible enemy we were engaged in fighting, and what hard trials were ahead for us.

"I've looked at your card," he said, "and to be perfectly honest with you I don't know what you're doing at this Post at all."

I would have had six or seven things to tell him in quick succession if I wasn't in the Army, but I *was* in the Army, so I didn't say any of them.

Then he said, "I suppose you know any man in the Army would give his right eye to be at this Post, and I'm sure you realize how lucky you are to be here."

I didn't think I was lucky, but I kept my mouth shut.

Then he said, "Because of the nature of the work we do at this Post our men enjoy privileges that regular Army men don't enjoy and never will until they are out of the Army—if they are lucky enough to get out of it, if you know what I mean."

I knew then what Victor meant when he told me they keep threatening you. He meant that what this man called a regular Army man might very well never get out of the Army because he'd get killed, whereas there was always a chance at this Post for a fellow to keep from exposing himself to the chance of getting killed, and the way to do it was to play the game.

Then he said, "If you want to get along here, I'd advise you to make a better showing than you've made so far."

He looked at my card and went over the facts which constituted my poor showing.

"Three and a half months in the Army," he said. "A month in

the hospital, two weeks furlough. Not a very good showing, is it?"

May God strike me dead if I didn't say, "No, sir."

Not only that, I even felt guilty for having gotten pneumonia and for having spent all that time in the hospital.

But mainly what I wanted to do was get home and lie down, and I guess that's why I agreed with him.

He kept me standing at attention for a long time while he mulled over in his mind what to do with me. And he hinted what he *might* do if I didn't make a better showing.

Then he said, "I notice that you came to this Post from California with Private Foxhall and Private Tosca. I suppose you've heard what happened to Private Foxhall."

I didn't say anything, so then he said, "All right, you're in Company D. You're on the Adjutant General's list. If you shape up all right, chances are you'll be at this Post for some time to come. I'll try to find a place to fit you in. If you don't shape up—well, I think you understand that since you're not a writer or a director or a producer—since you've had no motion picture experience of any kind—we can get along without you at this Post—if we *have* to. On the other hand—well, it's up to you."

God strike me dead again if I didn't go to work and feel grateful to him for his kindness, which only goes to show you what a complication human beings are, because there I was dying of agony, sick and tired and eager to lie down, full of contempt for this man who was so cheap, and then all of a sudden grateful to him for saying, "It's up to you." Grateful to him for acknowledging that *I* was involved, that I was an *actual* person. I even felt eager to make good, to prove to him that if something was left to me I was the kind of fellow who would go to work and please everybody concerned.

"Yes, sir," I said.

"All right," he said. "Think it over. One little slip, you know—" He snapped his fingers, and it seemed to me I understood what he meant, although later on I didn't understand at all and felt irritated with myself for ever having imagined that I did. I wanted to know what the hell he meant by snapping his fingers at me that way.

"That's all," he said.

I saluted, about-faced, and went back to the Sergeant.

"O.K. to go now?"

"You ought to fix a bunk for yourself," he said, "but O.K., you can do it Monday."

I left the building and took the subway to town. When I got home Victor was lying on his bed asleep. After a moment he opened his eyes. He didn't sit up or anything.

"Murder," he said.

Then he closed his eyes and went back to sleep.

I picked up the hotel Bible and after a while came to *Ecclesiastes* which tells us it's all vanity, but I guess we just can't help it. If we're willing to live, we're unwilling not to take pride in it, whatever the way of our living may be. But the lion doesn't know how handsome he is, and lives. And the eagle doesn't know his swiftness, and lives. The rose does not know the rose. It takes no pride in its perfume. It is not mortified by the stench of its decay.

But man knows the lion, the eagle, and the rose. He knows all things, and in the end the rot and shame of them bring tears to his eyes and mortification to his spirit.

Knowing's his vanity, but it's probably better than not knowing.

When I got pneumonia, that was my first taste of death, and I did not like it. I had never been sick that way before. That sickness was a school in which I learned much terrible and bitter wisdom. The Japanese boy who sat beside my bed I saw as my own self—speechless, patient, enduring and doomed. The dried-up little old orange he brought to me was the gift of God to men, the gift of men to one another—their understanding of one another—their knowing that before God they are nothing. In my sleep I learned many things which books do not teach, and I swore to myself to get up from my bed and remember these things. The words of my sleep came together into a mighty book whose language I had not learned and yet understood: *Breathe thou, and do not stop thy breathing. Go to the rose-gardens of the summertime and breathe the perfume of the thundering rose. Go to the wine tables of the town and take a cup of the purple plunging grape. Let thy right hand be a cup for the breast of thine own woman. Entwine the fingers of thy left hand into the fingers of her left hand, and the lips*

*of thy mouth hold to her own from the evening of that day to the
dawn of the next.*

But these are not the words I knew in my sleep. They are the
rot of them. Still, I am of the vain creatures, and the swiftness
which the eagle does not know is his I say is mine, and the hand-
someness which the lion does not know is his I also say is mine. I
am not in the world an orphan, but the son of many men, the
brother of most, and the seeker of their sisters. The lion does not
know me, but I know him. The eagle does not cherish me, but I
cherish him. The men who made me have forgotten who they
made, but I remember *them.* Pain and failure and dying made them
and me, but we are still alive. Even though there is no bother like
the bother of being alive, it is a good bother, for it swarmeth in
song, and the bother of my body swarmed to the body which is
woman's. I swore to myself in the fever of disease and dying that I
would get up from my bed and go to her, and I did, but hell, my
luck wasn't as good as it should have been.

CHAPTER 17

Wesley Takes Up with a Modern Woman

I MET a woman in a bar on 4th Avenue one night who asked me to
take her home when the place closed at two in the morning.

I had gone to the bar to see if an old Irishman I'd met there the
night before would be there again because he had seemed to me a
great man, and had talked as few men in this world are able to talk.

When he learned that my mother was Irish, from Blackrock,
County Dublin, and named Kathleen, he said, "Then you are
Irish too, and it's no matter where you were born, or for that matter
what you would *rather* be."

I told him my father was English, born in London, but the old
man said it was not so.

"It was Irish in London that set your father there on his feet.
What part of London?"

I told him I wasn't sure, but I remembered that my father had
spoken of the East End.

"Limehouse is where your father took his first look," the old man said, "and Limehouse is full of Irish. What's his name?"

"Bernard Jackson."

"Irish. And your mother's other name besides Kathleen?"

"Armagh."

"Oh Irish, and you've got the look of the Irish yourself. Where were you born and what's your given name?"

"I was born in San Francisco and my given name's Wesley."

"The town's Catholic and full of Irish, but the name's Protestant and Scotch. Who gave it to you?"

"My father."

"He must have had his reasons, but if he had no reason in the world, then it's no doubt at all he's Irish and not English."

Well, I'd gone back to see if the old man would be there again, but he wasn't there when I had my first drink and he wasn't there when I had my last, but the woman was there all the time, about three hours.

When she asked me to take her home, I was surprised because I didn't think a woman of her refinement would let herself do a thing like that, but I was glad I was mistaken.

Her home was an apartment by the river, East of 2nd Avenue, and there were two floors. The furniture was the kind you went out and took a lot of time to find because it was all old stuff that was very good to see and have around. She was a woman just a little over thirty, she had a son eleven years old at private school, her divorced husband was still her best friend, and she was very successful in her business, which was clothes designing. She was little all over but exciting because of the mischief in the way she looked out of her eyes and smiled and said the fool things she liked to say.

She poured drinks and I finished mine as if it were water.

Then she said, "Now—tell me about yourself."

I took the drink out of her hand and put it on the little table. Then I zipped open the tight-fitting coat she was wearing, and took it off. Then I did the same with the skirt, and she stepped out of it, but all the time she kept saying, "But you *must* tell me about yourself."

I didn't think there was anything to tell that couldn't keep, so I didn't say anything.

Upstairs I don't think I ever saw a nicer place for tomfoolery, not even in moving pictures.

At five in the morning I took a shower, kissed the woman good-bye, and reached the Post just in time for Reveille.

Victor Tosca and I walked three blocks to our regular restaurant for breakfast, to take our time about it and put nickels in the juke-box for music. The song we liked in that juke-box in those dark mornings of New York was *Why Don't You Do Right?* It was about somebody making a lot of money in 1922 and throwing it away on cheap women, and the *good* woman asking him why he didn't do right, and then telling him to get out of here and get *her* some money too.

We always put a nickel in the machine for that song as soon as we stepped into the place because the noise and comedy of it thawed us out and warmed us. There was an old Russian behind the counter who always seemed to become happy when we stepped into the place, as if we let him know the night was over. It was his own place and he was always complaining about the help because they weren't as devoted to the business as he was.

"Can't get them," he said. "Can't get good men any more. All gone. Got to do everything myself."

I told the old Russian to fix me four eggs and a lot of ham, and when we sat down to eat Victor said, "What happened to you last night?"

"Got layed at last."

"How was it?"

"Just fine."

"Who is she?"

"Woman I met in a bar."

"What sort of woman?"

"Society, sort of."

"No fooling?"

"What do you think happened to her?"

"What do you mean?"

"I mean—wanting *me?*"

"Why not?"

"You know I look like hell."

"You look all right. Are you going to see her again?"

"Tonight."

That night I had supper with the woman in her apartment. It was served by a Swedish girl and it was a fine supper. When the Swedish girl went home I went upstairs to sleep because I hadn't had any sleep the whole night before. There was a big Capehart phonograph behind curtains in the corner of the room and when I woke up I heard something wonderful that I found out later was by Brahms. It was a concerto for piano and orchestra, and I don't think I've ever heard such wonderful music. It made the whole world seem a little unreal, as if it were something every one of us was dreaming. The woman was lying on a sofa across the room and she was wearing something you could see through.

"Why don't you get out of those terrible clothes and be comfortable?" she said, so I did.

CHAPTER 18

Wesley Witnesses a Strange Sight, Receives a Number of Letters Addressed to the People of the World, and Is Visited by His Father

ONE MORNING in March I saw something happen that was very strange. I was standing at the open window of our place on the sixth floor of The Great Northern Hotel at the 56th Street end waiting for Victor Tosca to get into his clothes. In the hotel across the street I saw a room brightly lit-up and took it for the room of someone else who had to get up before daybreak. Then I saw a man come to the window of the room with a sheet of paper and an envelope in his hands. He folded the paper, slipped it into the envelope, sealed the envelope—and tossed it into the street.

I told Victor I'd see him out front and hurried down to see what it was.

The envelope was addressed *To the People of the World.*

At breakfast I told Victor what had happened, opened the envelope, brought out the letter and read it to him. "Dear People,"

the letter began. "I am writing to you every day because you are
going through hard times and I am not. I have a typewriter with
a good ribbon, plenty of paper, plenty of envelopes, and nothing
better to do. In this first New York Letter I shall only mention the
date (Monday March 21, 1943) and announce my intention to take
up in subsequent letters the various problems you know. I have
no problems, and I am in search of nothing for myself. I have no
ambition. I do not need any money. I am not unhappy. I am not in
trouble. I live as I please. I can therefore tell you what no one else
in the world can tell you. I shall drop my New York Letters from
various windows of various hotels in this city at the rate of one a
day—every morning just before daybreak. From New York I shall
go to another city, and from that city I shall go to another until I
have covered the whole country."

The letter was unsigned.

"Some fellow having a little fun," Victor said.

"He didn't look as if he was having very much fun," I said. "He
looked as if he'd been up all night writing these few lines."

"He's crazy, then."

"Maybe not."

"What is he, then?"

"I don't know. I'll know more when I get the second letter."

The second letter, which I read to Victor the next morning at
breakfast, said: "Now then. Your biggest problem is what to do
after you have had food. You seem to be avoiding the truth, and
that's not necessary. It is not actually possible to avoid the truth,
but in *seeking* to avoid it you plunge into foolishness and disaster,
whereas if you did not try to avoid it you would begin to have the
grace which is in you but lost in many hundreds of years of fret-
fulness. Please do not be fretful any longer. There is no reason for
your anxiety if you will sit down and begin to know who you are
by counting the things around you. Counting is a pure activity
because it does not try to make anything of anything. That will
come later. You must first know how to count. Count up to nine
the first time and let it go at that. Do not add, subtract, divide or
multiply just yet. You will get the idea when you begin to count."

"What do you make of this?" I said.

"How should I know?" Victor said. "Let's try what he says, though. We've finished breakfast, so let's count."

"This spoon," I said. "One. But before we go to Two, let's have a look at this spoon, and see what it is."

"No," Victor said. "He says not to do that. He says to start out by counting and nothing else. So, this plate with the left-overs of scrambled eggs, fried ham and potatoes on it—Two."

"O.K.," I said. "This cup of coffee, Three."

"The old man behind the counter, Four."

"What's that?" the old man behind the counter said.

"You're Four," Victor said.

"Four?" the old Russian said. "What's that?"

"Number Four," Victor said.

"What's the matter—why no music?" the old Russian said.

"This nickel for music," I said. "Five." I put the nickel in the machine and the woman began to ask the man how come he didn't do her right.

"This window," Victor said. "Six."

"This whole city," I said. "Seven."

"This whole world," Victor said. "Eight."

"All creation," I said. "Nine."

"Well, we made it," Victor said. "We may have started out with a spoon, but we sure got around to a lot more, didn't we?"

"I wonder what this fellow's driving at?" I said.

"What do you say we answer his letters?"

"What would we tell him?"

"What do you mean? We'd tell him we'd received his letters, and thank him for them."

"His letters are addressed to the people of the world."

"We're a couple of them," Victor said. "Somebody's got to pick the letters up from the street and read them. He doesn't say anything about a couple of Privates in the Army who sleep in the hotel across the street not being eligible."

"He doesn't ask for any replies, either."

"He's having a little fun," Victor said.

"What I want to know is why isn't he in the Army?" I said. "I saw him at the window yesterday morning. He's not too old, and he looks as if he enjoys pretty good health."

"Maybe he's in essential industry," Victor said.

"He doesn't work at all."

"How do you know?"

"He said so in the first letter."

"I guess he's 4-F, then," Victor said. "Lucky fellow."

The following morning when I went to get the letter somebody had got to it ahead of me. It was a pretty girl. I didn't know what to do, so I said, "Excuse me, I think that letter's for me."

"It says, *To the People of the World,*" the girl said.

"Well," I said, "do you want it very much?"

"I don't know," the girl said. "What is it?"

"It's nothing," I said. "It's a game. I get a letter every morning."

"Maybe *this* letter's for me," the girl said. "*I* found it."

"Do you want to keep it?"

"Maybe there's something in it," the girl said. "Maybe there's money in it."

"I don't think so," I said. "I'll tell you what. Open the letter and read it. Then if you want to keep it, let me read it, and I'll give it back to you. But if you don't want to keep it, I'll give you a dollar for it, if you don't mind."

"Why do you want it?"

"I don't know."

Suddenly it occurred to me to look up. There at the window was the man himself. I expected him to move away, so he wouldn't be seen, but he just sat there and watched.

I gave him a morning salute—nothing military—and he returned the salute.

The girl had to get to work at the Automat on 57th Street, so she began to go. I walked along with her, looking back every now and then to see if the man was watching, and he was. He was leaning out of the window.

"If this letter's worth a dollar," the girl said, "it's worth more."

"Well, keep it, then," I said. "But at least let me read it."

Victor hurried up and joined us.

"What's the matter?" he said. "Complications?"

"This girl got to the letter before I did," I said. "She's late for work, and if we don't hurry we'll be late for Reveille."

"Well, let's hurry, then," Victor said. "Let her have the letter."

"O.K.," I said, so we got a cab at the corner, drove across the 59th Street or Queensborough Bridge, and got to Reveille just in time.

At breakfast we tried to guess what was in the letter, but of course we couldn't, so during my lunch hour I got a cab and went to the 57th Street Automat to see if I could buy or borrow the letter from the girl. She was very busy but she said, "The letter's for me—and I want to keep it."

"Can I read it?" I said. "I'll hand it right back. I promise—and let me have some roast-beef with macaroni and baked beans."

The girl brought the letter out of her pocket. I asked her if I could sit down and read it while I had my lunch.

"Don't go away with it, though," she said, and I said I wouldn't.

Well, the girl was right, I guess. The letter was for her all right, or at least as much for her as for me or Victor or anybody else. It said: "Food is everything, therefore eat slowly and behold what you eat. Consider what a blessing it is to be able to eat. To hunger is to live. To satisfy hunger is to live beautifully. Satisfying the hunger of the body is always good, but satisfying other hungers is better. Know what you hunger for, for it is in not knowing the nature of your hunger that you suffer most. Do not let grass, for instance, be the substitute for glory, for if you hunger for glory, grass cannot satisfy that hunger for you. You must look into the matter of things. You must know the quality of them. If you boil the life out of grass, it will not even satisfy the hunger of the body. If you hunger for beauty, you will satisfy that hunger by opening your eyes and seeing that beauty is lodged in all things—but only if the eye is open. Do not close the eye. Do not satisfy the hunger for one thing with the food which can only satisfy the hunger for another. Take no substitutes. Learn to count. Learn to see. Know who you are. Know what *things* are. Thank God for the quality of things, and go to sleep as if you were nothing more than a creature of the field lying down to rest."

I handed the letter back to the girl.

"Thanks very much," I said. "What are you going to do with the letter?"

"Keep it," the girl said. "Read it until I understand it."

I decided to get the letter that would be in the street the follow-

ing morning, but when I got to the street, there was no letter. The
girl came by and said, "What are you looking for?"

"Nothing," I said. "If I give you a dollar, will you give me a
copy of the letter?"

"O.K.," the girl said.

I gave her a dollar and asked her if she'd leave my copy of the
letter at the desk of the hotel, and she did.

The next morning there was no letter in the street again.

At breakfast Victor said, "What's the matter, no more letters?"

"He's moved on," I said. "He said he would in his first letter.
I've considered the matter, and I've decided he's a writer who's
forgotten how to write, or become bored with his writing, or discovered that he can't really write, so he's having a little fun instead—making fun of himself, making fun of writing, making fun
of writers, making fun of everybody and everything."

"He must be unhappy about something," Victor said. "I'm unhappy about being in the Army. What are you unhappy about?"

"I don't know," I said.

But I knew I was unhappy about a lot of things, especially Pop,
because he'd gone off and gotten lost again. Lou wrote to me and
said Pop had been all right for a month—he had been fine—he had
helped Lou a lot in his saloon on Pacific Street. Everybody had
liked Pop and if he wasn't in the saloon they'd ask Lou, "Where's
Valencia?" Lou took to calling Pop Valencia because Pop was always singing that song, and he introduced Pop to everybody by
that name. He sent Pop to a tailor who'd made him three suits
and two overcoats, and he'd set Pop up in the three rooms over
the saloon. For a month Pop had been a great help to Lou, just
hanging around the place, and Lou had made so much money he
was going to make his place bigger—make it a big restaurant and
bar and keep Pop around all the time because Pop brought him
good luck, and everybody liked him. Then Pop didn't show up
one night, so Lou went to the rooms over the saloon and found
the three suits and the two overcoats, but no sign of Pop. Lou said
not to worry, though, he'd find Pop again. He said Pop was the
finest man he'd ever met, and he needed Pop in his new place.
Well, the last letters I got from Pop weren't like him at all. They

were like the letters a man writes when he doesn't want to say what he means. They were *cheerful*. I wasn't sure, but I thought I'd be seeing Pop in New York pretty soon.

The next morning I decided to see if there would be a letter in the street once more, and there was. The envelope was addressed *To the People of the World* the same as ever, only the words were written in longhand. I opened the letter and read: "F—— you, Jackson." I looked up and saw Victor leaning out of the window laughing his head off. He was still laughing when he came down, but he stopped and said, "Anything in the street this morning?" So then we laughed all the way to Reveille, all through Reveille, all the way to the restaurant, and all through breakfast.

When I got home that night the desk clerk said there was somebody in the lobby to see me. It was Pop asleep in one of the big chairs in the long hallway to 57th Street. I sat down beside him and waited for him to wake up. Pop looked pretty bad, but I was glad to see him again just the same. He didn't wake up for an hour. I didn't say anything and he didn't say anything. We just sat there in the hallway for ten or fifteen minutes, then I told one of the boys to get a bottle of Scotch from the bar and two glasses and some ice. I poured Pop a big drink and one for myself and then he said, "Before this War's over you'll be the same as me."

"That's all right," I said.

CHAPTER 19

Wesley Tells His Father About Young Life During This
War and His Father Tells Him About Young
Life During the Last War

I SENT a telegram to Lou to let him know Pop had come to New York to see me. Lou answered the telegram thanking God and said he was sending Pop's new clothes by Air Express. In the telegram was a money order for three hundred dollars for Pop to spend in New York. Lou said the building of his new place was coming along fine and he was counting on Pop being there for the opening in six weeks. He wanted to know if Pop would take an interest in the place for a percentage of the profits. He said he was writing in detail.

Three days later Pop's clothes came, and a long letter from Lou to Pop and me. I handed the letter to Pop but he handed it back and told me to read it to him. Lou was serious. He needed Pop in his business. He wanted to make a deal with Pop, with or without a written agreement. He was glad Pop was in New York, first because he knew Pop wanted to see me, and second because Pop could study the New York restaurants and bars and find out what they're like. He said a third interest in the business for Pop was O.K. with him and he wanted to know if it was O.K. with Pop, whose job would be to be in the place from eight o'clock at night till two in the morning—closing time. He said Dominic Tosca was the third partner in the deal, and he said that Dominic was all for having Pop in the deal too. He had talked to Dominic by long distance. He said he was making too much money for himself and Dominic anyway with the high taxes, and with Dominic in the Army he needed somebody with him—but he wouldn't have anybody except Pop. So how about it?

Well, Pop didn't say anything for a long time. He just got the bottle and poured himself a drink and I waited to see what he'd say.

"What do *you* think?" he said.

"I know Lou's straight," I said.

"Don't you think he's being kind? I don't do anything around the place."

"Restaurants and bars are funny places," I said. "People go back to a place where there's somebody they like to see. I know I do. I think Lou may have been kind to you and me at first, but I think he means what he says now. I think he needs you in his new place."

"I couldn't take a third interest without putting up some money," Pop said. "I don't know anything about business, but I know a third interest in a business like Lou's is going to be a lot of money."

"I think you ought to trust Lou," I said. "If you get too much money you can give it back to him sometime when he needs it. Do you mind staying there every night for six hours that way?"

"I always stay somewhere for six hours that way," Pop said.

"Do you drink much at Lou's?"

"Less than I do at other places. It's better stuff."

"What'd you leave for?"

"I got embarrassed. I thought I was in the way. I thought I ought to see you too."

Pop didn't say anything for a little while, then he said: "You've changed a lot since I saw you last. What's happened to you?"

"I've gotten older," I said. "The Army ages a fellow pretty fast. I caught pneumonia and went to the hospital too—that did something to me. And I met a woman in a bar."

"Pneumonia?" Pop said. "Why didn't you tell me?"

"I was going to."

"Did you get it bad?"

"Virus, they said. I thought I was going to die."

"Why didn't you?"

"What?"

"How did it happen you didn't?"

"There was a Japanese boy in the hospital who used to come and sit by my bed."

"Japanese?" Pop said. "Are you sure?"

"I know Chinese and I know Japanese," I said. "This boy was Japanese. He had just gotten over pneumonia too."

"What about him?"

"Nothing. He just sat there and waited. He left three little oranges for me. I never did talk to him or get to know who he was."

"Everybody hates the Japanese," Pop said. "Don't you?"

"No. Do you?"

"No," Pop said. "What'd he do for you that you think made you get better?"

"He just sat there. When I'd go to sleep I'd know he was sitting there, so I'd want to know if he'd still be sitting there when I woke up, and he always was. When he wasn't there I knew the worst was over and two weeks later when I was a lot better I used to go and sit by a fellow who was sicker than I had been."

"Who was *he?*"

"Fellow by the name of Leroy Harrison. I got his name from the card on his bed."

"What was *he?*"

"Negro boy."

"What happened to him?"

"I was discharged from the hospital before I knew how he was going to be."

"Did you leave anything for him?"

"I didn't think he'd like that, so I didn't."

"The Japanese boy left three oranges for you."

"I guess he knew I wouldn't mind."

"Did you eat the oranges?"

"Hell no. I'm keeping them."

"What for?"

"I just want to keep them. The skins have gotten dry and stiff."

"Did the Negro boy wake up and see you sitting beside him?"

"Three or four times."

"What'd you say?"

"Nothing."

"Do you think he wanted to see you sitting there when he woke up?"

"I don't know for sure, but I got the idea he did. *I* wanted to see the Japanese boy when I woke up."

"Did you smile at the Negro?"

"Hell no. Smile about what? The poor fellow was dying, the same as I had been."

"Did the Japanese boy smile at you?"

"Hell no. He had been dying not long ago too."

"I hope the Negro boy's O.K.," Pop said.

"I hope so too."

Pop didn't say anything for a little while again, and then he said:

"Who's this woman you met?"

I told Pop what I knew about the woman. He poured himself another drink—and one for me that time too—then he said, "Something's made you half-way handsome. I don't know whether it's the pneumonia or the woman."

"I think you're kidding."

"It's just as well."

We drank a while, and then Pop said. "Well, what do you think?"

"I think you ought to get in your good clothes and go around and study the restaurants and bars of New York for Lou. I think you ought to go in with Lou and Dominic."

"I don't mean that," Pop said. "I mean what do you think's going to happen to you in this War?"

"Who knows?" I said. "Did you know what was going to happen to you in the War you were in?"

"I had a pretty good idea."

"You're O.K. Do you want to have supper with me tonight at some place that you can look at for Lou?"

"Wouldn't you rather have supper with the woman?"

"No. I'm not sure I'm ever going to see her again."

"Why not?"

"I'm looking for somebody to marry and have a family with."

"That's a good thing to be looking for. You want a son, don't you?"

"Yes. How'd you know?"

"Every man does when he begins to understand that he may not make the grade."

"What grade?"

"I went through the whole War," Pop said, "scared to death I'd never see you—and that's one thing I had to do—I had to see you. But I hadn't even found your mother yet. I didn't know who she'd be or where I'd find her. I hadn't had a chance to get started in my own life, and there I was with a good chance of never getting started—that's the reason I made myself stay alive even after I knew I was dead—all banged up and good for nothing—an impostor of a man."

"You're no impostor, Pop."

"The minute we get to know how great the odds are against our ever becoming who we really are—well, then we go looking for the mother of our son, so if we don't make the grade, maybe he will."

"What do you mean who we really are. Who are we?"

Well, then Pop got angry, but not at me. He got angry at the whole world full of people who, not knowing who they themselves are, try to keep a fellow from being who he is.

"*Who are we?*" Pop said. "I'll tell you who we are. We're the Jacksons, that's who we are, and we've been walking this earth since the beginning of walking. It's no good trying to stop us from becoming human beings at this stage of the game because some day one of us is going to *make* the grade. I know it's not going to be me. Maybe it's not going to be you—but it may be your son. If something stops him, then it may be *his* son—but one of us is going to make the grade, and then the rest of us can turn over in our graves and go to sleep at last. But we won't rest until one of us makes it."

"We're human beings *now*, Pop."

"The hell we are," Pop said. "Look at me. Look at you. The most you can say for either of us is that we're trying—we're still trying. Human beings don't kill one another. I notice you're in the uniform of a man who is apt to aim a loaded gun at another man some day and shoot it. Human beings don't do that. Human beings don't ask other human beings to do it. They don't compel one another to do it. Human beings don't scare the shit out of one another all the time—yes, shit—because I don't mean anything else."

"Did you kill somebody in the last War, Pop?"

Pop didn't say anything for a long time.

"Who was he?" I said.

"He was dead by that time," Pop said. "He was *nobody* by that time. He had been a boy of eighteen or nineteen—but he wasn't anything by that time."

"What'd you do it for?"

Pop looked at me a moment, then lifted his glass and talked into it.

"For *you*, I guess. I know I didn't do it for myself. I don't want to be putting the blame on you, but *you* did it—if you know what I mean. I just had to do it. I didn't want to be finished with myself until I had seen you."

"Thanks, Pop. I'm sorry you had to do it, though."

"Some day you'll feel the way I felt that day. You'll do anything to stay alive, so you can see your son. Even kill somebody."

"I guess the fellow you killed felt the same way."

"I *know* he did," Pop said. "He didn't want to kill me any more than I wanted to kill him—we both saw that—but we were caught, and we had to go through with it. I never believed I'd ever be able to use a bayonet on another human being, but I did it."

"*Bayonet?* I thought you *shot* him from away off, somebody running for cover maybe."

"Hell," Pop said. "I'd never shoot a man running for cover. I know I never *shot* anybody—I never was a good shot, anyway—and I had a whole sky to aim at. But you and I—we stopped a fellow who wanted to see his own son. We've got to make up for that somehow."

"How?"

"I don't know—but *somehow*. Someday somehow you or I or your son—my grandson—we've got to make up for it. If it wasn't for this War, you'd be in a better position to do it, so just in case you fail, keep your eyes open for your own son's mother."

"I don't have much luck with girls," I said. "I'm clumsy and awkward and too serious about everything."

"That's all right," Pop said. "You'll find her. And when you do you'll know she's the one."

We got up and went to supper and talked about everything under the sun because Pop wanted me to know everything he had learned.

CHAPTER 20

Wesley Sends and Receives Some Letters, Gets a Desk and a Room of His Own, and Is Mistaken for a Writer by a Man Who Mistook Himself for One

IN NEW YORK I exchanged letters with Harry Cook. I wrote to Joe Foxhall. I sent a letter a week to Dominic Tosca telling him how Victor and I were getting along. I wrote to Lou. And of course I wrote to Pop. I guess that's why he came to New York to see me.

Letters mean more to a fellow in the Army than anything else—outside of getting out of the Army and going home. The reason for that, I guess, is that nobody is ever really *in* the Army. His body may be where he's stationed, but his heart's somewhere else.

In my letters to Pop I didn't tell him I'd been in the hospital with pneumonia because I didn't want him to get worried. About a month after I left the hospital I got to feeling all right again and I didn't mind the snow, the black skies, the rain, the sleet, or anything else. A fellow goes to work sooner or later and carries his own climate around with him.

Lou sent me a letter every Monday morning which usually got to me Wednesday or Thursday. He wouldn't say much but he'd tell me the things I wanted to know. There would be a Post Office Money Order in every letter. At first the money orders were for twenty dollars, then when Lou found Pop they went to thirty, but pretty soon they went to fifty. Lou said not to worry about the money—he was *lending* it to me and he expected me to pay him back some day. I knew he didn't want me to pay him back at all. He just didn't want me to feel embarrassed. But I knew I was going to pay him back. I would pay Lou back with the first money I made. I hadn't ever done anything for him—I had only been willing. I was glad Lou was making a lot of money, though, because you like to see a generous man with plenty of stuff to give away. A generous man with nothing to give away is just about the unhappiest man in the world.

You get to know people a little when you get letters from them. If you've met the fellow who writes to you—if you remember him and what you thought of him—well, when he writes to you you get to know him that much better, and his letters seem to be extraordinary things. They seem to come from something that's in every man in the world, and as far as I've been able to tell that thing is loneliness.

Man is a lonely creature. In spite of all the company there is for him in the world, he's lonely. He's so lonely sometimes he'll turn away from all the company in the world and take up with the dead —he'll read the books men who lived long ago wrote. Or he'll take up with the fields and the sky and the creatures of them, like Thoreau did. Or he'll turn to some little domestic animal like a dog, or a canary, or a parrot, or a turtle even, or a goldfish, or maybe a big animal like a horse. They say Arabs love their horses more than their wives. Or he'll take up with plants—in a little garden of his own, or if he has no garden he'll take up with little plants in pots. But who's he looking for all the time? He's looking for somebody to know him. Every letter I ever got had loneliness in it, and eagerness to be in touch with someone who was not a stranger, someone who remembered.

Harry Cook's letters were a big surprise because I expected them to be full of jokes and fun, and they weren't. They were full of longing and nothing else. Most people long for something they've already known—such as a home or a farm or some neighborhood of a town or city—but Harry's longing was for the stuff that was ahead. "The thing I'm hoping for," he wrote in one of his letters, "is to be let alone some day, so I can see if I can find out how to spend my life. If I had my way, I'd never grow old, and neither would anybody else—I'd just go to sleep some afternoon under some old apple tree and never wake up again."

Joe Foxhall's letters were not half as serious as his talk. He told me the little things that had happened to him and he poked fun at the officers he knew.

Dominic Tosca was interested in only one thing: How was Victor? Victor wrote to him more often than I did, but Dominic wanted *me* to tell him. Would I be staying with Victor if we got shipped? Try to work it out to stay with him, he said.

Pop's letters were the shortest. "I got your letter," he would scribble. "Read *Ecclesiastes* again—once quickly—then two or three times slowly." Or: "I got your letter—I'm reading Anderson—I think you'll like him too." So I'd write and tell him I was reading Anderson too and I'd mention some of the stories and Pop would write back and say, "Hans Christian is O.K., but I mean Sherwood."

I wrote to Cacalokowitz once too. He was a good fellow, just as I had expected, and he said he was sorry he hadn't answered sooner, but he had been working very hard training a new Company of men. "You'd be surprised," he wrote, "how much alike the men of every new Company are."

The reason I wrote so many letters was that they sent me to school to learn Map Reading and Army Organization, so I had a lot of time. I used to keep four or five sharpened pencils in my pocket and I used to keep a tablet with me all the time, and envelopes, so when everybody else was listening to the stuff about who's who in the Army and how to tell for sure, or how to get along when you're lost in the desert, I'd be in the back of the room writing to Pop or Lou or Joe Foxhall or Dominic.

After we'd finished school the Sergeant asked me if I wanted to do some typing for him and I said I did, so after that I had a desk and a typewriter and spent most of my time typing announcements and reports for him.

I had a little cubby-hole of a room of my own on the same floor with the writers, so I guess it was natural for them to think I was a writer too. Once in a while one of them would come by and sit on the end of my desk and say, "What are you working on?" I'd tell him, so then he'd say, "I don't mean for the Army—I mean for yourself. *I'm* writing a play."

CHAPTER 21

Wesley Meets the Army Film Writers and After Seeing Their Training Films Isn't Sure They Aren't the Real Enemy

THERE WERE about fifty writers in the writing department in New York. I had to type a list of them one day for the Sergeant, so I knew their names, but I didn't seem to remember having read a book by any of them. I took the list with me to the Public Library on 42nd Street one Saturday afternoon to look them up one by one, alphabetically. Well, only one of them had published a book. I wrote the number of the book on a slip of paper, the book was fetched for me, and I sat down to read it.

Well, it was a book all right—it was printed on paper and it had covers—it was a story too, but it was the most tiresome story I ever encountered in all the reading I've done. I read twenty pages at the beginning, ten at the end, and two in the middle, but it was tiresome no matter where I went.

I wondered what kind of writers these writers were. There didn't seem to be fifty writers in the whole country worth reading, but there they were—fifty of them at that place writing stuff for the government. I even saw the writer who'd had the book published, but he wasn't much to see or listen to. He was smart, though, and so were the other forty-nine. They were just about the smartest lot of fellows I ever saw. They talked about books and plays all the time and they had something clever to say about everything that was ever written. "Boil Shakespeare down," one of them would say, "and what have you got? A plot-stealer, an escapist, and a non-thinker." And they would go from one writer to another and knock holy hell out of him.

I used to look at them and try to figure out who they could possibly be, but I'd never be able to reach a satisfactory decision.

These fellows in the Army were the most patriotic I ever ran into—or at any rate they were the only fellows in the Army I ever saw who wanted to make chop-suey out of the Japanese and sauerkraut out of the Germans. Most of them had been at that Post at least two years, and a few of them were growing old there—they were settling down in their little homes in the country. They used to drive in from the country in the morning and drive back at night. They never did any routine duties like the rest of us because they had gotten enough stripes to get out of routine duties. They sometimes worked at home too, and that meant you wouldn't see them for a week or two.

Their Army work—which they attended to with considerable ceremony—was to write "treatments" and "scenarios" for one-reel or two-reel Training Films. At first the films had to do with specific problems, such as how to fire a rifle and keep it clean, but pretty soon when they had run out of stuff like that they moved on to the more artistic aspects of being a soldier. They showed a fellow how to kill somebody else with his bare hands, or how to face death bravely. They were very good at both of these assignments—full of the lust to kill, full of hate for the dirty little yellow-belly Japs or the cowardly Germans, and full of a most astonishing and superhuman courage in the face of death. But they always drove out to the country in the evening, and when everybody else got shipped overseas they were still writing scenarios for films encouraging everybody else to face death like a scenario writer.

They didn't like anybody to think any German of Germany or any Japanese of Japan was a human being. If somebody very innocently happened to ask them when *they* were going to go overseas and have a crack at the enemy, they would say that they had been trying for years to get over but the Medical Officer of the Post wouldn't think of it because of their sinus trouble, or their stomach, or their eyes; or they would say the Post Commander was forever fighting with them to make them stay at their typewriters because he felt the work they were doing was a hundred times more useful to the War Effort than picking up a gun; or they themselves would say their work was doing more to destroy the enemy than the action of a whole division of soldiers.

It was compulsory to see their films—even though the films were made at that Post, right under our noses—but only they themselves would leave the Theatre feeling satisfied and thrilled. The rest of us would be a little shy and embarrassed about all that bravery going on in the film, or a little sick about being encouraged to learn how to gouge out a man's eye; kick him in the balls or face; break his neck, back or arm; or stick a bayonet through him, and then, like as not, turn around just in time to save the life of a scared little fellow being choked to death by a great big German; and after having broken the German's back turning to the little fellow, putting a protective arm around him and telling him, "You see, Sam, there's nothing to it—and we're doing it for the right to say what we please, do what we please, and go where we please. Cigarette?"

Nobody but the writers themselves was ever convinced by that stuff and no matter how brave everybody was on the screen, the fellows who were going to be shipped overseas sooner or later had a tender spot in their hearts for the poor soldiers of the enemy who were always getting their eyes gouged out or their necks broken. Things like that hurt. If anybody really expects a fellow to do things like that, a fellow's liable to think there ought to be some other way to win the War. Maybe the fight promoters ought to agree on some kind of half-way human procedure. If everything got out of hand and both sides just couldn't stop doing all those ugly things, maybe they ought to stop the War and flip a coin for it.

I don't mind saying the stuff these writers turned out went to work and increased my estimation of the enemy. I found myself forgetting the enemy overseas. I began to look at these writers as the real enemy—a kind of danger likely to endure and be a nuisance even after the War had ended. I don't know who or what ever wins a War, but I have a notion it's a fellow like Victor Tosca who wants something else besides a Purple Heart, or Joe Foxhall who hates everything about an Army and a War, or Harry Cook who wants to be let alone so he can decide how to live his life in such a way that he won't get old but will lie down and go to sleep and not wake up, or the millions of fellows I don't know and never will know who get caught in the machinery of an Army and go out and get killed or have a little luck and come home half-way O.K. If movies can win a War, I guess they can avoid one too. And movies had twenty years to avoid this one. *Forcing* men to make an Army and fight a War is the way I think it's done, but I may be mistaken. All I know is that they sent for me and they sent for almost everybody else I've met in the Army. It was a national emergency all right, but I don't remember having helped make it—and nobody asked me to help avoid it when there was time to do so. They didn't ask Pop, either.

CHAPTER 22

*Wesley Is Banished to Ohio and Has a Farewell Drink
with the Modern Woman*

IT WAS just my luck to get sent on Detached Service the day after Pop and I had had supper together, but that's how it is in the Army. The minute you get used to the stuff you've got to put up with in one place, they go to work and send you to another. Chances are you're not needed in the new place any more than you are in the old, but everybody gets busy to see that you get there on time.

I told Pop to stay in New York and study restaurants and bars for Lou, but he said he'd study them where I was going. I told him there weren't any good restaurants and bars where I was going, so he said, "Where you going?"

"Ohio."

"One of the finest restaurant-and-bar states in America," Pop said, so I knew he wanted to go any place I happened to be going.

My train wasn't leaving until ten that night, so Pop and I got packed and went out for a walk. When I got back there was a letter on my duffle-bag addressed *To the People of the World*. I opened the letter and this is what I read:

"A lady telephoned and said it was very important for you to telephone her. I asked her to leave her name but she said you'd know who she was. The reason I've gone out is that I hate to say good-bye. Don't forget to count nine and drop a letter out of a window once in a while. I'll get it. Also don't try to avoid the truth because if you do you'll get syphilis. Well Jackson boy we've had some good times together and I hope we have some more. Take good care of Pop. Your Friend Victor. P.S. Don't think grass ain't important because it is—so don't forget to graze on a good green lawn once in a while. So long."

I telephoned the woman and she said she wanted me to be at her house for a little dinner party she was giving Saturday night. I told her I was being sent away on Detached Service and wouldn't be in New York Saturday night. She asked where I was going and how long I'd be gone. I told her I was going to Ohio, and my orders were for six weeks but that they might be extended for another six weeks. "When's your train?" she said.

"Ten," I said.

"Couldn't you take another train?"

"I'd be A.W.O.L. if I did."

"Can't you come here for just a minute before you go?"

"It's a quarter to nine now. By the time I get a taxi and get to the station it'll be train time."

Pop said, "I'll get everything on the train—go head."

Then the woman said, "Please come by for just a minute," so I said O.K. and hung up.

"I know what to do," Pop said. "I'll see you on the train."

The door was open, so I went in, but she wasn't downstairs. On the way upstairs I thought she'd be on the couch with almost nothing on, but I was mistaken. She was standing at the window looking out. When she turned around, damned if she wasn't crying.

"What's the matter with you?" I said.

Well, she couldn't talk for a while but pretty soon she said, "You think I'm crying because you're going away and I'm not going to see you for a while—maybe never again—but that's not why I'm crying at all."

"Well, whatever you're crying for, don't cry any more."

"Do you want a drink?" she cried. "Would you like to hear some music?"

"I've got time for a drink," I said, "and just a little music. I think you know the part of that Brahms piece I like so much."

"Of course I know," she cried. She poured the biggest drink I ever saw and got out the Brahms album of records and found the one she was looking for and put it on, so then it wasn't as bad as the crying alone, although it wasn't much better because that part of the Brahms piece that I liked so much was something like crying too.

"Do you think Brahms didn't cry?" she cried.

I took her in my arms and held her, but then she cried more than ever, so I went back to my drink.

"Do you want to know why I'm crying?" she said.

"I don't mind if I do," I said.

"It's because the old fools go to work and murder somebody like you every twenty years or so and nobody ever knows you were ever alive—and they'll do it again too. You've got to go to Mexico, that's what you've got to do. Not for *me*—I may be in love with you, but I'm not in love with you for *me*. You've got to run away before it's too late. They'll murder you, and I know who they are too. Old fools, and full of shifty ways and other things, and I guess you know what I mean too."

Well, that made me laugh and when I laughed she laughed too, so I took her in my arms and kissed her for that, but pretty soon she started to cry again.

"You think you're going to be luckier than anybody else and get out of it all right," she said, "but that's because you don't understand what kind of fools they are. They live to be eighty-eight, and they don't care how old you are when you get killed. You go away to Mexico and let them die of old age."

"I'm in a branch of the service that's not very dangerous," I said.

"The ship you go over in will sink and you'll drown," she cried. "Or they'll run over you with a truck. Or you'll fall off of something."

"No, I won't."

"You're going away to Ohio, aren't you?"

"Yes."

"Did you ask to go? Do you want to go?"

"No."

"Well, there you are," she cried. "Who's making you go?—who'll make you go where you'll be murdered too?—the eighty-eight-year-old fools, that's who, and I hate them, I hate them all—they never knew how to do anything all their lives."

I finished the big drink and poured another half as big, and while she was talking and crying the woman took off her clothes and I like to fell over I was so surprised. Then she stopped crying and looked at me the way that's so mischievous, and she was smiling, even though the tears were still wet on her face. So then she looked like a beautiful naked wicked little girl, and even though I wasn't sure the whole thing wasn't an act, I liked her for the way she was. She went to the telephone and arranged for a taxi to be outside her door at a quarter to ten, so at a quarter to ten we got into the taxi together because she wanted to ride to the station with me.

When I sat down beside Pop, the train didn't move for about three or four minutes, and then it began to move, and even though I didn't want to be going to Ohio at all, I was glad the train was moving because if you're on a train and you've got to go, well, you might as well get going.

CHAPTER 23

Wesley Tries to Tell Joe Foxhall What He's Gotten Hep to, and Pop Tries to Tell Wesley Something He Can't Remember

WELL, WHEN Pop and I got to Ohio the next morning, he found a room for himself at a little hotel, and I went out of town about nine miles to the Post. I spent the first day getting settled, but in the evening I ran into Joe Foxhall on his way to town, so we went out on the highway together to hitch a ride. We had to be back in bed by eleven, but that was better than nothing, and we were glad to see each other.

"Something's happened to you?" Joe said. "What is *it*?"

"Damned if I know."

"You look like somebody who's gotten hep to something worth knowing. What have you gotten hep to?"

We were standing there by the side of the road waiting for a ride when something strange and wonderful happened to me. For the first time in many days and many nights the voice of the singer broke forth in me crying *Valencia*, only this time I knew who the singer was.

"What do you know that's so wonderful?" Joe said.

"Who sings in you?" I said.

"Nobody," Joe said. "Bloody nobody."

"Well, then," I said, "I'm lucky, because my son sings in me."

"Your *son?*" Joe said.

"Yes," I said, "my own son."

A big truck slowed down for us and we hopped on. The driver said, "Last night I was high-rolling down this highway when one of those little midget cars came out from a side road and got in my way. It was so little I could barely see it, but it raced along like a scared jack-rabbit and by God it beat me to town."

When we got to town I told Joe I'd meet him at ten in front of the hotel where he was having supper with a girl he'd met and we'd take a taxi back to the Post. Then I went to Pop's room and found him lying on his bed asleep. When he woke up he said, "I wish to God I knew what to tell you."

"You don't have to tell me anything, Pop."

"No, there's something I've got to tell you. Something I remember from the days before you were born that I promised myself I'd tell you when the time came, but now I've forgotten it."

"You'll remember it one of these days," I said. "How do you feel?"

"I don't think I ought to go back to San Francisco."

"Why not?"

"I think I ought to stick with you."

"Why don't you go to El Paso?"

"I'd like to," Pop said. "I sure would like to, but hell—"

"Go see Mom and Virgil," I said. "You're all right now."

"Mom's all right," Pop said. "Virgil's all right. But you and I—"

"I'm all right."

"The hell you are," Pop said. "The *hell* you are. I was twenty-one years old in 1919 when I saw your mother and knew who she was and took her for my wife. I was twenty-one years old that year in San Francisco, but I was an old man, and I'm an old man now. I've waited all these years to tell you something I promised myself to tell you when the time came and now that the time has come, I've forgotten it. I've been lying here all day trying to remember, but I just can't. *You're* all right—sure. But the world's not, and one way or another a man's got to live in the world."

"I saw a Chinese restaurant on the way here," I said. "Let's go have some Chinese food."

"But where can a man go in the world to live?" Pop said.

"Anywhere's all right," I said. "Come on, Pop, let's go eat."

"One drink," Pop said.

CHAPTER 24

Wesley Meets The Writer and Writes a Scenario for a Training Film on the Beauties of Calisthenics for Him

OHIO WAS cold and white when Pop and I reached there, but early in May just before I got my orders to return to New York the sun came out, the snow melted away, and a lot of color showed up in the fresh new light of the year. The girls became adorable, and it was all I could do to keep myself from going up to every one of them I saw. It was all I could do to keep from hugging them and kissing them because they had gotten through another winter and were so lovely to see.

I got the same kind of job in Ohio that I'd had in New York, and I was thankful to get it because I had gotten used to having a desk and a typewriter. The work was easy, but there were formations and inspections and the same old round of duties—calisthenics, marching, classes of various kinds, and of course two or three Training Films to see every week.

I was given the bunk of a fellow who had just been packed off to a hospital for observation because of his interest in what he called *The Death Ray*. The fellows of that barracks claimed he was crazy all right, but to look at him, they said, you'd think he was as sound as anybody could be. He just seemed to believe there was a death ray hidden in the light of the world which science was seeking to understand and control. He used to tell the fellows he was working on the death ray himself and felt confident that very soon he would have something very big and secret to turn over to the War Department in Washington. He told the fellows, "I can't tell you much about it because it's the biggest thing in this War, but I think I've got the answer." The fellows said he'd gotten the idea from a comic strip.

Another fellow in that barracks used to spend all his time every evening shining his shoes. He had two pairs of Army shoes, two pairs of his own for dress, and a pair of leather slippers. The fellows in the barracks had agreed to take turns putting a pair of their own shoes beside this fellow's shoes, and every night in addition to his own shoes he would polish a pair for somebody else and never know the difference. He was a thoughtful fellow named Charles Blunden. I let him shine my shoes too, partly because it was the custom of the fellows in that barracks and partly because I knew Blunden needed a lot of shoes to shine. He'd take a good long time with every pair of shoes and no matter how dirty or muddy they had been when he had started on them, when he was finished they were almost like new. He used to enjoy looking at them when they were nicely polished.

There weren't so many writers at that Post. There were an even dozen of them, and they were not like the writers of New York at all. For one thing, being stationed at that Post was like banishment. It was like getting sent to Siberia if you were a Russian and had displeased the Czar or the Central Committee. All of the writers had been at the Post in New York originally, but they hadn't shaped up, as the saying is—they hadn't gotten along. A banished man is a bitter man, and a bitter little man is better than a cheerful little one, so I found these writers a lot more likable than the ones in New York, even though these writers weren't really writers, either.

Only one of them was a writer. I had heard of him long before I had gotten into the Army, so when I found out he was at that Post I got his books at the Public Library and read them. There were fifteen of them altogether. I found eleven of them before I left Ohio. They were all good books, but three of them were very good. I couldn't understand what a man like that was doing in the

Army. He was thirty-five years old, and he walked a little like a gorilla. He had the shoulders and long arms of one too. He was a funny fellow when you got to know him a little, but the expression of his face was always painful. He was always stumbling, but nobody ever saw him fall. Fellows who marched like soldiers were always slipping and falling, but not this man. He stumbled more than anybody else at that Post, but he never slipped.

The writers worked in what was known as The Production Building which was down a hill about a mile from where the barracks were, but this writer had asked if he could work in an old building near the Company Street, and they'd given him permission to do so. There hadn't been any heat in that building and he hadn't asked for any, but after a while a coal stove had been installed for him, and some of the junk in the building had been removed. When I was assigned some work to do the Company Commander couldn't find any space for me in the Orderly Room, so he told me to go to the building where the writer was and ask him if he would mind another desk and typewriter being installed there.

When I went into the building I found him standing at one of the windows looking out at the snow.

"The Company Commander wants to know if you'll mind—"

"Not at all," he said.

He didn't even wait for me to tell him what the Company Commander wanted to know. I knew he wasn't rude, though—he was impatient.

"I'll move the desk and typewriter in, then," I said.

"I didn't know you were a writer," he said.

"I'm not. I did some typing at the Post in New York, and they want me to do the same here."

"What do you type?"

"Duty Rosters. Announcements. Lists of various kinds. Reports."

"How do you like it?"

"It's O.K. I like having a desk and a typewriter."

"Come on in. You can put your desk over there. That's mine at the other end of the room. How long you been in the Army?"

"Almost five months. How about you?"

"Almost six. Do you like it as much as I do?"

"How much do you like it?"

"You don't like it either, then."

"I suppose somebody's got to make an Army."

"I had imagined it might not be me," he said.

In the afternoon of that day, which was my third day at that Post, I finished my work for the Company Commander and got up to yawn and light a cigarette.

"Any of that stuff secret?" the writer said.

"I don't think so."

"Mind if I look at it, then?"

I didn't mind, so he looked at the stuff, which was three announcements for the Bulletin Board, a Duty Roster, and a List of the Personnel at that Post.

"Excellent," he said. "And you've typed it all perfectly. Want to pitch pennies?"

We pitched pennies against a wall for about an hour. I won seven, although at one time during the game I had won about twice that many.

That night I told Pop I had met the writer, and Pop said, "Do you mean to say *he's* in the Army too?"

"Yes, he is," I said. "Do you know his writing?"

"Of course I know it," Pop said. "What's he *do* in the Army?"

"He's supposed to write scenarios for Training Films."

"For God's sake," Pop said. "You might as well ask Burns to write slogans for War Bond Posters."

"Who's Burns?"

"Robert Burns," Pop said. "You don't put a man like that in the Army. You let him alone to write what he wrote before the War and what he'll write after it—or you put a bullet in his head and be done with it."

One morning the writer got up from his desk where he had been trying to work and came over to my desk.

"Have you got any work to do?" he asked.

"No," I said. "I'm typing a letter to a friend."

"Well," he said. "I've been trying for three weeks to write a scenario on the beauties of calisthenics, but I don't seem to be able to do it. My mind keeps wandering off to other things. The Colonel in charge of The Production Department has been very patient with me, and I'm grateful to him, but I don't want to try his patience any longer. I'm most eager to please him, but I know I haven't got the stuff in me to do it. I've got too much other stuff in me. Will you give me a hand?"

"What can I do?"

"Write this scenario for me."

"I don't know how to write."

"You don't need to know how to write. All that's needed is a couple of hours of typing. I can't do it because I've learned a little about writing and it keeps stopping me. How about it?"

"I'll try."

"Thanks. I'll try to do something for you some time."

"When do you want me to start?"

"Could you start right now? I'd like to go for a walk. Have you any idea what to do?"

"Well," I said, "I've seen a lot of Training Films. I know the way they like to go about them."

"It's nine now," the writer said. "I'll see you at twelve. Will you have lunch with me at the Cafeteria?"

"O.K."

"Now, here's the source material the Colonel handed me three weeks ago. Look it over and see if you can take it from there."

"O.K."

He stumbled out of the building but didn't fall and I began to look over the Colonel's source material. I considered everything ten or fifteen minutes, then I began to write what I thought the Colonel wanted. I typed the whole thing by half past eleven, and it came to nine pages. The stuff seemed so silly to me I felt ashamed, but I didn't know what else to do about stuff like that. I thought I'd tell the writer I couldn't do it, but when he came back I was looking at the stuff.

"Any luck?" he said.

"Well," I said, "I've written *something*. It seems pretty silly to me."

"Let me look at it."

He took what I had written and went to a window and stood there and read it. I thought he was going to be polite and thank me and forget the whole thing, but when he came back he said, "I hope you won't be offended when I tell you you've written the best scenario for a Training Film I have ever read."

"Do you mean it's all right?"

"It's exactly what the Colonel wants. Now, I didn't write this, but it was *my* assignment to write it—"

"What do you mean?"

"I don't feel comfortable about my good luck in finding someone who can do my work for me—I feel deeply embarrassed about it and deeply grateful too. Is it possible, for the time being, for you and me to pretend that I wrote this?"

"Sure," I said. "It was no trouble at all."

"I'll hand it to the Colonel after lunch," he said.

After lunch he went down the hill to The Production Department, and I went back up the hill to my desk. I had gotten a letter from Victor telling me he had been shipped to a Camera School in Rochester, New York. He'd be back after six weeks—maybe we'd both be back in New York about the same time. Well, maybe Victor would be back in New York after six weeks, but I was afraid I wouldn't be, because the Sergeant had told me that once a fellow got sent to Ohio—always on Detached Service for six weeks, according to his orders—he was there for good.

"Don't think you'll get back to New York after six weeks," the Sergeant had said.

"Why not?"

"They don't like you in New York."

"How do you know?"

"If they sent you here, they don't like you."

"I seemed to be getting along all right."

"Somebody decided it would be better to get you out of the way. So forget New York. The next place for you will be overseas."

Well, I began to write to Victor, but I didn't think I ought to tell him I probably wouldn't be seeing him again—at least not in New York. I wrote a lot of other stuff instead. Pretty soon the stuff stopped being a letter and began to be a funny story about Victor and myself and Pop and Dominic and Lou. I had typed four pages when the writer came into the building.

"Well," he said, "the Colonel's thrilled with *our* scenario. He says if I can hand in one scenario a month like that he'll be very happy. I want to make him as happy as I can because before the War he wrote scenarios at Warner Brothers. Are you going to be at this Post for any length of time?"

"The Sergeant says I'm here for good. He says from here it's overseas. My orders are for six weeks, though."

"Mine were too," the writer said. "As long as you *are* here, do you think you could manage to do what you did this morning once a month?"

"I think so."

"What's that you're writing now?"

"Letter to a pal of mine."

"It's a little long, isn't it?"

"Every once in a while I write a long letter."

"Do you mind if I read what you've written?"

"Hell no."

The writer sat down and read as far as I'd gotten in the letter.

"Anybody ever tell you you're a writer?" he said.

"The preacher at the church I used to go to in San Francisco told me."

"I'm telling you too."

"I can write *letters* all right."

"Everything a man ever writes is a letter. Write a letter to everybody."

"What'll I tell 'em?"

"Tell 'em what you tell Victor. You're the first writer I've run into in the Army."

CHAPTER 25

Wesley Takes The Writer *to Call on Pop, Only to Find Him Gone*

ONE NIGHT I didn't get to town to see Pop because I'd been on Kitchen Police all day and hadn't gotten through until a little before ten when it was too late to go to town. The next night I went to town with the writer to introduce him to Pop, but when we stepped into the elevator, the elevator man said Pop had left the hotel.

I went to the desk and asked the man if any message had been left for me. He said no, so I asked him when Pop had checked out, and he said late the night before.

"Was he drunk?"

"He'd been drinking."

"Did he leave anything in his room?"

"No. He went out with a suitcase."

I thought Pop had been all right, and I thought he was going to go on being all right. I was so surprised to find him gone I thought it must be a mistake, so I sat down to wait for him to come back.

The writer talked to the man at the desk and pretty soon a waiter from the little bar at the end of the lobby came over with a bottle and some ice, and we had a drink.

Drinking, I got to believing Pop would come into the lobby any minute, but when it was ten o'clock and time to go back to the Post and we had almost finished the bottle, Pop hadn't come back.

"We've still got fifteen minutes," the writer said. "I'll get a taxi."

Pretty soon it was seventeen minutes after ten. If the taxi went as fast as it could go, we'd be at the Post a few minutes before eleven. But the writer didn't seem to be in a hurry, and I didn't want to go back at all. I was sick of the Army. I was sick of having to be on time all the time. I was sick of trying to be something I wasn't, something I not only didn't want to be but couldn't be—a prisoner. I said to myself, "Well, they can court-martial me—they can put me in the Stockade. I'm not going back until I see Pop."

Then it was twenty minutes after ten and I knew we'd never be able to make it, so that made me pour another drink. Let the trouble come, just let it all come, and let it be big trouble instead of little.

The writer went to get a package of cigarettes. When he came back he said, "We don't have to be back tonight, but we've got to stand Reveille at six in the morning. I telephoned to see who was Charge of Quarters, and it was Blunden. I told him you and I might not be able to be in by eleven—how about it? He said O.K., but he'd get in trouble if we didn't stand Reveille."

He went out to the taxi and paid the driver and the taxi went off. Then he came back and sat down and we went on drinking. When the bottle was finished we went out to find an all-night coffee place.

"If my father comes in while I'm out," I told the man at the desk, "tell him to wait here for me—I'll be back in a little while."

After we'd had some ham and eggs and coffee we went back to the hotel. All the way back I kept praying that Pop would be there, but he wasn't. We sat in the lobby of the hotel until five in the morning. We just sat there. We didn't say much until about four in the morning. We were pretty sober by then and I just couldn't keep quiet any more, so I told the writer about Pop, how he had always gone off all of a sudden without saying anything to Mom when they were together, or without saying anything to me when Mom had left him. The writer didn't ask any questions, he just listened, but I had the feeling that both of us were talking even though it was only me all the time. I told him I didn't know what it was that made Pop go off that way every once in a while, but it had been going on as long as I could remember.

At five I wrote a note to Pop and left it with the man at the desk, to give to him when he came back to the hotel. Then the writer and I took a taxi and went out to the Post to stand Reveille. When the taxi came to the Sentry Gate, the Sentry came out and drew his pistol. It was a pitch black morning with a drizzle of snow coming down. The Sentry had been fast asleep when the taxi had come up. He was scared to death and embarrassed about it, and his hand was shaking, but he didn't shoot us.

We stood Reveille, then went to the Mess Hall, but I couldn't eat. I sat down with the writer until he had had some coffee, then we went to our desks. I folded my arms and went to sleep.

That night I went back to the hotel, but Pop wasn't there. I sat down to write him a letter, but after I had written for two hours I knew it was silly, so I folded the pages and put them in my coat pocket and went out to see if I could find him in the streets.

I went from one bar to another, but he wasn't in any of them, and pretty soon it was after ten. I telephoned the Post to see who was Charge of Quarters. It was somebody I didn't know. I asked him if he'd do me a favor and not report me for not being in my bunk by eleven, but he said, "You're in the Army, boy—if you're not in your bunk by eleven, you're just naturally A.W.O.L." There are fellows in the Army who are like that. Well, I got so mad I just hung up and decided not to go back anyway. I might not even go back for Reveille. I might not go back at all. I might wait to be *taken* back by the M.P.'s.

CHAPTER 26

Wesley Goes A.W.O.L. Looking for Pop and Finds a Woman Singing Valencia *in the Snow*

I WENT from one part of the town to the other.

Around midnight snow began to fall, and the town became beautiful, even if I hated it. The new snow covered the dirty slush in the streets and everything turned white and grew silent. I went into a few more bars and had a drink or two in each of them and looked at the people and listened to what they had to say. Around one I thought I'd go back to the hotel and if Pop wasn't there I'd rent his room and go to bed—and keep the room for him to return to, if he came back—or keep it for myself. It was a nice room and it seemed like home to me.

On the way back to the hotel a woman came out of a bar, singing the way drunken women do—but she made my heart stop beating because the song she was singing was *Valencia,* and that's my song, that's the song I learned from Pop. I just had to take hold of her.

"Where did you hear that song?"

The woman stared at me and smiled, so then I put my arms around her and kissed her because I was so drunk and tired and close to her anyway.

"You've got to tell me," I said. "Where did you hear it? Somebody sang it to you, didn't he?"

"Come home with me," the woman said. "Goodness gracious, come home with me."

When we came to the entrance of a rather good-looking apartment building, the woman said, "My own place, I own the whole building." I took her in my arms and kissed her again, and she said, "Goodness gracious."

A Negro girl who was dressed something like a waitress in a good restaurant came hurrying to help the woman with her coat. She made a fuss over the woman, and then hurried up the stairs with her coat. The woman turned to me and whispered, "Now don't you be afraid. Come and sit with me and have a drink."

When we got to the second floor I saw a girl with long red hair come out of a room and go down the hall. She wore a very expensive-looking evening dress and looked so beautiful I said to myself, "How am I ever going to find a girl to be my wife when every girl I see seems so beautiful, no matter who she is, or what she is, or anything else?"

The woman and I went into a very big room with a lot of stylish furniture in it, and a baby-grand piano, and three telephones on a table. Pretty soon the Negro girl came into the room and closed the door behind her.

"Everything's just fine now, Miss Molly," the Negro girl said.

"Did O'Connor telephone?"

"He telephoned all right, Ma'am."

"What'd he say?"

"He said for you to phone him."

"Who's here?"

"Just Maggie, and she's going in a few minutes."

"All right, Daisy," the woman said. "I'll be here if anything comes up."

The Negro girl went off and came back in a few minutes with a big silver tray full of stuff. She put it down on a little table and went off again, and the woman asked if I liked water or soda and I told her water, so she fixed a drink with water for me. She was a handsome woman, with her hair rolled up from her neck, and her head round and proud. She was soft and plump with thick white arms, and small hands with fat little fingers. She was about the same age as the woman in New York, but she was another kind of woman altogether.

"When did you hear that song last?" I said. "I've got to know."

"*Valencia?*" the woman said. "I've known that song since I was a girl."

"You must have heard somebody sing it not long ago—last night maybe?"

"I don't think so."

"You *must* have. Try to remember. Nobody remembers a song like that for no reason. Who was here last night?"

"I never see the people who come here. I see only my friends." She lifted the receiver of one of the telephones suddenly and dialed a number and talked softly and seriously with somebody, and then hung up.

I took her in my arms again and kissed her, and she said, "Oh goodness gracious, boy."

"Maybe you heard one of the girls singing the song," I said.

One or another of the telephones would ring every few minutes and the woman would lift the receiver and talk softly but in a very business-like way and hang up. Pretty soon it was three o'clock, and I was so drunk I had almost forgotten about Pop. The woman and I went to a big room on the third floor, which was the top floor, and I said, "I've got to stand Reveille at six in the morning, so I'll just sit here until it's time to take a cab. I'm tired and I'm in trouble too."

"What kind of trouble?"

"I'm A.W.O.L. I was supposed to be in my barracks for bed-check at eleven, and now it's past three."

"Where's your home?"

"San Francisco."

"I used to be there," the woman said. "I had a place there too, once—the nicest place in town. Now don't you worry about anything. You're tired from being away from home, that's all, so lie down and go to sleep."

When it was almost time to go I began to shiver and my teeth began to chatter. The woman thought it was very funny and hugged me until I got warm all over and stopped shivering. She fixed a bath for me and gave me a card with her private telephone number on it and the address of the place, and she said to telephone her no matter what happened. She knew a big Army man and if I got in trouble, she'd telephone him and get him to fix things up for me.

I got a cab and went out to the Post and stood Reveille, but right after Reveille the Sergeant came up to me and said, "The Company Commander wants to see you."

CHAPTER 27

*Wesley Is Held Under Arrest but Is Too Tired to Care or
Notice Any Difference*

I WENT to the Company Commander's office and presented myself
to him, and he said, "Do you know how serious it is to be
A.W.O.L.?"

"Yes, sir."

"And yet you were A.W.O.L. last night?"

"I had reasons, sir."

"I didn't ask about any reasons. Were you in your bunk for bed-
check at eleven o'clock last night?"

"No, sir."

"Then you *were* A.W.O.L.?"

"Yes, sir."

"Sit on the bench in the Orderly Room until I send for you."

"Yes, sir."

I sat down and knew I was in for it for sure, but I was too tired to
care. Pretty soon the Company Commander came out of his office.
He called the Corporal over who was Charge of Quarters and he
said, "Corporal Bennett, when you went to Barracks Number 808
for bed-check last night, what was the situation?"

"All present or accounted for, sir, excepting Private Jackson."

"You're sure?"

"Yes, sir."

"You're prepared to testify to that effect?"

"Yes, sir."

Well, hell, I was so tired I didn't even care to be sore at the
Corporal. I just listened as if the whole thing was something interesting to know about.

"Private Jackson," the Company Commander said to the Corporal, "is confined to this building, under arrest, until further orders." He turned to me and said, "Have you had breakfast?"

"No, sir."

He turned to the Corporal. "Telephone the Mess Sergeant and have a tray of food sent over for *him*."

"Yes, sir," the Corporal said.

The Company Commander went back into his office and the Corporal telephoned the Mess Sergeant. Pretty soon Joe Foxhall came over with a tray of food.

"I heard the Mess Sergeant mention your name," he said. "What's the matter?"

"A.W.O.L."

"Who turned you in?"

"This Corporal."

Joe looked over at the Corporal.

"What's the matter with *you?*" he said.

"I do my duty," the Corporal said.

Joe was talking to the Corporal when I remembered the card the woman had given me, so I got it out and handed it to him.

"Telephone this number," I said. "Tell her you're calling for me, and say I'm in trouble all right—*plenty*."

"O.K.," Joe said.

Ten minutes later Joe came back into the Orderly Room, but the Company Commander was talking to the Corporal, so Joe just looked over at me and nodded and went out. I knew he'd telephoned her all right. I sat on the bench until half-past three in the afternoon, with the fellows finding excuses all the time to come into the Orderly Room to see me—under arrest for being A.W.O.L. At half-past three the Company Commander sent for me and after I'd presented myself, he said, "Return to duty."

That's all he said.

I went to my desk and fell asleep. Pretty soon Joe Foxhall woke me up and said, "What happened?"

"The Company Commander told me to return to duty. Give me back the card."

"Do you mind if I write down the telephone number and address?"

"O.K., but let's not make any trouble for her."

"Who is she?"

"Lady from San Francisco."

"I've been to San Francisco," Joe said. "My home's in Bakersfield, but when I went to the University of California in Berkeley I used to go to San Francisco every Saturday night."

"O.K.," I said.

Joe wrote the numbers down in a little book he had.

I got up and went to the latrine to shave.

CHAPTER 28

Wesley and The Writer *Discuss the Problem of a Scenario About a Deserter, Wesley Reads Some Magazines and Writes a Letter to Victor Tosca in Rochester*

AFTER SHAVING I went back to my desk to sit there and think. It seemed to me I ought to get a few things straight. What did I think I was doing? I hadn't had any sleep worth calling sleep in more than forty-eight hours. I had been drinking all the time. I had walked the streets for hours, and just because I'd heard a woman sing something I happened to know and like—something any number of people in the world might suddenly begin to sing for no reason—I had taken up with her.

Pop had gone off again, but he had gone off that way every two or three months for as long as I could remember, so what excuse was that for me to go off too? Was Pop right when he said I would soon be like him? I couldn't answer the questions because I was too tired. The real stuff had become like the stuff of sleep, except that in my sleep I always knew I was dreaming and would wake up. I knew I wasn't dreaming the real stuff. But I was so tired and so uncertain about what I ought to do next that I wondered if the real stuff wasn't dreaming too. Wasn't the real nothing more than *deeper* sleep? Wasn't it possible that everybody existed in an enormous sleep? How real was I last night, for instance, more asleep than awake and yet awake too? How real were the streets in snow in which the woman appeared, singing my song? How real was she with her round proud head and her fat white little fingers, and her talent for dialing telephone numbers and talking softly in a very business-like way? Was there a girl with long red hair somewhere in the world, busy with some strange action of living? Was Corporal

Bennett real? Was it a real voice that had said, "You're in the Army, boy"? And the little Company Commander who crossed his legs under the bench in the Mess Hall and tapped his little feet together when he ate, was he real? Was he real when he became the mighty voice of military law and order and said, "Private Jackson is under arrest"? Was it real that eight or nine million men of one nation were herded together into little groups like our own group, each man trying still to live his own life?

I went to the writer's desk to use his telephone. The card with the woman's telephone number on it was in my coat pocket. When I went to get the card out of my pocket I found the folded pages of the letter I had written to Pop the night before. I unfolded the pages, read the first few sentences, dropped the letter into the writer's waste-basket and telephoned the woman. I thanked her for getting me out of the trouble I had been in, and she said, "Come and have supper with me at seven."

"What's the name of the girl with the red hair?"

"Why?"

Well, I didn't know what reason to give—I didn't have any reason —but I had been thinking about her ever since I had seen her. I didn't know what to say.

"I don't know," I said.

"Do you like her?"

"I'd like to know who she is."

"Come and have dinner at seven and I'll tell you."

I sat at the writer's desk a few minutes longer and pretty soon he came shambling along and said, "Don't get up. You might as well sit in *my* chair at *my* desk because the Colonel has just handed me a new assignment."

"How much time we got?"

"A month."

"I'll write it tomorrow."

"No," the writer said, "let's go about these things the way the others do. Let's think about these things for two or three weeks— it's easier and it's the custom."

"What's this one about?"

"Desertion. The Colonel feels that this one's right up my alley. He said not to be afraid to make it strong—scare the hell out of them, he said. He suggested that I end the film with the fellow being shot for desertion."

"Who shoots him?"

I felt sorry for the fellows who were going to shoot the deserter. I felt sorrier for them than for the deserter himself. Since *they* were going to stay alive, and he wasn't, I wanted to know about *them*. There isn't much more to know about a man who's dead."

"*Who* shoots him?" the writer said. "You and I shoot him."

"But in the story," I said, "who shoots him?"

"You and I. That's why I suggest we think about this one very carefully. Do we want to shoot him?"

"Do you?"

"No."

"I don't, either."

"Why not?"

"Because the deserter might be me. Why don't *you* want to shoot him?"

"Because he *is* me," the writer said. "If I ever write of a deserter, it will be myself, and I will use all my skill to get him away and prove that he is right and a greater man than the millions of others who do not get away. I will make him the greatest American that ever lived." The writer stopped to light a cigarette. "As it is," he said, "we've got a very difficult problem on our hands. As soldiers, we must kill the man. As human beings, we must prove that he is right. I don't think we can tell the Colonel this is not the kind of story we—that is, I—can do. I think the Colonel is curious to find out several things. I think he is curious to know to what extent it is possible for me to be corrupted. If I kill the deserter, I think he is bright enough (however corrupted he himself may be) to know that I have accepted the necessity to become a moral crook. If I try to prove—or even succeed in proving—that the deserter (and not the Colonel or the Army or the government or the world) is right, he will believe I am mad, although uncorrupted. If I say, on the other hand, that I cannot write such a story, he will know I am a moral coward, and while the consequences will be insignificant insofar as my position in the Army is concerned, they will be considerable insofar as my writing after the War is concerned. So what are you and I going to do?"

"I'll kill the deserter for you," I said. "I'll make him strike his old mother in the face, so nobody will like him. I'll make him twist the arms of little children to take pennies out of their clenched fists. I'll kill the son of a bitch for you, don't you worry about that."

"Why will you do it?"

"Because I don't want *you* to do it."

"You forget," the writer said, "that the Colonel will think I wrote the story, just as he thinks I wrote the one about calisthenics."

"You can tell everybody the truth after the War."

"No," the writer said. "If I let you kill the deserter, it will be myself killing him. We've simply got a problem to consider for two weeks—or three or four. Or, for that matter, for two or three or four years. I'm afraid I shall not want to kill the deserter, consequently I can only hope that the Colonel will fall down very soon and die of a heart-attack. Then perhaps the whole matter will be forgotten."

The writer looked at me a moment, then said, "Don't worry about your father."

"O.K.," I said. "Can I look at these magazines?"

I took the bundle of magazines that was on the writer's desk and went back to my desk. There was an hour before Retreat, so I thought I'd look at the magazines. They were all kinds: *The New Republic, The Yale Review, The Infantry Journal, Secret Stories, Town and Country, The Atlantic Monthly, True Confessions, Theatre Arts, The National Geographic,* and two or three kinds of magazines full of color comic strips.

First, I looked at the magazines from the outside, then I turned the pages of each of them one by one, then I went back to read a little in each of them, beginning with *The Yale Review* because the print is so big. I read some stuff by a Professor who said that everything is grass, so that made me remember the fellow who had dropped letters out of his window, and that made me remember the letter Victor Tosca dropped out of our window for me and the note he left on my duffle-bag when I left New York and what he said about grazing on a lawn, so while I was reading the stuff about grass by the Professor I kept seeing Victor and myself and a lot of other fellows we knew on our hands and knees on the big lawn in front of the White House nibbling the grass, so then I said, "To hell with all this stuff about plant life and soya beans and carbohydrates and oxygen and nitrogen and all that other stuff that's in the world anyway whether we know it or not, the thing that counts in this life is fun—that's the only thing that counts."

I started to type a letter to Victor, to tell him that according to *The Yale Review* everything is grass, and the man who dropped the letters out of his window was right, and I'd see him in New York pretty soon maybe. I didn't feel tired any more and I was glad I was going to have dinner with the woman at seven because the best thing in the world *is* fun. The only thing that counts is eating and drinking and talking and laughing and sporting around. "Sure everything's grass," I wrote to Victor. "And you and I are weeds. We're the weeds by the railroad tracks, dirty and grimy but tougher than the steel of the rails. Remember nine. Give your money to the beggars who step out of limousines. Say your prayers and drop a letter out of a window for me."

CHAPTER 29

Wesley Has Dinner with the Woman Who Sang Valencia, *Meets Maggie the Girl with the Red Hair, and Goes to Sleep*

I HAD dinner with the woman at seven. After dinner the girl with the red hair came and sat with us to have coffee and brandy. Her name was Maggie. She made me feel the way I felt when I saw the girl in Roseville, so when she was gone I asked the woman all about her and she said, "Goodness gracious, talk to her yourself."

"Can a girl like that have children?"

"I think so. I think she can if she doesn't take care of herself. Why? Are you looking for somebody to have children with?"

I told the woman I was and she said, "Oh goodness gracious, I wish I were twenty years younger."

She told the Negro girl to tell Maggie not to go for a while.

"She'll be here any time you want to see her. Do you want to see her right away?"

"Can I talk to her?"

"Goodness gracious, yes," the woman said. "Go ahead and see her and get it started or over with."

"You mean *now?*"

"Unless you'd rather wait."

"I'll wait," I said, so then the woman and I sat there and drank coffee and brandy and talked, and damned if I didn't go to work and like her more and more all the time. She was all fresh and cool and smelling of soap and perfume and her own self, and very wise and generous-hearted. She was full of love for people of all kinds, just so they weren't crooked—the only thing she couldn't stand was a crook.

"If there's anything a big man in the Army can do for you," she said all of a sudden, "let me know and I'll get him to do it for you."

"I'd like to get back to New York when my six weeks are up, but the Sergeant tells me I'm out here for good."

"I'll get you back tomorrow if you like."

"Not tomorrow," I said, "I've got three more weeks to go. Do you think he could get two other fellows to go back with me?"

"I think so," the woman said. "You let me know who they are and when you want to go, and I'll tell him. He'll get you all back to New York for me."

Well, that made me feel pretty good because I knew the writer wanted to go back to New York, and I knew Joe Foxhall wanted to go back. I'd ask them first, though, and make sure.

About half-past nine I telephoned the hotel where Pop had had his room, but they said he hadn't come back. The woman asked me to tell her about Pop, so I did, and then I said, "Where do you think he goes?" She said I ought to be able to guess.

"We get them like that all the time," she said. "Some of them stay three or four days, but now and then we get somebody who stays a whole week. Rich men, as a rule—tired of the life they've been living, sick and tired of their families, and themselves too. They spend a lot of money, but money doesn't mean anything to them. They just want to forget who they are."

"Why?"

"Why not?"

"What's the matter with them? What's the matter with their families?"

"Nothing. They just want to have a little fun, and forget. It does them good to stop being good. Of course they're never really bad. Once in a while somebody'll get mean—ugly—unkind—but I tell them to be good or get out. Most of them are only tired. They only want to forget the things they can't forget when they're home. Who they are—the high opinion people have of them—all the things that are pleasant most of the time, but get awfully tiresome every once in a while. They all go back of course, and I read about them in the papers. When I was in San Francisco they were bigger men than they are here, but I've had some big ones here too."

The woman rang for Daisy who took me to a very handsome-looking room. Pretty soon Daisy brought a silver tray with a bottle of Scotch and two glasses and a bowl of ice on it, and after a while the girl with the red hair come in and we had a drink together and talked. I had to be in my barracks by eleven and no two ways about it. Whoever the big man in the Army was, I didn't want to be a nuisance to him. If he could get me to New York after my six weeks were up—and the writer and Joe Foxhall too—that was good enough for me. I didn't want any more trouble with anybody. I felt funny being alone with the girl with the red hair because she hadn't asked to be alone with me—the two of us hadn't wanted it to be so—and it didn't seem right. There was nothing about the way we had met to make either of us feel anything but awkward. I don't think she was dull—she was too beautiful to be dull—I think she needed what everybody needs before they can stop being dull. She needed something to happen to her in relation to somebody else. She needed to like somebody just when he seemed to like her very much and that wasn't happening with us at all, so pretty soon we decided to have another drink some time and then she stopped being dull and so did I.

A few minutes after the girl with the red hair had gone the Negro girl came into the room and said, "Miss Molly told me to ask you to come into the parlor." I went into the parlor, and the woman was talking on the telephone. When she was finished, she said, "Is Maggie the girl you're looking for?"

"I don't know. I don't think so."

"Why not?"

"I don't know. Maybe it's because I'm so tired."

"Why don't you go upstairs and go to sleep?"

"You got me out of some pretty serious trouble today," I said. "I don't want to ask you to do it again. I've got to be in my barracks by eleven."

"How long does it take to get out there?"

"Forty or forty-five minutes."

"That leaves enough time for one drink."

"It leaves enough time for more than that."

"Oh goodness gracious," the woman said. "Why do you like me?"

"Why do *you* like me?"

"I guess it's because when I saw you in the street, standing like a fool in the snow, staring at me as if I were the only woman in the world—"

"You were singing my song."

"—I almost believed I *was* the only woman in the world."

"I thought you'd heard Pop singing the song. I thought you'd help me find him, but at the same time I liked you a lot anyway because you knew my song—and then after that I guess you know why I liked you more and more. I'll never forget you. Why were you drunk last night? You don't seem like a woman who'd go out and get drunk."

"I was in trouble myself," the woman said. "I was in very serious trouble. Terrible things can happen to somebody like me. It seemed to me a terrible thing was beginning to happen last night, so I went off to be alone. When I saw you I was on my way back to find out. I'd know the minute I got back."

"What kind of trouble?"

"Goodness gracious," the woman said. "You *know*—of course you know, and I don't like to think about it. I like nice things around me, and nice people. Well, when you hugged me I knew you were in trouble too. I told myself that if I got out of *my* trouble—just this once again—it would be on account of *you*—and I'd try to get *you* out of *your* trouble."

"Well, you sure did," I said. "They could have put me in the Stockade for six months for being A.W.O.L., I guess."

"Ten years or more for me," the woman said, "and that's more time than I can spare. It would kill me, I know."

"*Ten years?*"

"This place is only my home now, and it's for sale. I've had enough good luck. I'm scared, now. I don't like District Attorneys or Judges or juries. I was on my way home to the worst trouble that could ever happen to me when I saw you last night. I needed somebody to hold me. I got Maggie to come here tonight especially for you. If you want to see her any more, let me know."

"I don't want to see Maggie any more," I said.

I got back to my barracks before eleven, got into my bunk, and then, oh *Valencia*, how I slept.

CHAPTER 30

Pop Sends Wesley a Letter Explaining the Mystery of His Disappearance, and the Woman Who Sang Valencia *Sings It Again, This Time Better Than Ever*

THE DAYS moved along, every one of them pretty much the same as the other, everything on schedule, and then one day I got a letter from Pop.

"I didn't mean to go off without leaving word with you," he wrote, "but I wasn't sure where I was going or what I was going to do, so I couldn't write anything at all. I wanted to let you know, but I couldn't tell you something I didn't know myself. I checked out of the hotel and went to the railroad station, but the next train to where I thought I was going wasn't leaving for three hours, so I checked my suitcase and went back to town. I didn't take a train until more than twenty-four hours later, although when I got back to town I decided not to go, after all. I decided to go back to the hotel after three or four days, and then something happened that I think you will understand, and that made me go. The place I had gone to was in some kind of trouble and they didn't know what was going to happen. They were getting everybody out of the place as fast as they could, but I was too drunk to move, so they all went off—but pretty soon one of them came back to take care of me. She brought me coffee, and after a while I ate some food that she brought, and then I felt sicker than ever, but she stayed with me and didn't care if she got in trouble or not. I tried to get well enough to go away, so she could go too, like the others, and not get into any trouble. Well, I had a bath and got dressed to go, and then she came and said the trouble was over—everything was all right again, so I didn't have to go—I could go to bed and sleep. I was glad the trouble was over and thought I would go to bed. The girl said she would go and get me something hot to drink that would help me sleep. When she opened the door to go I saw a woman and a fellow in uniform coming up the stairs and I heard the fellow's voice. When the girl came back I thanked her with all my heart for her kindness, but I said I had to go—because I had decided to go to El Paso, after all, where I am now—where I've been since early this morning. I walked past your uncle Neal's store and I think I saw your brother Virgil in there with him, but I haven't seen your mother yet. I want to see your mother, but I'm a little scared. I'm O.K. now, but if it hadn't been for that girl with the red hair I'm sure I wouldn't be here. Write to me right away just in case I can't make up my mind what to do, and I'll write to you again very soon."

Instead of writing to Pop, I sent him a telegram.

"No matter what," I said, "see Mom."

Then I wrote him a long letter and sent it airmail special delivery. The next day there was another letter from Pop. He said he had gone out and seen Mom. I sent a telegram in answer to that letter too, and then wrote another long letter and sent it airmail special delivery too.

For a week I got a letter from Pop every day. He said he was sure I'd understand what he meant when he told me that my brother Virgil was a better man than either of us or both of us put together, because of his mother. "You and I have been too long away from the kind of women who hold the world together, so look for your girl."

One day Pop sent a half dozen snapshots of Mom and my brother Virgil and my uncle Neal and himself, all of them in a group. I was thrilled to see them all looking so young and handsome, even though none of them smiled, as almost everybody does when a pic-

ture is being taken—but the thing that thrilled me most was how
well Pop looked with Mom and Virgil. He didn't look as if there
was anything the matter with him at all. He looked as if he
belonged with them, so I wrote and told him so, and I told him to
write and tell me all about Mom and Virgil and my uncle Neal. I
felt happier then than I'd ever felt in all my life, and I showed
the snapshots of my family to the writer and we sat down and
talked about the deserter and what we ought to do about him.

"If we got shipped to another Post," I said, "then we wouldn't
have to do this story about the deserter, would we?"

"No, we wouldn't," the writer said.

"Would you care to get shipped back to New York?"

"Yes, of course. New York's my home and my wife's home and
we want our son to be born there."

"Your son? How do you know it's going to be a son?"

"It's our first, and it's going to be a son," the writer said.

I went down the hill to The Production Building to find out if
Joe Foxhall wanted to go to New York too. He had a job something like mine because of his high I.Q. and his education—he did
typing for the writers and ran errands. I found him carrying six
Coca-Colas to as many writers.

"Joe," I said, "my time is going to be up here in a week, and—"

"That's what *you* think," Joe said. "You're here to stay, Jackson,
so forget it—there is no discharge from that War."

"*Ecclesiastes,*" I said. "There may be no discharge, but there's
such a thing as getting shipped. Do you want to get shipped back
to New York with me?"

"I was thinking of asking your permission to telephone that
woman myself," Joe said. "I wanted to ask her to get me the hell
out of the *Army*. One of these days I'm going to use one of these
Coca-Cola bottles as a weapon."

"I don't think anybody can get you out of the Army," I said,
"but there's a pretty good chance that you can get shipped back to
New York if you want to put up with that stuff back there again."

"It's no worse than the stuff I put up with here," Joe said. "Do
you want my serial number?"

"I've got it."

"O.K.," Joe said. "And many thanks. When do you think we'll know?"

"Where's the telephone booth?"

Joe showed me the telephone booth. I took a bottle of the Coca-Cola and went in and closed the door and Joe stood outside drinking from one of the bottles and waiting. The woman was very glad I telephoned because she had settled all her affairs—sold her place and everything in it—and was leaving town very soon.

"When?" I said.

"As soon as I get everything settled for you too."

"Where you going?"

"New York for a little while, then home to San Francisco. Now I'll telephone my friend in the Army and call you back—stay where you are."

I opened the door of the booth and Joe and I drank another bottle of Coca-Cola each, and then the telephone bell rang.

"It's O.K.," the woman said. "The three of you—in about a week." She gave me the name of one of the biggest and most expensive hotels in New York—and her own name, not the name on the card, and I said, "I didn't know you were married."

"Goodness gracious," she said, "I've got a son at school in Maryland and a daughter at school in Pennsylvania. My husband's been dead ten years. You telephone me when you get to New York. If I'm there I want you to take me dancing."

"I don't know how to dance."

"We'll go and watch the others dance. If I'm not there, ask for my forwarding address and write to me once in a while and let me know how you're getting along."

"O.K.," I said. "What are you going to do in San Francisco?"

"Read," the woman said. "I like to read. Take care of yourself, now."

"O.K.," I said.

I came out of the booth and Joe said, "What are you crying about?"

"Never mind," I said. "You smoke a cigarette in a telephone booth and it'll bring tears out of your eyes too."

CHAPTER 31

Wesley Sees His Name in Print for the First Time and
Doesn't Know What to Make of It

I WENT back up the hill to tell the writer. He was sitting at his desk
looking at some new magazines that had just come for him.

"I think we'll be going back to New York in about a week," I
said. "Joe Foxhall and you and me."

"If you say so," the writer said, "it must be so."

He handed me the magazine he was reading—*The New Republic*.
He didn't say anything but I knew he wanted me to see something
in it. What I saw across the top of the left hand page made me
sweat: *A Letter to My Father*. I read the first eight or nine words
of the letter and knew it was the letter I had written to Pop when
he had gone off—that I'd dropped in the writer's waste-basket. At
the end of the letter was my name.

"I had no right to do it," the writer said, "but I had no right *not*
to do it, either. I happened to look in the waste-basket for an envelope on which I'd written a title for a story, and I found your
letter to your father. I didn't tell you I'd sent it along to the magazine because I wasn't sure the editors would agree with me about
it. If it came back, I had planned to try it out on one or two other
magazines, but as you see it didn't come back—the editors agreed
with me. I have a letter from them asking about you and wanting
to see anything else you've written or happen to write in the future.
I told them not to say anything about you in the column about
contributors because I thought you ought to tell them about yourself the next time they print something of yours. I hope you're not
unhappy about any of this."

"I'm not exactly unhappy," I said. "But what about Pop? That
letter was written to *him*—I decided not to mail it because—well,
I didn't want to hurt him."

"I think your father will understand," the writer said. "That
letter isn't to him alone, you know. It isn't from *you* alone, either.
That's the way it is when a man's a writer. It's a good way but it's
also a bad way—good or bad, though, anything *you* write is for

reading. I feel as sure of that as I feel that anything *I* write is for reading. I know I took a hell of a liberty, but I think I did right, and after you read the letter I hope you will think I did right too."

I took the magazine to my desk and read the letter, every word of it—and then I read it again because I was so confused. It was exactly what I had written, word for word, but I had forgotten it—I had been tired and angry when I had written it—and when I read it in *The New Republic*—something I had never expected to see again as long as I lived—well, then, it was like the writer said: It wasn't as if *I* had written a letter to Pop, it was as if somebody had had to say something and had said it. I kept sweating and smoking cigarettes and feeling half-sick and half-crazy—and every time I saw my name at the end of the letter, at the bottom of the page, I couldn't understand what had happened.

I felt funny—lonely in a new kind of way—and a lot of other things. Who was I to write? What right did I have to write? If I could write things like that, I could write a lot of other things too. Did I want to be a writer? Did I want to go around being different from everybody else and see things differently and remember what I saw and write about them all the time? Would that be a good way to be or would it take all the fun out of everything? Was I different from everybody else? The writer didn't seem to be different from anybody else. He didn't seem to be watching and remembering all the time. Being a writer didn't seem to bother *him*.

Well, then, I don't know what happened because I began to cry. I didn't cry only on the inside the way you do when you won't let yourself cry. I didn't cry the way you do when you keep everything in except the water that gets your eyes to swimming. I really cried —but I got out of the building first and went out to a field where there were some trees and nobody could see me.

CHAPTER 32

Wesley Does a Heap of Powerful and Systematic Weeping

I GUESS I started to cry because I was a writer and there wasn't anything I could do about it, but pretty soon I cried about everything anybody ever cried about—as long as I was crying anyway. I cried about people being ugly when by all rights they ought to be so handsome that little animals would come up out of the earth to peek at them. I cried about the little animals peeking. I cried about Mom because she had been separated from Pop so long and was still the same—still his girl—and still loved him. I cried about my brother Virgil because there he was in the snapshot as big as me, with the face of a man who knows plenty but isn't making a fuss about it—a better man than me. There he was in the snapshot easy and friendly and not ashamed to be so close to his mother and not a stranger to his father, even though he had only just met him. There he was in El Paso, out there in the old sunshine, as easy as pie. I cried about my uncle Neal because I didn't know him and there he was in the farm-implement business with all kinds of ready information about the working of tractors and when to plant and when to harvest and all kinds of other things somebody ought to know something about. I cried about Pop because he was such a great man and such a fool, thinking he was no good—no good at all—just because it was the truth—just because he didn't know other things were the truth too. Sure Pop was no good, but how good did he think he had to be? How good is it possible to be? If you don't hurt anybody and don't want to hurt anybody, how much better than that is it possible for any man to be? I cried about Maggie because she had taken care of Pop and been so awkward with me I had thought she was dull. I cried about the woman who had come out into the snow singing *Valencia*. I cried about the Corporal who turned me in when he could just as easily not have. I cried about the Company Commander tapping his feet together under the bench as he ate his food. I cried about the Japanese boy who sat by my bed when I was sick in the hospital, and I cried about the Negro boy that I sat by—and I remembered the three dried-up little old oranges and cried about them and tried to remember what I finally did with them—left them on the mantle at The Great Northern Hotel—Victor Tosca probably threw them away. I remembered Jim Kirby the newspaperman and cried about him because he forced the Colonel to send Harry Cook and me to Alaska by airplane, and as long as I was in Alaska I cried about Dan Collins because he didn't look like an Eskimo, he looked like a bartender. I cried about Cacalokowitz because Lou Marriacci had badgered him so about having had sexual relations while off duty —and I cried about Lou because he kept lending me money every week—and I'd pay him back too—I got in a few tears about paying Lou back all that money. I cried about Harry Cook out there in Missouri singing *If I had my way, dear, you'd never grow old,* singing the song to some officer he didn't like, so then I cried about the officer because who the hell did he think he was? Who the hell was he when you got right down to it? Just another sucker, like everybody else, driving himself crazy because he had one little old gold bar on his shoulder—rank mad. I cried about Nick Cully singing *Oh Lord, you know I have no friend like you*—and how was Nick these days? I cried about the fellow going home in his little car to his wife the night I did Guard Duty and envied him because he was free and there was nobody in the world to bother him. I cried about the star that come out for me, to tell me I wasn't going to be killed in the War. I cried about the little cur-dog that yapped at the Colonel for imitating the President and denouncing the Democrats. I cried about the Colonel, and the President, and the Democrats—all those grown men acting like a gang of orang-outangs every time there was a convention to nominate the same man. I cried about the fellows who were always hoping they'd get nominated instead of the same man and then never got nominated and went home to their wives and children no different from what they had been when they left, except maybe a little more irritable, but always courteous about the man who'd been nominated again, calling him, most likely, Our Great President. So then one of those broken-down old tomcats you always see in the fields came creeping along through the grass thinking he was stalking a bird when I could see there wasn't any bird around for miles, his old tail sticking straight out behind him, just shaking with emotion, so I cried about him, and his tail too—and I looked to see if maybe there wasn't a bird he was going to catch, after all, so I could cry about the bird, but there wasn't—the old cat was just doing it to keep in practice—it was only calisthenics for him—or he'd gone mad. So then I looked at the magazine I'd brought along, *The New Republic,* in which at one time, according to Joe Foxhall, the greatest poem ever written was printed—*Ecce Puer* by James Joyce, so I took them in order and cried about *The New Republic,* then Joe Foxhall, then poetry, then the greatest poem ever written, then James Joyce, but I didn't stop to think what that left, I just knew there was still a lot of stuff I hadn't cried about yet, so I moved along to Woodrow Wilson and The League of Nations because Clemenceau had spit in his eye and the League had never worked. Suppose somebody else came along and spit in somebody else's eye who wanted to do the world a little good and the man had to go home brokenhearted because he had believed he could have done the world a little good and then somebody spit in his eye and on top of everything else Congress wouldn't work with him? I cried about Calvin Coolidge because he never hurt a flea. As long as I was out there with the big men, I knew I was in for a fine full unhappiness, so I decided to go about it in a systematic way and cry about the big politicians first. I started out with Ben Franklin but he had always had so much luck and had been so happy the only thing I could cry about was that he had died—he could have lived three years longer and invented the radio. After Franklin, I went along to Patrick Henry for saying "Give me liberty or give me death," because nobody seemed to know for sure which he got. Considering everybody was still asking for liberty, how come he didn't fall down and die on the spot? How come he just got up and made another speech a couple of days later and asked for some other alternative, maybe "Give me money or give me girls." So then I figured I'd had enough of politicians and started to cry about Edgar Allan Poe because of the lonely life he'd lived, always thinking up extraordinary mysteries to solve and at the same time writing painful poems to young girls. I thought I'd cry about one more writer and go along to some of our criminals, and the writer I picked was Longfellow—Henry Wadsworth—because he wrote *Hiawatha* and that really got me to heaving and sobbing because I hated Hiawatha. As long as I was among the Indians I couldn't pass up the chance to shed a tear for the beautiful Indian girl Captain John Smith took for his bride but I couldn't remember her name, so I cried for her anonymously. Then I cried for Jesse James the trainrobber because in the end crime doesn't pay no matter who you give the loot to—they'll shoot you down sooner or later if you take to crime. Then I cried for the Dalton boys, but couldn't think of

any more big criminals excepting a half dozen recent ones, so I cried about a boy who'd been caught in San Francisco ten years ago for stealing a little old dirty pig—but I remembered that he told them he had wanted it for a pet—so I cried a little about the difference that made, and then I cried a lot because nobody felt that that made any difference at all. So pretty soon away out in the distance I saw three little dumpy women in uniforms—culls, Victor Tosca called them—walking in step down the street—perfect little soldiers—fighting the War just like anybody else—so I cried about them because they were dumpy, because they were in uniform, and because everybody believed it was all right for them to do *that* but not all right for better girls to do what Maggie did, which was more or less what girls were meant to do originally, one way or the other —so the dumpy girls did it anyway, out of nervousness or confusion or the excitement of War, and tried to keep it among officers as far as possible. But when I saw the three of them throw a salute, well, then the tears just poured out of me because they didn't fool around with it, they threw the kind of salute that keeps winning the War all the time. It seemed to me then that there was the matter of small nations to cry about because what chance did a small nation have any more? So I cried about Iceland, taking the nations by islands first, then Ireland, then Australia, then New Zealand, then Tasmania, then Madagascar, then all the little islands of the Pacific, then Java, then Cuba, then Haiti, then Cyprus, then Ellis Island—what chance did the people of those islands have? So then that took me to the little nations on the mainland like Greece and Albania and Bulgaria and Roumania and Finland—how about them? Pretty soon I got to crying about science because hardly anybody ever does, so I took to crying about all those lonely men looking through microscopes all the time trying to find out everything it's possible to know. Then I cried about the things they saw through microscopes because those things are part of everything else and it's just as easy and important to cry about a jumping molecule as it is to cry about anything else that jumps. So then as long as I'd gotten down to the littlest things, I thought I'd cry about the biggest too, so I shed a tear for all creation, all the secrets in it that nobody knew—all the millions of years of time and light— and that was the most restful crying of all.

Pretty soon I stopped crying and blew my nose and read the letter in *The New Republic* again that I myself had written, but now it didn't make me cry any more because I knew it didn't matter one way or the other if I was a writer or not.

So then I *was* a writer, and except for the awful crying I'd done, I was no different from what I had always been, only I was pretty sore about the way things turned out for Woodrow Wilson.

CHAPTER 33

Wesley Reads in The New Republic *the Letter He Wrote to His Father*

THIS IS what I wrote to Pop that night in the lobby of the little hotel, and this is what I read in *The New Republic:*

"Bernard Jackson: Even though I don't know where you are or whether this will ever reach you, I've got to write to you because if you're in trouble, then so am I. I have never felt that I had to be loyal to you or that I had to feel proud of you or any of the other things good sons are supposed to feel about their fathers. You're my father and I'm your son and that's the end of it—good or bad's got nothing to do with it. I suppose some people would think you're a weak man because every now and then you've got to go off the way you do—the way you've just done again—and drink yourself through whatever it is that made you go off. But I don't think you're weak to do that at all. I think it's just naturally necessary for you to do everything you do.

"Then why am I writing to you? I'm writing to you because I think the time has come for me to try to straighten you out in myself, like you told me not so long ago you were counting on me to do. A lot of things happened to you in the last War that I can't even guess about because no man can guess what another man knows, not even if one is the son of the other. From what you've told me, though, I know the worst didn't happen to your body. Your body is still stronger than the bodies of most men. The worst happened to You—all of you, not your body, not your nerves, not your mind, not your heart, not your spirit, but to You Yourself. I

know you felt outraged by the War, and that you still do—*personally*. And I know the notion of my going through the same thing scares you because you have been counting on me to turn out all right—for the two of us. You are counting on me to have a son to pick up where I leave off—and I'm counting on it too. You told me you kept yourself alive through the whole War for one reason: to see me. Well, I want you to know that I have decided to do everything I can to keep myself alive so that I can see *my* son. I know you will not be shocked when I tell you that this decision is making a physical coward out of me, because that is the truth. In order to see my own son someday I am willing to be such a coward. The idea of physical cowardice scares the hell out of most fellows in the Army, but it doesn't scare me. I'd really begin to be scared if I found myself unwilling or unable to understand very clearly that under some circumstances and for certain reasons I am willing to be unwilling to die. I absolutely do not want to get killed—for any reason. I honestly don't think I would care if civilization itself (as they are always saying) ended, just so I stayed alive. I swear to God I think I *am* civilization. What the hell do I care what collapses as long as I don't? I don't believe any other honest fellow in the Army doesn't feel in his heart as I do. I know that I might get myself killed (without thinking about it) out of anger about what's true or right, for instance—but I don't think if that happened I'd have helped save civilization. I think it would be damned foolishness. If I've got to get killed in order to keep civilization going, then everybody's got to get killed with me. Since that cannot be, I've got to stay alive or civilization has got to collapse or it's got to be put on the sort of operating basis that will not ask you, then me, then my son to go out and get killed.

"Your good time has come—you can run out on all these things, and I'm glad you can. My bad time has come because I'm caught. The same old machine that caught you and squeezed the bajesus out of you and then let you drop, has caught me and it means to do the same to me, or worse—and I mean not to let it, if I can manage. You've got me, which I guess is something, but I haven't got mine, and I need it badly. You said there's no place in the world for a man to live and watch his children grow—the whole place is caught by the machine and can't get free. I think you're right, Pop. You and I haven't got enough money to buy our own world and put a fence around it and live in it. If we had enough money to do it I think we could make a nation of our own and establish a government of our own and be satisfied with our two acres and our two cents' worth of culture, but I think it's a good thing we haven't got enough money to do it, because nobody's got enough money to do it, and if everybody can't do it, its no use for us to do it. So then what are we going to do? How are we going to get along with ourselves? I mean, how are we going to get to be human beings, as you put it, if the situation simply will not permit it? Well, I don't know about you, but if you really meant for me to be an improvement of you, then I think I've got to find out how to get free of the machine and how to become human—no matter what the situation happens to be.

"I wish you were here now, so instead of writing all this stuff we could have a couple of drinks together. Now, I know why—"

And that's as far as I got in the letter, and that's where it stopped in *The New Republic.*

CHAPTER 34

Wesley Returns to New York Where He Meets Victor Tosca, Just Back from Rochester with a Philosophy, a Gift, and Some Written Observations

WHEN THE good day came the writer and Joe Foxhall and I returned to New York. Two or three days later Victor Tosca came back from Camera Repair School in Rochester and asked if I had any cameras to repair. He said he had been taught how to make minor repairs on complicated cameras and major repairs on simple ones, but he couldn't understand why they had decided to teach him stuff like that when what he was really interested in was yoga, so I figured he'd had a couple to drink and I was right.

He said he'd met a man in Rochester who had graduated from Harvard and had taken to finding out about the mysteries of life. This man was a Private in the Army, but being a Private hadn't prevented him from sitting down in various yoga positions in his spare time, and it hadn't prevented him from trying to teach the secrets he'd learned to other fellows who were at that school. Victor had learned more about yoga, he said, than about repairing cameras. He said the man had told him that cameras come and cameras go, but yoga's yoga forever. This man's name was Olson, and his family was rich. They lived in Boston, Victor said, but Olson planned to leave Boston after the War and go to India to continue his studies. Olson claimed there was a good chance that some day he would be able to learn the real truth about living. He said he was staying clear of America after the War because America was getting too rich and too powerful for him. He said he was interested in the truth, not money. He was interested in poise, not power.

Well, Victor and I had kept in touch with each other by mail and we had decided to get back our place at The Great Northern because it was like home to us and that's what we did. He came straight from Grand Central to the hotel because it would have been foolish to report to the Post at ten at night. He had been drinking from a bottle all the way down, and he handed the bottle to me. Besides telling me about the yoga-man, Olson, he kept singing *Everybody calls me honey*. Pretty soon he had the stuff out of his duffle-bag all over the place.

"I've brought you a present," he said. "Don't think I'd go away for six weeks and come back without a present. The trouble is I've forgotten where I put it, so I'll take a yoga position on the floor and get some poise because then I'll be able to remember where I put the present—it always works. That fellow Olson is going to help the world out some day."

I was feeling so glad to be back in New York and it was so good to see Victor again—especially since he was a little drunk—I said, "Help the world out of what?" Now, I know that that question doesn't mean anything, but it was the kind of question that seemed to be appropriate and Victor was very grateful for it.

"Help the world out of *what?*" Victor said. "Help the world out of its loneliness, that's what. Hand me the bottle and help me out of *my* loneliness, will you?"

So Victor took another swig, sitting on the floor in one of the several yoga positions he'd learned from Olson. His feet were crossed under him, his back was very straight, and every now and then he'd make his back straighter than ever.

"Loneliness," he said. "I've got your present around here somewhere. I know you're going to be very happy when you see it too."

Pretty soon he said he had gotten all the poise he needed and he believed he knew where he had put my present, so he got up and began searching through the junk he'd brought out of his dufflebag. He didn't find the present right away, but he found a copy of *The New Republic* and he opened it to where my letter to Pop was printed.

"Olson says you're a great man," Victor said. "Olson showed me this magazine. He says you've written something that's going to help the world out too. I've read it eight or nine times and I think Olson's right. I don't know much about anything, I guess, but you sure wrote something in that letter to Pop. I've got your present here some place. I'll find it with my old yoga poise any minute now." But next he found something else, and he said, "You know, if your pal's a great man—even if he doesn't know anything about the secrets of life—well, a fellow's got to be a great man too—so I've done a little writing myself—and here it is." He handed me a sheet of hotel letter paper. "It's not much," he said, "but it's got *something,* I think. It took me the better part of a whole night to write it. I guess you'd call it a philosophical saying. Go ahead, read it."

Well, I read what Victor had written. It was wonderful, but it just wasn't like anything I ever thought he'd write, which goes to show you you can't tell about anybody—he'll go to work and fool you on some point or other.

Across the top of the sheet of paper he'd written: "The Observations of Victor Tosca by Victor Tosca." Beneath this was written: "Part I."

And then, this:

"One day somebody said to me I want you to meet a friend of mine so I met him but there was something the matter with him. The next day I noticed that he didn't have any eyes."

"How do you like it?"

"It's very funny."

"There must be some sort of message in those words," Victor said, "because it took me a long time to write them. Of course it's the first writing I've ever done. I don't think I'll ever be the kind of writer you are. It's only a hobby with me—loneliness, that's my profession. But a little writing once in a while never did anybody any harm. Here's your present."

The present was all wrapped up. I cut the string and opened the paper and took the lid off the little cardboard box. Inside the box were the three oranges the Japanese boy had left for me at the Hospital. They had gotten drier and littler than ever, but they were good to see and I was glad I knew a fellow who would keep three dried-up little old oranges for me.

"I knew you'd like your present," Victor said.

"I sure am glad you saved them for me. What'd you do it for?"

"I'm no fool," Victor said. "I know about a few things. Do you think I ought to continue my career as a writer?"

"Sure," I said.

"Where'd you learn to write stuff like that?" Victor said. "When I first saw you I thought you must be a little foolish. I thought *I* was smart. Did you go to school to learn stuff like that? Let's go out and get drunk."

CHAPTER 35

Victor Tosca Urges Wesley to Write About Love, Telephones His Girl in San Francisco, and Buys a Rose

WE TOOK a cab to the bar where I'd met the woman because I liked that place. Besides, I believed the old Irishman might be there. I guess I wanted to go to a place where I'd met some people. I even hoped the woman would come by for a drink because it would be fun seeing her in the bar again. Well, the old Irishman wasn't there and didn't show up, and neither did the woman, but Victor and I had a lot of fun and we got good and drunk and he said, "Jackson, I've got to get my girl to come to New York—I'm dying of loneliness."

He went to the telephone booth and pretty soon he came back and asked the bartender for ten dollars' worth of change. It was almost one o'clock in the morning, but it was only after dinner

time in San Francisco. I thought he'd shout over the telephone, the
way most people do when they talk long distance, but he was very
quiet. After seven or eight minutes he came out of the booth and
sat at the bar and finished a double Scotch before he said anything.

"Write about love," he said. "Love's the only thing. Tell them
again and again, 'I love you.' *Tell* them, for God's sake, Jackson.
Tell them about love. Don't talk about anything else. Just keep
telling them the story of love. It's the only story. Money's nothing,
crime's nothing, War's nothing, nothing's nothing—the only thing
is love. So tell them about it."

I knew how in love he was, and I knew what love could do to a
man. Love could make any man great. Nothing else could do it, but
love could do it. I knew it was no good not being in love.

"Is your girl coming to New York?"

Instead of answering me he went back to the telephone booth.
After another eight or nine minutes he came back and said, "Yes.
I talked to her again. I talked to her in Italian. I forgot to talk to
her in Italian the first time, so this time I talked to her in Italian.
I told her in Italian. I told her mother in Italian. I told my mother
in Italian. They said all right, they'd come in a month, but I said
no, so then they said in a week, but I said no again, so then they
said, 'When do you want us to come?' And I said, 'Take the train
tonight.' And my girl started to cry and she said, 'All right, we will
start packing now and we will get on the next train.' Just write
about love. Just tell them about it over and over again. It's too
lonely without love. Promise me you'll write about love. I thought
you must be foolish just because you *looked* foolish. Promise me
you'll sing them the only song. Do you promise?"

"Sure," I said.

"On your word of honor?"

"O.K."

"Don't think I'm just talking," Victor said. "Don't think I'm
just talking because I'm drunk. I come from a family—a family.
Love's the only thing we know. I've got to belong to a family, not
an Army. For a while I had my brother with me—but that was on
account of a mistake, so they had to correct the mistake. Not good
to have brothers together in the same company. Why not? Brothers
understand one another. Brothers are brothers and they know.

Mothers and fathers and brothers and sisters and uncles and aunts
and cousins—they know. Everybody's got to have a family—got to
have love. You've got to promise me, Jackson—because you and
me, we're brothers too. I brought back the oranges, didn't I? I
wrote to you, didn't I? You're not Italian—you're Irish or something, but you and me, we're brothers. Dominic knew—he didn't
think you were foolish. That's what I thought—ignorant—didn't go
to school enough. But Dominic knew. He told me. He told me in
Italian. 'He's your brother,' he said. 'Don't forget.' I got all your
letters. I'm keeping them too. I know who you are. You get to understand things when you learn about yoga. Do you promise?"

Well, he was drunk all right, but drunkards say a lot more than
the words they say. I wasn't sure I knew exactly what Victor Tosca
was saying, but I think I was pretty close to it. I think he was
saying, *When my girl said they'd start packing right away and take
the next train, she knew why—and the reason is—you know the reason—you can't get away from it because the reason is—who wants to
think about the reason? We're brothers, so I'm telling you—the reason is I'm going to be dead pretty soon. I'm not scared—I'm not drunk
—I* know *the reason my girl and her mother and my mother have
got to come to New York. The fellow without the eyes—he's all
right—he doesn't know—he hasn't seen love—but I've got eyes and
I've seen love, and when you've got eyes and you've seen love and
know the reason—when you know the dirty reason—then time goes
too fast and you've got to get love on a train, you've got to make it
hurry, there isn't time enough for much, your eyes aren't going to
see much longer—love's got to hurry—there isn't time—because you
know, you know, you don't want to know but you know.*

"Do you promise?" he said again. "You understand what I'm
talking about, I know. You don't even *look* foolish any more. I
know you understand. Do you promise your brother? Tell them—
love. We'll never talk about this again, but you've got to promise
and know what you've promised and you've got to keep your
promise. You've got to keep it for your brother. You've got to shake
hands on it, and then we'll just drink and have fun."

"I'll try," I said, and we shook hands. Then Victor said, "I know
you'll do it."

Well, it was almost closing time, so we ordered one more each.

We drank to each other, but we didn't say anything. We just touched glasses and drank the last one straight, in one gulp, and then Victor started hollering his song as if he were the happiest man in the whole world.

Well, the bartender—how should he know what was going on? He didn't know. He just thought a couple of fellows had got drunk at his bar. It was nothing and he didn't care, so when we got up to go he smiled and said, "Good night, boys—come back again."

When he said that, Victor stopped singing and just looked at the bartender, but I knew what he was thinking. He gave the old man an easy salute, the salute you give when you're not in uniform.

"So long," he said.

He looked around the place without moving his head, then he walked over to the telephone booth and tried to put his arms around it, but of course his arms couldn't reach around it. He just stayed there that way a little while. Then he didn't look at anything any more—he just walked straight out of the place.

We walked all the way home, but he kept his promise, he didn't talk about it any more, he just sang all the time. On 57th Street near 4th Avenue there was an old woman in the street who was holding three roses in her hand. When she heard Victor singing she came up to him because the old women who go through the streets all hours of the day and night selling roses—they know fellows who are singing will buy a rose from them. She pushed the roses out toward Victor.

"God bless you, my boy," she said. "I've got a boy in the Army, a boy in the Navy, and a boy in the Marines. God bless you, my boy, and take care of you."

She was a little old dirty beggar woman, the kind that scare most people, the kind that people avoid, but Victor, he looked at her and spread his arms out, and then he embraced her, and she rested her head on his shoulder and he said, "Oh Mama—Mama." And then he kissed her, first on one cheek, and then on the other, and the old woman kept saying, "God bless you, my boy." Victor took one rose and gave the old woman all the money that came up in his hand out of his pocket, a lot of silver and a couple of pieces of currency. Then we hurried down the street, and I could hear the old woman still saying, "God bless you, my boy."

We went to an all-night cafeteria for coffee. Victor kept looking at the rose and he kept smelling it.

"You've got three oranges," he said, "but I've got something now too. I've got the rose. I took only one because you never want *roses* —you want the rose—the one rose. I've got something now too, and I'm going to keep it. I'm going to keep it as long as I— Something's going to happen to the oranges some day, and this rose is more than half-dead already, but I'm going to keep it just the same. What'll we do tomorrow night?"

"Get drunk."

"O.K."

"We could go back to that bar and—"

I suddenly realized what I was saying, and stopped.

Victor just looked at me and shook his head a couple of times.

"Let's go to a play or something," he said.

"O.K."

CHAPTER 36

Wesley and Victor Go to a Wonderful Play That Isn't Wonderful and Then Is Because of the Play Within the Play

THE NEXT night we went to a play that everybody said was wonderful and we sat in the first row. The play had been running three years. It was one of the biggest successes in the history of the American theatre. Every eight or nine months they'd change the actors and actresses in the play because by that time the actors and actresses would be all worn out from saying the same things over and over again every night. There were six or seven road companies of the play too, all over the country, so we felt pretty sure it was a wonderful play. Pretty soon the curtain went up and the play started. The scene was a living-room of a very fine house, and the people were very refined people. After ten minutes the play hadn't gotten wonderful yet, but of course it was a little early. We were sure it would get wonderful in the next two or three minutes, but it didn't, so pretty soon we started wondering if it was ever going to get wonderful.

It hadn't gotten wonderful by the end of the first act, so we went out of the lobby with some other people from the theatre to a bar next door and had a drink to help us wait. Then we went back and sat down and the curtain went up again, but again the play wasn't wonderful. Everybody was talking very clearly, and every once in a while somebody would get a little excited and we'd see some acting, but we always knew it was acting, and it was never wonderful.

What it was was this very clear-speaking man of fifty-five or so whose daughter seemed to be infatuated with a man who was known to be no good. The father didn't want his daughter to have anything to do with this man, and the daughter *did*—all through the first act. At the end of the first act we saw this man who was no good, but he seemed likable enough, hardly worth all the fuss.

In the bar next door during the first intermission we heard the people next to us talking about the play and how wonderful it was. They said the man who was playing the part of the father was great —he was really great—he'd been in the part longer than anybody else had ever been in it because the management kept raising his pay so he wouldn't leave the part. Everybody liked him so much the management just didn't want to let him go. The people said the play would always be a wonderful play, even without him, but *with* him—well, it was just that much better. Victor kept looking and listening, and then he said, "Are they talking about the play we're seeing?" I said they were all right, and he said, "Well, we've just got to pay closer attention because we're missing something. Do *you* think the play's wonderful?" I told him I didn't think it was wonderful so far, but maybe it would get wonderful in the second act, but if it didn't in the second, then it would for sure in the third. Victor asked if there was a fourth act and I said no, and he said, "That's good, in case it never gets wonderful."

During the second intermission we went back to the bar for another drink but we decided to make it two because the play still wasn't wonderful. There were some new people next to us now, and these people said the play was wonderful too. Victor said maybe we hadn't gone to school enough. All through the second act the father had succeeded in keeping his daughter away from the man who was supposed to be no good but seemed to be all right to us, but that was all. We went back into the theatre to see the last act.

I could see for myself how tired the man who was playing the part of the father was. Sitting that close to the stage I could hear him breathing hard—from being tired. I could also see that he hated the girl who was playing the part of his daughter, and I could see she hated him. Well, Victor and I had both begun to notice such things along about the middle of the second act, so then we forgot about the play we'd paid to see and began to watch the actor and the actress fighting with each other. We just couldn't miss any of it. It almost made the play wonderful.

About the middle of the last act something happened that Victor and I couldn't believe.

The moment on the stage was a tense one. It was a show-down between the father and his daughter. Everybody knew it was a show-down and they were happy to see the man who was playing the part of the father playing it so well. The daughter was going to have her way, after all, it seemed, but nobody was sure the father wasn't going to trick her into keeping away from the man who was no good. All during the play the father had been letting everybody know that he was the kind of man who might *seem* to be letting somebody else have his way, whereas in the end they didn't have their way at all—especially in big business deals. He always got his way, and he always did it in a way that pleased the other people because they always thought they were having *their* way—not at all. *His* way.

So this was the big moment. The father turned to his daughter and very clearly—so clearly that unless you were deaf you could have heard him in the last row of the gallery—he said, "Well, my dear, I've been an awful fool not to see things in their true light— not to see them as they really are—not to understand that you have your life to live as I have mine—that you *must* live your life —that you would not be my daughter if you did not *insist* on living your own life." He was going along at a pretty good clip, making everything more dramatic than it was, saying everything very fast because he had either really come to see things as his daughter saw them or was going to trick her—which made it just that much more dramatic—and then he said, "Why don't you f—— the man and be done with it?" And went right on talking very swiftly.

Well, I thought I had heard what the man had said, but I couldn't believe it. I looked at Victor and I knew *he* had heard what I had heard, so then we looked back at the people on the stage, but now the daughter was making a very swift and exciting speech, and the father looked the same as ever—a really serious man, very unhappy about the inclination of his daughter to throw herself away on a social climber of dubious morals. It was all over, as if it were nothing.

We looked around at the people, but they didn't seem to think anything odd had taken place. They were just sitting there the same as ever. We decided they were either half-asleep or they *had* heard what the father had said to the daughter, but inasmuch as it was such an unusual thing to hear from a stage—a thing that just isn't said—they hadn't believed their ears, and they were satisfied that the man had said something else which for some reason had reached their ears as they thought it had but couldn't believe.

The play ended and Victor and I got up and went to a bar.

We decided the man who had played the part of the father had become so bored with the part, and at the same time his hatred for the girl who played the part of his daughter had become so great, that he had made a private bet with somebody, a stage-hand most likely, that he would say what he had said and get away with it—and from all appearances he had won his bet.

CHAPTER 37

Wesley Celebrates His Nineteenth Birthday by Carving His Initials in the Arm of the Statue of Liberty

ONE DAY it was September 25, 1943, my birthday, and there I was nineteen years old. I had been in the Army a year. I had been in the East nine months, which is the amount of time it takes for a man who is scheduled to be born to be born. Christmas-time is the time of my beginning in the womb of my mother. Now, I had been in the world, on my feet, nineteen years. What did I have to show for it?

Nothing.

I went out to the Statue of Liberty and carved my initials on the stone wall of the arm that holds the torch. I don't know why I did it. There were some other initials on the wall, but I found a place where no one else had carved his initials and when nobody was around I put my initials in the stone, very big and clear: *W. J.* Underneath I carved the number "9" because I like to think that that's my number.

When I got back to Manhattan I walked all the way up 5th Avenue to St. Patrick's where I sat down to think. I can always think in a church. It's a Catholic Church, but I didn't care about that, and I thought a lot of things.

I considered my life and found it wanting. My life wanted many things, but most of all it wanted liberty, and I guess that's why I had gone out to the Statue. My life wanted to be free to shape itself. It wanted time. It wanted its wife.

I got up and walked home.

Pretty soon Victor Tosca came along to visit me. He had been married almost two months now and he and his girl were living in our old place, and I was living in a room on the floor above. His mother and his girl's mother, they lived in a place just like our old place, two floors below Victor's. We were all together every once in a while. One Sunday we went out to visit an Italian family in Brooklyn because Victor's mother wanted to cook for us. She cooked six different kinds of Italian things and we ate all day. We drank a lot of wine, and I wished to God I had a girl like Victor's.

When Victor came to visit me on my birthday I knew he had good news.

"My wife's pregnant," he said. "For a week now she's been nauseous in the morning, so I made her go to a doctor yesterday. This afternoon he told her she's pregnant."

"I wish I had a beautiful wife who was pregnant," I said.

"You'll find her."

"Where?"

"Where have you been looking?"

"Where can you look? *Everywhere.* I'm nineteen years old too, and pretty soon we'll be going overseas. You sure are lucky."

"I feel O.K. now," Victor said, "but I sure would like to be with her when it happens."

"I hope they let you stay that long."

"Some fellows have been at the Post two or three years."

"They're in Company A, you're not."

"How can I get into that Company?"

"You can't."

"Why not?"

"I don't know. You just can't. *Why not?* Why not a lot of things? You'd better *try* to get into that Company, though. You'd better try hard. Start trying tomorrow. Keep trying all the time. Find out what you've got to do, and do it."

"What do you mean?" Victor said. "What am I supposed to do —go and tell somebody I don't want to get shipped overseas because I want to be with my wife when my son's born?"

"Sure," I said. "Why not? Let them send somebody else. They don't need *everybody* overseas. You can stay here like a couple of hundred other guys who aren't going to get shipped from that Post. Who are *they?* Why can they stay? It's different with me. Pop's home and he's O.K. now. I might as well go and look around. I know I'll be lucky. I'm scared to death, but I want to go just the same."

"Why?" Victor said.

"Because it embarrasses me to be with all those guys who are never going to get shipped."

"Why does it embarrass you?"

"Because they want *you* to be shipped—and me—and the next fellow. They think it's very important for *you* to be shipped—but not them. It embarrasses me to see them. I don't want *anybody* to be shipped. I'm tired of being embarrassed. I've told the Sergeant I want to be shipped. He said, 'What's the hurry? You ought to be good for another year here at least.' I told him I wanted to be shipped. I suppose a lot of fellows get themselves killed that way— out of irritation. I think they'd rather take a chance on getting killed than go on hanging around with a lot of—"

"They're not bad," Victor said.

"Sure they're not," I said. "I'm just sore. They're good fellows—they're fine—but I hate their guts. I'll tell you why too—because they know they're safe. They know they're being looked after. They know they can always go on pretending among themselves that they are liable to get shipped any day, but they also know they can always go to somebody and just look at him and get it fixed so they won't get shipped."

"How do they get it fixed?"

"There's nothing to it if you know the boys and play the game. It's all correct. It's all according to Army procedure. *Everybody* doesn't have to get shipped. *Somebody* has got to decide who gets shipped and who doesn't. The boys who decide—well, they'll decide *you* have to be shipped. They don't know you. You're a name and a number to them. If it's a question of you or somebody they know—well, it's you. No harm done—there's a War on, you know. Try to get into that Company."

"I'll get shipped," Victor said.

"No," I said. "Don't be a fool. Give the matter a little time and attention. You ought to be with your wife when your son's born—every man ought to be with his wife when his son's born—but *you* especially."

"You're not sore at me for not telling the Sergeant I want to get shipped too, are you?"

"Don't be silly. I'm sore—but not at *you*. I mean this with all my heart—try to get along with the boys. I can't. I couldn't if I wanted to. But hell, I guess if I was married to a beautiful girl who was pregnant I'd break my neck to try to get along so I wouldn't get shipped. I'm scared to death even though I haven't got a beautiful pregnant wife. It would be a lot worse if I had one. I think I'd do anything to stay with her. I think I'd desert. I've been sore all day. I always get sore on my birthday. I guess I sound as if I'm sore at *you* too—but I'm not. Maybe you forget that you and I are brothers. I don't. I remember that all the time. That's why I'm telling you to try to figure them out—see if you can get along. Dominic would tell you the same thing."

"I know he would," Victor said. "He tells me that in his letters all the time. I'm no good at that kind of stuff, though. I'm just no good at it. I ought to try to work something out, but I know I'd only feel foolish, and get shipped anyway. Who knows? Maybe the War will be over before we get shipped. Or maybe, even without working on anybody, they won't ship us."

"You don't believe that and you know you don't."

"That's right," Victor said. "But it's good to think it might happen anyway."

"It won't, though. They're shipping fellows from our Company every week. I don't know why they've skipped us this long. We've been here nine months. Some of the fellows get shipped in three."

"Well," Victor said, "she's pregnant anyway. They can't take that away from me."

"I sure am glad about that."

"Come and have supper with us."

"No. I'm no good on my birthday. I'll be O.K. tomorrow, though. You go ahead. Tell her how happy I am about the good news."

"I wish you'd come."

"Got to be alone on my birthday. Got to think it over."

"O.K. See you in the morning."

So then Victor went along to his beautiful wife and I went back to my thinking, but all it came to was zero.

CHAPTER 38

Wesley Hears About a Man Who Refused to Crawl

ONE DAY we knew we were going to be shipped. A unit of twenty-one men had been formed, and in the unit was Victor Tosca, Joe Foxhall, the writer and myself. They gave us new inoculation shots, new orientation lectures, and new equipment, including carbine rifles.

Early in December they sent us to a place in New Jersey for special overseas training. We got up at four in the morning to be at the Post at five, and then drove out to New Jersey—battle dress, field pack, gas mask, helmet, and carbine. It was awful cold out there, and the whole thing seemed silly to me. It seemed like a fantasy. It didn't seem real at all. We went to New Jersey three times, each time for some special new kind of training. The first time we crawled a hundred yards over rough ground, under barbed-wire, while a machine-gun fired real bullets along our path over us. The racket of the machine-gun sounded ridiculous to me. While we were waiting our turn to crawl the hundred yards with the full pack on our backs, I had time to study the faces of a lot of the fellows who had just finished crawling. These fellows weren't happy. They weren't like the fellows at the Post who'd been there two or three years and would be there for the duration. These fellows looked lonely. They looked as if they wanted to talk to somebody they had known a long time—somebody out of uniform—and tell them something important. I don't think I've ever seen faces as lonely-looking as the faces of the fellows who had crawled the hundred yards. They all came back from the crawl walking slowly, nobody saying anything. Every once in a while a fellow would turn and look at the machine-gun which would be firing over some new fellows who were crawling.

The Sergeant who was in charge there told everybody to keep his head down. "We got orders to make this tough, and it *is* tough," he said. "Keep your head down and keep crawling—don't look up or around. Looking's dangerous."

I got to talking to the Sergeant and he said, "Between you and me, they're looking for a few casualties now and then because casualties prove the training's tough, and that's what they want the training to be."

I asked him if anybody had been hit.

He looked around to see if anybody was listening and then he said, "Three since I've been here—three in one month."

I asked him what had happened.

"Panic," he said. "Now and then you get a fellow who jumps up to run, but he doesn't get very far."

I asked him why the fellow on the machine-gun didn't stop firing when somebody jumped up.

"Not enough time," the Sergeant said. "Besides, he's not *supposed* to stop firing. Hell, one poor son of a bitch got twenty shells in him. If he'd dropped after he'd been hit once, they would have been able to save him, most likely—but the crazy son of a bitch just stood there staring at the machine-gun. I thought he'd never drop. I guess he got sore, the way you do when everything's all wrong anyway.

I asked the Sergeant if the fellow had said anything.

"Yeah," the Sergeant said. "He kept saying, 'Oh f——, Oh f——,' until he fell."

I asked the Sergeant if he thought the fellow had been scared.

"What do you mean?"

"Well," I said, "from what you've told me, I'd say he *hadn't* been scared. He just decided he wasn't going to do it, that's all."

"Why not?"

"Just didn't feel like it."

"Didn't feel like it?" the Sergeant said. "You've *got* to feel like it."

"No, you don't," I said. *"That* fellow didn't."

So then the Sergeant gave me a worried look.

"Anybody who does a thing like that makes a lot of trouble for everybody," he said, "and he scares hell out of everybody too—it's the worst thing there is for morale. When *you* start crawling, just keep your head down and don't get any crazy ideas in it."

"Don't worry," I said. *"I'm* going to crawl. I'm going to keep my head *way* down. But I think that fellow decided he just didn't feel like doing it."

"Why not?" the Sergeant said again.

"That's the kind of Army he was in."

"What do you mean?"

"He was in his own Army. He figured *this* Army was his enemy."

"A lot of funny guys in the Army all right," the Sergeant said.

CHAPTER 39

Wesley Crawls a Hundred Yards

AT LAST it was our turn to crawl, so Victor Tosca and I ducked under the barbed-wire, and right after us came Joe Foxhall and the writer. The machine-gun started rattling away at us, and the writer started talking. He talked the whole distance and what he said I'm not even going to try to repeat because it was so dirty. So then I

started talking to Victor, and every once in a while I'd holler back
to the writer, and pretty soon Joe Foxhall joined in. Then everybody in our outfit—all twenty-one of us—started hollering and
laughing and making fun of the whole business, even the Lieutenant who was in charge, crawling last. What happened was that our
whole unit got to feeling that our own Army was the enemy. That's
a strange feeling to have, but there's a lot of truth in it just the
same. After we'd crawled about twenty yards—well, I was pooped,
I was really pooped, and there was still so far to go. I stopped to
catch my breath, so Victor stopped too, so of course right behind
us the writer and Joe Foxhall had to stop. *Everybody* behind us
had to stop. It was O.K., though, because *everybody* was pooped.
There were three sets of pairs of fellows crawling ahead of us who
didn't stop when we did that time, but they stopped after another
ten yards, so we had to stop then too. We were keeping our heads
down very close to the ground most of the time. So many fellows
had crawled over the course that the surface had become soft and
powdery, and we inhaled an awful lot of dust. Every once in a
while I'd look up a little to see how much farther we had to go,
and then I'd look at Victor who kept saying one dirty word over
and over again, and then I'd look at the writer and Joe Foxhall, but
the Sergeant kept hollering, "Keep your head down, God damn it—
don't make trouble for everybody—keep your head down." So then
I'd duck down and say to the Sergeant very softly, "Thanks, and
go f—— yourself, Sergeant—you and your lousy trouble."

We kept crawling and the writer kept swearing and making fun
of us and the Army and the government and the War and the
world and culture and religion and art and science and statesman-
ship and nationalities and races and patriotism and propaganda
and empires and republics and the balance of power and spies and
secret service and police and penitentiaries and courts and judges
and lawyers and banks and insurance and the rate of interest and
foreign trade and embassies and voting and newspaper publishing
and the radio and *Time Magazine* (which he hated very much) and
oratory and history and geography and arithmetic and the public
school system and advertising and moving pictures and just about
everything else there is.

Joe Foxhall got into the game with the writer and kept protesting and saying that everything was good, don't be impatient just because you're on your belly trying to move in a way for which your body had never been designed—don't let that make you contemptuous of everything, have faith, I beg of you, be patient, this is for beauty, it's for truth, do not despair, crawl on, crawl on, crawl on—and then Joe hollered out at the top of his voice, "Oh worm of the world, crawl on!"

Well, Victor Tosca, he just didn't like it—it wasn't funny to him at all and every time I turned to look at him—hell, it broke my heart because I could see how *much* he didn't like it—not this crawling, not this little game—but *It*. He didn't like it, and I remembered the night we had gone to the bar together when he'd come back to New York from Rochester and he'd made me promise to tell them about love—and I knew he knew I was remembering that night because when we were a little better than half-way there he said, "Don't forget your promise—my wife's pregnant—they can't take that away from me—but don't forget—you gave me your word of honor."

And God damn me, I let myself *believe* him—I let myself believe what I should never have permitted myself to believe: that he was right, that he knew, that it was true. I got so sore at myself I told him to shut up, but after a while I said, "Don't you know a fellow can go to work and *make* something happen that might not happen at all—don't you know that? You can't let yourself believe you haven't got a chance."

Well, then he made me ashamed of myself because he laughed and said, "I'm only kidding, Jackson—we're just having fun."

But I knew he *wasn't* kidding. I decided to pretend that he was, though, so we got to hollering back to the writer and Joe Foxhall, and laughing, but we were pooped, every one of us was pooped, we were in a bad way. And then Victor and I were on the other side of the barbed-wire at the end of the course, on our feet again at last. We stood there and spit the dirt out of our mouths and lungs.

Then it was time to walk on a single-wire bridge across a stream, so we did that too, but that wasn't so bad.

The next time we went out to New Jersey we fired the carbine at moving targets, and the third time we just went out and fooled around because that visit was a mistake.

CHAPTER 40

Wesley Celebrates Christmas with the Modern Woman

WHEN IT was Christmas-time again we were all ready to be shipped, but we felt lucky to be able to celebrate Christmas in New York. I spent the whole week with the woman I'd met in the bar because I didn't know anybody else that well and I'd taken to seeing her now and then about two weeks after I got back from Ohio. Before that I'd spent a little time with the woman I'd met in Ohio, I'd taken her dancing at the Savoy in Harlem—but we'd only watched—and then she'd gone home to San Francisco. One night I got to remembering the music by Brahms, and even though it was very late I telephoned the woman and asked her if I could hear the music again and she said I could. I spent Christmas week with her, even though she knew I was always looking for the girl who was going to be my wife. She even hoped I'd find her, she said, because if I did, well, she'd be happy because she knew it meant a lot to me—and then we'd go to sporting around and *she'd* mean a lot to me. We'd both know it and have a lot of fun and laugh and drink and eat and like each other anyway.

Every once in a while she'd get serious and want to know what I was thinking, but I'd stop her and we'd go to sporting around some more which should have told her what I was thinking and probably did. All the music was wonderful, but my favorite was the Brahms piece—there was something by Grieg called *Lyric Suite* that I liked when I wasn't feeling very sporty—and I liked something by Beethoven that she called *The Appassionata*. I know the music when I hear it, but maybe I've got the name wrong. There was a lot of Mozart that was good to hear, and Haydn, and Handel, and Bach, and of course for good loud heart-breaking clamor we always liked Tschaikovsky. But Tschaikovsky always got me to feeling sporty no matter how heart-breaking it was.

Christmas week she got out a lot of phonograph records of old

hymns, but the one I liked best was the one in which they sing,
Fall on your knees, O hear the angel voices. Maybe I've got the
words of that line wrong too, but that's my favorite Christmas song.
She had a music store that specialized in finding old phonograph
records find *Valencia* for me, and one night when I saw her she
said she had a surprise for me and put the record on. Well, then
I really loved her. Women understand a lot and even if this woman
knew I wasn't in love with her the way I was going to be in love
with my own girl some day she was glad I could be in love with my
own girl that much because it almost came to being that much in
love with *her.*

It was a better Christmas than the one before, and besides the
happy times I had with the woman I saw a lot of Victor and his
wife and his mother and his wife's mother. I took them all little
presents and they all gave me little presents. By Christmas you
could see that Victor's wife was going to have a baby. It was a wonderful thing to see because she herself was so much like a child.
The pregnancy of Victor Tosca's wife was one of the most beautiful
things about Christmas that year. Victor was always happy when
he was with his family, and they were always glad that we were
going to be together. And they talked about the happy times we'd
all have together when we got home to San Francisco after the War,
and I had my girl too, and maybe a son too.

CHAPTER 41

Mrs. Tosca Recites a Letter to the President

ONE NIGHT Victor's mother and I were alone for an hour or so because I had dropped by at ten and Victor had taken his wife and
her mother to Radio City. Mrs. Tosca wanted me to sit down and
talk with her, so of course I did. Well, I guess I knew it was going
to happen sooner or later, but even so I was surprised when it did.
The poor woman began to cry while she was telling me about herself—starting with her childhood in Naples. She told me all the
adventures of coming to America, moving from New York to San
Francisco, meeting Victor's father, and how she fell in love with

him and married him and what a good man he had been and how they'd had so much happiness and so many children—eleven children, for God's sake, she said—and the last was Victor.

They hadn't believed they would have another because they hadn't had any for nine years, so when they knew there was going to be another they were both very happy. Victor's mother said she was very proud when she carried Victor. She told me he was the most wonderful baby she ever carried. She said she knew he dreamed beautiful dreams in her all the time because while she was carrying him she herself dreamed the most beautiful dreams she had ever dreamed—even more beautiful than the dreams she had dreamt as a little girl. Most of her kids, she said, were wild in her belly—Dominic was a crazy man, jumping all the time, playing tricks, having fun—but Victor—he was like a saint coming to the world. He would sleep all the time, and when he would wake up he would move so carefully, not to hurt his mother. He moved as if he was all lips kissing her, she said, and *she* was always kissing him and looking at Catholic pictures of the Holy Mother, and the Infant, and the beautiful Saints. When the time came for Victor to be born everybody thought it was going to be very difficult for her because of her age—forty-seven is no chicken, she said—but they were wrong.

He came so gently, she said, he was so beautiful, he was so full of love from the beginning.

She stopped a moment and then she said:

"You gonna kill it a boy like that, for God's sake?"

"He'll be all right, Mrs. Tosca."

"I pray to God," she said. "I say, take care my boy, for God's sake, don't let them kill it a boy like that."

She began to cry softly. "But I *know* my boy—I can tell it from the way he talk from his eyes. A boy like that with the enemies— he's got no chance. He's born for love, not to kill somebody. He's made for kiss. You gonna kill it a boy like that? You get my boy not to go—if he go I know I gonna see him no more. You get Victor to stay."

I told Mrs. Tosca the only way he could stay would be to get sick or desert.

"How you desert?" she wept. "How you do that?"

"You run away."

"What they do if they catch you?"

"Kill you."

"I gonna write it letter to President," she said. "Mr. President, I gonna tell him, do not kill it boy like Victor. Kill it your *own* boy to win the war—kill it *my* boy Dominic to win it—he's another fellow—he's my boy and I love my Dominic—but do not kill it a boy like Victor, Mr. President. You're big man, Mr. President, you understand these things, this is not politics, this is the mother who knows Victor from the belly—do not commit terrible crime. God will not forget crime like that. I gonna write it letter to President," she wept.

"Please try not to let Victor know how you feel, Mrs. Tosca."

"He *know*," she said. "*I* know, and *he* know—we understand. Who brought it his girl to New York to give him chance? His mother. Who know from his voice long distance what he's saying? His mother. Victor know. I know. What we gonna do?"

Well, hell, I didn't know what to say. But I knew she was right. Only it doesn't make any difference. There's nothing you can do. What do you do? When the time comes you load everything on your back, throw your duffle-bag over your shoulder, and go along, the way we did.

It happened in January. It must have been pretty tough for Victor to say good-bye to his wife and his mother and his wife's mother, but it must have been tougher for *them*. It wasn't tough for me to say good-bye to the woman. She cried a little of course, but what are tears like that? What are they to tears like the tears of Victor's mother?

CHAPTER 42

Wesley Leaves the Post in New York for the Embarkation Point and Refuses to Protect Himself from the War by Means of Government Insurance

ONE MORNING before dawn we were all set to go to the Embarkation Point which meant good-bye to America for sure. We stood around waiting to go from five in the morning until a little before eleven. The happy fellows at that Post who were not going arrived and were cheerful and full of farewells, but I didn't like it.

I didn't want anything unpleasant to happen to any of them. I didn't want any of them to catch cold or slip on the linoleum or drive their automobiles into trees or hit their fingers with hammers while hanging pictures on the wall or get an electric shock while fooling with the radio. I wanted them all to be happy, to have anything they liked, to do anything they pleased, to look at the War any way that was convenient or comforting—the only thing I didn't want was to have them say good-bye to me, to hear them talking to Victor Tosca and Joe Foxhall and the writer. In a Democracy everybody is the same of course. If there's a War and there's conscription, well, everybody gets conscripted. There was the writer right there to prove it. There he was the same as anybody else, loaded down with all the junk, all his straps in place, his duffle-bag packed, all in accordance with regulations. In a Democracy it's one for all and all for one, and the first law is the law of right. If it's time to ship men overseas, in a Democracy everybody gets shipped. What's right is right, and there's no two ways about it. No funny business. No trickery. No favoritism. No conniving. Everything straight. Everybody sincere and eager and straight—everybody eager to take his share of the load and carry it. So the happy boys came to say good-bye. I puked. I guess maybe I'm not sentimental the way they are. If they were going and I'd been there two or three years and wasn't going to go, I don't think I'd go around to say good-bye to them. I'd be ashamed to do it. I'd just go to my desk and write a new scenario showing them in two reels how to go out there and die like men, and then drive home as fast as I could and read the afternoon papers about the progress of the War. I guess I'd think they were suckers and let it go at that.

They got us aboard the trucks at last, but before the trucks moved off, the happy boys stood there and made cheerful remarks and offered suggestions. "Kill a German for me!" they said.

Pretty soon we came to the Embarkation Point and were taken to our barracks. We made our bunks. We stood in line to get chemical-impregnated clothes to wear in case of gas attacks somewhere. We listened to some more lectures. We filled out some more forms. We told them who to notify and send the money to if we got killed.

In the afternoon a Captain sent for me and asked me to sit down. He was very cordial. Now that I was about to go overseas he didn't mind letting me know that relations between officers and myself would be a good deal more like relations between men in civilian life.

He picked up a form I had filled out.

"I notice," he said, "that even though you've been in the Army over a year, and even though you're about to go overseas, you haven't taken out any insurance. Why not?"

"I don't want any."

"Why not?"

"I don't believe in it."

"Everybody else seems to believe in it."

"I don't. I believe in God. Besides I was under the impression that I had a choice."

"You have," the Captain said. "I just thought I ought to talk to you about it—for your own good. Just in case—who knows? Don't you think your father could use that money?"

"He wouldn't have it."

"Why not?"

"I believe my father would be willing to pay the *government* ten thousand dollars to see that I *didn't* get killed."

"Well," the Captain said, "we have to go according to the wishes of the greatest number of men in the Army. The vast majority of them insist on having this insurance. They don't *have* to have it, mind you, but—"

"I've filled out that insurance form seven times since I've been in the Army. If they don't have to have this insurance, why is it that every time I fill out the form and very plainly indicate that I don't want the insurance, I am sent for by somebody, such as yourself, who asks me why I don't want the insurance? I just don't want it. I just don't want to get killed, that's all. I hope you don't mind that I don't."

"Every man in the Army is free to do as he pleases in the matter of insurance," the Captain said.

I went back to the barracks, but I was so sore about the War and the Army and the poor Captain and all this rigmarole and shilly-shally about insurance that when I saw the crap game in the latrine I got out all my money, which was twenty-seven dollars, and when it was my turn to take the dice I put the whole amount on the floor and told the boys that I was rolling only once, win or lose. They didn't care about that, so I rattled the dice and threw them to the wall and when they stopped spinning my number was ten, which is a losing number. I hit them against the wall for a three, then a six, then another six, then an eight, then a four, then a nine, then an eleven, and then it was ten, so I picked up all the money and said, "They can take their lousy insurance and I think you know what they can do with it."

CHAPTER 43

Victor Tosca and Wesley Go Home on Overnight Pass from the Embarkation Point and Run into Happy Bedlam

IT TURNED out that we were luckier than we had expected to be because early in the afternoon of the second day the Barracks Sergeant said that half of our unit could go on pass to New York at six o'clock that night, and half could go the following night. The granting of passes would continue to alternate that way until further notice. We could stay on pass until Reveille at six, but if we weren't at Reveille at six, well, that would be just too bad because if you were A.W.O.L. from an Embarkation Point that was practically desertion.

That night Victor and I got passes and took the subway to Manhattan, but when we got off at 57th and 7th Avenue, Victor said, "Wait a minute—what the hell do I think I'm doing? I can't go back—it would kill my wife if I left her again."

We took a taxi to another part of town. We sat down at a table in a bar and began to drink, but pretty soon Victor said, "No—I've *got* to see her. She's six months along now. If I could have stayed just three months longer— A wife wants her husband to be around at a time like that. I've got to see her again. Will you go with me to see her?"

We took a taxi to the hotel and all the fellows who worked at the hotel were surprised to see us because when we said good-bye they thought they weren't going to be seeing us again until after the War, or ever.

Well, one fellow—Carlo—he took me to one side and said, "It's pretty bad up there—they're all sick in bed."

Victor asked the desk clerk to give him a key to his mother's apartment, so he could surprise them. We went up and Victor opened the door and went in.

Well, I'll never forget what happened. The three of them were in bed. Victor's wife and his mother were in one bed, and his wife's mother was in the other, and they were all sick, but when they saw Victor all three of them went crazy—they went absolutely mad. They jumped out of bed and ran to him and laughed and cried and hugged him, and kissed and kissed and kissed, and cried and laughed and talked and tried to make sense, and ran to me and kissed me, and Victor kept saying they would have to eat, they couldn't go hungry that way, for God's sake, they were all starving. He got Room Service on the telephone and told them to cut up six chickens—yes, *six,* he hollered—and boil them with chopped celery and a little rice—and bring up the whole business with five soup plates. But while he was trying to give the order his wife kept hanging onto him—she had gone mad—they had all gone mad— and she kept talking to him in Italian and kissing him—and his mother kept looking up and thanking God and laughing because there he was in front of her eyes again. A few minutes after he had given the order the telephone rang and everybody thought it was a reprieve or something but it was only the kitchen. They didn't have six chickens. They had five. "All right," Victor said, "if you haven't got six, cook *five.*"

Everybody got dressed, and Victor's wife laughed at herself because she looked so pale and the noise and happiness kept up so steadily that I had to say to myself, "These people think the War is over, I believe."

I tried to go away because I thought I ought to see the woman after what I'd seen, but I also wanted to go because it seemed to me they ought to be alone. But everybody was so deeply hurt that such a thing could even occur to me that I didn't bring the matter up again. First one of them and then another came running to me and kissed me on the cheek and laughed and cried. Was I crazy? Go away? For God's sake, Victor and I had brought them to life again. We would all sit down and eat. We would drink wine and talk. Go away? How could I think of such a thing? Victor's mother said I was her son, and his wife said I was her brother, and her mother said I was *her* son too, and hell, I said to myself, "I'll see the woman day after tomorrow maybe."

We had supper and it was very good. The chicken was tender and the broth was fine, and there was so much of it we sat at the table at least three hours. Victor sent for the waiter to heat everything again when it got cold. We drank wine and we talked. But all the time I kept worrying about when it would be time to go back. I knew it was going to be so bad for everybody to try to say good-bye all over again that I got to thinking of some way for all of us to stay together forever. Victor and I could borrow some civilian clothes from some of the boys who worked at the hotel. We could borrow somebody's car, and the five of us could drive to Mexico and stay there for the rest of our lives.

But I knew it was no good because gasoline was rationed. We wouldn't even get to Pulaski Skyway.

Pretty soon it was three o'clock in the morning. Then it was half past three. Then it was five minutes to four. It would take us about forty minutes to get out to the Post, but I didn't know how often the subway trains ran at that hour, so at a quarter after four I reminded Victor that we ought to be thinking of getting back.

Well, then it began again. They all went mad again, but this time it was from grief, not joy, and it was awful. I don't think I'll ever see anything so painful and beautiful again. For ten minutes it was the same as it had been when Victor had walked into the apartment, and then finally we got away. Victor promised to come home again as soon as he got another pass—day after tomorrow maybe.

CHAPTER 44

Wesley Puts a Gas Mask over His Face, Enters a Gas Chamber, and Breathes Gas

THE NEXT day we got a lecture on gas—how to protect ourselves against it—what to do if the kind that burns into the flesh got on us—how to put the cellophane mantle over us, and a lot of other stuff that was so complicated the demonstrator could hardly do it. The cellophane mantle was more than a mantle—it was a little tent to protect your whole body. Just to get the thing open took the demonstrator (who'd had a lot of practice) about three minutes and that's too long if there's gas around. Pretty soon the demonstrator was inside the tent. He had his pack on his back, his gas mask over his face, his helmet on his head, he was wearing his impregnated clothes, there were thick gloves on his hands, and now he was going to show us how to fire the rifle through the cellophane tent and go right on winning the War.

Well, it just couldn't be done, that's all. If it came to that, any man would rather get killed. He'd rather be dead than that cluttered. It was the most incredible thing I ever saw. It was an insult to the human body—especially when, after all that clutter and fuss, the demonstrator made it clear that you would be expected to run along and fire your gun.

After the lecture we marched to the gas chamber and went through it, but my gas mask leaked. I knew I was breathing gas, but I didn't say anything because it was my own fault. They had told us to make the straps very tight so the mask would be airtight, but when I tightened the straps and put the mask on, it hurt my forehead and half-choked me, so I loosened the straps. Now I was breathing gas. The Sergeant asked if anybody thought he was breathing gas, so I lifted my hand and he hurried over and tightened my straps, saying something through his gas-mask that I didn't understand. He was talking through a gas-mask—how could I understand?

We left the chamber, and when the signal was given, we ducked down to test for gas, then removed the masks and put them back into their canvas bags. The Sergeant asked how I felt and I said O.K., although my eyes were stinging. He said it served me right for not tightening my straps as I had been told to do. I told him I knew it served me right all right but if I tightened the straps enough to make the mask air-tight, then the mask hurt my forehead and choked me and I didn't like that any more than I liked gas.

Pretty soon we went through the chamber again because now it was another kind of gas. This time somebody else's mask hadn't been made air-tight and he was breathing gas. He started jumping around making for the door, so the Sergeant grabbed him and held him because if one fellow gets panicky in a gas chamber a few others who think they are breathing gas are liable to get panicky too and the first thing you know you've got a stampede inside a chamber full of gas and a lot of serious trouble because when fellows wearing gas masks get panicky it doesn't occur to them that flinging the masks off their faces to improve their breathing or running to an iron door that's bolted from the outside and wanting to get out doesn't make sense at all. The Sergeant got the fellow under control. The fellow stopped swinging his arms around and jumping, and nobody got hurt.

A couple of the fellows in our unit said they didn't want the passes they were entitled to because they had nowhere to go in New York, so Victor and I asked them if we could have their passes and they asked us what we'd give them for them. I spoke before Victor because I knew he'd say five dollars. I said we'd give them a pack of cigarettes, and it was a deal. So we went to town again that night.

CHAPTER 45

*Wesley Computes the Value of the Modern Woman, Takes
a Voyage, and Lands in England*

I TOLD Victor I'd meet him at the subway station at 57th and 7th Avenue at five minutes to five in the morning and we'd ride out to the Embarkation Point together. I told him I wanted him to go home alone. He wanted to know where *I* was going, so I told him.

I also told him I thought it would be nice if he took his wife to dinner somewhere—or all three of them—get them away from the apartment—take them to dinner and then to a show. He said he would.

"And go to bed with your wife. Hold her in your arms a long
time and talk to her. Last night was fine, but it wasn't what tonight
ought to be." I told him to get his own apartment back, or another
one like it, and take his wife there after the show and be alone
with her.

Victor went home to his wife and I headed for a telephone
booth. The first thing she told me was to hold the line a minute.
When she came back on the line she said she had gone upstairs to
the telephone in her bedroom.

"Where are you?" she said.

"In the bar around the corner. I'm on overnight pass."

"Oh, my God!"

"What do you mean?"

"I've got somebody downstairs. He's just come to take me to dinner. He's got tickets to a musical comedy too. I'll send him along
right after the theatre. Telephone me at a quarter after eleven."

"Send him along now."

"I couldn't possibly. I thought you were on your way to Japan."

"Who said anything about Japan? I'll have a couple of drinks in
this bar and see you in fifteen minutes."

"Make it a half hour. I've got to think of something to say. I
thought you were on the ocean somewhere."

"I'll be on the ocean somewhere soon enough, don't worry about
that."

"Telephone me in half an hour, just to make sure he's gone."

I telephoned her in half an hour and she said, "He was awfully
hurt."

"Anything to eat?"

"Cook's night out, but we can make something."

I walked around the corner and got a good welcome home. I
thought I'd want to eat right away. I thought I'd want to listen to
some music too—but the welcome was so good I let those things
go. I guess it was on account of having seen the poor demonstrator
trying to get into the cellophane tent.

I asked her if the dress she was wearing was new.

"No. Why?"

"I'm going to tear it off."

"That cost forty dollars," she said.

Then she said, "Those cost eighteen dollars—they're the best they make."

Then she said, "That's Belgian lace—twenty-five dollars."

"How much did *this* cost?"

"That was given."

At five minutes to five I met Victor in the subway station.

"How's the family?"

"Better," he said, "except my poor mother."

"What's the matter?"

"She says she's been praying ever since we left yesterday morning. She's sure her prayers are going to be answered and the War is going to be over before you and I get on board a ship—or somebody is going to send word at the last minute to keep both of us here."

"You mean *me*, too?"

"Yes, the two of us."

Well, that was O.K., having Victor's mother pray for me too.

"Why not?" I said. "It could happen, couldn't it?"

"No, it couldn't," Victor said. "How are things with *you?*"

"Just fine."

"Did you have fun?"

"I didn't eat or sleep, but when you feel good—or when you feel bad enough—you don't need very much food or sleep, do you?"

"I haven't slept, either," Victor said. "I held my girl and my baby in my arms all night, the both of them."

"How *is* your son?"

"He's beginning to laugh."

"No fooling?"

"She *says* he laughs. I couldn't *hear* him but my wife says she heard him all night. But what the hell's he *laughing* about? I wish to God I could be here when he comes out. I wish to God I could be with him when he begins to talk, so I could ask him. Find your girl, Jackson, get married, get her pregnant."

"Where'll I find her *now?*"

"We're going to England, aren't we?"

"That's what they say. We're not supposed to know of course, and I believe it's some sort of military misdemeanor for you to hint that we are—but I think that's where we're going."

"No girls in England?"

"Do you mean I've got to go to England to find a girl?"

"No," Victor said. "You've just got to go to England. As long as you're there, though, you can look around for one."

"I want an American girl."

"What's the difference? Anybody can be an American."

We got back to the Embarkation Point just in time for breakfast. After breakfast we both stretched out on our bunks and went to sleep. I don't know what Victor dreamed about, but for the first time in my life I dreamed about laughter. It was all over the place. It was in and out of everything. In my sleep I thought it was the secret all of us are trying to know. I wanted to remember the value of the secret (which was greater than the value of anything else in the world) so I could tell it to everybody when I woke up, but the secret began to lose its value and I began to wake up, and then the secret was lost and all I did was turn over and go back to sleep.

We stayed at the Embarkation Point sixteen days. Every morning there were rumors that we would go that night, and every night there were rumors that we would go tomorrow morning. They gave us Kitchen Police and the other duties of course. And they gave us a quick medical once-over: breathing mainly. They wanted to be sure none of us had stopped breathing. On the fourteenth day they stopped giving us passes, but Victor and I had gone on pass all the other nights. If somebody wouldn't make a deal with us, we used to make a deal with the Barracks Sergeant to get on the pass list. Once it cost Victor five dollars, but he got the money back from the Sergeant the next day shooting crap. We both shot a lot of crap, and we both won. On the sixteenth day we got aboard a truck and went to some docks somewhere and after two or three hours we went up the gang-plank onto the ship. Quarters were assigned, and they were very small. There seemed to be six or seven thousand men on the little ship. I didn't count them, but I could see there were a lot of them. They were all over the place, in all the little corners of the ship. But the ship didn't move. It just stayed there. Late one night it began to move at last, so Victor and I went out on deck. Snow was falling and the whole ship was white with it. We were glad to be going, as long as that was the idea. Pretty soon we got out to sea and everybody on the ship got sick. Victor and I got a little sick too, but not as sick as the others. The others got deathly sick. I'll never forget the way they got sick.

It was a large convoy of ships. Somebody counted thirty-seven of them, but there were more that couldn't be seen unless you had binoculars. There was a lot of gossip every day about submarines, but that's all it ever came to. It was a terrible voyage. It took a long time and a lot of things happened aboard the ship. One morning we saw land. It was Ireland. It was beautiful. That night we stopped at a dock in a town in Wales. It was called Swansea and we were in Europe. The next morning we got on a train and rode to London where we were taken in a truck to a building that was to be our barracks.

The whole voyage was like a dream. You go on voyages in your sleep from the time you're able to remember what you dream. Well, that whole voyage was like one of the dreams of travel of childhood.

Suddenly we were in London. It was the 25th of February, 1944.

CHAPTER 46

Wesley Thanks God for Hot Water in a Tub, Falls into Magnificent Sleep and Dreams a Rambunctious Dream

LONDON WAS cold and sad. None of us had had a bath in two weeks, so we were cold and sad too, and homesick and angry, because the barracks were cold and sad. We made mattresses for our bunks out of straw that was piled on the floor of the basement. I wasn't in the proper mood to fool with cold moldy sad straw, so Victor helped me.

"Let's get it over with and take a bath and go to bed and sleep," he said. "At least we're on land again."

"Call that a bed?" I said. "A little old moldy stinking straw to try to make a bed with?"

After an hour or so we had our mattresses ready, so we flipped a coin to see who got the lower. The bunks were double-deckers and next to us Joe Foxhall had the upper and the writer the lower, but they hadn't gotten any farther along with their mattresses than we had. Victor won and took the lower, but I didn't care about that because I felt so cold and sad I didn't care about anything.

Pretty soon the writer came from the bath, then Joe Foxhall, then Victor, so then I went and filled the tub and sat down in it and said a prayer.

"I thank God for water that's hot in a tub instead of cold in the ocean. I thank God for a little left-over soap to clean my stinking old hide with. I thank God for a chance to get out of all my straps and burdens and step into a tub of hot water and sit down there and ask them to take their whole world—excepting bathtubs—and drop it into hell and forget it, for it isn't worth remembering, except the tub and the water and the soap. I thank God for getting us across the cold water heaving and sobbing because the whole world is so hopeless and human beings are such fools. I thank God that we are on land again, in a great city, and here I am all free of my encumbrances, just sitting in the water. I thank God for getting Pop home to his girl in El Paso—to his son Virgil there —to his brother-in-law Neal of the farm-implement business. I thank God for getting Victor Tosca married to his girl in time to get her pregnant. I thank God for keeping me and Victor together because I am going to look after him all I can, no matter what—I am going to see if I can prove he's mistaken to believe he is going to be killed. I am going to do it for his mother, Mrs. Tosca, for whom I thank God because she is such a nice lady. I thank God for the woman I met in Ohio because she is such a nice lady. I thank God for the woman in New York because in spite of all her money and all her understanding of great music she liked me, and in spite of her age she had the body of a young girl. But most of all I thank God for this bath because it's bringing me back to life. I thank Him for this soap because it's getting almost three weeks of dirt out of my skin. I protest to the smell of the barracks because I never did like the smell of a place that too many fellows are trying to live in, but I thank God for most things. Amen."

Then I went and climbed into my bunk and fell right into the most magnificent sleep I have ever slept, but damned if I didn't go right on thanking God. I was in heaven in my old clothes, a civilian again, happy and free and not caring too much about anything, but thankful to the brim for all of God's blessings. And there was no end to them. As long as I was free there was no end to God's blessings. Everything I saw was a blessing, and I loved everything. I just stood there like I used to stand in San Francisco and I just loved everything. There was a flock of angels flapping their wings, coming along slow and easy and good-natured, and I loved them so much I went to work and flapped along with them. "It seems to me," I said to the nearest one, "I've seen you somewhere before." And sure enough it was Joe Foxhall, but instead of admitting it, Joe winked at me. So then I said, "I know *you*, Joe—hell, I'd know you in hell, let alone flapping around with angels. I bet you don't even belong with these angels."

"No?" Joe said. "Well, I'm flapping along with them, ain't I? So why don't I belong with them?"

"Well," I said, "you know damn well neither you nor I have got real wings like the rest of these angels and pretty soon they're going to find out and shoo us away."

"Angels don't shoo other angels away," Joe said.

"You ain't no angel, Joe," I said.

"Oh no?" Joe said. "Want to see me flap ahead of everybody else in this outfit?"

I had the notion all the time that I was dreaming, but I didn't feel like bothering about that, so everything was fine. I told Joe not to go flapping ahead of everybody else because he wasn't a real angel and might fall on his face, but Joe went ahead and flapped ahead of the real angels and fell flat on his face. I swooped down beside him, and the flock of real angels flapped away, but all of them turned their heads to look at us. I recognized every one of them—I knew every face I saw—but I just couldn't remember who they were by name. I remembered one, though—Mrs. Tosca—and the others were people like her.

I helped Joe to his feet.

He tried out his arms and legs to see if he was O.K. and it turned out that he was.

"I guess there's going to be snobbery wherever you go," he said.

We went walking along, laughing to ourselves, and all of a sud-

den there was a fellow standing in some sort of a wagon who seemed
to be waiting for us. He seemed to be the writer—and sure enough
he was, only he was wearing clothes people haven't worn in a
couple of thousand years.

"Well, if it isn't old Shakespeare himself," Joe said. "What are
you doing in that chariot?" He didn't say anything about the
clothes.

"I don't walk," the writer said. "I never walked hardly in my
whole life. Always went by chariot. Hop on. I'll give you a ride."

Joe and I jumped onto the chariot and the writer hollered out in
some foreign language to the four white horses and hell, they just
lifted themselves off the ground and took the chariot along with
them away out into the sky, going like mad straight for the sun.
Well, I didn't know if that was a good thing or not, but the writer,
he was hollering at the horses in the foreign language, and singing,
and cheering, and then he turned to Joe and me and he said, "Shit,
boys, this is the life—this is the way to live—not walking or crawling
on the earth."

"You can drop me off at the Public Library in San Francisco,"
I said. "I've been there, and by God, it's good enough for me."

"Just roll me up to the door of the Dreamland Ballroom in
Bakersfield," Joe said, "and I'll be much obliged to you."

"You mean you don't want to go for a *real* ride?" the writer said.

"Just San Francisco," I said.

"Just get me to summertime dancing in Bakersfield," Joe said.

So then the writer didn't get sore or anything, he just hollered
something more in the foreign language to the horses, and wham!
—there we were swooping down out of the sky on the Public
Library in San Francisco with all the old faces looking up to see
me—all the old philosophers who used to stand in front of the
Public Library and ask one another to listen to reason—all of them
hollering up to me and glad to see me again. "Well, look at that,"
they said. "Here's *The Ugly Kid* himself coming back in a chariot."
The chariot stopped right at the front door and there was a hell of
a commotion of greetings and laughing and philosophizing and running about to get a look at the chariot and me. They asked me what
is life and what is death, but I didn't know, so I started to cough.

"O.K.," the writer said. "Say good-bye to your friends, so I can take Joe to Bakersfield." I said so long to the boys, and we drove straight up into the sweet Californian sky, down the great San Joaquin valley to Bakersfield, and rolled right up in front of the Dreamland Ballroom. A couple of boys in zoot suits came prancing and romping with a couple of girls to say hello to Joe and ask him where he'd been. Joe took a girl in his arms and went to waltz with her but the music stopped, so he kissed her, and it seemed as if he meant to kiss her forever. I guess he would have kissed her forever if she hadn't broken away from him and run off. Joe said, "Kissing's the best way to wait," and got back on the chariot and we drove off again, but pretty soon the chariot wasn't a chariot any more, it wasn't a handsome open carriage racing along in a blaze of light, it was something rattling and bouncing and we were *sitting* inside of it, we weren't standing in it, and hell I knew what it was: it was an old Army truck, and now Victor Tosca was sitting next to me and we were on our way to the ship that was going to take us overseas.

Well, that was no fun at all, so I almost woke up, but soon I was fast asleep again, and it was better than the Army truck, but not much better because it was that place in Ohio I went to with the woman who sang *Valencia,* and there was Pop surrounded by six or seven of the most beautiful girls in the world. He was drunk and full of big talk and all kinds of elegant manners. "Pop," I said, "you ain't Don Juan or anybody like that—what are you doing here?"

"What am *I* doing here?" Pop said. "What are *you* doing here? I'm surprised at you."

"I came looking for you," I said. "I didn't come for sport. I came to fetch you away. You better go home, Pop."

Just to show you how it is with sleep, Pop went along. So then *I* was the show-off, standing around with the beautiful girls and talking the same big talk.

I went along that way in my sleep, none of it making much sense but all of it deep and yet not so deep I didn't know all the time I was lying on a straw mattress I had just made in the city of London, dreaming. Even while I moved from one foolish episode to another, I kept remembering that I was sleeping and I kept thinking, "Well, look at the stuff a fellow will go to work and dream—me driving Pop away from the girls, so I can have them myself. I guess I've slept about an hour maybe, so pretty soon I better get up and get dressed and go out and look at the city because it must be a great city. I'll get Victor Tosca and we'll go out and look at it."

So then I came to wakefulness, but I didn't open my eyes. Little bits of dream came and went a while longer, not enough to make anything like a story, maybe just a crowd of people going by in front of The Great Northern Hotel: a mother nagging at her little boy who said, "But I don't want to—and I *won't*." Well, I knew I'd *heard* that. I wasn't dreaming, I was remembering. Then a taxi-driver said, "You could spend your whole life in this city and never know the half of it." Well, that was remembering too because a taxi-driver in New York had told me that one day. Next Mrs. Tosca was crying and saying, "You gonna kill it a boy like that?" That was when I opened my eyes. I leaned over and looked down at Victor who was asleep. I guess I was still a little asleep too, because I said to Mrs. Tosca, "No, Mrs. Tosca—nobody gonna kill it a boy like that."

"What are you mumbling about?" the writer said.

Then I was awake.

"How long have I been asleep?" I said.

"Ten minutes," the writer said.

"Ten minutes?" I said. "Is that all? Are you going to sleep?"

"Can't," the writer said. "Too tired. Want to go out and look at London?"

Well, Joe and Victor were asleep, so we decided not to wake them up. It was about five o'clock in the afternoon, but it was almost dark. It was almost night-time already. The building we were in must have been a hotel before the War because there were a lot of little rooms in it, and a couple of pretty good-sized ones. Ours was so little there was room for only two double-deckers in it, so it was only the four of us there in the evening darkness. While I was putting on my clothes I began to remember the stuff I'd dreamed. I looked at the writer to see if he looked like the fellow on the chariot, and he did—he looked like a Greek who belonged on a chariot. I had never noticed that before. I thought I'd tell him about the dream, but I decided it would take too long, so I let it go.

While we were getting dressed Joe Foxhall woke up and wanted

to know what was going on, so we told him we were going out to
see London. Joe got out of his bunk to go with us. I didn't want
to leave Victor alone, so I went and talked to him quietly until he
opened his eyes. "We're going out to look at London," I said.

Pretty soon Victor opened his eyes and said, "Wait for me."

CHAPTER 47

*The Writer, Joe Foxhall, Victor Tosca and Wesley Go to Soho for
Supper and There Compare Personal Snapshots*

THE FOUR of us went out into London and got lost. The night itself
was pitch black and of course there were no outside lights on anywhere, but Joe had a flashlight, so we didn't fall down any stair-
ways or bump into any telegraph poles like so many people were
always doing, according to the gossip we'd heard. The writer suggested that we go to Soho, to one of the restaurants there, and have
ourselves a fine supper. We decided to do that, but it took us a long
time to get to Soho. The writer had been to London before, but he
only knew how to get around in a taxi. The few taxis that were in
the streets wouldn't stop to pick us up, so we began to ask people
how to get to Soho. The people we asked told us. They took a long
time and were very accurate, but one would tell us one thing, and
another another. After we'd followed the directions of five different
people, we got to Soho at last, and pretty soon the writer found the
restaurant he remembered. We waited our turn for a table, then
sat down and ordered a bottle of wine. We had a glass each and
began to celebrate. The whole supper didn't amount to much on
account of the rationing, but we were across the cold water, we'd
had baths, and we were together, so we felt pretty good. We started
remembering America right after supper. The writer remembered
his son who was now five months old to the day, born on the 25th
of September. Well, that's my birthday too, so I told the writer, and
he said, "Christmas, you know—that's what does it." He passed a
snapshot of his son around, the way all fathers do, I guess, and by
God his son looked just like him and was scowling just like him.
We all got to talking about being in love and having your wife

pregnant and then having a son or a daughter and I said to myself, "I've got to find *my* wife." The writer asked Victor about *his* wife and her pregnancy. Victor showed us a snapshot of her taken a couple of days before we had gone to the Embarkation Point. She was very pretty, and you could see she was pregnant.

"I was luckier than you," the writer said. "I was lucky enough to be with my wife when my son was born. I saw him a few minutes after he came out. And what do you think I discovered? I discovered that the new-born infant is an old man. He is older than any living man in the world. It takes time for this old man to get around to his own little infancy—about a month, I'd say. And then of course he loses his age and begins his life as if he were the earliest man in the world instead of the latest. He starts from scratch as if he hadn't come to his breathing from thousands and millions of years ago."

As long as everybody was showing pictures I showed the snapshots Pop had sent me of him and Mom and Virgil and my uncle Neal. Then Joe Foxhall came out with a snapshot of a girl in a bathing suit who was oozing sex. Everybody looked at the snapshot and passed it around until it got back to Joe and he looked at it too, but nobody said anything, so I said, "Who's that, Joe?"

"Damn if I know," Joe said. "I saw it in Woolworth's. It only cost a dime, so I took it. Some girl in the movies who isn't famous yet, I guess."

"Well, what do you want with it?" I said. "You don't know the girl."

"What's that got to do with it?" Joe said. "It's patriotic to carry the picture of some c—— around with you. You see that whole page in *Yank Magazine* every week all covered with some naked piece, don't you? What for? Because we know what we're in the Army for. It's for *her*. I'm as patriotic as the next man. I carry my little naked reason for being in the Army around with me all the time. I don't have to see my reason in *Yank Magazine* every week. I like my reason to be *mine*, not everybody's. I paid ten cents for my reason in Woolworth's and it belongs to me and nobody else. It's very clever of the War Department to invent *Yank Magazine's* most popular feature, you know. If you're going to kill them, show them a little ass and tits first, don't you know? Give the boys something to beat their roots about every week. As I see it, you could show the boys a kind of picture on that page every week that might be a little more relevant to their circumstances."

"Isn't it what the boys want?" Victor said.

"I'm one of the boys," Joe said, "and it's not what *I* want. Who decided it was what the boys want? But to hell with it, let's go out and prowl around the streets of London."

CHAPTER 48

The Boys Visit Piccadilly Circus, See the Bombed-Out Families of London Living in the Subway Stations, and Learn a Little of the Lore of Flak

WE WENT out and started to prowl. We prowled from Soho to Piccadilly Circus where all the street-walkers work. The place was like a sore. Everybody had a flashlight, so you got flashes of everything but not enough light at one time to give you anything like a real picture of what was going on. The sidewalks were jammed with soldiers and English girls, swarming together as if they were red and white corpuscles in sick blood. The girls kept moving all the time, stopping to exchange a few words with somebody, and then going along with him, or going on alone. You could hear all kinds of talk, soft and loud, and laughing and hollering and singing, and then a girl would say something dirty to two or three soldiers in a group who'd hurt her feelings, and the soldiers would shout something back at her, but you'd never see the girl or the fellows, and then some more people would come along and take their place.

In the midst of all this the Air Raid siren started to wail, and a lot of the people in the streets started hurrying to the shelters, but a lot of them *didn't*, too. A couple of our M.P.'s told us it would be a good idea to duck down into the subway station right there—Piccadilly Circus. It was a *real* sight down there. Along the walls of the station bombed-out families had their little homes—double-decker bunks with sometimes a little bit of carpet in front of them. You'd see a whole family: father, mother and two or three children, the kids asleep and the father and mother talking quietly in spite of all the people around, as if they were in their own parlor. The place didn't smell very good, but the people were used to it. Every once in a while a train would roar up and stop. A lot of people would get off, a lot would get on, and a woman in overalls who worked on the train would holler at everybody to step lively, move along, hurry up there now, and all that. We wandered around while the anti-aircraft guns fired away at the airplanes, and the airplanes dropped their bombs, and we saw a lot of people keeping their homes together away down under the streets of London in the subway stations—in the underground, as they call it a little more accurately than we do. Well, the trains came and went and came and went, and then one train came that was headed for Cockfosters, so Joe suggested that we go out there, and hell, we'd got across the water safe and sound, and the city was being bombed, and a lot of people were hanging onto themselves under the ground that way, so a train headed for Cockfosters seemed very funny to us. We started to laugh about that and make jokes about it and the English people smiled and said to one another, "More Americans—always laughing." There's nothing funny to the English about a place being called Cockfosters. Cockfosters is somewhere where people live, and nobody in England thinks it's a joke at all—you've got to come from America to think it's funny, and of course it really isn't, but we thought it was the funniest thing in the world.

The station had three or four levels, so we explored every one of them, and then went up to the street, but the raid was still on. We could see the lights in the sky and hear the guns popping away as if it was a children's celebration, but the M.P.'s told us to stay off the streets because too many people were getting killed by falling flak—it was more dangerous than bombs. We decided to take a chance anyway. We walked down Regent Street to Nelson's Column in Trafalgar Square, and the writer said, "George Bernard Shaw used to take his morning walk around this Square." But the guns were making so much noise we could hardly hear him.

Joe and the writer got to talking about London, how rich it was in literary lore and all that, so Victor and I just listened. Every once in a while we'd think we'd hear some flak coming down, so we'd duck into a doorway for cover, but we didn't find any flak. Later on we hardly saw a fellow in the Army who didn't have his hunk of flak. Every fellow had a long story to go with it, mainly lies. He'd tell you the flak, by some miracle, was shaped in the form of a six-legged elephant, and he'd count the legs for you, show you the trunk and the tail, and stand there and just admire a piece of steel that had been knocked red-hot off a big shell a mile in the sky. Every fellow I ever saw who had a piece of flak thought he had lived, as the saying is. I just couldn't help telling one fellow whose piece of flak was only twice as big as a dollar to fit it into his head somewhere and see how it looked there. After that he went around telling everybody the flak had dropped on his head but through some miracle hadn't killed him. Some fellows don't care if people believe them or not, just so they've got the flak and the story to go with it.

After a while it seemed as if the raid was never going to end, so we decided to walk along close to the buildings and head for home, but the M.P.'s kept badgering us all the time to duck for cover. They claimed *they* were O.K. out in the streets because of their steel helmets. I asked them how it would be if the flak missed their helmets and hit their shoulders. They said flak always hit a man on the head, and told us to duck for cover—but we kept moving along toward our barracks anyway, and after about forty-five minutes we were there, so we went up—we were on the fifth and top floor —and got into our bunks and talked a while and then went to sleep.

We were in London. We'd seen some of the city and how wonderful the people are, even though they'd been bombed out of their homes and were living in the subway stations. There were bombs again the second night. The writer and I happened to be on the sixth-floor terrace of a friend's apartment, so we watched the whole show, crouching down to be away from falling flak which we could hear every now and then hitting the roofs and the street. It was an awful sight, but very beautiful too if you didn't keep in mind that the purpose of it all was to destroy buildings and kill people. The anti-aircraft guns started pounding away soon after the alarm sounded, and we could hear people running for air-raid shelters but couldn't see them. The big lights went on all over the city and searched through the sky for the airplanes. You could hear the airplanes humming along very high whenever the guns stopped for a minute. And you could see the flares the airplanes were dropping. The flares would drop in groups of three, falling and going with the wind very slowly, making a lot of light so the aviators would know where to drop their bombs—if the guns didn't get them first. Pretty soon the purple-pink-red-black rockets began to push up into the sky, climbing like fireworks and filling the bowl of the sky with their awful wonderful light. It was like a celebration, not a War. The writer's friends that we had visited had gone down into the shelter of that building because they didn't like any of that stuff, but the writer had asked if he could stay and watch, so they told him he could if he was crazy, so I asked if I could watch too. The writer's friends told him not to be a fool, though, at least keep covered, don't stand up on the terrace, don't lean out to look at anything, and stop watching as soon as possible—get off the terrace and come downstairs to the shelter. Well, we watched until the raid was over, which was an hour and a half. It was a beautiful sight, and we didn't get hit by any flak and no bombs fell near us. We saw where one had fallen, though, because that area was on fire. We found out later that three or four other areas had been hit and were on fire too. The newspapers never gave any information about such things, so the only way you could know was to see for yourself, or listen to the gossip, but the gossip went off into all kinds of directions. If you left it to the gossip all London was burning, even though you couldn't see any sign of it—that would be the next day, in the afternoon, and the gossiper would mention some part of London that was far away—"Out in Elephant and Castle, everything's on fire." It wasn't so, though.

CHAPTER 49

The Writer *and Wesley Settle Down in Their Own Office*

OUR SECOND day in London was big and busy, and we began to get an idea what we were in for. There was a formation in the afternoon, and the Sergeant gave us the talking-to that new arrivals in London always get. He told us not to forget that we were visitors in London, that it was up to us to make a good impression on the

English. No rowdyism, no bad manners, no wild spending, because wild spending was the mark of a fool in a country like England where everybody had put up with so much for so long. He told us the English had been getting along on a great deal less than our people, and nothing was more rude than for American soldiers to come to London and throw money around as if they were million-aires. He told us what our formations would be. He told us what our duties would be. And he asked us to pay particular attention to our appearance—be bright and sharp all the time. After the formation Joe Foxhall came upstairs with the information that it was not inconceivable that we might be able to move out of the barracks to a place of our own, if we wanted to, because others had done it, and while it was not exactly authorized, it was O.K. be-cause barracks space was badly needed. Joe said he was working on the Sergeant and felt that in two or three days he might be able to make a deal—maybe get us off the working list too. That was the best news we'd heard in a long time.

The third day we were told where to go to work every day. It was a red brick building near Grosvenor Square. The writer and I got a cubby-hole of an office with two tables, two typewriters, and a telephone, so we settled down there. Across the hall Joe Foxhall and Victor Tosca settled down in another office pretty much like ours, only without a telephone, and only one table and one chair. There was nothing special for them to do anyway, so they just hung around and talked.

When we had gone back to New York from Ohio the writer had got me established as his collaborator. We did one scenario that we didn't mind doing because it was on how to load stuff into box-cars and wouldn't get anybody killed. We considered five or six others that were meant to encourage others to get killed, but we never did any work on them because we didn't want to. I did the work on the box-car one, but you didn't need to be a writer to do it. We were pleased when we learned that the scenario about box-cars wasn't made into a Training Film, after all. They used some-body else's scenario. They didn't make the one we wrote on calis-thenics, either. We were always pleased when they didn't use any of our stuff.

The writer and I wrote letters and talked. The writer answered the telephone. Every once in a while somebody wanted to interview him. He would try to get out of it, but they'd be stubborn and the Public Relations Office would give them permission to interview him, so then somebody from one of the London papers would come up to our office. I'd move to go, but the writer would make me stay. The interviewer would ask the writer the kind of questions they usually ask George Bernard Shaw or H. G. Wells, but the writer would just take it easy and answer the questions.

They wrote down everything he said, and everything he said was good to hear because he always managed to tell the truth no matter how hopeless it seemed to be at the time. He introduced me to everybody who came to interview him and said I was his collaborator. "If you want to know the truth," he said, "he's a better writer than I am—nineteen years old."

Well, then the interviewers would think he was kidding because he had a reputation for saying things that could be taken two or three ways at once, but he would always tell them he wasn't kidding, so then they would say, "Do you mean to say *you* think somebody else in the world is a better writer than you are? We thought you thought you were the best writer in the world."

So then the writer would say, "I'm better than most, but he's better than I am. When I was nineteen I wasn't half the writer he is. You'll be hearing from him if he lives."

They'd ask him what he thought of the English, and he'd say, "I always liked the English—but now I like them more than ever." They'd want to know why and he'd say, "Because I know them a little better. They're no better and no worse than any other people, but I like them a little better than I like most other people on account of their writers. I hate their politicians, but I like their writers."

Every now and then he'd tell me to write a short story in three hours—he'd give me three hours to do it in, and after I'd done it he'd go over it with me and show me where I'd gone wrong and where I hadn't, and in that way he taught me a lot. He told me not to think I had to be ignorant because I hadn't gone to college. He claimed I wasn't ignorant, and sometimes my writing sounded as if I thought I was. I told him that that happened by itself, so then he said not to let it happen by itself. Let right things happen by themselves. The more right things a man encouraged to happen by themselves, and the more wrong things he kept from happening by themselves, the better he became as a writer—but more important than that, the better he became *himself*. The only thing that mattered about writing was that it improved the writer first, and therefore might be apt to improve the reader too.

He told me a lot of things from day to day, but I didn't just sit there and listen to everything he said without putting in my two cents' worth. I listened all right, but I had a few ideas of my own too, and most of the time he liked them. Whenever anybody asked him if he was writing anything, he'd say he wasn't, so then they'd ask him why and he'd say he couldn't be bothered as long as he was in uniform—he was waiting for the War to end. There would be plenty of time to write then. So then they'd ask him if he was going to write about the War, or about the Army, and he'd say, "For God's sake, don't ask silly questions. I'm not a journalist, I'm a poet. I write about everything." They wouldn't know what to make of it because the whole world was jumping with American writers and newspapermen who were busy writing books about the War. There wasn't a newspaperman in London who hadn't come out with at least one book about the War. A lot of them had come out with two or three, but the writer, he was waiting for the War to end. He said he was waiting for the hysteria to stop, so he could take up his work where it had been interrupted. He said, "The most hysterical people in the world are the Americans—the most naive and the most excitable. The calmer they seem the more excited they are."

CHAPTER 50

The Writer *Solves the Problem of What to Do with the German People*

PRETTY SOON other literary things began to happen. There were story conferences with high-ranking officers. The writer and I always went, and I always listened to everybody. The writer was right all right—they seemed calm, but they were actually jittery.

The first meeting we went to was a dinner, followed by informal discussion. The writer and I were the only Privates at the meeting. The rest were Captains up to full Colonels, and a lot of civilians, some of them a good many years younger than the writer—draft-dodgers who had government jobs with big money and nothing to do but eat and talk. I never wanted to go to these meetings, but the writer said I had to go—it was my duty to go, because *he* had to go. It was my duty to him, he said. He said the stuff was too embarrassing for him to cope with alone. Well, at this first meeting everybody got filled with food and the bottles were brought out and everybody started to drink. The atmosphere was pleasant, and there was a nice cordiality in the air. Then the young civilian who was sponsoring the discussion on behalf of the government introduced the topic to be discussed, namely: *What to do with Germany after the War.*

Well, the writer kept his mouth shut a long time, as long as he could take it, I guess. I could see how unhappy the talk was making him, because these little men—in uniform and out of uniform—all of them full of big talk and none of them ever concerned about anything before in their lives, and not really concerned now—were playing a game—puffing themselves up and being important. Well, they went to work and chattered about what to do with fifty or sixty million people. Every one of their proposals was monstrous. You got the notion that these people believed every German was a criminal. At last somebody made the mistake of asking the writer for his views.

Well, the writer looked around at everybody. I could see how sore he was, and then he said very quietly, "The thing to do is to kill them one by one until they have all been killed. They're too big a problem for any other solution—at least for *this* group."

Nobody said anything, so then he said, "May I ask why we are discussing this problem at all, and who has asked us to do so? Because if we are serious—and we *seem* to be—this problem calls for a tremendous amount of hard work by all of the finest men in America—work that will not be finished after fifty years or even a hundred—and I had no idea our country was eager to assume such a responsibility. If we are ready to assume such a responsibility I'm afraid I can't offer to accept any share of it because I have other plans for my time after the War. In the first place I think the job is important enough to attract the energies of men better fitted for the work than any of us here. If we're here to eat and drink and talk, and our talk isn't to be taken seriously, I suggest we discuss what we are going to do with ourselves after the War, for we shall all of us be in a much better position to devote our time and energy to that problem than to the other one—which I seem to feel is the problem of the German people themselves. Is anybody here a German?"

While he was talking I thought he was going to get himself into a lot of trouble—but no such thing—nothing came of it at all—everybody just forgot what he said the minute he'd said it, and they went right on throwing the old crap around, as the saying is. I got a lot of drinks out of it, so I didn't care. I knew they'd never do anything about themselves, let alone the Germans, so I didn't take part in any of the talk at all, although the fellow who was throwing the party on behalf of the government asked me for my opinion every now and then. I always said, "Shit, don't ask me." Then I'd go freshen up my drink.

I learned a lot from that first meeting about the kind of people who go to work and set themselves up as the representatives of a whole people—like our people, the Americans, for instance—and as far as I can tell they are an inferior order of human beings. Governments just don't seem to attract the kind of people who are embarrassed by so much crookedness and frigging around.

CHAPTER 51

The Boys Take a Flat in Pall Mall, Wesley Writes Some Letters, and Receives One from His Uncle Neal Full of Good News

ONE DAY Joe Foxhall said he'd come to an understanding with the Sergeant, and if we could find a place to stay, and the four of us wanted to stay together and share expenses, we could move out of the barracks to our own place and have a little more privacy. We all wanted to stay together, so we went to work looking for a place, and two days later we moved into a three-room apartment, a parlor and two bedrooms with two beds in each bedroom, and a fine big bath with a shower. Victor and I took one room, and Joe and the writer took the other—with the parlor for all of us. It was O.K. The place was called the Locksley Mansion. At one time it had been a pretty good place. It was on Pall Mall which is the street of the London clubs, two blocks from St. James's on the right and two from Trafalgar on the left.

Joe went to work and wangled a ration book from a Lieutenant who wanted a bottle of Scotch (which Joe got for three pounds from a friend of the elevator boy's at the building where we had our offices). After that we could get the people who ran the Mansion to send us breakfast, lunch, or supper. We were all set, and we had plenty of time to think about the Invasion. We figured it would begin in about two weeks, by the middle of March, but of course it didn't.

The Invasion was the only thing that was on anybody's mind in London, in England, and in America too, most likely. It was in all the papers. Everybody was always trying to guess when it would begin, and then pretty soon the rumor got around that there wouldn't be any Invasion—the Invasion was going on all the time from the Eastern or Russian front, and from the air. We were keeping the Germans confused and worried—*that* was the Invasion.

So now we had our own place to live in, and we had our "offices." After a while everything became more or less official or authorized or proper because the writer and I were expected to go to meetings at night, and since we were writers, we were supposed to be in a position to work at any hour of the day or night at home. One day the writer told me that he and I were all set, and he was trying to fix it for Joe and Victor too. The writer and I always had some scenario or other to look at and study, but he told me not to take any of it too seriously. He told me to read it and know about it, and be ready to answer questions about it—but to write letters to my friends, and a story once in a while.

I wrote to Pop, I wrote to Mom, I wrote to Virgil, and Uncle Neal, and Lou Marriacci, and Dominic Tosca, and I wrote to the woman I knew in New York, and to the one who'd gone home to San Francisco from Ohio, and I wrote to Victor's mother, like I'd promised to. I told her what good luck we'd had and how nice things were turning out for us, and how lucky Victor and I were.

I wrote to Harry Cook and Nick Cully and Vernon Higbee and one more letter to Cacalokowitz. I got letters back from every one of them, but the most wonderful letter of all was the letter from Mom. Her handwriting was so beautiful, and she said such wonderful things to me—I fell in love with her.

The letter from Victor's mother, written for her by Victor's wife, was a wonderful letter too. She was praying for Victor and me all the time, and God bless us again and again, and look after Victor because Victor would look after me.

Well, Uncle Neal—hell, I didn't even know him, but he told me more that I wanted to know than Pop and Mom and Virgil put together because I guess they didn't know how to put it. He said Pop was working for him, and was a great help to him—people liked Pop, he said. Old grouchy customers who used to be a lot of trouble were no trouble at all after Pop had loafed around with them and got to finding out about their lives and farms and problems. Pop had a car, he said, and was always driving out to call on the people he'd met in the store. He wouldn't go out to sell anything, he'd just go out to loaf around with them and visit the farm, but pretty soon the people would turn around and order more stuff than they'd ever ordered before. They wouldn't order from Pop, they'd order from my uncle Neal. A lot of new people were coming to the store because the people Pop had visited had introduced Pop to them. My uncle Neal admitted that he himself wasn't a drinking man, but he said Pop was always taking somebody old or new out of the store to a bar and sitting there with him and having a drink, and after that they were good friends, and when the people came to the store it was different from the way it had been. He said he didn't think Pop had the slightest idea what he was doing—he had no head for business at all—but he was so friendly people just naturally liked him. He went on to say that he was sure Pop and Mom were together for good now. The dry warm climate seemed to agree with Pop. He had a lot of color in his cheeks now. My uncle Neal said he was glad Pop was O.K. again because he had always wondered why his sister wouldn't think of getting Pop out of her life and settling down with somebody else—but now he knew. He said he just didn't know what to do with all the money —the same as Lou Marriacci had said—so Pop was getting his share and always would. Pop and Mom and Virgil had moved to a house of their own, with ten acres of good land on it, and my uncle Neal, he'd gone to work and gotten married too, at last. He said they were all waiting for me to come to El Paso and have a good long holiday —but I knew I'd never stay anywhere in the world very long, except my own city, San Francisco, where I would live with my own wife and family. But I was glad Pop was settling down in El Paso.

Well, Virgil wrote to me too. He told me about a couple of hunting trips he and Pop had gone on—and the time they made Mom go too, and the good time they all had.

The woman in New York wrote and told me she was going to write to me at least twice a week, and she kept her word. She typed her letters and they were always nice to read because they were full of stuff only she and I knew about and understood, so I wrote back to her two or three times.

Harry Cook and Dominic had finished their special training long ago. They hated their work but pretty soon they were going to be shipped—most likely to the Pacific. They both told me so, and Dominic kept asking about Victor. He told me to have some snapshots taken of Victor and me in London, so we got one of our own photographers to take a half dozen and we sent them along to Dominic. I told Victor to send one of each to his wife and his mother too. I got a half dozen of each and sent them to my people —to Mom, and the woman in New York, and the one in San Francisco.

CHAPTER 52

Wesley Finds His Girl, Jill Moore of Gloucester

AS OFTEN as possible I made Victor Tosca go out walking with me. One Sunday we walked all the way to Limehouse, down East India Dock Road and through Pennyfields, which is the Chinatown of London. I told Victor Pop had been born somewhere in the East End of London. I looked at everything carefully because hell, maybe Pop had looked at the same things. If there was an old church, I'd know Pop had seen that all right, so I'd look at it a long time. There were a lot of bombed places—that part of

London got it bad in the Big Blitz—the poor people always get it worst.

Victor and I did a lot of walking in London. We'd walk to Regents Park one evening, down the Strand the next. Down Whitehall or up to Hyde Park. Past St. Paul's and down Threadneedle Street. Past Old Bailey to the Liverpool Street Station. Across the bridges: Waterloo, Westminster, London, Blackfriars, Tower—all of them. Because it was the best city I ever saw to walk around in.

But hell, I hadn't found my girl, and that's what I wanted to do. I'd gone to Piccadilly Circus a lot of times to see the girls trying to make profitable deals with the boys, and I made a few myself, but the girls made me so sad I didn't want them any more.

One night while I was hanging around Piccadilly Circus watching the show a little girl came up to me. She was so young I couldn't believe my eyes, and I didn't like it at all. I thought she must be fourteen or fifteen. She didn't have the manner of somebody who knew what she was doing, so I told her to take a walk with me. We went down to St. James's Park and sat on a bench and talked. Pretty soon I got to feeling that this might be *my* girl —but I hated the idea that she had been in Piccadilly Circus and had come up to me that way because if that was a true thing, she *couldn't* be my girl—even if she had been meant to be—because I wouldn't allow it.

I told her to tell me the truth—not to lie to me for any reason because I hated lying. I told her I liked her, and if it was true, well, I'd be broken-hearted but I'd still like her. She said she had come from Gloucester to London that afternoon—she had run away from home. She was hungry and didn't have any money. One of the girls of the street advised her to do what she had tried to do. She said the girl had promised to let her use her place if she had had any luck. I told her to take me to the place.

We walked half a mile to a doorway, and the girl rang the bell, but there was no answer. We went to a fish-and-chips place and ate some, and then went back to the doorway and rang the bell again and a woman came to the door. I gave the woman a pound note and stepped into the hall with her. I told her to tell me about the girl. She said she hadn't seen the girl until a few hours ago. She said the girl was in London without any money, a little fool like so many others these days—so she'd taken pity on her and told her she could stay with her overnight, and maybe make a pound or two for herself if she had any talent for it.

I thanked the woman and took the girl back to St. James's Park to think things over. Well, I liked her. I wasn't sure I liked her as much as I thought I'd like *my* girl, but I knew I liked her a lot. She said she was almost seventeen, but looked younger because her family was poor and they never ate very much—it was because she had always been a little hungry.

I took her home. The writer was sitting in the parlor reading. Joe and Victor had gone to bed. I asked the writer what I ought to do about her. He said she ought to take a bath and go to bed—sleep on the couch in the parlor. I told her to take a bath and I gave her a pair of my pajamas. The writer and I fixed the couch up into a bed. Pretty soon she came out of the bathroom in the pajamas and got in bed.

She had a sweet little face with the upper lip lifted away from the lower in a kind of child-like perplexity, and all sorts of soft thick yellow hair tumbling down. She was all small and white, with the hands of a baby, and little baby legs and feet. But what she had that broke my heart were big staring blue eyes—the amazed eyes of a scared little girl in a crazy and ferocious world. The writer closed the parlor door, and I asked him to go for a walk with me because I wanted to talk to him about her. He went to the bathroom first, and called me over, because she had washed all her clothes and hung them up to dry, and he wanted me to see that.

We went out into the street and I told the writer about her.

"She came up to me in Piccadilly Circus just as if she were a street-walker. Well, I couldn't believe that, so I took her to St. James's Park and we talked a long time. She's almost seventeen, but she looks younger. She's run away from home because the family's poor and she can't get along with her mother—her father's dead. Do you think she's lied to me?"

"All you've got to do is look at her," the writer said. "She hasn't lied to you."

"Well, what shall I do about her?"

"Marry her."

We walked along and I kept remembering the girl and the

things she'd told me and her eyes staring at me and her little clean hands after her bath, and her feet, and hell, I didn't know for sure—but she *seemed* to be my girl. It seemed to me I'd found her at last, and all I had to do now was make sure. She was everything she ought to be that I could tell about so far, so all I had to do was find out about everything.

And I had to find out if *she* liked *me*.

I reminded the writer of the Army's ruling about soldiers marrying English girls—how your Commanding Officer had to investigate the matter, which took two or three months because they liked to discourage English-American marriages, and had to give his approval, and all the other red-tape.

"Just marry her," the writer said.

"What do you mean?"

"Find out if she's the girl for you. Find out if she thinks you're the man for her. Find out if you love each other enough to want to get married and have children and live together for the rest of your lives. Forget the Commanding Officer. Let me know what you decide and I'll figure something out."

"What do you *really* think of her?"

"I think she's wonderful. From what I've seen of her, I think she's your wife. I think you're both very lucky."

CHAPTER 53

Wesley and Jill Visit Mrs. Moore Who Gives Her
Daughter's Hand in Marriage

SHE WAS my girl all right. We spent a week going for walks and talking, and all I ever did was hold her hand once in a while. I didn't kiss her or touch her because I was in love with her the way children are in love with one another. She met Victor Tosca and Joe Foxhall, and everybody understood what was going on, but in order not to get things complicated we agreed not to let the people of the Mansion know about her, so she always had to get up very early and unmake her bed on the couch and stay out of sight until the breakfast table had been set, and then we'd all sit down and she'd have breakfast with us.

I took her home to Gloucester one afternoon because I wanted to meet her mother.

They had a dirty little old flat on a dirty street, and there were five other children, only one of them older than my girl, a brother who was home on leave from the Army.

He was about my age, and he looked a little like his sister, but he was a sad boy. He was sad from poverty.

"What do you want with my sister?" he said.

"I want her to be my wife."

Pretty soon her mother came out of another room. She wasn't a bad-looking woman, she was just poor and tired and she'd been sick or something—for years, I mean.

"Who are you?" she said.

"My name's Wesley Jackson."

"What are you doing with my daughter?"

"I've come to ask your permission to marry her."

"Can you support her?"

"Yes, I can."

Well, then she asked me to sit down. All of us sat down and talked, and she asked me a lot of questions about my family and my religion and a lot of other things mothers want to know about when somebody wants to marry their daughter. She seemed more curious about me than concerned about her daughter, but she wasn't a bad woman at all—just poor and not much hope for any kind of improvement for herself or her family. I could see she had been a handsome woman at one time, and a pretty good mother too, but things had gotten too tough for her. The boy who'd come home on leave improved a lot as time went by and pretty soon the mother said, "When do you want to be married?"

"Right away."

"She's not seventeen yet."

"I thought you might write a note for me saying that you approved of the marriage."

"What do you want me to say?"

"Just say, 'To Whom It May Concern: I approve of the marriage of my daughter Jill, born such and such a date in such and such a place, to Wesley Jackson, born in San Francisco, September 25, 1924.' And sign your name to it."

She went to a table and got out the family Bible and a tablet of lined writing paper and a bottle of ink and a pen. She turned to the part of the Bible where she'd written down the births and deaths in her family, and she wrote the note and handed it to me.

"To Whom It May Concern: I approve of the marriage of my daughter Jill, born 11th September 1926 in Gloucester, England, to Wesley Jackson, born 25th September 1924 in San Francisco, America. My family name is Scott and I am from Dundee. My husband Michael was Irish but a Presbyterian. He was a fisherman, lost at sea six years ago. Peg Moore. Gloucester, 17th March 1944."

Then the woman opened her arms to her daughter, and Jill went crying to her mother, and they kissed, and the woman sniffled a little and blew her nose and then opened her arms to me too, and I kissed her cheek and she kissed mine. Then Jill kissed her brother who was home on leave, and one by one she kissed her two younger sisters and two younger brothers, and then we said good-bye.

On our way back to the railroad station I took my girl in my arms for the first time, and tears came to my eyes because of the tears in hers. I kissed her tears, and her mouth, and I knew I had found my girl at last because the singer of my song was singing it now—he was really singing *Valencia* now. My heart was heaving in me and I thanked God for my wife and her mother and her brothers and her sisters and her father drowned in the sea. I thanked God especially for Michael Moore, whoever he was, for I was full of the love that embraces even the dead.

CHAPTER 54

Wesley Jackson of San Francisco Is Married to Jill Moore of Gloucester by Joe Foxhall of Bakersfield While Victor Tosca and The Writer Act as Witnesses

ON THE train coming back to London I knew I was married and had my wife and would some day have my son too, because I had the note from my girl's mother in my pocket and my girl by my side—*oh beauty!* my own angel by my side. And I loved the touch of her beside me, and the smell of her, and the sweet stillness of her. I was so happy I almost thanked God for the War, for getting me drafted, for getting me across the ocean when He did, for setting me down in London, for making me go to Piccadilly Circus to see the show—because if those things hadn't happened I wouldn't have found my girl. I asked God to forgive me for having hated the people I had hated. I couldn't hate them any more because they had sent me to London where I had found my wife.

Pretty soon we were home again. The writer was in the parlor reading a story he had asked me to write, so I handed him the note I had gotten from my girl's mother. After he had read the note I said, "We want to get married right away—tonight."

"Sure," the writer said.

Just then Joe Foxhall came in and I showed him the note too, and the writer said, "Joe, do you know anything about marriage ceremonies?"

"What do you have to know?" Joe said.

"Well," the writer said, "I think Jill and Wesley ought to have the best kind of ceremony there is."

Jill knew how it was in the Army—about getting the approval of the Commanding Officer and all the other red-tape—so we had agreed to have a ceremony of our own. There was no Bible in the apartment, so Joe telephoned the staff and asked them if we could borrow their Bible. Old Dan, who was the all-around man of the building, brought us a Bible, and Joe went looking through it for something to read to us. Then Victor Tosca came home and I showed him the note too, and we were all ready for the ceremony. I had bought a ring that morning, and it was in my pocket. I was shaking all over with nervousness because this was the most important day of my life—it was the day I had been waiting for for so long, and there I was with my beautiful Jill, all pale and staring, waiting to perform her part in the ritual. Victor was so happy he told us to wait a minute and ran out. Ten minutes later he came back with two bottles of champagne. Old Dan brought a bucket of ice and five champagne glasses. He saw Jill for the first time and nodded to her. I asked him if there was a vacant apartment in the building for myself and my bride. He congratulated

Jill and me, and said there was a very little apartment that he could let us have for six or seven days when it would have to be given to some people who had reserved it, so I gave him three pounds and asked him to get some flowers and put them in the apartment—red roses.

Well, I was a mess. I didn't know whether to laugh or cry I was such a mess. Pretty soon Joe said he was ready, and then I really got excited. Joe had the writer stand beside me, and Victor beside Jill, and Joe stood in front of us and began the ceremony. It was the most beautiful ceremony I ever heard. I don't know how much of it was from the Bible and how much of it was from Joe's head, but the things he said were just right. I couldn't hold back the tears, because finding your girl and getting married to her is the toughest and most beautiful thing in the whole world, and now at last I had found my girl and I was getting married to her.

It was time then to put the marriage ring on my bride's finger, so I did, and Joe said, "In the eyes of God, and in the eyes of one another, you are now and henceforth until the end of this world— Wesley Jackson of San Francisco and Jill Moore of Gloucester— husband and wife, and of any issue father and mother."

Joe closed the Bible and I took Jill in my arms and kissed her, and then one by one the writer and Joe and Victor kissed her, but Jill started to cry and that made me cry too. But the others, they were so happy they got us to laughing at the same time. Victor opened a bottle of champagne and filled the glasses and everybody drank to Jill and me. And I drank to everybody—to a long and happy life to Victor Tosca, and Joe Foxhall, and the writer. Then I drank to my bride, and she drank to me. We drank until there was no more to drink. Pretty soon Old Dan came with the key to my own apartment, so the boys told me to take my bride home and carry her across the threshold.

CHAPTER 55

Wesley and Jill Cleave Together for a Son, if It Is the Will of God

I TOOK Jill by the hand and went off, but we didn't go home then, because I wanted to go out into the streets of London with my bride. We walked up Regent to Piccadilly Circus where we'd met. We stood exactly where we'd stood that night. We walked to St. James's Park and sat down where we had sat and talked. We walked to the place where the woman lived and I rang the doorbell. When she came to the door I said, "We're married now and I've come to thank you for your kindness to my wife when she was alone." I wanted to give the woman something for her kindness but I didn't have anything to give except money and I couldn't give her money at a religious time like that. The woman just stared at us, and I'm not sure she understood what I was talking about, but maybe she did too. We walked back to Piccadilly Circus, down Haymarket, and there at the curb was an old man sitting at a broken-down old piano. I went to him and when he finished the piece he was playing I said, "Could you play a song called *Valencia* for me?" So the old man played *Valencia*, and *oh beauty!* I hugged my girl and I said to her, "That's our song—that's the song of our life together." I gave the old man a quid of English money, and turned away to go walking through London with my partner, adoring everything in the city, and all the people of the streets.

When we got to the door of our home I lifted my bride off her feet and carried her across the threshold. We were then, until the end of the whole world, husband and wife.

It was a beautiful home, with red roses all around. There were two bottles of wine on the table—from Victor and Joe and the writer. I opened one of the bottles and poured a drink for my wife and one for myself, and pretty soon Old Dan came to ask what we'd like for supper. Well, I was too excited to eat, but I knew Jill ought to eat—she ought to eat a lot from now on—so we ordered a lot of stuff and one by one the old man brought them and set them on the table in front of us, and my bride and I, we sat and ate and looked at one another.

I ate and ate and looked at my darling Jill.

That night I held her in my arms until it was morning. Then we got up and drew back the black-out curtains and looked at the new world, and it was good to see. Then I sent Jill back to bed. When she was asleep again I went to her and adored her lovely sleeping face and kissed her lips, and it was the same the night of that day too, and the next night. It was the same many nights— until I knew the time had come for Jill to be with her husband—to be truly wed to him, to take unto herself his heart's delight in her, to mingle it with her own in him, to see if their smiling together might be, by the grace of God, themselves together in their own son.

I had bought a Bible for my family and I wrote down in the Bible the time Jill and I were first together: "The night and morning of Saturday and Sunday March 25 and 26, 1944—for a son, if it is the will of God."

We did not cleave together again, waiting to know, and when the time came we began to know. We knew a little more the next day, and more the next, and then Jill felt nausea one morning, so I took her to a doctor. After several visits he said it was so, and I loved London more than I loved San Francisco even, because it was the city in which the life of my son had begun.

After that I wasn't the Wesley Jackson I had been. After that I was a husband and a father, and the meaning of all things changed for me.

CHAPTER 56

Wesley and Jill Find a Home, Receive Gifts of Love and Money, and Are Stunned to Find Themselves So Happy

JILL FOUND a small apartment for us on Charles II Street. She fixed the place up until it was like herself, and then it was truly our own home. There was a little kitchen in it, and she got breakfast for me, and supper. She wouldn't let me send anything out to the laundry because it took too long and she wanted to do it anyway. She got more beautiful every day, and the more beautiful she got the more amazed I felt about my wonderful luck.

I wrote to Mom and told her everything because that kind of news belongs to a mother before it belongs to a father. I sent her some snapshots of Jill and me, and I told her Jill was pregnant and we hoped and believed it would be a son. I wrote to Mrs. Tosca too because I knew she'd be glad to hear I'd found my girl at last. She'd asked me about that and I'd told her I'd been looking a long time but just didn't seem to be able to find her. I wrote to Lou Marriacci and told him too, and my old pal from San Francisco Harry Cook—and I sent them all snapshots of Jill and me.

Well, the letter I got back from Mom was so beautiful Jill cried when she read it. And Lou—the crazy fool—sent me a wedding present of five hundred dollars. I didn't know how I was ever going to pay him back, but he said not to give it a thought because his new place was making too much money anyway. He said I had brought him the best luck of his whole life. He said he missed Pop very much, but was glad Pop was O.K. and home again.

Pop had been sending me money every week for a long time, but now that I was married he made it a big lump of money. I had Jill open a bank account, and I made her buy herself all the clothes she had enough rationing coupons to buy.

The writer and I sat around every day in our office and talked about everything. Every three or four days he'd tell me to write a story, so I would write one, and after he'd studied it, he'd tell me what I'd done. He claimed I was getting better all the time. Victor Tosca and I would sit around somewhere and talk about our lives and the way we felt about being lucky enough to have a beautiful girl apiece, and a son on the way—if it was the will of God, a son —but if it was a daughter, well, I loved Jill so much I wasn't sure I wouldn't rather see a little girl like her instead of a son, but I hoped it would be a son anyway. And Joe Foxhall, he was always around grumbling because all of us were married and he wasn't.

The days of beauty kept piling on top of one another, and Jill and I were so happy neither of us could believe any of it was true. Sometimes when I'd come home she'd be fooling around in the kitchen crying, and I'd ask her why and she'd say, "Because I never even dreamed I could be this happy. I never knew anybody could love anybody the way I love you, but when I see you I think you love me more than I love you, and it makes me so happy I think I'm dreaming. I think I'm dreaming all the time—because look at Mama. What kind of happiness did poor Mama ever have?"

I told Jill to take twenty-five pounds out of the bank and go for a visit to her mother's, but she didn't want to go. It took me a week to make her go. I knew going home that way would make her mother very happy, and I wanted anybody we knew to be happy. I knew Jill wanted to go back too. I told her if I ever got hold of any money I was going to send it to her mother. I told her I was going to have the bank send her mother a little every week anyway —five pounds. It wasn't much, but I knew it would mean something to her mother. And that's what I did. When Jill came back from that first visit she told me how happy we had made her mother, and how proud her mother had become of her, and how happy she was that Jill was pregnant. I guess that made me just about as happy as anything has ever made me. I told Jill I wanted her to visit her mother at least once every two weeks. Every time she came home after a visit to her mother's she'd be happier than ever.

They'll tell you happiness is the end. They'll tell you when the fellow marries the girl, that's it, that's all, that's the end, but don't ever believe them because it's not so, it's not the end at all, it's the beginning, there is no beginning at all until the fellow marries the girl, until the girl gets pregnant and more beautiful every day, until the fellow's heart expands with adoration for the girl and the life in her, and for all life. That is the beginning, that's not the end. When the fellow and the girl have become one another, when they are the same person, well, then life has begun, and forever after there is no end—there just naturally can't be any end when the two of them are together and the same person because in the nature of things that's it, that's the idea, that's what all the shouting's about, that's Death knocked on its ass, that's life goosed into blessed galloping, that's Christmas come, that's the Kingdom on Earth as it is in Heaven, that's the song and the dance, the old river laughing, the ocean all happy, the wind full of kisses, the sky open arms, the tree jumping for joy, the rock all humming, the night gone whispering, the day come strolling. If they tell you happiness is the end, if they say it's dull, if they say no good ever came of it, no art or greatness, don't believe them, they've never known happiness. If they tell you kissing's for fools, tell them they lie. If they tell you adoration's for the ignorant call them sons of bitches and tell them they lie. If they tell you tenderness is weakness, tell them they are not men. If they tell you pain's better than pleasure, tell them no, it's the other way around. The good things are the beginning. The bad things are not the end—they are only stuff trying to reach the beginning. The right things are the immortal things. And nothing's so right as love. Victor Tosca knew. Joe Foxhall knew. Love is it. Love is the great number: the one and only. It's three, seven, nine, eleven, and all the numbers rolled into the wonderful one. Love God. Love your wife. Love your son. Love your neighbor. Love your enemy, the son of a bitch—love him anyway. Give the poor man a chance—love him.

CHAPTER 57

Wesley and Jill Discover a Saint in Fitzroy Square

ONE SUNDAY morning Jill and I went out to walk. When we came to Fitzroy Square we saw a man in a long coat standing at the middle of the street preaching to the people in the houses. He was in rags, a man of medium height, about fifty-five years of age, with a battered old hat which he took off now and then, and a great head covered with white hair. We heard his voice before we saw him, and we knew he was a Saint. I have never heard another voice as moving as the voice of this man. I have never heard such noble anger so magnificently mingled with tendernesss and concern. Jill was afraid of the man, and even I was afraid to go too near him. It wasn't that we thought he was crazy, which would have been easy to do—it was simply that his anger had such grandeur, as if he did not dwell in this cheap world, but had come about in our streets from a better place and could not bear to see the littleness all around him—the meanness, the stinginess, the nagging, and the pathetic vanity. He shouted as if his best friend were God and no one else. The tone of his voice humbled the heart.

Well, London's London, and London's full of strange and great people. I took Jill by the hand to within twenty yards of this man and we stood in the street and listened to him. The people got out of their Sunday beds and came to their windows and looked at him, and then went back. Every now and then he would break into song.

Then he would roar at the people: "Get up, people of the false world. Get up, broken ones and be healed." Then he would sing a few lines of another song that had just occurred to him:

> *Brightest and best of the sons of the morning!*
> *Dawn on our darkness, and lend us Thine aid!*

Then he would shout some more: "Awake! Awake! Salute the happy morn. Why do you choose the way of Death when the way of Life is so near at hand? Get up, you dead—get up and be born." Then he'd sing again:

> *Thy Word is like a glorious choir,*
> *And loud its anthems ring;*
> *Though many tongues and parts unite,*
> *It is one Song they sing.*

When he came to the word "loud" he roared it louder than all the other words in the song. In their houses the people knew greatness had come to their street, for soon, not knowing what else to do about it, they wrapped coins in paper and tossed them into the street for the man.

I have seen many in London who go about singing for money. When the coins have been tossed to them, wrapped in paper, they hurry to pick them up—but not this man. He would pick the money up all right, but not until he was ready to do so. He had to have money in order to stay alive, but that wasn't what he was out in the streets for. It happened that people tossed money to him, and it happened that he picked the money up when he got around to it, but he was no beggar. He was a Saint. He was a citizen of the true world.

Little by little the man came closer to us. I knew Jill was not afraid any more, so the man and I talked. He said his name was Berry, and he said he'd been going through the streets of London talking to the people for more than twenty years. He was almost sixty. He said he was not a Christian alone, but a believer in all good men, religious or whatever. He believed in anything that would help bring the people to life—get them out of their poverty, lift them out of their sloth, push them into beauty, carry them along to truth and greatness, kick them out of their awful confusion and forgetfulness, drag them away from their sickness. He was for anything that would help the living to become alive.

I asked him if he had ever been an actor, because he used his voice so magnificently, and he was shocked. Of course he hadn't been an actor, he said. What theatre was big enough to hold his voice?

"Now," he said. "I'll talk and sing again, and you listen."

He went to the center of another crossing, and beginning gradually his voice mounted and mounted in speech until Jill and I heard the great roar of truth that was in his voice. He turned to us and without lowering his voice he said, "No theatre in the whole world could hold a voice like that, but England's my home."

CHAPTER 58

The Writer *Meets the Saint of Fitzroy Square and Tells Wesley About Money and Manners*

I WAS sure the writer would like to know of this man and hear his voice, so when he was finished again and came over to talk with us some more I asked him if he would come to the building where the writer and I had our office and let us hear him there—tomorrow afternoon. He said he would, and the next day around three in the afternoon I heard his voice and waited to see what the writer would think.

Well, the writer listened a moment. Then he went to the window and lifted it. After a moment he hurried out of the office. I saw him in the street waiting to talk to the man. When the man was finished the writer put something in his hand and they talked. Then the writer stood over to one side while the man began again. The people in the street stopped to listen. The man did something to every one of them with his voice and his words. I saw the writer studying the people. Everybody gave the man money. He was in front of the building about forty-five minutes, and the people never stopped giving him money. I was afraid something terrible would happen to him with all that success. He must have taken in three or four pounds, maybe more. I thought perhaps I had done a terrible thing to ask him to come there because a good man ought not to be in a position to understand the results of his efforts in terms of the most obvious kind of success—the amount of money he has attracted to himself. The greatness of this man was so much a part of his aloofness that I was afraid success might begin to mean something to him, impurify his spirit, wreck his grandeur, and send him to thinking about the worthless things. He himself must have considered these things too, for he never came back to that street. In Fitzroy Square he was even more magnificent because no fuss was made about him.

When the writer came back to his desk he said he believed he had seen and heard one of the great men of our time, so then I told him I had found the man in Fitzroy Square while I was walking with Jill and had asked him to come to our street because I was pretty sure the writer would want to know about him.

"I didn't know what else to do," the writer said, "so I gave him a pound. I know *that* was wrong."

"He can use the money."

"Of course he can, but he's out there trying to deliver people from the oppression of money, so what do the people do—what do *I* do? Give him money. That's not it at all."

So then we talked about money, and the writer said, "Some day you're going to make a lot of money—you're not going to *try* to make it—it's just going to happen. Well, when it does happen, don't pay any attention to it, don't get interested in it, don't be taken in by it—don't want more, don't be unhappy when less of it comes to you. Be above it. Don't ever let yourself be rich or poor. Money can drive even a good man into bankruptcy."

I wanted to know how I was going to make a lot of money, so I asked the writer and he told me.

"By writing," he said. "You're a good writer now, but pretty soon I think you're going to be a great writer."

"How do you know?"

"I know, that's all."

Well, when it's something as wonderful as that, and it's about yourself, a fellow wants to know more about it, so I said, "But what makes you think so?"

"I've read everything you've written that I've asked you to write," the writer said. "You're a better writer now than most writers ever get to be, and you haven't even started yet. Writers don't like writers. They're afraid of one another. Not me. I like writers. I don't like people who insist on writing who aren't writers. You're a writer. When you get around to making all that money, don't pay any attention to it—just go on being the millionaire you are anyway."

"Millionaire?"

"Sure," the writer said. "You're a born millionaire. You're the kind of millionaire who doesn't need a dime to go with it—hardly. Just try to get through this War O.K., that's all."

I told the writer I was trying all the time, so then he handed me back the last story I had written for him, but he didn't say anything, so I said, "Well—what about it?"

"You're on your own from now on," he said. "I've got nothing more to tell you about writing."

That made me feel pretty good, so I said, "What do I do now?"

"You'll know," he said. "In the meantime let's go get a beer." We went down the street to The Running Horse and had some beer and played the marble game in the corner for half a crown a game, and talked about the Invasion.

I didn't like the Invasion at all. I wished the whole War would fall down and die, but I knew it wouldn't. The War would fall down and die *eventually* and everything would come to about the same as ever, but not until the War had done its damage and made fools of everybody. It would all come to the same thing that it would have come to if there had been no War at all, but now that there was a War and everybody had got tangled up in it, well, they had gone to work and made themselves believe once they got out of this War, why then it would come to something really extraordinary—but I didn't believe that at all. I didn't think that that was the way anything got to be extraordinary or right or good or improved or great or honorable or true or human at all. I thought the War was only an unhappy thing that men had allowed to come to pass and would one day fall to pieces and die and leave everything important pretty much where it had been before the unhappy thing had been allowed to come to pass. I just didn't believe in War. I don't believe in it now. And I never will believe in it. I think it's just the poor excuse of failures. It's all right for the germs of Death to go to war in a man's body with the germs of Life—that's nature—but men are not germs.

CHAPTER 59

Wesley and Jill Hear a London Street Beggar in Song and Speech

ONE SUNDAY morning around eight a fellow stood in Charles II Street where Jill and I had our home and began to sing. His singing woke us up and made us very happy because he sang *You'll never know just how much I love you. You'll never know just how much I care.* I took Jill in my arms and hugged her and kissed her, so then the man was finished with his song and went to work picking up the coins people had wrapped in paper and tossed out to him, but as he did so he made a little speech.

"Ladies and gentlemen," he said. "I don't like coming out here this way on a Sunday morning to sing to you for money, but my wife's in the hospital in considerable pain. I thank you, Ladies and Gentlemen—good luck and God bless you."

Then he sang *When the lights go on again all over the world.* As he sang he moved down the street so he would be near a new building and get some new money. After he'd sung this song I heard him make the speech again. It was beautiful, because in the second speech he added something new.

"Ladies and Gentlemen," he said, "help a fellow in my case." He moved a little further down the street and started singing *I'm a Yankee Doodle Dandy.* That was funniest of all because he was no such thing, he was a London cockney, a serious-minded bounder, about twenty-five years old. In his third speech I heard him say, "Ladies and Gentlemen, I am a Veteran of the last War—fought at several different places and won several different decorations." Well, the only decoration he was wearing was his red nose, but he had a good voice and I know everybody liked him as much as Jill and I did. We knew he was a liar, but there are some liars you can't help liking. We hoped he'd come back next Sunday, and he did. He sang the same three songs and made the same speech three times with only a few changes in the speech each time.

The people of the streets of London are my favorite people. Jill and I used to look for the old man at the piano in Haymarket and get him to play *Valencia* for us, and there was a banjo and clarinet team that used to come by around sundown playing *Whispering Grass* that we liked very much. The whole city was full of a strange kind of beautiful singing.

One Sunday when the singer came to wake us up with the song, *You'll never know just how much I love you,* we woke up all right and hugged and kissed and waited for his speech all right, and sure enough he said it the same as ever, only when he got to the part about his wife being in the hospital in considerable pain something stopped him. I ran to the window to see what it was. Well, it was a London bobby who had taken him by the arm and was pushing him gently--which I didn't think was necessary at all. He was back again the following Sunday anyway.

But the best music of all was the music we sometimes heard just before nightfall, long after sundown, when the shadow of night was coming into everything. This music came from the trumpet of a Scotsman who could really blow a horn. His music was so pure and lonely it made me feel I had lived more than a thousand years. Soon after his solo it would be night, and like as not the airplanes would come over to bomb London. The sirens would wail the alarm and everybody would take to shelter, but Jill and I had agreed that the only shelter we wanted was one another's arms and that's the only shelter we ever took. It was the best shelter there is and we were never afraid because we couldn't believe any bomb would come to hurt us--and none did. The guns would rattle away in the night--sometimes so close they shook the whole building-- the bombs would fall and explode--but we weren't afraid because we were together.

London was always good, it was always the best city of them all, better than San Francisco even, better than New York, better than Chicago--because London was where Jill came to me, and that is the kind of thing that makes you love a city. I never would have gone to Gloucester, but Jill just *had* to come to London—because I was waiting there for her. I know I would have liked London anyway, even if I hadn't found Jill there, but having found her, I shall always love London more than any other place in the whole world. It's where my life began. No matter how far away from London I ever go, and no matter where Jill and I die, we will always be somewhere in the streets of that sombre, proud and beautiful city.

CHAPTER 60

Wesley and Jill Go to Windsor and Win a Lot of Money on the Races

ONE SATURDAY I thought I'd take Jill for a little holiday in the country, so she fixed us a picnic lunch, and we got on a train at Victoria Station at noon and went to Windsor, to see the races.

There was a man on the lawn there standing at the center of a large circle of people and he was making a speech, so Jill and I stopped to find out what he had to say. He said he wasn't like some people he knew—blokes who had no business-standing. He was a man who was well-known for the past nine years, a man who knew them all —Selfridges, Claridges, Tattersalls. He said he wasn't interested in money. To prove it he brought a handful of coins out of his pocket and tossed them on the lawn in front of him one at a time and said, "Half a crown, crown, seven and six, ten, twelve and six, fifteen, seventeen and six—a pound. I'm not here for money. I could go to any of my friends and without saying a word—not one word, Ladies and Gentlemen—get any amount I cared to mention." He talked on and on and finally got around to the point, which was this: that he had a card on which he had written down the numbers of the winning horses in the next five races. Well, I wanted that card, but he wouldn't say how much he wanted for it, so I asked him. He said he wanted half a crown. I gave him half a crown and went to bet a pound on the first number which belonged to a horse called *Turning Home*.

Jill and I crossed the lawn track with a lot of other people and went to the inside of the track, to the rail near the end of the race. A fellow there got to telling me about the races and how you had to know what you were about in order to pick a winner. I told him I had paid the tipster half a crown for his card and had bet a pound on *Turning Home*. The man said *Turning Home* didn't have a chance, but I didn't care. I liked the tipster's speech. Pretty soon the horses came galloping up the track on their way to the starting gate, and I saw my horse. He seemed to have so much life I told Jill to keep my place while I went to one of the bookies in the inner field to bet two more pounds on him. The man gave me seven to one. I went back to Jill and the man beside us reminded me that my colors were red shirt, green cap. Pretty soon everybody said the race had started. We couldn't see anything because the starting gate was around a bend. After a while the horses came around the bend, but they were so far away I couldn't make out one color from another. They kept coming closer and closer, and then they were climbing the track because that's how it is in England—the tracks rise gradually toward the end—and away out front I saw a red shirt bobbing along on top of a horse and above the red shirt I saw a green cap, so it looked as if *Turning Home* was out in front. The man agreed that this was so, but he said his horse would overtake *Turning Home* in the next thirty yards, but his horse didn't. *Turning Home* galloped in about fifteen yards ahead of any other horse. I went and collected my money, and then bet it all back on the next number on the tipster's card which turned out to be a horse named *War Son*. What could I do but bet my money on a horse with a name like that, considering Jill was carrying a War son right then? Well, the odds on *War Son* weren't as great as they had been on *Turning Home,* but they were good odds just the same, four to one. I told Jill if *War Son* won we'd quit for the day and go somewhere nice by the Thames and lie down and take a nap and eat our lunch. Pretty soon the horses came galloping along on their way to the starting gate, then the race started. It was too good to be true, but it *was* true: *War Son* just naturally galloped in first, away ahead of the others, not even breathing hard. I felt so wonderful I hugged Jill in front of everybody at Windsor. When it was official I collected my winnings, eighty-four pounds, which comes to about three hundred and thirty-six dollars in American money.

I put the money in Jill's hand.

"That's for you."

I knew she would pay her mother another visit soon and take the money with her, and that's what I wanted her to do.

On the way out we passed the tipster who had sold me the card for half a crown. He was beside himself with pride, because so far two of his selections had come in. I liked the man for having been so lucky in his first two selections, because he had brought me so much luck—and nothing makes a fellow who's in love so happy and so much more in love than having good luck. (I kept the tipster's card, and the next day I looked in the paper for the results of all the races. I was sorry to see that the next three horses he'd picked weren't even in the money, but I was a little glad too because I hadn't bet them.)

Jill and I found a nice place by the Thames to lie down on. The grass was fresh and clean and green as only English grass is green. There were a lot of little wild flowers all around, winking and laughing to themselves, and bees humming favorite songs, and butterflies killing time, and grasshoppers jumping around, and a lot of other insects, and hell, it was the most wonderful time I could ever want because out in the green, out by the Thames near Windsor, out by the race track there, my beauty, my darling Jill was the fairest flower of all creation. I winked back at the flowers and thanked them as if they were God for having me around that way—out in England, out where the Kings and Queens had strolled, out by the lazy old Thames, out with my lovely English girl. After we had slept in the green of Windsor and wakened and kissed and played games involving clouds and their shapes and what they'd change to, we ate our lunch. Then Jill took off her shoes and stockings to run bare-footed in the grass and dance for me, and oh Jill, I love thy blessed little feet. I chased her and caught her and lifted her off her feet and set her down in the green grass of England and kissed her feet because they were so twinkling and funny and serious. I kissed every toe of each foot, each sole, each arch, and each ankle, so Jill kissed my Army shoes to make me laugh, and I laughed, and the flowers winked and laughed and didn't care about the lousy War. Jill ran off again and I chased her and caught her and brought her back—so where was the girl who had come up to me in Piccadilly Circus? Where was that unlaughing astonished little girl now?

We walked to Windsor, to the city itself, up to the Castle, then down to the river to watch the boys and girls rowing there. Then we got on the train and came home, and oh England was lovely then, England was sweet then, her fields were the greenest fields I ever saw, her trees and bushes and boughs were the sweetest I ever saw, for England's Jill was my Queen, and I was King of a whole new world.

CHAPTER 61

Joe Foxhall Introduces His Friends to The Shaking Girl

WHEN I went to live with Jill, that left Joe and Victor and the writer together in the flat on Pall Mall. Well, the writer liked to read all the time, or he had to go to one or another of the baloney banquets, as he called the meetings (and half the time I had to go with him, although I kept trying to get out of that stuff it bored me so), so that left Victor and Joe to pass the time. I was glad about that because I had given Victor's mother my word that I'd watch out for him—and I'd *meant* to keep my word—but I hadn't known I was going to find my girl and marry her and make my home in London and wait for my son to be born. I hadn't known those things, and I had broken my word. But Joe Foxhall turned out to be a better pal to Victor Tosca than I could ever be, so I didn't feel so bad about having broken my word. Joe got Victor to laughing and having fun, and that's something I hadn't been very good at doing, so I figured Joe Foxhall, without promising anybody anything, was not only watching out for Victor but making him laugh, which is plenty in War or Peace.

Well, everybody we knew who'd come over to England (excepting Victor and the writer) had gone to work and found a girl to help him pass the time while waiting for the Invasion to start, and sure enough, Joe Foxhall found a girl too.

One night I happened to go into The Polish Club with the writer for a drink after we had been to a very big baloney banquet that had made us sick to our stomachs and ashamed of America.

We were standing at the bar when Joe Foxhall came from the back room and said, "I'm glad you two are here because I want to introduce you to somebody I met in Green Park tonight." Well, he had had a few to drink. He was feeling pretty good, but you could see he was not especially grateful for the kind of luck he had had in finding who he'd found.

"You understand," he said, "that I *like* a girl who is trembling all over with excitement all the time, and by God I've found her. So come along and meet her."

We followed Joe into the back room, which was sort of like an exclusive place—you'd think it would be exclusive for Poles, considering the place was called The Polish Club, but it wasn't—it was exclusive for Americans, and not even for all of *them*. The Poles had stopped coming to the place when the Americans began to arrive. There at the corner table in the back room was the most incredibly sexy piece anybody ever saw. She was all a-tremble from head to foot, just as Joe had said. Her whole face was a kind of beautiful blur. Joe had warned us, so the writer and I weren't surprised, but I'll never forget how big and warm and juicy and all a-tremble she was. She could talk all right, but there wasn't much point to it—she didn't really need to. Her voice was all a-tremble too. I felt half-sore at Joe for keeping her waiting—only I didn't know until later (when he told me) that she was that way all the time, at any hour of the day or night, no matter where she was or who was on hand or how inappropriate it was to be that way. She was just naturally a shaking woman.

Victor Tosca was sitting beside her, but hell, Victor had the best manners in the world, and you'd never guess he even suspected the woman of trembling. He had been chatting with her the way gentlemen chat with beautiful calm young women with whom it's a delight to chat—women who make one feel more and more at ease and worldly.

The writer and I sat down and had a drink and listened to Joe. He talked the way a man does who is serious and sore and happy and irritated all at the same time. I didn't think the woman had the slightest idea what Joe was saying half the time, but that didn't matter one whit. And Victor kept everything neat and easy-going by maintaining his good manners.

When we had gone I asked the writer if he wasn't tired of being away from his wife so long, and he said it was bad, but at the same time it was good. It was all right, because it was out of separation and denial that so much good had come into the art and experience of man.

I went on to the door of my own house and found poor Jill weeping as she sewed clothes for her son, so I took her into my arms and whispered the little poem I'd written to her that day. I used to write something to her every day—either a letter or a poem or a forecast of the future or something ridiculous about history because I knew it would make her laugh, so this night I whispered to her something I had half made-up and half stolen from a poem I'd read somewhere once.

> *Up and down the Thames,*
> *All around the Strand,*
> *Holding hands with Jill—*
> *That's the life for me.*

Jill laughed a little but soon went back to crying, so I just had to go on, even though I had nothing more written and had to make it up:

> *Standing in Trafalgar,*
> *Strolling by Old Bailey,*
> *Holding hands with Jill, my Jill!*
> *That's the life for me.*

CHAPTER 62

*Wesley and Jill Explore the Streets of London Waiting
for the Invasion to Begin*

LONDON IS the loveliest city in the whole world for those who love one another. Jill and I loved every bit of the city and found beauty and tenderness in everything that was part of it. Coming to Trafalgar one Sunday morning we looked up and saw a word we had seen many times before, but now it was so beautiful to us that I took Jill in my arms and kissed her and said the word to her as if it meant all the secret loving things of the heart that no other word could ever say.

"Bovril."

Then I whispered in her ear something else I had just seen in the Square:

"We shall have Moussec wherever we go."

Jill loved the words and whispered, "Whatever Moussec is to you, Moussec is to me too." That made me roar with laughter because Moussec is such a funny word, and Jill said it so sweetly and wickedly.

"*You* are my Moussec," I whispered.

"Then you're *mine*," Jill whispered.

We went for walks as often as I was free to go. One evening we finished the supper Jill had cooked and went out to stroll, going along to Trafalgar, across to Charing Cross Station, down the Strand to Waterloo Bridge, across the Bridge, and through the old streets to The Imperial House, all shattered and broken by time and bombs, and yet for all its damage and forsakenness, still proud since 1865 when it was put there—still The Imperial House. Then we went down to the docks of the Thames and along the narrow streets, all empty of people but a lovely garden to us—along Bankside to Clink Street, past Black Friar's Bridge, from there to St. Mary Overie's Wharf, and on to Number One London Bridge where a fine cockney man took us through the Shelter and showed us where five hundred bombed-out families were living in white-washed dungeons, waiting for the War to end. He told us about Guy's Hospital, about the man himself, who was the stingiest man in the world as long as he lived—letting you into his house to pay a visit, if you insisted, but after you were seated and he knew where you were he would blow out the candle so the tallow wouldn't be wasted, and you'd sit in the dark to visit with him—long years ago. But when he died he left all his money for the hospital—Guy's Hospital, but we didn't go to see it.

We went along to Denmark House to look at the two cherubs at the top, all lovely and fat. Then we crossed London Bridge and went down the steps to the Fishmongers' Shops along Lower Thames. Then up Upper Thames to Fye Foot Lane where we stopped to chat with a bobby who told us that according to Stowe's Survey of London published in 1665 or somewhere along in there the name of the Lane had been Five Foot Lane, but it had come to be called Fye Foot Lane, which was just as good, if not better.

We saw the majestic ruins of London, and loved the weeds and flowers that had come up where the wreckage had been cleared away. Beside the Bank of Afghanistan we came to a place that had been bombed. Away up on the top floor of the building was a door half open onto what would have been the living room of a flat, for there was the fireplace against the wall.

"The man came home," I said to Jill, "expecting to go to his parlor and sit down by the fire and read the evening paper. He opened the door and saw nothing left of his parlor—all of it gone. He was so confused he said 'What's this, now?' "

(So the next time we passed that way Jill looked up at the door still half open and clutched my arm and whispered, "What's this, now? What's this?" I held her and comforted her and told her not to be afraid, it was only the War, and the War be damned.)

We came to a tailor's shop standing amidst the ruins of many great buildings, but the shop was still in one piece. Out in front of the shop by the doorway we saw a half-filled sand-bag tossed upon the sidewalk most carelessly and I said to Jill, "That's what did it—that half-filled sand-bag—that's what protected the tailor's shop. Every morning he would unlock the door of his shop, go in, fetch the half-filled sand-bag and toss it out by the door—for protection against bombs—and only across the street the mighty buildings with their thousands and thousands of tightly packed sandbags piled one on top of the other would be on fire or falling to pieces—but not the little tailor's shop."

We looked at the half-filled sand-bag, and it seemed so delightful to us that we laughed inside and knew each of us was laughing.

At home we'd remember it suddenly in the middle of the night, in the middle of a raid, and Jill would say, "Toss the sand-bag outside our door so we'll be protected tonight." I'd get out of bed and take a pillow from the couch and drop it outside our door, and Jill would dance with delight because she knew nothing would ever touch us.

We had all kinds of wonderful things we knew together that nobody else in the world knew and these things kept us full of laughter and love all the time. Almost every day something new came along to join the other things and make everything that much more wonderful.

But we were scared—Lord God of Heaven, we were both scared to death, for the War was coming, and we knew it. We knew it would get to us sooner or later and I knew if anything happened to finish me before my time—oh bloody hell, that would be a sinful thing, that would hurt, that would make me haunt London forever looking for Jill or the ghost of her. That would not only take me, it would take her. And with my Jill would go my son too—my son would be dead too—nobody would know of Jill or my son or me—we would be finished forever and aching everywhere with hatred and amazement because we had been stopped just when we had begun, just when it seemed that our chance had come, our chance, as Pop had said, for one of us to be abroad in the world who would be a human being at last. We were scared, and it was awful. I knew how awful it was for me and I knew how awful it was for Jill because almost every night she whispered to me, "If anything happens to you—" and then started to cry— "If anything happens, I'll kill myself—I can't help it, I will—I couldn't live one day after you. Don't let anything happen—please don't." And every night I said to Jill, "God will take care of me, and you, and our son," because hell, I knew nobody else would bother.

I knew Jill prayed for us all the time. I don't care what anybody else thinks, I believe in prayers. I guess I believe more in Jill's prayers than in anything else on earth or in heaven. I believe in love, and things of love pray all the time. I believe in prayers, in numbers, in omens, in all the things that are apt to make foolish disaster go along with itself—spend itself exploding upon things that do not dream or love. I believe in superstition, and I believe in truth, but most of all I believe in love. I don't want somebody else to be hurt so that I may be spared—I want *all* to be spared—but I know love is the only answer to disaster, and I hope the day will come when every man in the world finds his love, hears the singing of his song, sees his son, and is protected by the everlasting arms of God.

CHAPTER 63

Wesley Meets Lords, Ladies and Millionaires, Finds Them
Wanting, and Tries to Make a Speech

THE BALONEY banquet the writer and I had gone to the night Joe
Foxhall introduced us to the woman he had picked up in Green
Park was big stuff, so of course there were some big people there. I
had asked the writer to leave me out of it because I hated to leave
Jill alone at home when I didn't know how many more days and
nights I'd have with her, but the writer said, "They want *both* of
us there tonight because everybody has read your piece about London in *Time and Tide* and they want to meet you. You're not
going on account of *me*—I'm going on account of *you*."

Well, somebody had asked the writer to write a piece about London for *Time and Tide,* so one day he told me, "I'm going to write
one, but I'd like you to write one too."

We each wrote one, and he read mine and I read his.

He said my piece made his piece look sick, so he wasn't going to
send in his piece at all—he was going to tell them he hadn't found
time to write a piece yet—later on, maybe—and he was going to send
my piece in instead.

The piece came out in *Time and Tide,* but it didn't bother me
the way the piece in *The New Republic* had bothered me. It didn't
bother me at all. The Ministry of Information wrote to me asking
permission to use it in a magazine published in the East for English
soldiers, and later they asked permission to use it over the British
Broadcasting Company. They made such a fuss about it I went to
work and almost got proud of myself. They sent me little checks of
token payment for the different uses they made of it. I gave the
checks to Jill because according to the writer my piece about London was what it was on account of her.

The meeting started with cocktails, then came supper, and after
supper came an informal discussion of *The Role of English and
American Films in the Post-War World.*

I got introduced to some mighty big people. I shook hands with two Lords, three millionaires, five Ladies, a lot of writers and producers and directors of films, and a lot of government people of England and America. I was disappointed in both the Lords and all five of the Ladies. The Lords couldn't hold a candle to Joe Foxhall, or Victor Tosca, or the writer, and I couldn't understand what the millionaires had that made it possible for them to become millionaires—to get hold of all that money and know how to keep it. They didn't seem brighter than other people. If anything, they seemed less bright. So then how had they come to get hold of all that money? What was the secret? The Lords were probably born with their money, and the Ladies with theirs, but what about the millionaires? Was it possible that there is something besides wit and intelligence and humanity a man's got to have in order to become a millionaire? If it's wit and intelligence and humanity that make a man rich, then Joe Foxhall ought to be one of the richest men in the world, richer than the fellow in India, the Maharajah of something or other, who had the biggest diamond in the world and more cold cash in gold and silver than any other man in the whole world. And yet Joe had no money at all. So what did these millionaires have?

Well, I had a lot of time during cocktails and dinner and during the discussion to look at them carefully, to listen to their talk— formal and informal—and it seemed to me they had a number of special qualities which Joe Foxhall could never permit himself to have. For one thing they just didn't give a damn about the truth, although in their formal speeches they pretended that they did. For another, they were very fearful of the right coming to pass because I could see they knew if the right came to pass they would not be as rich as they had been. And then it seemed to me that they were men to whom the making of money was the big thing in life—it was more important to them than learning the truth, than becoming truly great (as Joe Foxhall was great, and it seemed to me Victor Tosca in his way, and the writer in his), than living generously, than cherishing others and not wanting them to be so bitterly denied—and in many other things which are first in importance to truly good men. The millionaires just naturally weren't whole men and didn't give a damn that they weren't.

The two Lords were feeble-minded. I didn't find out until they got up to speak, for their manners when I met them were excellent.

That left the writers and producers and directors of films and while I must say they were a little superior to the millionaires there wasn't anything much to them either—at least nothing I could discover during cocktails, dinner and discussion. One was chipper and happy and delighted with the work he'd done—he'd just directed a picture that people seemed to like. Another was stuffy and pompous about the importance of films after the War, and there was no real wisdom in him—he just insisted that better films would have to be made if any of us expected the War not to turn out to be in vain. Another was full of anecdotes about the great actors and actresses he had worked with in his twenty years as an English producer of plays and pictures. An American Major who had been a director of pictures was very cautious about what he said, and then a young American civilian who was connected with the Office of War Information made the worst speech of all because it didn't mean one blessed thing, although he used words like "augur" and "vestigial" and I don't remember what else. It seemed to me that even though he was taken for somebody important, the whole thing was a mistake from away back and he had come to be in his present position largely because he had been with the O.W.I. so long.

Then the writer was introduced. It was his turn to say something, so of course he was in terrible pain. He got up from his chair where he had been all stooped over from agony and he straightened himself out, and he said, "I have always felt that there is little mischief in gatherings of this sort if the food and drink are good, and I have always taken everything that has been said at such gatherings with a grain of salt, so I hope everyone who has made a speech will forgive me if I continue to do so. I agree that we have a chance to do rather pleasant things for people with films, but it seems to me the main idea with the people who matter in the making of films—the people who own the companies that make the films and the theatres that show them—is to make money—and anything else any of us say is so much chit-chat. I would feel very pleased, though, if in spite of everything, we managed to make a nice, honest, human picture now and then."

Then it was close to eleven o'clock and I thought the meeting would come to an end, but the Chairman got up and began to make a speech about somebody that was so full of flattery and nonsense I felt sorry for the poor man. I lost my breath when I discovered he was talking about me. I was scared to death and I kept sinking lower and lower in my chair at the table because I never heard such lies about anybody in the world in all my life—all on account of the little piece I had written about London. The fellow who was talking about me had only met me a couple of hours ago, we hadn't exchanged more than two dozen words, he didn't know me at all—he didn't know about Jill and our son, he didn't know about Pop and Mom and Virgil and my uncle Neal or anything else —and yet there he was making the sweat pour out of me with the terrible lies he was telling. I sank lower and lower in the chair until almost the only thing left of me above the table was my head, and my eyes were studying the tablecloth and the fine woven design of flowers in it—great big roses—so I studied them in the hope of not hearing any more of the lies. I didn't know what I would do when he was finished. I couldn't see how I would ever be able to get to my feet and be the incredible fellow he claimed I was—which was all written down on a pad of notes he held. He claimed I was a man who would not only be heard from, but had already been heard from. He said that in spite of my recent arrival in London I had said things about the city and its people which every Londoner felt deeply but did not have the magic talent of words I had and therefore could not say. He said he was thankful as an Englishman, and as a born Londoner, that I—an American—a Private in the American Army—had come to London and seen the city, not with the eyes of a stranger, not as a visitor might see it, but as a Londoner saw it.

Well, I never made a speech in my life. I hated speech-making, but it seemed to me there was only one thing to do and that was to make a decent stab at it, so when the man was finished and everybody had stopped applauding, which embarrassed and thrilled me at the same time—thrilled me because every man is such a fool when you get right down to it—well, I got up and said, "My father was born in the East End of London, so I am not altogether a stranger to this city. I have gone back to the streets my father knew as a boy and I have looked at them, and it seemed to me that I knew them. My father handed me the books of England and Lon-

don which he loved, and I read those books and loved them. I saw
London in my sleep long years ago, and I made up my mind to get
back to my father's city some day. I wish to God it hadn't taken a
War to get me over here because I don't like Wars, but I'm thankful that I did get here when I did, because (*remembering Jill, whom
I missed so terribly now*) I have found in this city the treasure
I have searched for all my life. (*I looked at the writer and he knew
what I meant. By his smile I knew he was happy about what I was
saying, so that made me feel a little better, although mainly I felt
like the awfulest fool in the world, even though I was saying things
that were true and meant a lot to me—I guess I just didn't like saying them in public that way. So then I went on.*) It embarrasses me
to say that I am in love with this city, for it seems such a false thing
for anyone to say, but I am in love with London, and I will never
stop being in love with it."

I sat down and by God everybody applauded as if I had just
made the Gettysburg Address, and the writer said, "You made the
best speech of the evening."

Pretty soon the meeting was over. Just before the writer and I
got away one of the millionaires came over and introduced himself
to me (as if we hadn't been introduced during cocktails—I guess he
didn't get my name or something) and he said, "I liked your piece
in *Time and Tide* very much. I think you could do a great story
about London for me. You must come and have lunch with me
soon and talk about it."

Well, the writer and I went along, and he told me the man was
one of the biggest men in the moving picture business in England,
and it was no little thing for him to ask me to lunch, but I said,
"I don't like him."

"Why not?" the writer said.

"I think he's a crook."

"He is," the writer said. "But you're going to learn that a lot of
important people in the world are crooks. The way to go about it
is to forget that they're crooks and see if you can do something
you want to do anyway, and let them have it for all the money
they're eager to pay you for it."

"I don't like him," I said. "The only thing I want is for the War
to be over."

CHAPTER 64

Duncan Olson Arrives in London and Tells Wesley the Secret of Yoga

ONE DAY Victor Tosca came into the office where the writer and I had our desks and typewriters, and with him was a big fellow with a bright round face all covered with freckles.

"This is Olson," Victor said. "He just came over to be in time for the Invasion."

I shook hands with Olson and knew he was the yoga man, not only because I remembered that he was but because he looked as if he was hep to something special. He was the calmest fellow I ever saw and the most easy-going. The writer had gone along with some Colonels and Majors to talk about a film everybody wanted to make about the Invasion, so the three of us sat around and talked. Olson wanted to know what I knew about yoga. He was surprised that I didn't know anything about it because he said I was a true "student." He said I knew about yoga all right. I just didn't know I knew about it. I didn't care about that because maybe it was so. He said Victor had a lot of yoga in him from birth but also didn't know it, and he said I had searched after the truth and found some of it—which was yoga—and it didn't matter that neither Victor nor I knew about yoga, although it wouldn't do us any harm to find out.

"Well, what is yoga exactly?" I said.

"Yoga," Olson said very slowly, "is knowing the higher truth or finding it out, and cherishing it—that's all."

Pretty soon the writer came back. I thought he would be amused with the three of us sitting around talking so big—none of us more than twenty years old—but if he was amused, he didn't show it. Olson told the writer how much he admired the writer's work, and the writer was very polite, although I know he never enjoyed having anybody tell him stuff like that. I know the writer thought he was one of the best writers in the world, and I guess he was too, but I know he didn't like people to crowd him with their approval. I guess the reason for that was that in his heart, even though he knew he was one of the best writers in the world, he knew he wasn't half good enough, so that made any approval from others irritate him a little. He was always very kind to me about my writing—and to anybody who happened to send him a story in the mail —or anybody who called on him with a story—but he didn't like anybody to be nice to him about his writing. I could see he liked Olson a lot, though, and was even a little pleased that Olson liked his writing. Pretty soon Joe Foxhall came into the office and shouted and laughed and went along, and when he was gone Olson said, "I'm sure that man isn't always that way. What's happened to him?"

Well, we knew what had happened to Joe but we didn't know how to put it. We knew the truth and thought it was fine. We thought it was funny too, because Joe himself thought it was funny. Nobody said anything for a moment, so then the writer said, "Joe's accepted a kind of happiness for himself recently that he knows isn't quite the real thing but will do for the time being—I think that's what's happened to him."

Olson wanted to know more, but we couldn't come right out and tell him. The Shaking Girl had changed Joe superficially, but he was still the same deep down underneath and just about the best fellow anybody could ever know. Pretty soon Olson (understanding truth as he did) understood that we didn't want to say anything more about it, so we went on to other topics and had at *them*.

Olson said he had been in England only a week, and only three days in London because they'd kept everybody on the ship four days for some reason or other, but he was living at Claridge's now and he'd be much obliged if we'd visit him any time. He didn't drink, he said, but there was always anything any drinking man might care to have—so I knew he was the son of a rich man all right because in the first place you've got to know somebody in order to get into Claridge's, and in the second place you've got to be in a position to pay for it, and it costs a lot of money. He said he didn't want it to get around that he was living at Claridge's because somebody might not like it. He wondered if he might say he was living on Pall Mall where Victor and Joe and the writer were living? Everybody said that that would be O.K., so Olson's name

went on the list with Victor's and Joe's and the writer's and mine
as being billeted on Pall Mall. I had kept my name on that list too
because I couldn't tell anybody I was married and living with my
wife, considering the whole thing had been attended to among ourselves and was not in accordance with Army procedure.

CHAPTER 65

*Jill Pretends to Be an Opera Singer Who Is Too Good for Wesley,
and Accepts the Admiration of All England*

JOE FOXHALL made me buy his portable typewriter for ten pounds
because he needed the money, didn't need the typewriter, wasn't a
writer, and I was (he said). I was glad to have it because it was a
fine machine. I started keeping a daily record of my life with Jill
because it seemed to me my son would want to know about his
father and mother when his mother was carrying him. I wrote
everything down for my son, telling him how I met Jill, and called
on her mother and got her permission, and I described the marriage
ceremony, so he'd know the whole truth about everything. Jill
loved to read everything I wrote. I taught her how to use the typewriter and asked her to write to our son too, and keep the record
alive when I wasn't home, because when I got home again I'd want
the story to be complete, both for me and for him, and once I was
gone I wouldn't have a chance to keep very much of a record.

Jill loved the idea, and pretty soon she got so she could type
pretty nicely. The things she wrote were so wonderful I knew our
son would be thankful to her some day for thinking so much of
him and writing everything down for him to read when he got
around to learning how. She wasn't too good at spelling and always wanted to improve, but I told her not to think about it because her spelling was better than the correct spelling. She'd write
"sence" for "sense," "rediculous" for "ridiculous" and "sivilisation"
for "civilization," but I knew what she meant, and I knew my son
would too. At first Jill didn't write much because she wasn't very
good at typing, and mainly she'd say how much she loved me and
couldn't believe she wasn't dreaming, but pretty soon all the lovely

things began to come into the story, and best of all was her wonderful comedy.

Sometimes when I'd come home after a meeting, she'd put on airs and be too good for me because she was an opera singer. She'd shoo me away and stand on the couch as if she were on the stage at Covent Garden and she'd sing in Italian—she sang more beautifully than anybody ever sang at Covent Garden—and then she'd step down from the couch as if the leading tenor had held his hand out to help her and she'd bow to the people and throw them kisses and accept bouquets of flowers and hug them and go off—but on the way, she'd stumble on purpose and almost fall, and lose her elegance and laugh at herself and come and lie on the floor to laugh with me.

And then sometimes instead of being an opera singer she'd be a ballet dancer, and she'd dance and dance with the son of our life in her. Never in all the world was anyone so light and graceful, never was anyone so twinkling and delicious, and I kept asking myself how I had ever been so lucky as to find her, how had such a precious thing come to pass? How had such a lunk as me come to have for my bride a girl so adorable, and how could she love me with my foolish face and my notion that yes, by God, some day I would be great? I *would* be great—maybe not a writer, but maybe *even* a writer. In any case I'd be great to my son, and if it was the will of God to spare me, to my daughter, and then to my second son, and then to my second daughter, and to their mother whose love for me was in everything she ever did, even in her anger with me, even in the fights we sometimes had.

If I was irritated with her for not hurrying out into the sunlight of a Sunday morning because she wanted to make herself more beautiful—sit and put creams and powders all over her face like a little girl playing grown-up—and hollered at her to hurry up for the love of God—and we'd fight—well, even then she'd make me laugh at myself for not understanding that when she went out to walk with me she wanted to be the prettiest girl in the world and just couldn't be rushed because whether it was true or not she was *going to be* the prettiest girl in the world and if I didn't like it, well, I could go walk alone. So then I'd grab her and we'd wrestle. She'd jump up on the couch to remind me that she had the devoted admiration of society, especially opera-lovers. The handsomest men of England were forever begging her to notice them. She'd sing an encore and thank everybody for loving her so much, for agreeing with her that she was the most beautiful girl in London—and hell, what could I do but love her and laugh at myself because she couldn't get dressed as fast as I could? And then late at night, after all the fun of walking through London, she'd lie on my shoulder and I'd feel her belly to see how my son was getting along, and she'd whisper, "If I'm lovely to you, it's only because your love has made me so." And I'd shout to my son, "Do you hear the words of your mother? Do you hear your lovely mother's lovely words?" And I'd adore her for being such a sweet girl for me, and such a delicious starting place for my son.

CHAPTER 66

Joe Foxhall Writes a Poem to His Son and Reads It to Wesley and Jill and Their Son

ONE DAY Joe Foxhall came to the writer and me and handed the writer two sheets of paper.

"Here is the first poem I have ever written that I am willing to let anybody read," he said.

The writer read the poem and handed it to me, and I read it. *To My Son*, Joe called the poem, even though he had no son, wasn't married, hadn't found the girl to be his wife, and was still having the affair with The Shaking Girl.

"What about it?" Joe said.

I looked to the writer to say something first, and he did.

"It's one of the finest things I've ever read," he said. "I feel about my son as you feel about yours. Only I didn't know you had a son."

"I haven't," Joe said.

"I didn't know you were expecting to have one, either," the writer said.

"I'm not," Joe said. "But surely a little bad luck like that shouldn't keep me from fatherhood, should it?—at a time like this when the chances to improve one's luck get poorer and poorer.

You've got a son. Victor's expecting one, and so is Jackson. I haven't even found my girl yet, and I don't think I'm going to find her before this War's over. But I *am* a father the same as any of you."

So then Joe turned to me. He didn't say anything, but I knew he wanted to know what I thought of what he had written.

"I'd like to make a copy of this," I said, "so I can read it to my son tonight."

"Your son's not born," Joe said.

"I want to read it to him anyway. His mother's born, and he's on his way. I think he ought to hear this while he *is* on his way."

"Will you do me a favor, then?" Joe said. He was very serious now, not the way he had been for so long. I never saw him more serious. "Will you let me read it to your son?"

"Sure," I said. "My son's no stranger to you. Sure you can read it to him."

"Thanks," Joe said.

I took Joe home with me that night. I told Jill about the poem Joe had written to his son—and how he didn't have a son and wasn't expecting one because he hadn't found his girl—but wanted to read the poem to our son, which was his in a way too, because he was our friend. Jill understood, and after supper she sat on a chair at the center of the room, and Joe read the poem to his son:

> *The tree brought down*
> *And treated into paper,*
> *I take for stone*
> *On which to say so little*
> *For the chance I have to say so much.*
>
> *But what is there to say*
> *Excepting yes and yes?*
> *What stone, what paper's needed for that?*
> *I say it with my eye on waking,*
> *Sleep says it to my dead,*
> *My hand says it to all hands lifted*
> *In crime or held forth in compassion.*
>
> *I cannot speak the language of no.*
> *Love's my language.*

Nothing less will do.
When all is said and done
That others say and do
I stand in sacred stupor saying this:
Oh I love you.
Oh blessed infant of my ignorance,
Child, child, and my own son,
Say yes for me,
For I am now better than half among the dead.
There's time for you, and better than time
The chance you'll get from the chance I took,
Which now, a little improved, is yours,
Through her whom I more than love,
Whom I adore, the mother of Truth,
And our best chance of all.
I took the chance and wrote the only book
That all my looking gave me leave to write.
If that book's neither day, nor morning, nor noon,
If it's all night and then more night,
If in it's none of heaven's blessed light,
Give me the light of thy young eyes.
My time was possibly a time of night.
I saw what heavenly things I saw
In night time's light.
I know there were other things,
For I saw other things, but as they had no eyes
They were forgot, for only that is truly seen
Which in its turn can see.

The tree which you shall climb,
From which you shall fall,
Which (brought down and treated into paper)
Shall be the stone on which you'll carve your words—
That tree is almost all there is to us—
Yourself, myself and your son—
But not quite all.
There is the forest, too.
The trees are other kinds,

For other treating—
But all together they are the only tree.
There is no forest in the paper—
The paper's either stone on which to say yes
Or stuff in which to wrap debris.
I've said my name to God too often.
I now say yours.
Ben Ben Ben Ben, my son,
In loving you I love all men—
The tree of them, the paper,
The stone and alphabet.

There is no more.
Say everything else, but also say yes.
Love's our language—nothing better will do.
To all things, all things, Ben, say I love you.
And better things adore.

Nobody said anything for a long time, then Jill went to Joe and kissed him on the cheek, and I loved her for knowing the beauty of what he had said to his son, which she and I had said with him to ours. And I know my son heard Joe's message, for his mother heard it and kissed Joe. I don't know what kind of a poem Joe wrote—maybe it's not a good poem at all. But I think I know what he said to his son in that poem, and I like a man who understands things so well that he can talk to a son that's not even scheduled to be born. I like a man who tells you by talking about the forest that the world is made up of all kinds of people and that every kind has its own purpose, great or little, and the whole thing may come to nothing, but just remember that if it comes to love, it comes to a lot. It comes to almost everything. Everybody likes to think a man who writes a poem is a fool, but it's not so—people talk poems—they live them—they dream them—and Joe Foxhall, he wrote one. He wrote one that he was willing to let a few others see. Then he went along to The Shaking Girl.

CHAPTER 67

Wesley Learns There Is No Truth Excepting It Is from Love and
The Writer *Receives a Mimeographed Letter*
That Fills Him with Irritation

ONE DAY I got a letter from Pop.

"I have just gotten up in the middle of the night," he said, "because I now remember what I promised to tell you when the time came but couldn't remember in Ohio. Here it is: 'There is no truth, no beauty, no right, no heaven, no God excepting it is from love.' Now I'll go back to sleep."

That was all. Well, I got to thinking about it. There I was with my Jill. There I was coming to be a human being at last because of her sweet love for me. And there was Victor Tosca and his beautiful wife and his wonderful mother, and Victor asking me again and again to promise to write about love. And there was Joe Foxhall with his poem saying, *When all is said and done that others say and do, I stand in sacred stupor saying this: oh I love you.* And now here was the message Pop had salvaged for me from the last War. What it came to was what I had come to know in my own way, and Victor in his, and Joe Foxhall in his. It came to the same thing: *There is no truth excepting it is from love.* That's all. I knew this was no little accidental thing that might happen to me and not to somebody else—it happened to everybody, it belonged to everybody. It was in Olson, in his searching after the truth. It was in the writer, in his regard for every moment of goodness in all people, in all things. It was in the woman I had met in New York, and it was in the one I had met in Ohio. God forgive them, it was even in the sons of bitches I hated. It was even in *them* in one form or another. But thinking about it scared me, for I knew we had come to hard times—bitter and lonely and evil—and I knew the times might be too much for love.

Well, the song hummed on and on, waiting to know. One thing came after another, but none of us knew. We sat and waited, each of us thinking of his own chance. We talked and laughed and drank beer and had fun and were happy, but we were waiting. We didn't know. These might be our last days. We all knew *that*. That was something none of us could forget. The times were the hard times, and we had come to them. The bombs came to the good people of London and took some of *them* along—surely unwilling to go, and a little surprised to be going so swiftly, because there was so much more to do—there was so much more love in them still.

One morning the writer handed me a mimeographed letter that had just been brought to him by a special messenger. It was getting closer and closer to the time for the beginning of the Invasion —everybody said so, everybody was sure the time was coming—so a boy came running from the Office of War Information to hand the writer a mimeographed letter. He made a terrible face and handed the letter to me.

I read the letter and thought it was wonderful. I thought the man who had written it must be a great man. By God, it was one of the holy epistles: *It has been suggested by several members of our monthly dining group, that, during this period when enemy action has made it impractical to meet at the P.E.P. Club as is our custom, that I organize a little surprise for Robert Samson, our indefatigable secretary, in the way of a token of appreciation for what he has done in organizing our dinners. I have accepted the suggestion, and I know you will want to respond. I don't know exactly what sort of present would be most appropriate, but I am certain that if each of us Americans who had shared the excellent Dutch Treat Hospitality of this group, contributed, say, three shillings, we would be making a very fine gesture indeed.*

The monthly dinner, as you probably know, was the outgrowth of a practice, initiated in 1942, of introducing interesting newly arrived members of American missions to a group of British officials concerned with American affairs who met regularly at the P.E.P. Club. It soon became apparent that such a useful informal gathering would be desirable if a small group met monthly to discuss a significant current topic related to our life and work in the U.K. A few members of the American Forces were included. When Henry Stanton returned to Washington, Carlton Cummings and I inherited the duty of attracting appropriate Americans to the meeting, in addition to the regular veterans who, as it were, got in on

*the ground floor in 1942. However, it has been Robert Samson who
has held the group together, made it a useful and often genuinely
important, and always interesting, forum. I know you will agree
that this contribution to Anglo-American acquaintance, discussion
and understanding should be acknowledged.*

*Could you, if you agree, try to get three shillings to me before
the end of this week? Thanking you in advance, I am, Yours sin-
cerely—*

"That's a nice letter," I said.

"It's one of the hideous documents of this War," the writer said.

"The man wants three shillings from everybody for a little
present for Robert Samson."

"I haven't had a letter from my wife in ten days, so a small
English boy comes running with this letter."

"If you weren't waiting for mail from home, you'd agree that this
is a beautiful letter, wouldn't you?"

"Yes, in a very special and ghastly way."

"I think it's innocent and touching."

"These are the men who are going to get the American and
English people to understand one another. They're charming.
They're sweet. You say hello to them, and that's the end of it,
isn't it? The P.E.P. Club. Our indefatigable secretary. Our life and
work in the U.K. What's the U.K., a ukulele?"

"You're just sore because you haven't gotten any letters from
home lately. You'll get some letters this afternoon maybe."

Sure enough in the afternoon there were seven letters for the
writer, so after reading them and laughing all the time he said,
"Hand me that letter again, will you?"

He read it again and handed it back.

"You're right," he said. "It's sweet and innocent, and no harm
to anybody. I'll send him the three shillings before the end of the
week and I hope the f——ing indefatigable secretary enjoys the
ninety-eight cent pipe they give him for having been in on the
ground floor since 1942, so to speak. And so to speak, I think you
know what I'd like him to do with the pipe."

He typed a note to the man who had sent the letter to him and
in the note he explained why he could send only two shillings and
sixpence, instead of three shillings—namely, that he had not been

in on the ground floor since 1942, hadn't taken part in any useful, genuinely important or interesting forum that he could remember, hadn't met the indefatigable secretary—and consequently felt that two shillings and sixpence was all he could afford for an appropriate gift for the son of a bitch, and he wouldn't be sending that much if he hadn't just received seven letters from home.

CHAPTER 68

The Mystery of the Man Who Dropped Letters Out of Windows Is Solved

AND THEN one day, best of all, Victor Tosca brought me a copy of *Stars and Stripes* and said, "Read this, will you?"

It was a newspaper story about a fellow who had been arrested in the city of Flagstaff, Arizona, by agents of the Federal Bureau of Investigation who had been searching for him for over three years as a draft evader. The story didn't seem worth reading, so I was about to put it down when I happened to look at the photograph of the man. It seemed to me I had seen the man somewhere before, and I could see that Victor believed I ought to be very interested in the story, which was a long one, so I went on reading. Pretty soon I got to the part that made me know who the man was. He was the fellow who had dropped letters out of the hotel across the street from The Great Northern. I studied the photograph, and there he was, exactly the same as he had been the day I had got to the street a little too late and was trying to buy the letter for a dollar from the girl who worked in the Automat.

Well, Victor was having himself a grand time. I could just see him laughing inside and feeling wonderful, but on the outside he was very quiet.

The fellow's name was Walter Marples. The newspaper story said F.B.I. agents had followed a unique sequence of clues back and forth across the country, from East to West, South to North, crisscrossing all over the place: unsigned letters dropped out of hotel windows. Finally they had caught up with him and nabbed him just before daybreak Sunday morning May 21st in a room overlooking the street in the Monte Vista Hotel of Flagstaff, Arizona. The fellow wasn't surprised at all and said, "Too late. I was thirty-eight three days ago, and the Army isn't taking men over thirty-eight."

I looked at Victor. He barely winked and said, "Go ahead, Jackson, count nine."

Then he couldn't hold it in any more and began to jump around with laughter.

The man looked serious in the picture, and in the story he sounded serious. He wanted to know why the F.B.I. men weren't in the Army considering they were so well trained in the use of fire-arms, and he wasn't. He said he had kept away from draft boards and all such things because he just didn't like War for himself personally. He said he felt a grave responsibility to the people of the world and couldn't see his way clear to shirk that responsi-bility at a time when the people were in such desperate need of the truth. He said he had dropped letters out of hotel windows just before daybreak in every state in the union—more than a hundred cities, more than three hundred hotels. He said he had never stolen anything or broken a true law in his life.

At the end of the newspaper story the reporter wrote that even though Marples was past thirty-eight he had a score to settle with the government—especially if the government could prove that he wasn't insane, which the government felt sure it could do. Even so, there seemed to be considerable admiration between the lines for Walter Marples.

Well, I started to laugh with Victor, so the writer wanted to know what the trouble was. Then he read the story and started to laugh too, but made me stop laughing long enough to tell him what I knew about the fellow, and what the fellow had said in the letters I had found.

The next day Olson (who'd heard about it too) brought us a copy of *The New York Times* and showed us another story about the man. This story was even better than the one in *Stars and Stripes* because it quoted from half a dozen letters the reporter had managed to steal from the F.B.I. men, and the stuff was wonderful. Olson said the man was a searcher after yoga. The story in *The Times* said Marples had gotten very angry at the government for trying to prove he *wasn't* insane because, as far as he was concerned, he was one of few sane men left in the world—so why did the government insult him with an investigation to prove he was something that he most certainly was? The story went on to say that his saying he was sane was making the government take special pains with the investigation because it was more than likely that the man had a record of insanity.

Several days later there was another newspaper story to read. It was in the Magazine Section of the Sunday *Times,* two full pages written by one of the top feature writers, and three excellent photographs of Marples. But he didn't have any record of insanity, and neither did his family. In one of the photographs Marples was sitting in the bend of a curved table with his back to the camera. Across the table were six of the ablest specialists of the country, one of them a woman. It was the funniest picture I ever saw because Marples didn't like having pictures taken behind his back and he had turned to look. The six specialists looked insane, whereas Marples looked only human and a little irritated. Between the lines of this story there was again a lot of admiration for Marples, although it seemed to the feature writer that the man didn't have a chance with the specialists. They were bound to put him down for mad and send him off to an institution, and sure enough the following Wednesday Olson brought another copy of *The Times* to us with another story about Marples, written by the same feature writer. Marples had been adjudged insane and was being taken to an asylum. He had managed to write one more letter to the people of the world, however, which he had sneaked to the feature writer, who had printed it in full:

"To the People of the World: Of course the mad say I'm mad, but don't you believe them. They think that if they put me in an insane asylum I'll go mad, but I won't. I intend to do a great deal of reading, and I shall consequently have more to tell you. They have taken my typewriter away, but that won't do them any good because if I can't get my letters written, I'll make them shorter than ever and have some inmate who is about to be discharged from the asylum memorize them and pass them along. I don't know how long I'll be in the asylum. I'm thirty-eight now, but even if I'm in the asylum ten years—even if the War lasts that long and everybody goes on being so insane that they think *I'm* insane—I'll only be forty-eight when I'm free again, and I'll have a lot to say about things. So wait for me. Don't trust anybody else unless it's somebody you love very much, who loves you very much. This is not the end. This is only an interruption. I will think of you always."

With this story there was a picture of Marples handcuffed to two F.B.I. men, one on each side of him. The F.B.I. men looked insane, but Marples looked something like a Saint, which the writer of the story claimed he was in a way. He gave the facts of Marples' life. He was born in Cairo, Missouri, the son of poor but upright parents. He went as far as the sixth grade at the Cairo Public School, whereupon he took a job as a farm hand in order to help maintain the family which consisted at that time of six younger brothers and sisters. At the age of seventeen he went to sea, sending the better part of his wages to his father and mother. He went to sea not to escape his responsibility to his family but because he felt the need to broaden his horizon. While at sea he discovered the writings of the Saints, as he called them, and he meant, of the American writers, Thoreau, Emerson, Melville, Whitman and Mark Twain. He did not consider himself a writer—could not allow himself so much vanity, but he believed his messages, some 393 of them since the beginning of the War, had not only reached the people of America but also the people of Europe, Asia and the various Islands. He did not feel that he was a martyr, for he had not suffered. He did not mind going to an asylum for the insane until the world got back its sanity because he was sure he would meet some sane people in the asylum and learn many good things from them.

Well, there it was, and Victor and I and Olson and the writer and Joe Foxhall thanked God for the fellow because if ever a man looked decent and talked as if he might actually be one of the few balanced men left in the world it was this fellow who had been nabbed by the law in a little old hotel in Flagstaff, Arizona. We were pretty sure most of the people of America felt the same way about him, too. The writers of the newspaper stories admired him, so we felt maybe there was some hope for the people of the world after all.

"Don't trust anybody unless it's somebody you love very much, who loves you very much," he said.

That's telling them, Marples old thirty-eight-year-old pal, old pal. Our best prayers are with you.

CHAPTER 69

Jim Kirby Tells Wesley of the Death of Dominic Tosca in the Pacific

ONE DAY the telephone rang and a fellow said, "I want to talk to Wesley Jackson." Well, it was Jim Kirby the newspaperman who had gotten Harry Cook and me to Alaska by airplane, and he said, "Where can we meet right away?" I told him we could meet at The Running Horse, so I ran down the street and pretty soon he came into the place in his War Correspondent's uniform.

"I just flew in to cover the Invasion," he said. "I was out in the Pacific. Who do you think I saw out there?"

"Harry Cook," I said. "How is he?"

"He's O.K.," Jim said. He swallowed a whole glass of lager. "He's O.K., thanks to a man named Dominic Tosca that I never met."

"What about Dominic?"

"He died before I got there. I saw Harry in the hospital and he told me."

"What did he tell you?"

"He told me Dominic Tosca saved his life and lost his own."

"Has his family been notified?"

"They won't be notified for some time yet. It happened only two weeks ago. Harry's O.K. He'll be able to walk again after a while. They're sending him home to San Francisco. He gave me your A.P.O. Number and the name of your outfit, and told me to look you up and tell you. He said, 'Tell him the guy who saved my life was a guy I didn't like, who didn't like me. So why did he do it?' "

"He did it for his brother Victor," I said.

"They came to the hospital to give him a decoration for saving Harry's life, but he drove them away, and then died. He would have lived a day or two longer, they said, if he hadn't gotten so sore. Harry said he swore an hour and then Harry thought he'd gone to sleep, but he'd died. I wrote a story about it, but I didn't use his name or Harry's. I wish to God he hadn't died. I wish I'd met a fellow like that."

"Dominic's mother," I said, "when she wrote to the President told him he could kill Dominic for the War if he had to—but not Victor. So Dominic's dead, he's been killed, so now they can't kill Victor too."

"What are you talking about?" Jim said, so I told him about Mrs. Tosca and Dominic and Victor.

"But hell," I said. "What are you going to do with a fellow who just knows he isn't going to get out of this War alive? His brother's dead. That's enough for one family. His brother didn't *have* to get himself killed. He did it for Victor, but suppose they kill Victor too?"

Jim Kirby told me the whole story of Dominic's death, and he told me how things were in the Pacific, and they were no good. He was glad to be in Europe because if he got killed over here it wouldn't be as bad as getting killed out there, where Dominic had gotten killed. He had to hurry along, but we agreed to meet at The Polish Club later that night.

Well, when I went back to my desk I just couldn't think. I had thought Dominic was a hoodlum when I had first seen him, but when I knew him a little better I knew he was the best brother any man ever had—he was such a good brother to Victor that he went to work and exposed himself to danger he didn't need to expose himself to in order to help a scared fellow nobody else would help. I was glad my pal Harry Cook hadn't been ashamed to tell Jim Kirby the whole truth about what had happened because if he hadn't told the truth I'd never have known what kind of a brother Dominic was to Victor. I had always thought nothing could kill Dominic Tosca—but Jesus Christ, love kills a man too, doesn't it? Loving somebody enough kills a man too, doesn't it? Love killed Dominic Tosca, didn't it? Harry didn't get things all jumbled up— he didn't lie about anything just because his life had been saved and now he was going home to San Francisco—his town and Dominic's town—and have a chance to figure out how to live the rest of his life. He didn't make it wonderful or silly. He was hurt and exposed and nobody would help him, not even his best friends, because it was foolish. He called out to them and *begged* them to help him, but they wouldn't do it. They liked him all right—they were his friends all right—but hell, you can't do something foolish when it's liable to do nobody any good and cost you your own life besides. Those fellows didn't love anybody the way Dominic loved Victor. Harry wasn't their brother, but Harry was Dominic's brother—Harry was Victor Tosca.

Pretty soon Joe Foxhall came into the office and wanted to know what was the matter with me. I hadn't figured to tell anybody what I knew, but I just had to tell Joe because the stuff was bothering me too much, so I made him sit down and I told him the whole story. He remembered Dominic all right, and Harry Cook, but he hadn't known the things I told him about Victor and his mother and his wife, and how Victor had made me give him my word to write about love and nothing else—because he knew he was going to die. Joe didn't know what to say, but felt so bad about Dominic —and all the rest of us too—that tears came to his eyes. Joe promised not to let Victor know about Dominic. He said he would take Victor out and they'd have some fun.

I went to The Polish Club after supper to have a drink with Jim Kirby, so we sat at the bar and drank one after another. Pretty soon Jim said, "Harry said you'd want to know about the fellows you used to know. I've got it all written down here somewhere."

He brought out a little leather-bound note-book and read the names of a lot of fellows I knew a little, who were all O.K.

"How's Nick?" I said.

"What's his last name?"

"Cully."

"Cully," Jim said. "Nick Cully. Here it is. He's dead."

Well, hell fire—I was glad all the other fellows were O.K., but Nick—for God's sake, what did Nick have to go and get killed for?

> *O Lord, you know I have no friend like you,* he used to sing.
> *If Heaven's not my home, O Lord, what will I do?*
> *Angels beckon me to Heaven's open door,*
> *And I can't feel at home in this world any more.*

I felt so mournful and sore remembering Nick's song I couldn't talk for a long time. I just kept hearing him sing the song.

"What happened to Nick?"

"Accident," Jim said. "He was out on some kind of patrol, and some Americans in another outfit shot him."

"Who else is dead?"

Jim read three other names, and among them was Vernon Higbee's—oh bloody bloody bloody—Vernon presented me with the first letter I ever got—the letter from the Preacher of the Seventh Avenue Presbyterian Church in San Francisco. Was Vernon dead too, for God's sake?

Jim said when you got around as much as he did you got used to a lot of fellows you knew in the morning being dead in the evening, but I said, "That's something I don't get used to."

I got to feeling lonelier and lonelier, so I thought I'd go home to Jill because pretty soon I wouldn't be seeing her for a long time, or maybe ever again. Jim told me a lot of things he'd found out about the War. He told me how much more he hated it now than ever before, and how much he'd hate people if they didn't straighten things out after the War. He got a little drunk and excited and said by God, he'd spend the rest of his life telling them they were liars every time they lied. He told me about fellows he'd met in hospitals—fellows with murder in them, who hated everybody—hated their own mothers and fathers and wives and children—paratroopers and Rangers and fellows with all kinds of decorations. They were good for War all right, but they weren't good for anything else, and pretty soon the War would be over—so what then? He hated everybody connected with the War. He hated the actors and actresses who went around trying to be funny or sexy or palsy-walsy for men whose friends had been killed, who might be dead tomorrow themselves. He hated the newspapermen who talked about the special fighting qualities of "our boys" and how "our boys" did things this way, and didn't do them that way, and were the best in the world and loved a fight. "What about our boys who are dead and can't tell us anything about it?" Jim wanted to know.

Jim was full of hate, but it didn't seem to me as if he would ever be able to do very much about anything except sit at a bar and cuss at everybody.

The news he'd brought from the Pacific was the worst I'd ever heard, and I didn't like it. It made me lonelier and more scared every minute. Dominic Tosca. Nick Cully. Vernon Higbee. Hell, they were all dead—and does anybody know what it means to be dead?

I went home to Jill and took her in my arms and cried, because I can't understand what it means to be dead—all I know is I don't like it for the fellows I've met in the world, I don't like it for the fellows I haven't met, and I don't like it for me.

CHAPTER 70

The Invasion of Europe Begins

WELL, APRIL and May went along, and the days of June began, and they were bright sweet days—but then one morning—Saturday, June 3rd—Joe Foxhall and Victor Tosca and Duncan Olson and three other Privates and a Lieutenant and a Captain went off, and everybody knew the Invasion would begin very soon. I asked the Captain why I wasn't in Victor's unit, because I wanted to be with him, but he said the rest of us would follow soon. Victor's unit was going over on a special assignment. They'd return to London soon after we'd gone over. Then they'd go over again, and we'd all be over together, till the end of the War in Europe.

Three days later we knew the Invasion had started. It was all over London, but there was no noise or excitement. There was a kind of holding of the breath. Everybody seemed to be praying, even the people in the streets. You could see it in their faces and the way every man went about his business. Would the damn thing work? That was the question. After all that preparing would it work?

I went home early in the afternoon of that day and took Jill to walk through the streets with me once more. We went past St. James's to Green Park, out to Piccadilly, and there we heard the clarinet and banjo team wailing away on *Whispering Grass*. I went up to them and gave them half a crown and asked them to play *Valencia* for me, so they did. But I couldn't go away, I wanted to hear my song again, so pretty soon, after they'd played two other songs and moved a block down the street, I gave them two half crowns and asked them to play it again. They played it three times, and then Jill and I went home and sat down and couldn't talk and I kept wondering "How's Victor and Joe and Olson, for God's sake? Where are they now?"

The next day it was our turn, so we went off, and I didn't even get a chance to say good-bye to Jill. I'd told her it would be that way, so be sure not to worry. I'd be O.K.

So we went to the War, but what the hell is a War? It's the same thing, and I couldn't understand why we weren't getting killed. I expected the War to come tearing at us the minute we set out for it, but it wasn't that way at all. We got on trucks and got off trucks, we got on boats and got off boats, we got on trucks again and got off trucks again, we walked and stopped—and all the time I expected the War to come out of the sky like a hurricane and have at us, but it didn't. Once we got into France and out along the country roads every man thought he was near home because the countryside looks like home wherever home happens to be. France seemed like California to me. There were fellows in our unit from Virginia and Nebraska and Louisiana and Oregon, and they all thought France was like home. Europe seemed sweet and peaceful in the countryside of northern France. There were birds around, and insects, and all the sweet smells of things growing, and French children, and girls, and old women, and young men of one sort or another, and cattle and horses and dogs—it was the same, there was nothing different about it.

"Where's the War?" everybody wanted to know. "We're all O.K. Where's the War?"

Well, the War was down the road a piece. Death was down there, too. Down the road was the same kind of place we were in, but the War was there, and we weren't. We passed through a village, and then another, and then a pretty good-sized town, but everybody was busy living. Nobody was busy dying.

It was the same the next day, except that we took moving pictures of some enemy dead, and some prisoners, and some stuff in town. We took pictures of troops hurrying by in trucks, or walking, or people coming back to their homes, or anything that seemed interesting and worth having on film.

The next night we were closer to the War. We began to dig in, in case we needed cover during the night, and then at last the War came to us. Everybody threw himself on the ground and expected the worse, but it was only one shell—a big one that wheezed and howled from a good way off. It scared us plenty. We didn't get up from the grass and dirt for a long time. I studied the grass and ate some of it. The shell hit the slope of the hill behind us and sent a lot of the earth flying all over, but none of the stuff hit any of us, so after that we had been in the War. We had been in it for sure—a shell had come close to us—but it wasn't much worse than London being bombed, except that it was out in the open. We all felt better after that because we had tasted enough War to let us know how it was and we had come through O.K., every one of us—nobody even a little hurt—but we didn't like it, and everybody calculated that if we had been on the slope of the hill, instead of down in the valley, well, then, some of us would have been hurt and some of us would have been killed.

We finished digging our slit-trenches and practiced diving into them and tried them out for comfort, and then it was night. We had eaten our field rations and they had tasted good because we hadn't eaten them very often and we had been very hungry, but they weren't home cooking—they weren't food at all. They were scientific stuff based on energy units, and they didn't care to be anything else.

We didn't run into anybody we knew, but we saw a lot of different outfits. I got to believing Victor and Joe and Olson were O.K. because we were so O.K., but the next night we weren't so very O.K. Our own planes came over to bomb the enemy, only they went to work and dropped the bombs on us. We hit the dirt again —we didn't have any slit-trenches that night—so we just hit the dirt and waited. The noise and nonsense were awful, but I couldn't believe stuff like that was ever going to kill me or anybody like me— any man in the world—but I was mistaken. Not far from us some fellows in another outfit had two dead and five wounded. I didn't know those fellows and I didn't go over to see them like some of the fellows in our outfit did because I don't like looking at a man in terrible pain, or a fellow about to die and nobody to talk to worth talking to.

But I knew it could happen as easy as anything. It might not be the way you thought it would be—it might be a silly surprise—but it could happen like nothing. A lot of fellows die in a War from things that go on all the time—all kinds of accidents, all kinds of mistakes, all kinds of miserable happenings on account of stupidity. We'd heard stories about such things ever since we'd gotten over. The countryside was full of fellows who'd gotten theirs for no good reason. In the first landings a lot of fellows got washed overboard and were drowned. A lot of fellows who weren't tall stepped off the landing boats all loaded down with their junk and didn't come up again—there wasn't time to fish for them—everybody just kept piling off and hoping he wouldn't sink so deep he wouldn't come up again. You move fast when it's time to move and the miserable and horrible things that haunt your sleep come to seem like nothing. You keep moving, and pretty soon you're walking in Europe.

CHAPTER 71

*Wesley Dreams of Facing the Firing Squad, Wakes Up,
and Is Captured by the Germans*

ONE NIGHT I dreamed a dream that scared me a hundred times more than anything ever scared me when I was awake. I don't know what had happened, but they had taken Victor Tosca and Joe Foxhall and Duncan Olson and me to a wall to shoot us. I didn't know who it was that was going to shoot us—I just knew that unless something unbelievable and beautiful happened in less than two minutes we were finished, and that would be the end of Jill for me, and my son, and Pop, and Mom, and Virgil, and Uncle Neal—and I didn't like it. But there they were with their rifles, waiting to shoot us. So then they came to blind-fold us. One after another Victor and Joe and Olson took the cloths and tied them around their eyes. I took the cloth they offered me and was about to tie it around my eyes too, when I said to myself, "I'll be damned if I'm not going to see as long as I can, even if it's only another minute." I wouldn't put the cloth over my eyes, so the man in charge said it was all right. He marched back to his men and started to give orders. The first row of men went to one knee when he gave the first order. On the second order both rows lifted their rifles to their shoulders and aimed at us—at *me*—and Jesus, blessed Jesus, I didn't like that at all. The man was giving his orders in cadence—one, pause; two, pause; and the next was three, but there wouldn't be any pause for me after that. I had no time at all, but I had time enough to feel fear and rage and anger enough for everybody in the world, and all the time I expected to hear the guns and see the flash of light, and then move on to the next thing, which I didn't want to move on to, because I was going alone—without Jill, without my son. I didn't want to go because I didn't know that place and I knew this one and liked it. I liked this place with all my heart and soul, and I wanted it for as long as I could have it, and the time it takes for a bullet to travel from the muzzle of a rifle to my head didn't seem time enough to me. I kept wanting this place and expecting to be in the next, and then I woke up sweating and thanked God for sparing my life, and cursed the world for making me dream a dream like that.

The next day I got to brooding about the meaning of the dream. Sometimes I decided it meant I would be killed for sure, and sometimes I decided it meant I'd be spared.

I kept trying to get news of Victor and Joe and Duncan all the time, but there just wasn't any. Then some gossip came through that some of the boys in that unit had been killed and some injured, but I paid no attention to it because you always hear too much gossip in a War and all it does is bother you. The War seemed to be going slower than it was supposed to, but everybody said everything was fine. The worst news was about London and the flying bombs. That put me to worrying about Jill night and day because it had been all right for us to stay in our house during a raid when we were together because we *were* together, but I didn't want her to stay there alone. I wrote to her and told her to send for her mother, or if her mother couldn't stay with her, to send for a brother or a sister. But I never knew when she'd get my letters because I'd heard the mail was slow, and I'd gotten none from her.

My partner was a cameraman named Graham who had joined our unit in England because he was an American by birth. His parents were English and he had lived in London most of his life, but inasmuch as he was technically an American he had chosen to go into our Army, and he'd taken his Basic Training at Lichfield. He was one of the most English fellows I ever saw, but he was a good fellow and we got along fine. Sometimes we'd get sent off for a day or two to get some special pictures, but Graham would forget his assignment and think of something else, and I'd go along. At first everybody had some kind of classification. I had come to be classified as a writer, but when the time came to go to the War and we had gotten to it, well, it didn't matter what you were classified. I went along in a jeep with Graham and a driver named Vanhook. My job was to help carry the camera and get it set up, and sometimes I tried to get the people involved under control, so they wouldn't act up just because there was a camera looking at them. Vanhook drove and watched and helped out. Graham was in charge. He had a pistol in a holster and loved the War and was never so happy as when it seemed things were going to get exciting. He was always disappointed to learn that none of our fellows had been killed or injured, but for all that he was a nice fellow and very eager to get results. I'm sorry about the way things turned out for him, but I guess he meant to do the right thing.

We had been out two days and two nights and we'd photographed what we'd been sent to photograph and a lot of other things besides—flowers in the field, French peasants smiling at us, beautiful girls holding baskets full of tomatoes, and anything else Graham took a fancy to, all of which I liked too. It was time to get into the jeep and go back with our stuff, but on the way Graham got an idea and told Vanhook to turn off the road because he thought if we went about ten miles out of our way we would get some real stuff. Vanhook turned and drove the jeep where Graham told him to go because Graham was a Sergeant and Vanhook was a Corporal. Pretty soon we came to an outfit that was resting for the evening. Graham told them what we were after and asked them where we could find it, and they told him. So we drove on and pretty soon we were there. It was called the front, but it was the same as ever, except that every once in a while there'd be a big shell and we'd hit the dirt and wait. Graham decided to go down the road two or three miles from the front and set up the camera in a nice place and wait, because he'd heard there would be some tanks coming along, and some others from the enemy to meet them, and he'd photograph the battle. He hoped we'd find a nice hill with some trees, so we could set the camera up nicely.

We found a nice spot all right. It was quiet and peaceful, and except for the shelling every two or three minutes, you wouldn't know you were in a War at all. We got out our field rations and sat under the trees and ate them slowly and kidded around and felt pretty good because it was a cool green spot and the camera was all set and chances were we'd see some good stuff along about daybreak.

Well, it just goes to show you how unaccountable the mysteries of living and dying are because there we were as peaceful as we could be, eating and talking and feeling glad, thinking we'd get our stuff in the morning and scoot back to our outfit and have been in the War better than ever and none the worse for it when all of a sudden somebody said very quietly in very good English, "I'm afraid you boys are my prisoners, so just stand up with your hands over your heads."

Well, hell, I didn't even look around—that was good enough for me. I thanked God my rifle was in the jeep because I didn't think I wanted to shoot anybody who spoke such good English and was so calm about taking us prisoners—if it wasn't one of our own boys playing a joke on us. Joke or no joke, I got to my feet along with Vanhook and my hands were over my head—and it seemed awful silly too.

Pretty soon a young fellow came strolling out where we could see him. He was the enemy all right, but the only way you could tell for sure was from his uniform and helmet. He was alone, it seemed, and he had a pistol in his right hand. All of a sudden I heard a pistol shot and knew it wasn't the enemy's pistol because he'd hit the dirt and hadn't fired yet. So then he fired, and Graham fired again, and the enemy fired again, and then Graham groaned and fired once more, and then we heard him fall. We didn't turn to look at him, though. The German got to his feet very slowly and waved to his men, and then six more of the enemy came along. He put his pistol away and went over to look at Graham while his men examined the jeep and took the rifles out of it. Then the

officer came to Vanhook and me and told us it was O.K. to sit down
and finish our supper.

"Your friend," he said, "was very foolish. He made an awful big
target standing there that way. I don't think he's a very good pistol
shot, either. I only meant to stop him, but I'm afraid I can't help
being accurate with the pistol. What are you up to out here where
you don't belong?"

Well, I knew we weren't supposed to answer any questions—just
give our name, rank, and serial number—but I guess Vanhook forgot because he said, "Pictures."

"Who told you to come here?"

"Graham," Vanhook said, and he pointed to poor Graham lying
on the grass.

"Who told *him* to come here?"

"It was his own idea."

"A very poor idea," the German said. "Have you got any American cigarettes?"

We had brought along a couple of cartons apiece, so we got them
out and he said, "May I have a pack? I'm very fond of Chesterfields
—smoked them all the time I was at Cornell." He turned to his
men and said a few things to them in German just as casually as
he was talking to us. One of them stood guard with his rifle at
parade rest, and the others gathered around and looked at us and
smiled, and we knew they wanted cigarettes too, but we didn't say
anything because the officer was in charge.

"Do you mind if the boys have a pack each, too?" he said. "You
can refuse, you know. You'll be wanting them pretty soon."

We said they could help themselves, so the officer told them to
take a pack each and they did, and everybody was sitting around
smoking.

"It's rather odd," the officer said, "that you fellows should be
taken prisoner by us when so many of our fellows are being taken
prisoner by you. Your unlucky friend should have acted on orders."

We sat around ten or fifteen minutes, then the officer got up
lazily and talked to his men in German. They lifted Graham off
the grass and loaded him into the jeep and put an overcoat over
him. Then he asked Vanhook and me to break the camera down
and load it into the jeep, so we did. Then he told us to sit together

in the front. He'd sit behind us. He asked Vanhook to drive slowly because it was a pleasant evening and we had a nice drive ahead and he wanted to look at the countryside. He gave some more orders to his men, then we drove off. Vanhook drove very slowly and it took us more than an hour to get to where we were going, which was an open stockade.

"This is for tonight only," the officer said. He asked us to get our personal stuff together and go with him. He left us with another officer in a little shack and he said, "I'll say good-bye to you now—and thanks for the cigarettes."

Well, the officer at the desk was an old man, very tired, but he spoke good English too. All he asked was name, rank and serial number. At the time it never occurred to me that everything was so different from the way they'd said it would be in the Training Films. The six German soldiers weren't sore at Vanhook and me at all. The officer shot Graham all right, but there was nothing else he could do, and he didn't enjoy doing it at all. The officer had hit the dirt the way he was supposed to do in order to be a smaller target. Graham had had enough time to do the same thing, but he hadn't done it.

Later on I asked Vanhook if it hadn't been our duty to run for our rifles when Graham had started shooting, and he said it hadn't occurred to him and a good thing it hadn't, he said, because if we had run for our rifles we would have been shot too, and then they would have gotten all the cigarettes. I asked him if the stuff had scared him much and he said it hadn't, so then I asked him why it hadn't scared him, so I could compare his reasons with my reasons, and sure enough we had the same reasons. First of all it was so peaceful out there that Vanhook didn't think anybody would feel like hating anybody else or shooting him unnecessarily. When he'd heard the officer's voice he knew the man was serious but not excited and wouldn't shoot if you didn't make him shoot—so why make him shoot? I asked him if he thought Graham had done right and he said, "I think Graham thought his chance had come to be a hero—I sure am sorry he got killed, but any good soldier will tell you he did the wrong thing."

We spent the night in that stockade, out in the open, getting acquainted with the other fellows who were there. Most of them had gotten captured pretty much the way we had—by having some-body take them where they had no business going, but they said it wasn't half bad and the Germans seemed to know capturing us was mainly a waste of time for them because we were moving down on them all the time.

The German guards had picked up a little English from our fellows and were friendly and carried on conversations about the same old things—home and girls and our side and your side and to hell with all Armies, take a look at my daughter, have you got anything to swap?

CHAPTER 72

Victor Tosca Tells Wesley of the Death of Joe Foxhall

THE NEXT day they took us in trucks to another open stockade about a hundred miles away, but I'll be damned if I knew where we were. I kept thinking of Jill and wondering how I'd ever get a letter home to tell her I was captured but O.K., considering it takes such a long time through the regular channels.

The new place had a lot more fellows, so Vanhook and I strolled around looking to see if there was anybody we knew or anybody who'd seen anybody we knew. It was a pretty big place and chock full of us, mostly in groups of six or seven, talking and telling stories or gambling, so it wasn't easy to get a good look at every-body. Every once in a while there'd be a fellow sitting on the ground just thinking—homesick most likely and hating to be inside barbed-wire that way, as if he were a head of cattle.

It was too surprising to surprise me because I hadn't figured on it at all. There on the ground, just sitting, was Victor Tosca. I was so glad to see him I decided to sit down beside him and wait for him to know who it was. The place was too jammed for anybody to pay any attention to anybody else, so when I sat down beside him he didn't budge. I waited a long time feeling fine because I could see he was O.K., and that's all I wanted to know. I just sat beside him and didn't say anything because I thought he'd look

around to see who it was and we'd have ourselves a laugh. I decided
that even if he didn't turn around for an hour I'd just sit there,
because that seemed to me the way to do it, better than making a
fuss, because who knows what he'd gone through? Except for Graham eating his supper one minute and being dead the next, what
had happened to Vanhook and me wasn't anything.

Well, Victor didn't turn and I didn't budge. We just sat there
and I got to wondering if maybe something wasn't wrong with him
because it was more than ten minutes that I'd been sitting beside
him and if he hadn't budged or turned to see who it was in ten
minutes maybe something was the matter.

About ten minutes later when he turned at last he saw me all
right, but I decided not to say anything. After a minute or two
more he turned and looked again. This time he kept looking.

"I sure am glad to see you," he said. "I kept thinking it *might* be
you, but I couldn't believe it. You O.K.?"

"Sure. How about you?"

"I've gone a little crazy."

"That's O.K."

We got up together.

"I've got something to tell you," he said.

When we found a private place to talk he looked at me a long
time and then he said, "Joe's dead, Olson's badly hurt, and do you
know that silly, twitching, jumping Lieutenant who went over with
us? Well, he's O.K., and I'm O.K."

Then he said, "This is what I want to tell you. Joe did it for
me. I haven't talked to anybody in nine days. Nobody knows him—
but you and I know him—so I can tell you. I still don't know what
the hell happened, but all of a sudden he knocked me down, and
then I heard a lot of crazy noises. All hell broke loose and I kept
hearing the crazy noises—loud and soft, loud and soft. Pretty soon
all the noise stopped, and there was Joe sitting on the ground looking at the grass. Most of the left side of his face was gone, and his
whole left arm—just bone and muscle dangling there—and his left
leg naked and bloody to the foot. Olson was limping around, full
of shrapnel—but that twitching Lieutenant—he was O.K., and I
was O.K."

Victor waited a minute and then said, "I've gone a little crazy. I don't know what to do about Joe because he's dead now. I looked at him, but what I saw didn't look like Joe any more. But it *was* Joe, and he was looking at me. I kept myself from getting sick, so he wouldn't know he looked so awful.

"He scared the hell out of me," Victor said. "He told me to sit down a minute, but you should have seen his face when he tried to talk.

" 'That was a good breakfast we had in Chicago that time, wasn't it?' he said.

"Then he started to laugh, but it wasn't laughing. He was just crying fast. Pretty soon he stopped crying and said to tell The Shaking Girl that he loved her. He said to tell you to remember—that's all he said—remember, so I guess you know what he wants you to remember. Then he told me about Dominic—yes, I know Dominic's dead. Then he asked me if I'd sing that song to him, and hell, I just sat there and made up my mind to try to sing it. But my voice wouldn't sing, so then I decided to talk it. I got as far as *Everybody calls me*— Then Joe whispered 'Ben, Ben,' and choked and twitched and fell over and tried to live a minute more and then stopped. That's the end of Joe Foxhall, so where is he now?"

Victor didn't say anything for a minute. Then he said very softly, "I thought I was going to get killed. I was ready for it. I believed it would happen right away. I kept waiting, and I was waiting when Joe knocked me down and took my place. But I didn't want Joe to take my place. I didn't want anybody to take my place. But *Joe* was waiting too. He was waiting with me all the time. He wanted to get to me before the War did—and he made it. He *just* made it. A War doesn't give you much time. I've gone a little crazy, though, because I know I ought to be dead, but I'm alive, and Joe's dead. I don't think I'm going to get killed any more. But what am I going to do about Joe?"

CHAPTER 73

*Wesley Studies the Various Groups in the German
Prison Camp*

VICTOR AND I stayed captured by the Germans until the last day of
August when they went off and left us. We saw a lot of stuff in that
Prison Camp—some of it funny and wonderful and beautiful, and
some of it terrible and ugly. The Germans didn't say anything to
us when they left. They just packed up in the night and went off,
and the next day we waited and waited, but the Germans were
gone. There were over a thousand of us cooped up inside barbed-
wire, and we'd been there a long time, so when it got around that
the Germans had gone and left us—well, we turned into a mob.

Victor and I had met in that Prison Camp the day before the
Fourth of July, so we had been there together almost two months.
The Fourth of July was celebrated, but not very successfully. Somebody tried to put on a show, but it didn't work. When a fellow
got up to make a speech everybody told him to skip it. They were
rude to the fellow, who had only meant to do something right. The
show was supposed to be a kind of stage show—a little vaudeville—
but nobody wanted to bother with it, so after a half hour it fell to
pieces and everybody went back to waiting.

I'll mention the terrible things first and get them out of the way.

One night a boy cut his wrists and was found dead in the morning.

And one afternoon two paratroopers who had been pals got irritated with one another because one of them said a certain girl they
both knew had been had by six of their friends (not counting themselves) and the other said she had been had by only five. The sixth
was also a paratrooper but a fellow one of them hated, so he didn't
want that paratrooper to have had the girl too. His pal kept saying
that he *knew* he had had her too, so the fellow who said the girl
had been had by only five took his pal by the throat and began to
choke him. But his pal had been taught a few things about hand-
to-hand fighting too, so they almost killed each other. When they

had been separated they agreed through the fellows speaking for them that one of them would stay on one side of the stockade and the other on the other, because they insisted that if they ever met again they would kill each other—and they meant it too, although they had been pals and had been through a lot of campaigns together. They kept their word, and each of them stayed on his side of the stockade. They never spoke to each other again.

There were a half dozen little fights every day because everybody was so tense, but the fight between the paratroopers was the only serious one.

The fellows divided up into little groups which were held together by the ties that have always made men feel related.

For the most part, fellows who had been in the same outfit stuck together because they had the same things to remember and talk about.

Then there were little groups that were held together because the fellows came from the same city and liked to talk about home or people they remembered.

Then there were groups that were formed because the fellows had had the same trades or professions in civilian life and liked to talk over the circumstances of their work in the past and prospects for the future.

Then there were regional groups. Southerners liked to stay together because they felt the same way about Negroes—and Negroes liked to stay together because they knew how the Southerners felt, or didn't want to be bothered. There were only nine Negroes in the stockade. Only three of them were Southern and weren't college graduates—but the other six were fond of the three who weren't as educated as they were.

Fellows from the Far West—California, Oregon and Washington —felt close together.

Then there were fellows who happened to have the same last name. Sometimes there would be only two and the name would be unusual and they would try to understand how they had come to have that name—Menadue—and yet weren't related and didn't know the same people.

Or there would be two fellows—one from Tennessee and the other from North Dakota—whose last name was Rosevar. They would take up with one another and talk about their families and get to be pals because their names were so unusual, and yet they weren't related.

There were seven Smiths, and they called each other Smithy, and so did everybody else. The four or five Browns got along nicely and were often together.

Then, fellows with the same temperament seemed to like hanging around together—comedians especially, but a lot of fellows who were serious-minded stayed together too.

Fellows feeling homesick would hang around a lot, but as soon as the feeling was gone they'd go back to another group. As soon as they weren't quite as homesick as they'd been, they'd take up with the sporting crowd, for instance, which was always busy with little athletics that didn't require running or a lot of space: Indian wrestling, standing broad jump, distance spitting, and stuff like that.

Or they'd take up with the prophesying group and prophesy this and that.

Or they'd take up with the dreamers—fellows who liked to discuss what romantic things they were going to do after the War.

As soon as a fellow with a cold got over his cold he'd leave his pals with colds and go along to one or another of the other groups, such as the discussers of current events, politics, religion, Communism, or philosophy.

Then there were size groups: little men, medium-sized men, and big men.

Or appearance groups: handsome men, not quite handsome men, plain men, or strange-looking men.

Then there were personality groups.

Fellows with a long record of conquests liked to hang around together and compare notes and go over each success in detail.

Fellows with the attitude that women are meant to be stalked and taken like any other animal not easy to stalk and take enjoyed one another's company.

Fellows who believed their wives were lonely worried about them and stayed together.

Fellows who felt sure their wives hadn't been true to them after so much separation spent a lot of time together wondering whether they ought to get divorced, forgive and forget, or catch the son of a bitch (or the several of them) who took their wives away from them while their backs were turned and they were fighting the War. But even among themselves these fellows were divided because some of them sympathized with their wives. The fellows who didn't sympathize with their wives would be irritated with the fellows who did and would consider them poor specimens of manhood, and the talk would get pretty heated and confused sometimes.

Then there were the fellows who had had very few women.

And the ones who had had none—but this group was very small because they were shy about it.

Then there were those who probably hadn't had any women, but liked to say they had, and understood one another and got along all right.

Then there were the men with one child, and the men with two, and the handful with three or more. The man with seven children —Orin Oakley, of Kentucky—belonged to no group at all. He just sat and invented names for famous men. One of the best was Rearview Mirror.

Then there were the men who went after women a lot but admitted they hated them and only liked to bring them down a peg, especially the proud ones—make them fall in love and then let them suffer. These men liked to discuss the pitiable conditions to which they had reduced many a vain hussy—made them humiliate themselves; made them write letters, send telegrams, telephone all the time; made them leave their husbands; made whores out of them; made them beg to be loved; made them go mad, and so on and so forth.

Then there were groups made up of cynics—fellows who were sure the world was shot to hell for good, and hated humanity because it stank.

Then there were the laughers; the moaners; the travelers; the stay-at-homes; the foolish; the wise; the gamblers; the readers; the chess crowd; the dice boys.

There were all kinds, but no matter how they broke themselves up, they were all one thing: prisoners.

They were captured by the Germans, and they were captured by the Americans—and they didn't like being captured by anybody.

CHAPTER 74

John Wynstanley of Cincinnati, Ohio, Puts on a Straw Hat and Plays the Trombone, Enchanting Enemy and Friend Alike

THERE WAS a fellow in the stockade named John Wynstanley who had a trombone. He'd carried it with him from his home in Cincinnati, and he'd kept it in the War two years. He was a little bit of a fellow with a grave preoccupied expression on his face. He didn't look more than sixteen or seventeen years old, although he was past twenty.

Everybody knew he had a trombone, but Wynstanley wouldn't bring it out of the case and play it because he said he couldn't play it unless he had a strawhat on his head. He had always had a strawhat, and he'd brought it to France with him, but somebody had stolen it.

If somebody would get him a strawhat, he'd play the trombone.

Well, nobody had a strawhat, so the only thing to do was take the matter up with the Germans. There were three or four of our fellows who could speak German, so one of them told the Guards what was needed, but the Guards said they didn't have a strawhat. They said they'd like to hear somebody play the trombone all right, but where would they be able to get a strawhat?

The Guards were told to scout around, and tell their friends, and see if they couldn't find a strawhat somewhere because Wynstanley couldn't play the trombone until he had a strawhat on his head. Maybe he really knew how to play the trombone, and if he did, it would be worth it.

The Guards said they would look into the matter.

After a while everybody decided Wynstanley couldn't play the trombone. They decided he had invented the story about the strawhat, so he could get out of being exposed.

Wynstanley prided himself on being a good trombone-player,

and he didn't like the slur, so on the evening of Sunday, July 9th, he brought the trombone out of the case and put it together. Everybody gathered around and waited—at least three hundred fellows.

Wynstanley wet his lips and pressed them against the mouthpiece and slided the trombone back and forth a couple of times to get it moving smoothly.

Then he began to play something that just about brought heaven into that miserable place. But, sure enough, he stopped playing and said, "Got to have a strawhat on my head—can't play worth a damn without a strawhat."

So then everybody knew he wasn't kidding. They ran over to the Guards and told them for God's sake, send to Paris for a strawhat because this boy knows how to blow the trombone, so the Guards said yes, they had heard him and would try their best.

Nobody badgered Wynstanley to play the trombone without a strawhat on his head after that because there is something almost religious about a man who knows how to cope with a horn, especially a trombone, and is able to bring music out of it. Everybody had a lot of respect for Wynstanley for having lugged the trombone half across the world, and after he had played enough to let everybody know he wasn't bluffing, they knew this wasn't any ordinary fellow, this was somebody special, and the only thing to do was get him a strawhat.

Wynstanley showed some of the fellows a snapshot of himself when he was nine years old. He had a trombone to his lips and a strawhat on his head.

"Always wore a strawhat when I played," he said.

Well, the song Wynstanley had started to play that night was *You'll never know just how much I love you,* and hell, it was wonderful—it was just naturally out of the world—and he went on to *You'll never know just how much I care*—just as easy and heartbreaking as anything could be, but when he came to the next few bars, well, he just couldn't go on.

Instead of being impatient with him—instead of thinking he was affected or silly—everybody took to feeling sympathetic. They tried to comfort him, and they said, "That's all right, Johnny—you'll get your strawhat, and then you can really play." Everybody could see he *wanted* to play, but was too good to let himself play poorly.

Well, the days and nights dragged along and the groups formed and broke up and re-formed and changed and were abandoned and new groups came along. But everybody had all kinds of stuff going on inside himself that was all his own, and there was no grouping of that stuff at all.

And everybody knew John Wynstanley was there with his trombone. Everybody had heard enough of the song he had started to play to want him to finish it, but nobody tried to rush him into doing a poor job.

One day one of the Guards told one of our fellows who knew German that according to some gossip he'd heard another Guard was returning from leave in Paris, and he was bringing a strawhat with him.

So everybody got happy about that and the news was carried to Wynstanley.

"When's he coming with it?" Wynstanley said.

"Any day now," somebody said. "Does it have to be any particular size?"

"It ought to fit," Wynstanley said, "but if it's straw and I can get it on my head, it'll do."

So then along with all the other waiting—waiting for the War to end, waiting to be captured back by the Americans, waiting to get to some place where we could get our mail—we started waiting for Wynstanley's strawhat to arrive.

Waiting's waiting and it's no trouble at all while you're waiting for a lot of important things to wait for a few unimportant ones too.

At last the fellow who'd been to Paris came back and sure enough, he'd brought a strawhat with him. He said he wanted to give it to Wynstanley himself. He came inside the stockade, and the fellows who spoke German walked along with him to Wynstanley who was sitting on the trombone case, the way he always sat. If he got up to walk, he carried the case with him by the handle. He took the thing with him wherever he went. Well, Wynstanley looked up at the German who'd been to Paris because the German was carrying a package and maybe there was a strawhat in it.

The interpreter said to Wynstanley, "He's brought you a straw-hat from Paris—his name's Trott von Essen."

"Ask him," Wynstanley said, "can I keep the hat? I'll pay him what it cost and something for his trouble."

So the interpreter talked to Trott and then said to Wynstanley, "He says it's a pleasure—you can have the hat—glad to do it."

"Ask him," Wynstanley said, "what he'd like me to play because the first song I play has got to be for him—for getting me the hat."

So then the interpreter talked to Trott again, and then said to Wynstanley, "He says finish the song you started to play about two weeks ago."

"Tell him," Wynstanley said, "it's a deal and let's have a look at the hat."

So the interpreter told Trott, and Trott broke the string of the package and brought out a brand new strawhat with a red band on it, and a little cluster of red and green and purple feathers stuck in the band.

Trott handed Wynstanley the hat, and Wynstanley just held it and looked at it a long time.

Then he put it on his head.

It looked very good on him. He looked like a civilian all of a sudden.

Then very slowly Wynstanley opened the case and put the trombone together and slided it back and forth a couple of times. Then he went to work and played the song like nobody in the whole world had ever played it before.

It was the most magnificent thing anybody ever heard. He played it through three times, each time just a little better than the time before.

Wynstanley had been hungry to play and nobody needed to tell him to go on—he just *wanted* to play, and he did. It was the finest thing that happened in the whole War. Trott von Essen was so proud of his share in the event he would hardly talk to the interpreters.

Everybody had a favorite song he wanted to hear, and Wynstanley promised to play them all one after another—if he couldn't play them tonight, he'd play them tomorrow. If you could whistle or hum the tune, he'd pick it up and play it for you, he said. He didn't care what the tune was or whether he'd heard it before, just whistle it or hum it and he'd listen, and play it for you. He told the interpreter to ask Trott if there was any other song he'd like to hear, so Trott thought a minute, and remembered one, but didn't know the name of it. He'd heard one of our fellows singing it one night and he'd liked it, so Wynstanley told the interpreter to ask Trott to hum the song, or whistle it.

Trott hummed a few bars, and Wynstanley smiled and said, "Hell, that's _I'm thinking tonight of my blue eyes_. That's one of my own favorites."

Wynstanley played that song too, and if he was good on the first one, he was better on the second. The German was just as happy and proud as he could be. He wanted to know from the interpreter what the song was about, so the interpreter told him. He asked the interpreter to teach him to say _blue eyes_ in English, so the interpreter did, and he went off saying the two words over and over again.

After _Blue Eyes_, Wynstanley played _Oh the moonlight's fair tonight along the Wabash, from the fields there comes the scent of newmown hay_, and damned if every fellow listening didn't have tears in his eyes and go to work and blow his nose and wonder how so much beauty could come out of a little old battered-up piece of plumbing like John Wynstanley's trombone.

I don't know what the fellows in the American Army are fighting for, or what they think they're fighting for, because I haven't asked every one of them, but I think I know what they love—every last one of them, no matter who they are or what group they belong to—they love truth and beauty. They love it and need it and want it and tears come to their eyes when they get it.

And they got it when John Wynstanley of Cincinnati, Ohio, played the trombone. They got it when that great American—that great man of the world—put the strawhat on his head and let them hear the message of love and truth and beauty.

And I don't know what's American as against what's something else, but I know there is no man in the world capable of resisting truth and beauty like the truth and beauty that came out of Wynstanley's trombone on the evening and night of Saturday, July 22, 1944.

I know the German Guards couldn't resist that truth and beauty, because, having got a hint of its enormity one of them had fetched Wynstanley his strawhat. And I know the men named Rosevar and Menadue couldn't resist it; or the men named Smith or Jones; or the men who came from the South and had a special attitude toward Negroes; or the Negroes; or the fellows from the Far West; or the men who were cynics; or the ones who hated women; or the ones with toothaches; or those with colds; or the athletic ones; or the ones who despised the world; or those who had no religion; or the paratroopers. I know everybody in that Prison Camp and everybody outside of it who heard Wynstanley could not resist the truth and beauty he brought out of his trombone—and they were all the same in the presence of that truth and beauty, so what's all this talk about some people being no good by birth, and others being very good by birth, and others being fair to middling by birth? What kind of talk is that?

CHAPTER 75

Wesley and Victor Escape from the German Prison Camp, Only to Be Captured by the Quartermaster Corps

THE GERMANS packed up and went off Thursday night, August 31st, but we didn't know we were free until Friday morning, and that's when we became a mob. Everybody found out the Germans had gone, but even so, we were still prisoners. We were prisoners of the barbed-wire. Things were crazy for a good hour or so, but after that they were all right.

Everybody wanted to get on the other side of the barbed-wire, and they were in a hurry to do it. But the first fellows who were on the other side didn't have anything to do, so they waited for the others. A few fellows tried to take up the responsibility of leadership, but it didn't work because being led means getting imprisoned again, and the main idea was to escape imprisonment, so every man was for himself.

There were a dozen newly made tunnels under the barbed-wire and a lot of fellows were standing in line waiting their turn to crawl under the barbed-wire to their freedom, but a lot of others just stood around wondering what was next. Twenty or thirty fellows didn't even leave the Stockade when there was plenty of time to do so because there was no hurry, and it was just as comfortable inside as out. The Germans had left a lot of field rations stored away, so there was plenty of the same old stuff to eat. But nobody knew what to do after eating. That night almost everybody stretched out and went to sleep outside the barbed-wire, but not very far off from it. It was a prison all right, but they had lived there for some time, and they knew what it was like and didn't know what it would be like if they went off. A lot of fellows went off too, mainly in groups of three or four, but some of them came back after a while. A lot didn't come back, though, and every now and then you'd see a fellow go off alone, but you'd never see him come back.

The next day Victor and I loaded ourselves down with field rations and went off to get somewhere. We found a stream and took a bath with soap and washed our underwear and socks and waited for them to dry. We set out again and talked and felt free but not free enough because the War wasn't over, we'd only gotten past some barbed-wire. If we didn't have so many things on our minds we might have been satisfied to be away from the herd and just spend some time enjoying it. But Dominic was dead in the Pacific and Joe was dead in Europe. A lot of time had gone by since we had come to know they were dead. Enough time had gone by for us to forget they were dead and go on as if they were still alive, only separated from us. Dominic had been separated from us a long time before we learned he was dead—he had been separated from us since the night he got on the truck with Harry Cook and Nick Cully and Vernon Higbee and went along to Missouri, and Victor and I went to Roseville, and that was a long, long time ago. I hadn't seen much of Joe Foxhall since the night he'd read his poem to his son. So I stopped thinking he was dead. I guess that's how people get over feeling so bad about their friends who are gone. I guess you go to work and forget they're dead, even though you know you'll never see them again.

But every once in a while the unbelievable news that they *are* dead would come to me and I'd know it so painfully I'd feel sick because I wanted to know Dominic better, and I wanted to see Joe Foxhall the rest of my life.

Pretty soon Victor and I came to our own fellows in trucks, so we got a ride and tried to get to some place where we could be returned to our outfit. For three days we went from one place to another, getting rides. Then one day we found somebody who knew about our outfit, but all he could tell us was that he believed they had accomplished their mission and returned to London. Well, that was good news because if there was anything we wanted to do it was to get back to London too.

We tried to do that, but damned if we didn't get taken prisoner again—this time by the Quartermaster Corps, just because the Major we had gone to for some information on how to get back to our outfit took it into his head that inasmuch as we were eager to get to London, he'd keep us with *him*. We didn't say anything, but three days later when he gave us a pass to go to town, we didn't report back. We went to Cherbourg, and after days and days of hemming and hawing orders came through for us to return to our outfit in London, so then Victor and I just wept for joy. We just naturally wept, although it sounded as if we were laughing.

CHAPTER 76

Wesley Comes to the End of His Story

AT LAST we came to Waterloo Station in London, but there were no taxis, so I said, "Come on, let's walk—or run—or something. Let's not just stand here." We started to walk and run, because, oh Jesus, I wanted to see Jill again. We walked and ran across Waterloo Bridge and up the Strand, so then Victor said, "You go ahead —I can't run any more."

I ran on and Victor walked, and pretty soon I was almost home. Pretty soon I'd see my girl again and take her in my arms and see how my son was getting along—but when I turned into Charles II Street I began to die because it was all in ruins. The building Jill and I had lived in—it wasn't there any more.

I guess I went crazy because I kept walking back and forth across

the street from where our building used to be—where we used to
live—because I was afraid—I was afraid to ask anybody about it. I
was afraid to even *think* about it. I guess I must have stayed there
a long time because pretty soon it was night. But I couldn't go away
and the song was sick with agony in me. It was fierce with aching,
and I didn't know what to do.

But I knew I was dead if Jill was dead—and I didn't want to be
dead. I began to cry because hell, suppose we were both dead
now? Suppose we had both died while I was gone? So where was
the star that had come out for me to tell me that I would be spared?
What good was the star to me now?

Pretty soon an old man who was begging came to me. I gave him
a pound, and then changed my mind and gave him two pounds
because I didn't want to be dead.

"Why are you crying?" he said.

"I used to live in the building that used to be across the street,"
I said. "I used to live there, but it's been bombed. I don't know
what's happened to my wife, and I'm afraid to go and find out. I'm
afraid. Do you want another pound?"

He said if I gave him another pound my wife was all right—not
to worry—so I gave him two more, which was all I had, not counting the change I had in my pocket.

"Your wife's all right," he said. "Don't worry about it. Have you
any more money?"

"Only these coins," I said. I gave him the coins because if Jill
was all right, I didn't want any money. The beggar went scraping
on down Charles II Street. He turned every once in a while to look
back at me as if he wasn't sure he hadn't tricked me in order to get
a little money, so I said to God, "Please don't let the old man be a
liar—please let Jill be alive. I forgot to ask you to keep Jill alive
when I made the bargain about the star because I hadn't met Jill
then, but if Jill isn't alive, it's no good my being alive, so please
keep the bargain, even though I didn't know how things were going
to turn out. Please keep the true bargain."

Well, then a taxi came up like thunder and lightning and the
writer jumped out and grabbed me and said, "Your wife's in
Gloucester."

Well, what do you do when God keeps a bargain? What do you

do when He keeps a bigger bargain than you thought you had made? What do you do when you know He will always know what you mean, even if *you* don't, and will stick to His agreement? You thank Him, don't you? I wasn't even polite to the writer—I just got down on my knees on Charles II Street, and I said to God, "I thank You, and I'll go on thanking You as long as I live."

I jumped up and got into the taxi with the writer, and he told the driver to take us to Paddington.

"Why?" I said. "I want my mail. I've got to see my mail."

"Here's your mail," the writer said. "The last train for Gloucester leaves in twenty minutes. When Victor told me you'd gone home, I thought you'd hurry along to find out what had happened, so I sat there and waited. Then I had a hunch what had happened to you, so I got a taxi to get you home. The gossip was that you and Victor were dead. I kept writing to your father and I kept telling Jill whenever she came to London that you were O.K., so now it's O.K. I sure am glad to see you. Our whole unit is being shipped back to New York. Jill was visiting her mother when your house was hit."

"When did it happen?"

"The night you left London. She had planned to stay home all the time you were gone, but she kept crying because she just couldn't be there without you. She came over to our old place on Pall Mall and told me everything—so I got her into a taxi and took her to the station and put her on the train. The next morning your whole street was a shambles."

We got to Paddington just in time for the writer to buy a ticket and get me on the train, so then I was on my way to Jill at last, but I just had to thank God all the way.

I just kept thanking God with all, all, all, all, all my heart, all my soul, all my blood and bone, and all the juices in me for getting Jill out of our house the way He did—for making her love me so much that she couldn't stay in our house one night without me. I thanked Him for putting people in the world like the writer to know what to do and how to do it right away and not fool around —somebody else might have told Jill to go back home and not be afraid. I thanked God for putting fellows like Joe Foxhall into the world—even if it was only for such a short time—and fellows like

...ic Tosca. I had so much to thank God for I just couldn't do
...hing else.

And then the train stopped in Gloucester, and I went walking to
my life, which God had so carefully kept for me.

It was one o'clock in the morning when I got off the train, and I
adored the city that gave me my bride and my life—I loved Gloucester—and when I came to the door which would be opened to me,
I kissed it, and then knocked softly, and then Jill came to the door
and opened it to me.

I held her in my arms and kissed her and bumped upon my son
in her because he was pushing out so far now.

And Jill laughed and cried, and her mother came out in her old-
fashioned nightgown, in her bare-feet, which were just like Jill's,
and she cried and laughed too, and Jill's little brothers and sisters
came out in their nightgowns and we all laughed and cried, but
pretty soon we stopped laughing and just cried because all of a sudden I knew the soldier—the big brother—had been killed and would
never come home again. Nobody said anything about it, but all of
a sudden I knew he was dead. I'd only seen him once, but I cried
and cried because a fellow like that had been killed.

Jill made tea and her mother and her brothers and sisters set the
table and put all kinds of things on it. We all sat down and tried to
eat, and tried to talk but couldn't. Every once in a while somebody
would break out sobbing and run away from the table and come
back after a few minutes, and then somebody else would go, and
come back, and I was out of my head with happiness and thank-
fulness and agony and anger—all together—because if so many
things could be right, why couldn't just a few more be right too?
Why couldn't the big brother come home too? Why couldn't Joe
Foxhall come home too? Why couldn't Dominic Tosca come home
too? Why did some have all the luck—like me—and others none?

Pretty soon the brothers and sisters wandered off to bed, and Jill
and I sat and talked a long time with her mother, and oh she was
a beautiful woman—she was a Queen like her daughter Jill. She
didn't cry any more. She talked about her darling son Mike, but
she cried no more. She told us about her lovely life—patient, patient, patient—and the child she lost in childbirth before Mike was
born—and the one she lost before Jill was born, but after that lost

no more, but lost her man, and now her darling Michael—and for what? To make a good home for her man and her children and watch them grow and be good people. So then she kissed us both and went to bed.

I took my wife and held her in my arms a long time, and then I said, "Jill, I died tonight when I saw our house in London gone, because I was afraid you were gone too, and that killed me—and Joe's dead—yes, he's dead, Jill—and your bother Mike's dead—all these things killed me."

But my lovely Jill said, "Mama says it's a boy. She felt him, and she knows. She says he'll be born on Christmas Eve or Christmas Morn."

"I'll be alive again when he's born," I said.

We were too excited to go to sleep, so Jill put on her clothes, and we went out to walk and watch the break of day in Gloucester, and oh the world's too lovely for death. The world's too sweet for murder. Breathing's too good and seeing's too wonderful. Human beings must not murder one another. They must wait for God to take them in His own good time.

MLib